A Ration Book Wedding

JEAN FULLERTON

CORVUS

Published in paperback in Great Britain in 2020 by Corvus, an imprint of Atlantic Books Ltd.

Copyright © Jean Fullerton, 2020

The moral right of Jean Fullerton to be identified as the author of this work has been asserted by her in accordance with the Copyright, Designs and Patents Act of 1988.

10 9 8 7 6 5 4 3

A CIP catalogue record for this book is available from the British Library.

Paperback ISBN: 978 1 78649 609 6
E-book ISBN: 978 1 78649 610 2

Printed in Great Britain

Corvus
An imprint of Atlantic Books Ltd
Ormond House
26–27 Boswell Street
London
WC1N 3JZ

www.corvus-books.co.uk

To my Fullerton family who are no longer with me but whose anecdotes and experiences of WW2 are sprinkled all through the Ration Book series.

Chapter one

FRANCESCA FABRINO, FRAN to her friends, grasped the lever just above her and pulled it down, watching through the Perspex lens of her goggles as the drill bit bore a hole into the solid cylinder of metal. Feeling the tip of the bit reach its goal, she quickly released her hold and allowed the spring to raise the mechanism. She pressed the pedal by her right foot and the component – designed to allow the propellers of a Lancaster bomber to turn – popped out and joined the others in a wooden crate to her left. Pushing away the tendril of ebony hair dangling in her vision, Fran shifted her foot across to the other pedal, stamped on it and released another plug of aluminium into the drill bed, then repeated the process.

She, with at least two hundred other women and girls, was deep beneath the ground working in the newly opened Plessey factory. The factory, which had previously been used to assemble field radios and wirelesses, ran along the tunnel of the Central line between Leytonstone in the west and Newberry Park in the east.

Francesca was working in the aircraft engine component section under Wanstead station. She and the other women operating the machinery sat facing the platform wall with the dome of the tunnel arching over them. Behind her ran the narrow-gauge railway used to ship the finished components to the collection shafts from where they were taken to the surface. Although she was in one of the deepest sections of the tunnel, at five hundred feet below street level, the vibration of the German bombs above could be felt. She'd been allocated to work at the factory when she'd signed up a couple of months ago when the new war conscription act meant all women between the ages of eighteen and fifty, without dependants, were required to register for war work. As she was twenty-four and single, she had volunteered for factory work to ensure she didn't get drafted into the ATS.

It wasn't that she would have minded being in the ATS. Not at all. In fact, if the truth were told, she'd have preferred to be up top driving a petrol wagon or ferrying supplies to army bases rather than deep beneath the earth, but her father had been through enough and she didn't want him to worry any more than he already did, so she'd opted for the safer option of factory work.

Feeling the sweat trickling down between her shoulder blades, Francesca yanked down on the lever again. A fine spray of lubricant drenched the fresh metal plug and curls of aluminium escaped as the drill bit deep again. As she released the lever the hooter, signalling the end of the shift, blasted out. Giving a silent prayer of thanks, Francesca stamped on the pedal and ejected the metal component. She flicked the red switch off and the whirling drill ground to a halt. Yawning, she stepped away from the now-idle machine then turned towards the double doors of the exit.

The cream-tiled changing room, which was situated between the two platforms at the bottom of the stairs, was already abuzz with women changing into or out of work clothes. Francesca yawned again. Moving her goggles up to her forehead, she removed her ear plugs. She squeezed her way through the half-dressed women to her metal locker on the far side of the room. Looping her mother's crucifix out from beneath her clothing, Francesca took the key dangling alongside the cross and slid it into the lock.

'Cor, I thought that night would never blooming end,' said a woman's voice as Francesca opened her locker.

She turned to see Joan Dunn, a jolly blonde who worked on the machine three along from her on the assembly line.

'At least in the old factory you knew when the sun came up you'd soon be done for the night,' Joan added, as she opened the metal door of her locker.

'I know.' Francesca stowed her goggles and ear protectors on the top shelf. 'But it was worst for them up top. Still,' she continued, unbuttoning her overalls, 'at least we've got a day off tomorrow.'

In the dim light from a forty-watt bulb above, Joan's blue eyes rolled Heavenwards. 'Praise the lord.'

'For what?' asked Daisy Willis as she joined them from the factory floor.

'For strong, handsome men and gin,' Joan said. 'Although I've not had much of either lately.'

Francesca smiled. 'And for a day off.'

'Oh yes,' said Daisy with feeling as she removed her goggles. 'Got anything planned?'

'Just a date with my bed for about ten hours,' Joan replied. 'Then off down the market to join a queue.'

'Are you after anything special?' asked Daisy, sliding the straps of her tan-brown dungarees off her shoulders.

'No. Whatever's on offer,' Joan replied, untangling herself from her work clothing. 'What about you?'

'I'm having me hair done,' said Daisy. 'Then going up West to the Trocadero with a few of the girls from seven section to see if we can catch ourselves a couple of rich GIs.'

'Well, you watch out that you don't end up being the one "caught".' Joan winked. 'They don't call 'em over-sexed for nothing, you know.'

Daisy laughed and looked at Francesca. 'Why don't you come with us, Fran?'

'Oh, I don't know,' she replied, lowering her gaze as she stepped out of her boiler suit.

'Come on, it'll be fun,' urged Daisy.

Standing in her knickers and brassiere, Francesca laughed. 'I'm sure, but I promised to give Dad a bit of a hand in the cafe.'

'I'm sure he can manage without you, especially –' Daisy's eyes twinkled '– if it meant you hooking up with some rich American with an Italian grandmother.'

'It would make his day,' Francesca replied. 'But I'll give it a miss this time if you don't mind, Daisy, as I don't want to play gooseberry.'

Her friend laughed. 'Well, if you change your mind, we're all meeting at Bow Road station.'

The radio's pips, heralding the morning news bulletin, cut through the changing-room hubbub.

'Cor, is that the time?' Daisy said, shoving her arms in her coat. 'I'd better dash or I'll miss my tram.' She slammed her locker door shut. 'Have fun and I'll see ya.'

'Not if we see you first!' Francesca and Joan called back in unison.

Daisy waved cheerfully over her shoulder. 'And don't forget, Fran,' she said, gathering up her handbag and heading to the door, 'seven o'clock at the station.'

Francesca smiled, but didn't reply.

She turned back and unhooked her light-blue dress from the peg inside. Slipping her gown over her head, she whipped off her head scarf and shook out her long ebony tresses.

'You know I used to have hair as long as that,' said Joan wistfully, as Francesca brushed out the tangles ten hours bound inside a scarf had caused.

Joan's pale eyes softened. 'You really should think about meeting up with Daisy and her mates and having a bit of fun up West.'

'Maybe another time,' said Francesca, deftly winding one coil over the other as she plaited it.

'It's not as if you've got a sweetheart,' Joan persisted as she took her coat from her locker.

'I know,' said Francesca, taking her rucksack from her locker and shoving her dirty overalls in it. 'But I'm just waiting for the right man to come.'

'I don't say it ain't important you find the right one,' agreed Joan. 'Cos if you don't, you're blooming well stuck with 'em until one of you's pushing up daisies, but—'

'Which is why I'm not going out looking for him,' cut in Francesca. 'And with my brother Giovani in the army, Dad needs me around so I'm happy to wait.'

'Well, I hope he don't take too long for your sake,' Joan said. 'Because, believe me, there's nothing quite like having a strong, handsome man to keep you warm at night.'

'So I've heard.' Taking her three-quarter-length red coat out of the narrow metal closet, Francesca put it on, then closed the door and locked it. She picked up her haversack and turned to Joan. 'Now, I'd better get my skates on or I'll miss my bus. See you Saturday.'

Emerging from the brick-built entrance of the underground factory some five minutes later, Francesca drew in a long, slow breath of early-morning air. It was the last Friday in February and after ten hours or so breathing in the hot, subterranean atmosphere of the factory, the chill of the frosty morning revitalised her.

She was standing in Cambridge Park Road. Wanstead's common, with its ancient gnarled oak, was in front of her and Wanstead Flats, which were now dotted with ack-ack guns instead of grazing cattle, beyond that. Above her head, in the bare branches of a tree, a few birds warbled away, welcoming the lightening eastern sky behind the houses.

If you ignored the ARP control post with sand bags surrounding it, the sticky-tape criss-crosses on every windows, the silver barrage balloons squeaking against their anchorages and the signs directing you to bomb shelters, you could *almost* forget there was a war on.

To her right along the High Street, people were already out and about, either going to work or making a start on their morning tasks. A milk float being pulled by a horse, its food bag fastened to its halter, steam puffing from his sweating haunches, plodded along the street while the milkman darted back and forth replacing empty bottles on the doorstep with full ones. The draymen on top of the Charrington's wagon were rolling barrels down a plank and into the floor trap of the vast Victorian gin place on the corner opposite. The greengrocer was out in front of his shop trying to make an artistic display of his limited supply of vegetables while the butcher next door placed trays of off-rations offal in the window.

Francesca's weary gaze flickered across to the clock hanging above the jeweller's shop opposite The George.

Twenty past. Blast!

On cue, the 17 tram came into view. Gliding silently on its tracks it disappeared around the corner and onward to Leytonstone. Adjusting her haversack on her shoulder, Francesca sighed. Oh well. It was only a mile to walk to her connecting stop at the Green Man and at least it wasn't raining.

Francesca jolted awake as the 25 came to a halt outside the main postal sorting office on Whitechapel Road.

'Whitechapel station and London hospital,' called out the conductor from his position on the back platform.

Forcing her eyes open, Francesca grasped the upright metal pole on the back of the seat in front and hauled herself to her feet. Trudging between the seats on the lower deck, she made her way to the platform at the back of the bus and stepped down, narrowly avoiding colliding with the three boys dressed in Sir John Cass uniforms who jumped on.

The section of Mile End Road between Cambridge Heath Road to the east and Vallance Road to the west was known as The Waste and was home to one of the oldest markets in East London. It was a Friday, so the stalls and shops were already bustling with women, sporting scarf turbans on their heads and wraparound aprons beneath their coats, searching for bargains.

Before the outbreak of hostilities, the stalls offered all manner of goods for sale: clothing from the local factories, home-made pickled herrings, fresh bagels and rabbits in their fur caught on Barking Flats or Hackney Mashes. Now, sadly, after three years of rationing and the German navy torpedoing merchant ships in the North Atlantic, there was much less for the cash-strapped housewife to choose from.

Amongst the early-morning bargain-hunters were ARP wardens, who were handing out government leaflets. Alongside them two matrons in the green uniforms of the WVS doled out tea and toast to a grimy-looking Heavy Rescue team who had just finished their shift of digging people out of the ruins. That said, as far as Francesca could see, all the shops that flanked Whitechapel station were still standing, as was the brewery and the Blind Beggar Pub on the corner.

However, although she was glad to see that the old shopping area had survived the night, as always after being away from home all night the building she was most happy to find in the exact same condition as when she set off to work the night before was her father's cafe.

The cafe, called Alf's, sat on the corner of Brady Street and would have been open since the crack of dawn, ready to feed the army of night workers who had just finished their shift. As soon as the blackout ended each morning, her father rolled up the window blinds. Even at this distance Francesca could see people sitting inside enjoying their breakfast.

Francesca stepped off the kerb and crossed the road to join the throng on the other side of the road. The door to the cafe opened as she reached it, so Francesca stood back to let two postmen come out, then stepped into the warm fug.

Her father Enrico had taken over the former pie and mash shop just a year ago, after he and her brother Giovani were released from an alien internment camp. Although they couldn't run to the expense of changing the black and white tiles that lined the walls, her father was able to add a bit of Italian flavour to the eating house by suspending a selection of battered copper pans from the ceiling behind the counter. However, pride of place was given to a painting of Ponte Vecchio in Florence, where the Fabrino family came from. It had been painted by Giovanni and now hung on the wall at the far end of the cafe, surrounded by ornamental plates.

This morning, as always, Francesca's father was behind the marble counter. Through the hatch behind him she could see Olive, stirring pots and loading plates with buttered toast and scrambled egg.

Olive Picaro and her husband Victor lived in the Peabody buildings behind Balmy Park at the top of Cambridge Heath Road, a five-minute walk away from the cafe. They'd been bombed out of their coffee shop in Bethnal Green Road almost the same day as Francesca's father signed the lease on the cafe. Enrico had offered them both a job and they were now firmly part of the fabric of the cafe.

As the warmth of the room spread through her – the smell of coffee, fried bread and braised kidneys filling her nose – Francesca turned her attention back to her father at the till. Although only halfway through his fourth decade, Enrico looked at least ten years older and whereas her Mediterranean colouring was a warm olive, his was sallow. He'd never been a robust man, but after their fish and chip business on the Commercial Road was torched by a rampaging mob the night Mussolini declared war on Enrico's adopted country, her father's spirits had never quite recovered.

With his sleeves rolled up and a long white apron covering his clothes, Enrico was taking orders and money at one end of the counter. However, when he spotted her as she walked in, his golden-brown eyes – so like Giovani's – grew warm. Taking a cup from the upturned pile at his elbow, he opened one of the enamel tins behind him.

Wending her way through the customers, Francesca lifted the counter flap and joined her father on the business side of the counter.

'Morning, Papa,' she said, giving him a peck on the cheek.

'You're late, luv,' he said, as he ran the spout of the enamel teapot along the lines of mugs on a tray.

'I had to walk to the Green Man,' she replied, unbuttoning her coat. 'Then a bomb had landed smack bang in the middle of the road by the Plough so the bus had to go all the way down Danes Road before it could get back to Maryland Point. I tell you, Dad, I'm so tired I could beat Rip Van Winkle hands down in a sleeping contest.'

He regarded her thoughtfully for a moment. 'It's not right you working like a mole under—'

'Papa!' Francesca gave her father a long-suffering look.

He opened his mouth as if to speak, but then thought better of it and pressed his lips together.

Two plates of liver, sausage and fried bread appeared in the hatch. Taking the tea towel dangling from his apron straps, Francesca's father wrapped it around his hands and picked up the order. Sliding past her he took it over to a couple of ARP wardens at the window table.

As he returned, a yawn stole over Francesca so she put her hand over her mouth.

'I have to go to bed before I fall down,' she said, tiredness dragging at her eyelids.

She turned to make her way through to the parlour and spotted a folded copy of the *Herald* lying on an empty table. She picked it up and continued towards the family parlour behind the shop.

'Wait.'

Her father spooned three heaped tablespoons of cocoa into a mug, then stirred in hot milk.

'That's got to last us until next Wednesday,' she protested, as he added two teaspoons of sugar from their weekly catering rations.

9

'You deserve it,' her father replied, handing her the frothy hot drink. 'I put a jug of hot water in your room half an hour ago so it should still be warm.'

'Thanks.' Francesca gave him another peck on the cheek. 'Give me a shout about two, Papa, and I'll help you with the afternoon rush.'

He nodded as a plate of kippers arrived in the hatch.

Tucking the newspaper under her arm and clutching her hot drink, Francesca waved to Olive, who was now busy flipping bacon, scrambling eggs and doling out bowls of porridge, and headed wearily up to the first floor.

Although the sun had only been up for an hour, her bedroom was warm from the cafe below. It was simply furnished with a single brass bedstead, wardrobe, dressing table and washstand. Thankfully, even though the wallpaper with its pink and blue flowers and entwining greenery was a little old fashioned, the colours were still sharp. She'd also found a pair of second-hand curtains down Petticoat Lane which matched the green of the foliage so, even with the blackout blinds visible behind them, the room looked bright and cheery.

Closing the door, she put her hot drink on the bedside table, threw the newspaper on the bed and then kicked off her shoes, wriggling her toes to ease their stiffness. As her father had predicted, the water in the enamel jug on the washstand was still warm and, after stripping to her underwear, she had a quick wash and changed into her nightdress. Throwing back the patchwork counterpane and blankets, Francesca upended her two pillows and slipped beneath the cool sheets. Resting back onto the metal framework between the two bed knobs, she picked up her mug of cocoa and opened the newspaper.

Although the appointment of Sir James Griggs as the new Secretary of State for War was splashed all across the front page, the story that caught her eye was the one beside it; about the

Eighth Army's desperate attempt to hold on to Benghazi in North Africa.

Taking a sip of her cocoa, Francesca let her gaze drift onto the photo sitting beneath the lamp on her bedside table that had been taken four years ago, in 1938, at the annual St Patrick's Day dance at the Catholic club, adjacent to St Breda and St Brendan's church.

It was of Francesca and her very best friend in the world, Mattie Brogan, and her brother Charlie. She and Mattie were wearing their new dresses, made specially for the occasion, and both had wide, happy smiles.

But it was Charlie, Mattie's older brother, standing on the other side of her best friend that Francesca's gaze returned to again and again.

In truth, she needed no photo to remind her what the man she'd held a torch for since she was just six years old looked like. However, since the day he'd slipped a ring onto Stella Miggles' finger, just over a year ago, Francesca had been training her heart.

She'd been schooling it not to conjure up that quirky sideways smile of his or to remember his rumbling laughter at the opening bars of a song or the whiff of Burlington aftershave and she was working hard to forget the memory of his arms around her as he gave her a brotherly hug. She was very pleased that now she could go days without imagining what it would feel like to have his mouth pressed onto hers or to have his arms around her. Of course, he did still invade her dreams almost every time she closed her eyes, which was annoying, but…

Her gaze started to drift back to the photo, but Francesca forced her attention back to the newspaper and scanned an article about a new food called Spam. She was about to turn the page when something caught her eye.

The cup hovered halfway to her mouth as she read the advertisement at the top right-hand corner.

The British Broadcasting Corporation's Overseas Service
requires young lady for clerical and general duties.
Must be able to read Italian and speak it fluently,
preferably as their mother tongue.
Please apply to Miss Kirk, European Service,
Bush House, the Strand, WC1.

Cradling her cup between her hands, Francesca reread it and then looked back at the photo of Charlie Brogan, dressed in a suit with one of his flamboyant waistcoats beneath and a neckerchief tied at a jaunty angle at his throat.

The yearning for him niggled at her, but Francesca cut it short.

Joan was right. As Charlie flipping Brogan could never be hers, perhaps she needed to start looking for a big, strong, handsome man somewhere else. And perhaps the BBC Overseas Service would be a good place to start.

Chapter two

REGARDING HIMSELF IN the small oblong mirror that dangled from a piece of string in front of him, Bombardier Charlie Brogan in the Royal Artillery ran his fingers over the four-day bristles on his chin. Ideally, he'd like to have a shave, but he was down to his last two razor blades and the saints in Heaven only knew when he'd get another pack; he'd have to leave his beard for another day. Not that it mattered. Stuck in the middle of the North African desert, hundreds of miles from civilisation, it wasn't as if he had a string of social gatherings to attend. If he'd kept his tally correctly, today was the last day of February but days of being surrounded by nothing but dunes and flies, one day often merged into another.

He picked up the bucket of water at his feet, raised it and tipped half of it over him, enjoying the sensation of the cool water over his hot naked body.

Setting it back on the scorching sand, he took the bar of coal tar soap balancing on the shelf in front of him and rubbed it into a lather all over his chest. As he scrubbed under his arms, he looked over the top of the improvised khaki canvas cubicle that served as a shower. His Royal Artillery regiment's Howitzers were over to the right and although it was only two hours since dawn, having had the full benefit of the North African sun on them ever since, you could probably already fry an egg on the breach block.

Between the assorted tanks, lorries and personal carriers, men dressed in the sand-coloured tropical uniform of shorts and loose open-necked shirts were checking equipment, replenishing machine-gun belts and repacking shells into metal cases.

Charlie raked his soap-laden fingers through his hair and poured the remaining water slowly over his head, rubbing vigorously to remove the soap, then secured a towel around his waist.

Pushing back the canvas, he stepped out. Taking his uniform from the hook, he picked up his right boot. Upending it he shook it, then banged it a couple of times against the iron pole of the shower block.

Satisfied no scorpions or red ants had taken up residence in his footwear while he'd been at his ablutions, Charlie shoved his foot in his unlaced boot. After repeating the action with his other boot, he strolled over to the oil drum lying on its side a little way off. He'd scrubbed his smalls out before showering and had laid them there to dry. Stopping in front of it he shrugged on his shirt to protect his shoulders from the blazing sun.

They had been warned on the troop ships before they landed about the dangers of the sun. Some of the poor sods with fair or red hair looked like they'd been deep fried, and several had to be hospitalised with second-degree burns. But with his darker skin and having been out in all weathers since he was twelve helping on his father's rag and bone wagon, he'd fared better than most and was now so tanned he could almost pass for a local. Well, he could if it wasn't for the fact that at six foot one, he towered over them and he'd yet to see an Arab with blue-grey eyes.

Taking his lighter from the top pocket, Charlie flipped his shorts over his shoulder and picked up his pants. Holding the elasticated band taut over his knuckles he flicked the lighter into a flame then ran it across the fabric, hearing the satisfying crackle of bursting lice eggs as the aroma of scorched wool drifted up. Satisfied that the heat had completed what no amount of washing could, Charlie shook them out then, gathering up the rest of his now-dried clothing, strolled back to his tent. Ducking beneath the overhanging flap of canvas, he walked in.

Ginger, who was called that not because of his colouring but because his surname was Rogers, looked up from his copy of *Striperama*. 'Blimey, corp, we thought you'd fallen down the plughole.'

'Or been captured by some randy sheikh on account of you smelling like a bleeding tart,' added Smudge, who was sitting on the cot opposite, paring his toenails with his knife.

The tent that had been Charlie and his gun crew's home for most of the past two years was octagonal in shape and had a central pole where the primus stove and crew provision were stored. The camp beds faced inwards with the heads towards the outer walls and the feet towards the middle. Each man had a narrow metal locker about three foot high next to his bed on which were stuck photos of wives and children, if the owner were married, saucy pin-ups if they were not. Each man had a lockable chest for his personal gear stowed under the bed. The sides of their abode were rolled up to let in the air, but, as any breeze likely to come their way would be scorching, the interior of the tent was only a degree or two cooler than the outside.

'We might be called the Desert Rats but you don't have to smell like one,' Charlie replied, as he reached his bunk.

'I don't know why you bother,' said Thin Jim, who was sitting crossed-legged on his bunk and playing Patience. 'Five minutes in this heat and you're sweating like a pig, anyhow.'

Feeling his backbone starting to prickle already, Charlie couldn't disagree. Dropping the towel over the end of the bed, he took his pants from his shoulder.

The tent flap opened and a wiry youth, who looked too young to shave never mind fight the Hun, stepped into the tent.

'Post for gun crew eight?' he asked, his pale eyes casting over them.

'That's us,' said Charlie, crossing the space in two strides. 'Brogan? Anything for Brogan.'

'I'm not sure,' said the young man reaching into his bulging bag and shuffling through the pile of correspondence he was carrying. 'Robinson, Crow, Riley—'

'Come on, man,' snapped Charlie, his heart thumping painfully in his chest. 'It's been almost two weeks since the last delivery from home so there must be at least one.'

'Give the boy a chance, Charlie,' said Smudge, waving a fly from his face. 'He's doing his best.'

Charlie took a deep breath and tried to master his impatience.

'Brogan.' The youth grinned and pulled out a small package and a letter.

Charlie took them and looked at the writing on each.

A pang of homesickness swept over him as he read his name, written in his sister Mattie's bold hand on the parcel, but it was the squiggly writing on the letter that took the tension from his shoulders.

At last!

Returning to his bed he quickly finished dressing, then, having pulled up his socks high enough to foil any sand fleas from having a nibble and tied his bootlaces tight, Charlie flicked a couple of sand beetles off his covers and made himself comfortable. As he opened his wife's letter, the post boy who was about to leave glanced at the photo fixed to the door of Charlie's locker.

'I can see why you were so keen for a letter, chum,' he said, a smirk spreading across his beardless face. 'I'd be keen to hear from a bit of skirt with knockers that size.'

The other men in the tent fell silent and Charlie felt their uncertain gazes on him as he regarded the young lad standing two feet away.

'Sorry, *chum*,' he said, fixing the lad with a look that had stopped seventeen-stone bruisers in their tracks. 'Are you talking about my wife?'

The colour drained from the youth's face. 'Er…sorry. It's just

16

that…you know, she's nice-looking…pretty, you know. I didn't mean nothing by it. No offence, chu… Sir.'

Charlie held the quaking lad's stare for a few moments more, then smiled. 'None taken. But you should be watching yourself, boy. Next time you might find yourself up against someone who's not as even-tempered as me.'

The post boy nodded like a rag doll being shaken, then scurried out of the tent.

'Even-tempered!' snorted Ginger. 'That's a laugh. Don't forget it were me who was with you in that bar in Winchester when you panned that fella for calling you a thick bastard from Paddyland.'

Charlie shrugged. 'He's just a boy pretending to be a man.'

He turned his attention back to his letter and silence descended again as the four men read about the loved ones they'd left behind – the ones they were fighting for in this insect-infested desert of North Africa.

As he read about his wife's daily struggle to feed her and their son, Patrick, because of rationing and shortages, her exhaustion from working in the ball bearing factory at night and caring for a lively eight month old by day, plus the nightly bombing raids, guilt tugged at Charlie's chest. No wonder she hadn't written to him since before Christmas. He knew Stella had never been much of a one for writing, but three months without a single letter was a bit much…

Brushing away a fly crawling over his knee, Charlie returned to his correspondence. His smile widened as he read about his son, Patrick, sitting up all by himself, his fretful nights with his teeth and how his mum had rubbed whiskey on them to numb the pain.

As always, he was told not to worry because although the Germans still bombed the London docks most nights, Patrick's granny, Charlie's mum Ida, took him to the Tilbury shelter at the end of Cable Street on the nights Stella worked.

Charlie moved on to the last paragraph. Along with saying how much she loved and missed him, Stella then went on to give such a detailed description of how she would be welcoming him home that it must have made the censor blush; it certainly caused a jolt in Charlie's crotch.

His gaze shifted from the letter to the photo of his wife with his son in her arms. Patrick had been only five months old when it was taken and the letter had taken a month to catch up with him. It arrived with his Christmas present of socks, chocolate, writing paper and envelopes. A lump caught in Charlie's throat as he thought of all the little things about his son's first year he'd missed. His attention shifted to the woman holding the child, his wife Stella.

She was wearing a skin-tight evening dress with a plunging neckline that showed off her cleavage. Perched on a bar stool, she had one high heel on the ground and the other on the footrest. Patrick, dressed in a knitted matinee jacket and leggings, was held tightly by his mother as he balanced on her raised knee.

The lad was right. Stella had an amazing figure and she'd never been short of male attention. When she'd turned her sights on him, she'd caught his attention, too. After all, he was a man with blood pumping in his veins, wasn't he? Of course he'd heard the whispers about her but then he was no angel either, so he'd shrugged them off. However, as he'd got to know the woman beneath the generously endowed figure, his interest had quickly waned, but it was too late. He was not a man to shirk his responsibilities so, two months after she told him she was in the family way, he'd made a respectable woman of her.

It wasn't the best start to a marriage, but Patrick was born four months later on the twentieth of June, a month after he'd shipped out from Portsmouth to North Africa. He'd received the letter telling him of Patrick's birth while he was trudging across the desert towards Cairo and although he'd never set eyes on his son, he'd loved him from that moment. He'd been raised in a happy, loving family and Charlie was determined that for Patrick's sake, and any other children that came after, he would make a go of it with Stella.

'Right,' said Ginger, folding his letter and tucking it into his top pocket. 'Who's for a brew?'

'Count me in,' said Smudge.

Shoving his disheartening thoughts about his marriage aside, Charlie swung his legs off the bed and sat up.

'And me,' said Charlie, putting Mattie's letter aside to read later. 'And you'd better do one for Ted as he should be back from Stores soon.'

Waving away the flies circling the jerry can containing the fresh water, Ginger refilled the kettle then placed it on the primus stove and lit it.

Charlie reached beneath his bed and extracted the metal box that contained all his personal belongings. Unlocking it he tucked his letters and parcel inside. However, as he sat up again, a commotion on the other side of the compound caught his attention.

'Oi, oi, something's up,' he said, rising to his feet. The others looked around as Charlie went to the door and stepped outside.

Shading his eyes from the glare, he saw plumes of sand rising up. There was a second or two pause, then the throaty sound of tanks, lorries and jeeps revving up drifted across in the blistering air. Men were shouting and dashing back and forth now. The sharp blast from a whistle sounded out, followed by a couple of horns tooting.

'Is it the Windmill Girls come to give us a show?' shouted Smudge from inside the tent.

'No!' Charlie shouted back. 'But you can forget having a cuppa, cos after five weeks of moping around this godforsaken wilderness, we're on the move!'

Pandemonium broke out behind him and by the time he'd got back to his bunk the other chaps had already stowed their gear and were starting to pull up the guy ropes.

'Come on, Brogan, look lively,' Ginger shouted, cutting through his thoughts. 'Or we'll win the war without you.'

'Don't worry about me, chaps,' he said, grabbing his backpack that was leaning against the locker. 'I'll be in Benghazi before the lot of you.'

A shell exploded somewhere to the right of Charlie's truck as the battle sergeant standing in front of them signalled them into their position at the end of the newly formed artillery line. His battalion had broken camp four hours before and they had been travelling east to meet the enemy ever since. With handkerchiefs secured over their noses and mouths to keep out the sand thrown up by the vehicles travelling over it, he and the five men sitting behind him in the Bedford looked more like bandits from a Western than a crack gunner team.

Jamming the gears into reverse, Charlie swivelled around in the driver's seat and looked over his shoulder through the canvas arch at his rear. He turned the steering wheel back and forth with his right hand and swung the seven-pound gun to face the German Afrika Korps. The enemy were situated behind the ridge just to the east and had the advantage of the high ground where, judging by the ferocity and accuracy of the shells exploding around them, they had been in position waiting for them.

Hitler's crack troops were very different from the hotchpotch of conscripts Mussolini had sent to seize British possessions in North Africa. The Eighth Army had gone through the Italian defences at Tobruk like a hot knife through butter, many of the ill-trained and ill-equipped men surrendering without so much as firing a shot. However, now the Germans had arrived to assist their allies, the British had a fight on their hands to prevent Field Marshal Rommel's Panzer divisions pushing them back into the sea.

A shell, probably a twelve-pounder by the flash of light, exploded to the left of them, sending the canvas awning covering the men flapping as the munition sucked in the air.

Charlie yanked on the handbrake.

'Right, lads!' he shouted, over the sound of exploding armaments and the returning fire from the British guns. 'Let's get this bugger in position and give the Jerrys a taste of their own medicine.'

Ginger, who was at the back of the truck, unhooked the tailgate and kicked it down. He jumped out and the rest of the gun team did the same. Charlie felt the back of the truck lift as they unhooked the artillery gun from the towbar.

A German shell landed some hundred yards in front of him and peppered the windscreen with sand and pebbles. Getting back into the Bedford, Charlie revved the truck's engine again, then circled the vehicle around behind his pals who were getting the gun into position and breaking shells from their cases. Churning up sand as he went, Charlie sped off to where the transport lorries and armoured personnel carriers were parked away from the front line. A shell whizzed over his head and a light tank at the rear of the formation burst apart in a ball of flames, sending fragments of metal high into the air.

Coming to a stop, Charlie pulled on the handbrake. He picked up his tin hat, leapt down from the cabin and slammed the door behind him. Over on the right flank his crew were already returning fire, the five men working like a well-oiled machine, loading and then standing aside as the gun spat out its shell at the enemy.

With debris and twisted metal flying all around him, Charlie hurried back to join his comrades. Another mortar shell exploded behind him but, mercifully, landed short of the line of armoured vehicles waiting to take the infantry forward once the German guns had been silenced.

Above the noise of gunfire, Charlie could hear a low rumble as the British tanks made ready for the offensive, the smell of diesel from their exhausts mingling with the burnt phosphorus of the armaments giving the air a sour taste.

Halfway across the open space between the lorries and guns, a mortar shell burst in front of him sending up a shower of grit. Tucking his chin in to avoid the dust from getting in his eyes, Charlie continued, the ground beneath his feet shaking as missiles crashed to the ground.

However, just as he had nearly reached his destination, something flashed in the sky. Charlie looked up to see a dart of light streaking across the dusty plan. The missile hit an armoured tank just fifty yards away, destroying it as if it were a child's toy.

A combination of hot sand and spent sulphate blasted Charlie in the face as distorted curls of metal, like giant hornets scorching the air, whizzed past him.

Something thumped into Charlie's left shoulder, spinning him around. He tried to get his balance but pain like a burning javelin cut through him. Gasping, he stumbled forward and then the world turned black.

'Does that hurt?' asked Major Frederick Willard, the senior officer in charge of the battalion's field hospital, as he prodded around the dressing on Charlie's left shoulder and chest.

'A little,' Charlie replied, through gritted teeth.

Looking over his half-rim spectacles, the consultant gave a grim smile. 'I'm not surprised. That bit of metal went through your shoulder muscles like an apple corer.'

It was just after two in the afternoon and three days since Charlie had been struck in the shoulder by flying shrapnel. Truthfully, he had very little recollection of the past seventy-two hours, thanks to the morphine he'd had pumped into him since the medic carried him from the battlefield. However, when the nurse arrived carrying a loaded syringe an hour ago, he'd refused it, which after ten minutes of the major's poking and prodding, he was beginning to regret.

He was reclining on a narrow hospital bed in a long camouflaged, painted tent a few miles outside Algiers. Around him were a dozen or so other wounded soldiers swathed in bandages or staring blindly up at the canvas ceiling.

The sides of the ward were pegged down in a somewhat futile attempt to keep the flies out, so the temperature inside was hotter than the sun. Charlie, like most of the other patients, was lying on top of the prickly army blanket and wearing only his underpants.

'What about this?' asked the consultant, pressing on the ball of Charlie's shoulder.

'About the same,' Charlie replied, as a streak of pain shot down the inside of his arm.

Major Willard, a stout man wearing a white coat over his sand-coloured desert shirt and shorts, stepped back a few paces.

'Keeping it straight, raise your arm up,' he said, his eyes fixed on Charlie's shoulder.

Looking straight ahead at the tent pole opposite, Charlie clenched his teeth and raised his left arm a few inches before pain forced him to abandon the attempt.

'Not bad,' said Major Willard. 'Not bad.'

The flaps of the tent at the far end opened and a red-headed Queen Alexandra nurse, dressed in battle fatigues like the doctor, came in carrying a large buff folder.

She spotted the major and hurried towards him.

'The X-rays you asked for, sir,' she said.

'Thank you, nurse,' he replied, taking them from her.

Her eyes flickered over Charlie's chest. She gave him a shy smile and fled the tent.

Pulling the large black negatives from the folder, Major Willard held them up to the square of ventilation mesh above his head.

'Benghazi, wasn't it?' asked the consultant, as he studied the X-ray plates. 'Where you copped a lump of metal in your shoulder.'

Charlie nodded.

'Jerry put up a stiff resistance, so I hear,' said the consultant without looking around.

'You could say that,' Charlie replied, as the memory of the SS 3rd Panzer division's sudden onslaught flitted through his mind.

Major Willard lowered the X-rays and then shoved them back in the file.

'What's the verdict, sir?' asked Charlie.

'To be frank with you, Mr Brogan, you're lucky to be alive. If that lump of metal had gone in two inches lower, it would have gone straight through your heart.'

'But it is healing?' said Charlie.

'Indeed it is.' The consultant's substantial eyebrows rose. 'Surprisingly well, too. However, it will be some time before you are fit to return to active duty so we've decided to ship you home to recuperate.'

'How long for?'

'With an injury like that I don't see you being fit for front-line soldiering until the end of the summer,' Major Willard replied. 'You'll have a few weeks in an army hospital to rebuild the muscles and give those bones time to start knitting together and then you can go home to recover fully.'

'Home!' said Charlie. 'You mean to my family?'

'Yes,' said Major Willard.

The major's gaze flickered to the photo of Stella and Patrick propped up on the locker. Charlie's gun crew had sent it to the hospital along with his personal effects and one of the nurses had kindly set it on the locker beside him while he'd been unconscious.

'We've sent a telegram to your wife telling her of your injury and that you'll be returning to Blighty.' His bushy moustache lifted as he smiled. 'I'm sure she'll soon have you fighting fit again.'

Charlie grinned.

'I'm sure she will.' He saluted. 'Thank you, sir.'

Major Willard returned the salute, then moved on to the next bed.

Charlie lay back on the pillow until the pain from his poked and prodded shoulder subsided a little, then he turned his head and studied the photo of his wife and son.

Tears pinched the corners of Charlie's eyes. Thanks to a flying tank fragment, not only could he look forward to enjoying Stella's warm welcome home but, more importantly, he would soon be able to hold his son for the first time.

Chapter three

AS THE BASS drum thumped out the pounding beat, Stella Brogan, or Salome of the Mysterious East as she was billed on the hoarding outside, wriggled her way to the back of the stage. Standing with her back to the audience she paused for a few musical bars as the wolf whistles and guttural sounds of the hundred or so men packed into the BonBon club grew louder. Then, clasping the fabric to her breasts with her left hand, she reached behind with her right and snapped open the clasp on her sequined brassiere.

As the roar of male voices became even louder, urging her to turn around, a fizzle of excitement shot through her. Stella's Scarlet Kiss lips curled upwards in a satisfied smile. Holding her pose for a second or two, she slowly swayed from side to side, setting the fringing at the top of her skimpy knickers shaking. Then, as the drummer hammered out a military roll, Stella spun around to face her audience.

The stage of the club wasn't large, so she was no more than ten feet from the front row, which was a sea of khaki and Air Force blue and leering faces.

Placing one high-heeled foot in front of the other, Stella sashayed to the edge of the stage; cigarette smoke swirling around her ankles and the smell of beer and spirits rising up.

Taking a step to the left, she lowered the cup of her brassiere enough to let the men craning forward get a glimpse of her 40 double-Ds, before swinging around and doing the same to those crowding around the other side of the stage, then turning her back on them again.

Drumming her heel on the rough floorboards beneath her for a second, she paused. Then, in a swift movement, she flung the brassiere into the stage wings where it was caught by one of the stage hands. Pivoting on her heels, with her arms outstretched, Stella turned to face her audience.

A deafening roar filled her ears as she stood naked except for her sequinned G-string. Letting a sensual smile widen her lips she paused for a moment, savouring the wave of rampant desire flooding over her. Placing her right hand over her pubic bone, she gave the room full of men a lavish look then snapped the clips each side to release the garment.

The room went wild as the men, on their feet and arms outstretched, lunged towards the stage screaming, 'Get them off!'

Stella gave her audience a wide-eyed, innocent look as the incessant beat of the drum continued, reflecting the pulsating atmosphere of the room. She waited for a second or two, then whipped away the garment and flung it to one side.

With one foot in front of the other, her legs pressed together and a smile across her face, Stella flung her arms wide once more and stood naked except for the modesty G-string that barely covered her pubic hair but, as total nudity wasn't allowed, allowed Tubb Harris, the proprietor of the club, to keep his licence.

After another couple of thumping beats the cymbals crashed and the garnet-coloured velvet curtain fell across the stage.

Ignoring the stage hands and prop boys lurking in the wings, Stella turned on her heel and stomped off, snatching her dressing gown from the hook at the back of the stage as she passed.

Something that sounded like a steam hammer crashing into the pillow beside her brought Stella to her senses.

Pushing back the tangle of lacquered hair from her face she opened one eye and struggled onto her elbow. She peered at the clock sitting above the bedroom fireplace.

Ten thirty on a Monday morning!

She flopped back onto the pillow.

For God's sake! she thought, trying to focus on the fluted glass lampshade dangling over the foot of the bed.

It had been a good night last night in the club. Mainly because along with the khaki and navy uniforms of the British servicemen, there was an increasing number of smart dark-olive American ones. All of them were wildly enthusiastic about the entertainment she and the other girls had to offer, both on stage and off.

They were loaded too, with a poor grasp of what the going price for a bit of company was. She'd made it home as the all-clear sounded just before dawn with three five-pound notes stuffed down her brassiere.

Sleep stole over her again, but, just before it enveloped her, the hammering on the front door knocker started again.

'All right, all right!' she shouted, forcing her eyes open again. 'I can hear you.'

Throwing off the sheets and blanket, Stella, still wearing the underwear she'd gone out in the night before, dragged herself upright.

The floor shifted under her feet and made her head spin, so she gripped the bedpost for a few seconds until the dizziness subsided, then, snatching her dressing gown from the foot of the bed, she stepped over the discarded cocktail dress and staggered across the room to the door.

As she made her way downstairs, Stella gripped the banister tightly and placed her bare feet carefully on each tread. By the time she reached her front door the rhythm of the metal knocker perfectly matched the pulsing pain across her forehead. Clutching the front of her dressing gown together across her breasts, Stella opened the door.

Standing on the pavement outside were two of her neighbours, Minnie Wallace, who lived two down, and her sidekick Elsie Griggs, who lived across the street at number 4. Both were in their mid-fifties and wore the standard housewife's uniform of a faded wrap-over apron and headscarf fashioned into a turban with a scrape of grey hair peeking out on their foreheads. Minnie was as lean and as knobbly as a hop vine in January and had a face that could curdle fresh milk. Elsie, despite three years of rationing, still had to swing one leg around the other to walk.

Behind them, milling about in the street, were half a dozen housewives pretending to sweep their steps and wipe their windows but who were, in fact, watching in eager anticipation what was happening on Stella's doorstep.

'Oh, you're up then,' said Minnie, pure mischief glinting in her close-set eyes.

'Is it any wonder with you two hammering on my bloody door,' snapped Stella. 'What do you want?'

Minnie pulled a manila envelope out from her apron pocket. 'The postman shoved this in my letterbox by mistake.'

'Well, couldn't you just have shoved it through my letterbox?' asked Stella, as a lock of lacquer-stiffened hair fell over her left eye.

'Well, we would have but it's from the War Office,' said Minnie. 'And it looked official. We thought it might be something about your husband—'

'Your husband,' echoed Elsie.

'Yes, your husband Charlie, who's away fighting for King and Country,' said Minnie.

'He was in the same class at school as my Larry,' added Elsie.

'In North Africa, isn't he?' asked Minnie, her eyes boring into Stella.

Stella didn't reply.

Minnie tutted and shook her head dolefully. 'Poor Charlie. I said to his mother only yesterday, "Ida, your Charlie's a regular hero, he is."'

'Regular hero,' Elsie repeated.

Pain sliced behind Stella's eyes and she rubbed her throbbing temples.

'Rough night at the ball bearing factory, was it?' asked Minnie sarcastically, her eyes lighting up like a fox catching the whiff of a rabbit.

'Hard at it all night, were you, Stella?' sniggered Elsie.

'Doing your bit for our boys, were you?' added Minnie.

Lunging forward, Stella snatched the letter from Minnie's hand and slammed the door shut.

'She looks like she's been dragged through a hedge backwards,' Elsie shouted through the door.

'More like been shagged backwards, if you ask me,' Minnie shouted back.

Stella gave the two women on the other side of the door a two-fingered, rude gesture then, clutching her letter, slouched into the kitchen.

Rummaging around in the cupboard she located a couple of aspirin and, finding the least dirty cup in the sink, swallowed them down.

Crossing to the kitchen table she picked up the three fivers from her brassiere and, shoving them into her handbag, retrieved a pack of Bensons & Hedges and her lighter.

Placing a cigarette between her lips, she flicked the lighter.

Taking the smoke deep into her lungs she waited for the familiar uplift effect as the nicotine reached her brain. Feeling relaxed and holding the cigarette in the side of her mouth, she turned the envelope over and slid her finger beneath the flap.

Holding it towards the kitchen window to see, she skimmed down the page but, as she got to the second paragraph, she pitched forward and started coughing.

'Bloody hell!'

Struggling to steady her breathing, Stella reread the letter then coughed as nausea surged again. She forced it down and, snatching the pair of stockings she'd draped on the back of the chair to dry the day before, she ran out of the kitchen and back upstairs.

Thirty minutes later, after tidying her make-up and hair and pulling on her navy pencil skirt and cropped white jumper, Stella walked out her front door. Putting on her sunglasses to dim the early March sunlight, and ignoring the gathering of women across the street, she slammed her front door.

With a look of grim determination on her face and her handbag over her arm, Stella tottered off towards her mother-in-law's house three streets away. She arrived at 25 Mafeking Terrace some ten minutes later.

Like Alma Terrace where she lived, Mafeking Terrace ran between Cable Street to the south and the Highway to the north, just a few minutes' walk from Shadwell Basin and London Dock.

Like most of the roads on the Chapman Estate, the narrow street was lined on both sides by three-up three-down workman's cottages. Every front door opened straight on to the pavement, while at the rear, each house had a small square paved yard with an outside toilet. As ever, no matter what damage a night of bombing did to the brickwork and windows of the dwellings, come morning a housewife who wanted to be counted as respectable by her peers would be out at first light to scrub a half circle on the pavement in front of their front door. And the bleached flagstone in front of her mother-in-law's house showed that, despite last night's visit from the Luftwaffe, Charlie's mother, Ida Brogan, had been out with her bucket and brush.

A faint sneer lifted Stella's painted lips.

Deliberately stepping in the middle of Ida's cleaned pavestones, she lifted the freshly polished knocker and struck it twice.

Of course, she could have just slipped down the alleyway between the terrace houses and entered the house through the back, as was customary for close friends and family. However, apart from the fact she wasn't going to endanger her nylon stockings – given to her by a grateful GI a couple of nights ago – by navigating her way through the junk in the backyard, she always forced her in-laws to get up and open the front door for her. After all, she doubted Winston Churchill went around the back of Buckingham Palace when he popped in to tell the king how the war was going.

Ignoring the glances coming her way from the handful of women standing around in the street gossiping, Stella grasped the knocker once more and smashed it down on the stud beneath.

After a few moments her mother-in-law, Ida, opened the door.

Ida Brogan was halfway through her forty-fourth year and was a couple of inches shorter than Stella. With her chestnut hair and brown eyes she looked very like her eldest and youngest daughters except she was about two dress sizes bigger.

She was wearing her forest-green WVS dress under a wraparound apron, lisle stockings and stout brown lace-up shoes.

Ida looked startled when she saw Stella and glanced at her wristwatch. 'You're early.'

'I'm not putting you out, am I?' Stella replied, feeling half a dozen pairs of eyes boring into her back.

'No…no, come in.' Ida stood back.

Stella marched into the hall. Holding her breath as she passed the door to the front room where Queenie Brogan and her moth-eaten parrot lived, she walked into the family's parlour.

As always when she entered her in-laws' main living area, Stella wrinkled her nose. Not because it smelt, credit where credit was due, no germ stood a chance against Ida's scrubbing brush and bucket of bleach, but because the room reflected her father-in-law's profession as a rag and bone man perfectly.

In truth, it was nothing more than a jumble of dilapidated

furniture which should have been chopped up for kindling long ago. Ida also had a collection of cheap china figurines on the mantelshelf, which Stella would have thrown straight in the bin. If that wasn't enough to make you shudder, on the far wall a massive bookshelf was crammed full of dusty copies of boring books including an old, scruffy edition of some encyclopaedia. Charlie had tried to explain how the different books linked together once but, quite frankly, she'd put the whole room on a bonfire. Jerimiah Brogan might style himself as a removal man but, in truth, he was nothing more than a rag and bone man and a Paddy one too.

'I was just making the boys' midday meal, so the kettle's boiled if you'd like a cuppa?'

The boys were eleven-year-old Billy, who was in fact the kid Ida's sister Pearl had abandoned in the lobby of the old workhouse in Bancroft Road – Ida had fetched him out two days later and had raised him as her own ever since – and ten-year-old Michael, who no one had known existed until last September. He was Jerimiah's boy by the woman who had been Ida's best friend. She'd pitched up before Christmas, dying and asking Jerimiah to take Michael. Anyone else would have sent the bastard to a bloody orphanage but Ida, fool that she was, not only forgave Jerimiah for having it away with her so-called friend, but had also welcomed Michael into the family.

If that wasn't enough, one of her sisters-in-law, Mattie, was married to some chap hardly anyone ever saw. The other, Cathy, was married to a convicted Nazi who was on parole in the army. And the younger one, Jo, was engaged to Tommy Sweete, whose brother Reggie was doing time for manslaughter.

Honestly! What a family. And they had the bloody nerve to look down at her for being an exotic dancer!

'No, ta,' Stella replied. She looked around. 'Where's Patrick?'

'Having his morning nap upstairs,' Ida replied. 'If I'd known you were coming earlier, I would have kept him up.'

'That's all right,' Stella said, forcing a smile.

It wasn't, of course. Usually, she tried not to collect Patrick much before two, which meant she only had to look after him for a few hours until Ida arrived at five thirty. Ida always changed him before Stella collected him so she could plonk him straight in his cot; that way he didn't bother her while she did her hair and waited for her nails to dry.

Quite often, especially if she'd had a busy night and needed a little afternoon doze, she'd only just finished giving him his tea when Ida arrived. Usually there wasn't time to change him but it didn't matter because if he was wet her mother-in-law would do that when they got to the shelter.

It wasn't that she didn't love him or anything, because she did, it's just that like all babies he was messy and she couldn't afford to have her clothes mucked up by dribble and sticky fingers. After all, she had to look her best when she turned up at the BonBon.

'I came around a bit early because I got a letter from the Ministry saying Charlie's been injured and is being shipped home—'

'Injured!' Ida screamed and gripped the armchair beside her. 'Charlie's been injured! How badly? Is he all right? How do you know—'

'Because I got this,' Stella cut in as she held up the Ministry's letter. 'He was hit in the shoulder two weeks ago and he's being shipped home to recover.'

'Charlie's coming home—'

The door from the kitchen opened and Jerimiah's mother, Queenie, walked in.

Mrs Brogan Senior, somewhere in the middle of her seventieth decade, barely reached Ida's shoulder and weighed in at no more than six stone. Never one to follow fashion, Queenie Brogan was dressed today in a fern-green dress, which was more or less completely covered by an apron similar to her daughter-in-law's but that was so old whatever colour it had been had faded long ago.

Her black lisle stocking were gathered around her ankles, and the hobnail boots she wore looked much too heavy for her sparrow-like legs to lift off the floor.

She tried to let on she had second sight, but Stella refused to believe the old woman's claim to be in touch with the 'spirits'.

Old, shrivelled and as mad as a crate of monkeys she might be, but when Queenie Brogan's piercing black eyes fixed on her, Stella struggled to hold the old woman's unwavering stare.

'You're a mite early, aren't you?' Queenie said, giving Stella the once-over. 'I thought you'd still be sleeping it off, recharging all that energy you used up jigging about starkers on that there stage.'

'And good morning to you, Mrs Brogan.' Stella smiled sweetly. 'Pleasure to see you as always.'

'What do you want anyway?' the old woman replied. 'Cos I know you're not here for the want of seeing that sweet child of yours, that's for sure.'

'Our Charlie's been injured,' said Ida, before Stella could reply. 'But he's all right.'

'Praise the Sweet Mother of God,' said Queenie, scraping a bony finger across her chest in the sign of the cross.

'Amen,' said Ida, crossing herself too, then looking at Stella. 'When's he landing?'

'It says his hospital ship is arriving in about a week or thereabouts at Southampton. He'll be transferred to a military hospital close by for assessment before they send him home.'

'Well, as soon as we know where he is we can go and visit him,' said Ida. 'Take him some—'

Stella's mouth went dry as an image of her mother-in-law sitting at Charlie's bedside came into her mind.

'I don't think you should,' she said, hoping only she could hear the alarm in her voice.

Ida's mouth dropped open. 'But—'

'Because he needs to rest,' Stella continued, feeling sweat prickle between her shoulder blades under the old woman's unreadable stare. 'You know, give him a chance to regain his strength.'

Queenie studied her closely for a moment, then her wrinkled face screwed into an ugly expression that would have done a gargoyle proud.

'You're a feckin' liar, so you are, Stella Miggles!' she shouted. 'You must think we're a couple of eejits. You don't want Ida to visit Charlie because you're afraid she'll let slip what you've been up to while he's been defending King and Country.'

Stella's heart thumped painfully in her chest as an image of Charlie's furious face loomed into her mind.

'I'll bet he'll be mighty pleased when he hears how you've been doing your bit for the war effort by flashing your bloody tits each night in the BonBon club,' the old woman continued. 'When I think that our poor lad—'

'Right. Now, you listen to me, you old bag,' snapped Stella. 'He's not your "poor lad", he's *my* husband, do you hear, mine! So I don't want you –' she jabbed her finger at Queenie and Ida '– or anyone else telling Charlie about my job—'

'Job,' sneered Queenie. 'More like on the job, if you—'

'My job,' Stella repeated, glaring at the women opposite her. 'Because I'm going to explain everything myself. Do you understand?'

'I'd like to be a fly on the wall when you do.' Ida laughed.

Stella's mouth pulled into a hard line.

'Do you understand?'

Ida sighed. 'I suppose so, but—'

'Good,' Stella cut in. 'Because I swear, as God is my witness, if any of you try to come between me and Charlie, I'll move away and I'll take Patrick with me.'

The colour drained from her mother-in-law's face.

'We promise we won't say anything, will we, Queenie?' Ida said, looking pointedly at the old woman standing beside her.

'No, we won't tell Charlie,' said Queenie, with a gummy smile as her false teeth were reserved for Sunday. 'Sure, won't he find out soon enough that he's married to a trollop.'

'We won't say anything, Stella, honestly,' said Ida in a tight voice. 'And I'll make sure the girls don't either, just don't...don't... take Patrick away.'

'I won't,' said Stella. 'As long as you remember it when Charlie does come home. Now we've got that straight, I'll collect my son from upstairs.' She smiled serenely at the two women glowering at her from the other side of the room. 'I'm sure once I've had a chance to welcome Charlie home properly and after he meets *our* son, he won't listen to a word either of you have to say.'

Chapter four

HOLDING THE HAIRBRUSH in her right hand, Francesca ran it through the thick rope of gathered hair draped over her left shoulder. She did it again then, satisfied all the tangles were out, she started plaiting it.

It was close to eight in the evening and as the final customer had only just left, her father was still in the cafe setting everything out ready for the morning.

She, on the other hand, was in the family parlour at the back of the shop. Dressed in an old skirt and jumper, she was just in the process of getting her wayward hair in order before heading off for another mind-numbing night shift punching out washers.

No more than twelve by fifteen foot, the living quarters had a wrought-iron fireplace with an over-mantel mirror above, two chairs either side, a very old chaise longue with a tartan blanket draped over it and a circular fringed rug covering the terracotta tiles. The door to the backyard was covered with a blackout curtain, as was the small window beside it. Beneath the window was an ornately inlaid wooden Italian cabinet on which were half a dozen sepia photos of her parents' families wearing their village costumes and staring solemnly as they stood against painted backgrounds.

Pride of place in the middle of her ancestors was the tinted portrait of her late mother, Rosa, her rosary draped over one corner of the frame. Mercifully, it had survived the chip shop blaze, but the original wooden frame had been so badly charred her father had had it remounted in silver gilt one. Standing alongside her mother's portrait was the photo of her brother, Giovani, looking very dashing in his Pioneer Corps uniform. It had been taken before he was sent to Scotland last year.

'Is it that time already,' said her father as he came through the door and into the back-of-the-shop lounge carrying a well-earned cup of coffee.

'I'm afraid so,' Francesca replied.

'It's not right,' said her father. 'A woman's place is in the home, not—'

'Papa, how many times have we been through this?' asked Francesca.

'I know, I know,' he said, waving her words away. 'But what has the world come to?' He continued. 'In our village, a respectable man's daughter spent their days learning to cook and run a house, alongside her mother, as is fit and proper. A man would be thought to be a poor provider if his womenfolk had to labour in someone else's fields.' He sat down.

'When did this arrive?' she asked, as she spotted a large manila envelope with her name on it tucked behind the mantelshelf clock.

He shrugged. 'Olive must have put it there after the afternoon post arrived.'

Francesca opened the letter and her heart lurched as she scanned the page.

'My grandfather would have had to take to the mountains with shame if my mother had taken in sewing, let alone spend twelve hours underground,' her father carried on. 'I don't suppose I'd mind so much if my daughter worked in a nice clean office, but a factory—'

'I've got an interview!'

He looked puzzled. 'Interview? What interview?'

'Oh, Papa.' Crossing the room, Francesca knelt in front of him and rested her hands on his knee. 'I wasn't going to say anything because, to be honest, I've got a snowball's chance in hell of getting it, so I didn't want to get my hopes up or yours but I thought nothing ventured nothing gained, so I applied for a job—'

She told him about the BBC Overseas Service advert.

'And I didn't say anything,' she concluded, 'because I didn't want you to be disappointed if—'

'My daughter working for the BBC,' he said, looking wondrously at her.

'I haven't got it yet,' Francesca pointed out.

'But you'll be perfect,' he said. 'And it will give you a chance to use your typing at last.'

'Yes, Papa.'

Of course, she tactfully didn't point out that she'd only gained her Pitman's typing and shorthand certificate because she'd refused to take over her mother's domestic duties when she'd left school and gone to secretarial college instead.

'The Italian section.'

'Yes.'

'I imagine there might be a few young men from the old country working there too,' he said.

'I should think so, but,' she added, to stop her father moving on to white weddings and bambinos, 'I have to pass the interview yet, so let's not count our grapes before the vine flowers.'

Her father studied her for a moment then his bony, work-worn hand ran gently over her cheek.

'You have your mother's looks,' he said softly.

Francesca smiled.

'And her brains,' he added, placing his hand over hers and giving it a squeeze.

She laughed and, rocking back on her heels, stood up.

'I'd better get off or I'll have my wages docked for being late.'

Picking up her knapsack with her clean boiler suit inside, Francesca went to the back door and took her coat off the hook.

'Don't sit up too late,' she said, as she shoved her arm in the sleeve.

'I won't,' he replied.

'And make sure you go straight down to the basement if the sirens go off,' she continued, buttoning her coat.

'I will,' he said. 'Now you get off before you miss your bus.'

Crossing the space between them, she gave him a peck on the cheek and then, slinging her work bag across her, she strode across the room and out of the door.

The next day, holding her hat with one hand to stop the March breeze whipping it away, Francesca hurried past the shops of Stepney High Street. It was the middle of the afternoon and she'd been up and dressed for little over an hour.

Bobbing impatiently on the spot, she waited on the kerb until one of McGuire's coal lorries had passed, then she sped across the road to St Dunstan's wrought-iron gates. Turning south towards the river she continued on past the ancient graveyard and the alms houses towards Mattie's home in Belgrave Street, which was just a fifteen-minute walk from her mother's house in Mafeking Terrace.

She and Mattie had been best friends since they were four and a half and had sat next to each other in Miss Gordan's class at St Breda and St Brendan's infant school. A shade shorter than Francesca, Mattie had her older brother's dark looks. In truth, Mattie was more a sister than a friend as Mattie's mother, Ida, had taken Francesca firmly under her wing when her mother died six years ago and then after the dreadful night when her home was razed to the ground and her father and brother interned as enemy aliens, Ida had taken her in.

Before the war the two girls had pooled their clothes for nights out dancing, however, Mattie would be hard pushed to fit into any of Francesca's dresses now as she was very pregnant.

Francesca stopped at Mattie's front door and knocked. After a moment or two Mattie opened the door holding a grizzly Alicia on her hip. She gave Francesca a querying look. 'I thought we were meeting up tomorrow to go shopping.'

'We are,' Francesca replied. 'But I've got some good news that won't wait.'

'All right, then come in and you can tell me over a cuppa.' Mattie held back the door and Francesca stepped in.

'Should you be carrying her in your condition?' asked Francesca as she stepped into the hallway.

'You sound like my gran,' said Mattie, closing the door.

She set her daughter on the floor and Alicia toddled off down the hall towards the kitchen.

'I'd better catch her before she pulls the cupboard open,' said Mattie, waddling after her daughter.

Taking off her jacket, Francesca hooked it on the hall stand then followed her down the hallway to the kitchen.

Unlike the old workman's cottage that Mattie had lived in as a child, the one her husband Major Daniel McCarthy had bought just after they married had three good-sized bedrooms and a separate lounge and dining room, a modern kitchen with a gas ascot, which provided hot water on tap. If that wasn't enough to make the neighbours green with envy, Mattie also had a bathroom, with an immersion heater and an inside toilet.

'I notice a bomb took out half of Trafalgar Gardens last night,' said Francesca, as she walked into the kitchen. 'The Heavy Rescue team were still digging when I came past.'

'Poor souls,' said Mattie with feeling, turning up the gas under the simmering kettle. 'The milkman said it was a high-explosive bomb and I believe him because I felt it land at about four-ish. Shook the sides of the Morrison shelter and made the tins on the shelf rattle.'

Like the cafe, Mattie's house had a basement, which Daniel had reinforced and kitted out as a shelter. Major Daniel McCarthy was away defending the country but whereas most of the thousands of men called up were stationed in far-flung outposts in the Far East or with the army in North Africa, Mattie's husband, a SOE operative, was deep behind enemy lines working with the French Resistance.

Even though Mattie said the cage-like shelter he'd installed made her feel like a hamster, she and Alicia spent their nights safe from the Luftwaffe's nocturnal visits.

Francesca sat down and Alicia, having tired of moving the kitchen dresser handle up and down, trotted across the Lino towards her. Catching her, Francesca planted a kiss on the child's soft cheek while Alicia buried her face in Francesca's hair and gave her a hug in return.

'She's such an angel,' said Francesca, enjoying the feel of the child in her arms.

'You wouldn't have said that if you'd seen her create about having her nappy changed an hour ago. Now,' she said, placing a mug of tea in front of Francesca, 'what is this wonderful news that won't wait until tomorrow?'

Francesca drew the manila envelope that had been on the mantelshelf the night before from her jacket pocket. 'I've got an interview for a new job.'

Mattie's eyes opened wide. 'You never told me you were applying for something else.'

'I didn't tell anyone, not even Papa,' Francesca replied, 'because, honestly, I didn't think I stood much of a chance.'

'What is it then?'

'A clerical assistant at the BBC, don't you know,' said Francesca, in her best plummy voice.

Mattie's eyes stretched even wider. 'The BBC! That's blooming brilliant.'

'Yes it is, isn't it?' It's in the Italian section of the Overseas department.'

'I didn't know they had one,' said Mattie, rolling up the wet nappy in yesterday's newspaper.

'They haven't, not yet,' Francesca replied.

'What will you be doing?'

'I'm not too sure,' said Francesca. 'But it sounds as if I'd be a general assistant helping with the recordings and things.'

'Oh my goodness,' said Mattie. 'You'll be perfect.'

'I haven't got it yet,' Francesca replied.

'They'd be idiots not to take you,' Mattie replied. 'And such an opportunity. Plus,' she continued, 'you'll be able to wear something nice to work instead of overalls.'

'Oh, I didn't think of that,' said Francesca, thinking with sudden panic about the handful of utility dresses and jackets hanging in her wardrobe.

'Don't worry, you can borrow a couple of my suits,' said Mattie, guessing her quandary. She ran her hands over her swelling stomach. 'It's not as if I can fit into any of them.'

'How are you, and the baby?'

'I'm tired and the baby's lively,' Mattie replied. 'But the midwives at Munroe House think I'm due at the end of May rather than the middle of June so now I'm just praying Master or Miss McCarthy stays put until after Jo and Tommy's big day. Talking of which, I'm hoping Jo and I can buy the material for her dress sometime this week so, as I'm not really in any condition to crawl around the floor or lean across tables, would you mind giving me a hand cutting Jo's dress out?'

'Of course not, I'd love to help.' Francesca picked up her cup. 'Any word from Charlie?' she asked, nonchalantly blowing across the top.

Concern flashed across her friend's face. 'Actually, Fran, he's been wounded—'

'Wounded!' Francesca's heart thumped painfully. 'How? He's all right, isn't he?'

Mattie's hand closed over her arm. 'He's fine. Well, as fine as he can be with a busted shoulder.'

'When?'

'About two weeks ago,' Mattie replied. 'We only found out yesterday when Stella came to pick up Patrick.'

'Where is he now?'

'On a troop ship steaming home,' Mattie replied. 'Mum was all set to visit him when he landed but Stella said she couldn't because—'

'Because she wants to make sure no one tells Charlie what she's been up to,' said Francesca, as an image of Charlie's feckless wife flashed through her mind.

Mattie nodded. 'According to Mum there was a right row.'

She recounted the argument.

'I bet Queenie tore her off a right strip,' Francesca said, imagining Mattie's ferocious pint-size grandmother giving Stella a tongue-lashing.

'She did,' Mattie replied. 'In fact, Gran was still cursing and swearing when I arrived half an hour after Stella left. Mum's so terrified that Stella will take Patrick away that we've agreed not to say anything to Charlie.'

'But he's bound to find out,' said Francesca.

'Of course he will,' her friend replied. 'But I think her plan is to get to him first and... and sweet talk him round,' continued Mattie. 'To be honest, Fran, as much as I love my brother, he's the bloody idiot who got himself into this mess, so he'll have to be the one to sort it.' Mattie's gaze ran over Francesca's face. 'If only...'

She didn't say: *If only my brother had fallen in love with you,* but Francesca knew her friend was thinking it. After all, hadn't she thought the same herself a thousand times?

Damping down the ache rising again in her chest, Francesca forced a smile. 'Well, whatever happens, the good news is he'll finally get to meet Patrick.'

*

Francesca was pretty familiar with Oxford Street, but when she came out of the underground station the following Monday morning it took her a couple of moments to orientate herself.

The department stores had taken a battering the same as the rest of the capital and, by the looks of the rubble scattered around and the soot-blackened faces of the Heavy Rescue crew drinking tea by the WVS canteen on the other side of the road, the night before had been a busy one. Although they were all still trading, thanks to the Luftwaffe many of the elegant late-Victorian facades had been partially destroyed, or, as in the case of John Lewis, which now stood like a tumbledown castle just west of her, completely destroyed.

Peter Robinson, which stood on the north-east corner of Oxford Circus, was still open to customers but remained boarded up since it was gutted by a high-explosive bomb a year and a half ago. Now, instead of mannequins wearing the latest summer fashions, the rough boards covering the shop windows had posters urging people to save fuel, salvage rags and there was one showing a soldier chatting in a pub above an image of a boat sinking that read: *Loose Lips Sink Ships.*

Even though she was kitted out smartly in Mattie's best navy suit with the pink blouse she'd bought for her cousin's wedding beneath, Francesca still felt sick with nerves. Her mother's pearl broach was pinned on her jacket, just above her heart for luck, and she had polished her black lace-up brogues until they shone so brightly they now reflected the morning sunlight as she stepped out onto the pavement. The ensemble was topped off by a perky little hat from Rose Hats that had taken her fancy; two clothing coupons and half of last week's wages.

Hooking her handbag over her arm and checking her hat was still on straight after being squashed in a Central line train for half an hour, Francesca turned north and, crunching shards of glass as she went, headed towards Broadcasting House.

The British Broadcasting Company was like a family member to every man, woman and child in the country. The programmes on the Home Service marked out the day with news bulletins and when you wanted the children out from under your feet while you made the evening meal there was *Children's Hour*. There were radio dramas such as *The Old Lady Shows Her Medals*, or politics with *In Parliament This Week*. The government used it to prompt people to observe the blackout and turn lights off, while Churchill popped up regularly to remind the weary, sleep-deprived population what they were fighting for.

It seemed fitting, therefore, given its prominence in the nation's life, that the main hub of all this entertainment, education and information should be housed in a grand art deco building that stood like a Portland stone ocean liner opposite All Saints church. The nautical imagery of the building was enhanced by the sandbags, stacked to head-height to protect the ground-floor windows, that looked like light brown waves rolling back as the building sailed on.

Broadcasting House hadn't escaped the Luftwaffe's attention and had received a broadside in the form of a five-hundred-pound high-explosive bomb as the masonry on the fifth floor testified.

There was a brick wall blocking the stylised doors leading into the lobby so, instead of walking through the main entrance, Francesca joined the queue of people entering the sole usable door to one side. Taking her courage in her hands, Francesca walked into the BBC's vast lobby.

The whole of London seemed to be there. A woman in high heels and a luxurious fur, holding a long cigarette holder aloft, glided across the polished marble tiles to the lifts at the far end, surrounded by a bevy of reporters. Three chaps in morning suits strode towards the stairs carrying violin cases under their arms.

'Excuse me!' A youth with slicked-back hair and carrying a stack of gramophone records shot past her.

'Sorry,' said Francesca.

She stepped aside.

'Out of my way, girl!' boomed a voice over her right shoulder.

Francesca turned to find a tall man with wild grey hair, black-rimmed glasses and wearing a baggy tweed suit ploughing towards her.

She leapt back and he swept past, followed by a worried-looking woman taking notes.

'Can I help you, miss?'

Francesca looked in the direction of the voice.

A plump woman in a tight jumper with scarlet-painted lips and her blonde hair styled into victory rolls was regarding her with a bored expression as she sat behind the reception desk.

Dodging past a couple of men in light brown overalls pushing a trolley with a tangle of wires on top, she went to the reception desk.

'I'd be grateful if you could,' said Francesca, snapping open her handbag and taking out the letter. 'I have an appointment with a Miss Kirk at eleven.'

'Room twelve, third floor, fourth door from the right,' the woman replied, waving vaguely behind her. 'Next!'

'Er, where—'

'I said, room twelve, third floor, fourth door on the right,' repeated the receptionist.

Spotting a sweeping flight of stairs to the left of her, Francesca made towards them.

'You want the stairs on the right,' the young women called out after her.

Francesca moved away, clutching her letter, and walked around the curved lobby area to the right, spotting a set of stairs which, although not as grand as the main ones, had less traffic.

She started upward, but as she pushed the door open she was confronted by a man in his shirtsleeves. He had a set of headphones around his neck and was holding a clipboard.

'Sorry, miss, you can't come this way, we're recording,' he said.

'But I have an interview at eleven with Miss Kirk.'

'Sorry, you'll have to go back down to the next floor and walk along to the middle flight of stairs,' he replied, his arms stretched out to bar her way.

Francesca sighed and trudged down the stairs she'd just come up until she got to the floor below. Pushing open the heavy door she stepped into the corridor but was immediately confronted by a crowd of people who were talking loudly in what she thought was Russian.

Francesca spotted a staircase just beyond the press of people.

'Excuse me,' Francesca whispered, trying to squeeze past a couple of elegantly dressed young women.

Giving her a disdainful glance, they shuffled forward a little. Francesca pressed on but was then blocked by an enormous man, wearing an expensive suit and too much cologne.

Francesca pressed herself against the wall. 'Excuse me.'

He gave her a sniffy look and then turned back.

'I'm sorry,' she said, trying to squeeze past. 'If you don't mind, I—'

'Sir, if you please,' said a deep voice from behind her. 'This young lady is *trying* to get past.'

The man blocking her path looked around and across the top of her head.

A tight smile lifted his fleshy face. 'My apologies.'

He stood aside and Francesca squeezed past and then, once she'd cleared the crowd, she turned.

'Thank you so much for—' She stopped.

The man standing behind her was tall and slender with olive-coloured skin like her own and liquid-brown eyes. A Hollywood starlet would envy his cheekbones, eyelashes and the abundance of his jet-black hair. He was immaculately dressed in a three-piece suit. Small diamonds twinkled in the gold cufflinks at his wrists, which matched the pin anchoring his club tie in place.

'My pleasure,' he replied, with a hint of an accent and a flash of white teeth. 'Miss…?'

'Fabrino,' Francesca replied.

'It was my pleasure, Miss Fabrino, there's always a melee when Prince Ivan Romanov visits,' her rescuer replied. 'Can I direct you?'

'I have an interview with Miss Kirk at eleven o'clock,' Francesca replied.

He raised a well-shaped eyebrow. 'For the clerical post in the Italian section.'

'Yes,' said Francesca.

Something flashed across the back of his eyes, then he smiled again.

'It's been lovely to make your acquaintance, Miss Fabrino.' He took her gloved hand and bowed over it. 'But if you'll excuse me.'

'Of course,' said Francesca.

He smiled again, then he turned and dashed up the stairs two at a time.

'Thank you again, Mr…' she called after him, but he had gone.

Adjusting her handbag and checking her hat again, Francesca followed the corridor he had disappeared down at a more leisurely pace.

Fifteen minutes later she was perched on the edge of one of three not very comfortable chairs outside room 12. A woman, a redhead in a flowery dress, dark-green jacket and saucer-style hat with artificial cherries fixed around the brim, had been called in almost as soon as Francesca took her seat and had yet to reappear. Biting her lower lip, Francesca studied the solid wooden door for a moment or two, then glanced at her wristwatch.

A young woman carrying a notepad hurried past and disappeared into a room further along the corridor just as a man, with a pencil in hand and his eyes glued to the manuscript in his hand, came out of another. He strolled past her muttering and then headed through the door at the far end as a telephone rang behind one of the doors.

Francesca was just about to glance at her watch again when the redhead stepped out, followed by a stout woman wearing a Donegal tweed suit over a plain white blouse with a bow tied at her throat. Her tightly permed steel-grey hair resembled a motorcycle helmet and she had a pair of thick horn-rimmed spectacles balanced on the tip of her nose.

'Thank you for attending, Miss Turnbull.' She gave the redhead a professional smile. 'And we will let you know.'

The young woman left, her heels echoing as she walked down the stairs. The woman in tweed turned her attention to Francesca.

'Miss Fabrino?' she asked, studying her over the top of her glasses.

Francesca stood up quickly. 'Yes.'

'I'm Miss Kirk.' The professional smile returned. 'If you would follow me.'

Opening the door again, she walked through with Francesca just a step behind. They entered a room with half a dozen desks, each occupied by a young woman bashing away on a typewriter.

'This way if you please, Miss Fabrino,' said Miss Kirk, opening a door at the far end of the room and ushering her in.

Francesca found herself in a high-ceilinged room, illuminated by box-shaped wall lights. The cream walls had brown-and-tan-painted panels at regular intervals around the room. There was a long sideboard with three drawers placed against one of the walls, on top of which stood an abstract metal sculpture at one end and a silver tray with a decanter and glasses at the other.

At the far end of the room was an oval-shaped table surrounded by four chairs, each with a blotter and notebook placed on the table in front of them. In one of the chairs sat a thick-set man in his middle fifties scribbling furiously on a pile of papers. A cigarette dangled from his lips, peppering his multicoloured striped jumper with ash. He was completely bald but made up for this by having the bushiest eyebrows she'd ever seen. He raised his eyes and regarded her with mild interest as she walked in and then, flicking his cigarette in the general direction of the overfilled ashtray, returned to his task.

In total contrast, next to him sat a slightly built man in his early forties, with short sandy-coloured hair, pale eyes, a clipped moustache and a charcoal suit that had clearly been made for him. However, Francesca's chin nearly hit the floor when she saw the occupant of the next chair: none other than her rescuer from the third floor. He didn't look up but continued scanning the file in front of him.

'Please take a seat, Miss Fabrino.' Miss Kirk indicated the solitary chair in front of the desk.

Gathering her wits together and tucking her skirt under her, Francesca sat down, placing her handbag on the floor by her feet before resting her hands on her lap.

'Now,' said the older woman, as she took her place on the other side of the table. 'You've applied for the clerical assistant post with the BBC's Overseas section; the Italian department, to be precise.'

'Yes I have,' Francesca replied.

'Well, before we start,' continued Miss Kirk, 'perhaps I should do a few introductions. I am, as you already know, Miss Kirk and I'm responsible for the broadcasting schedule, at the far end is Mr Whyte, who is our sound and recording engineer.' Lighting a fresh cigarette from the stub of the old, the technician raised his hand. 'Then we have Mr Carmichael, who is from the Ministry of Information.' The man with the sandy-coloured hair and expensive suit took off his round spectacles and started polishing the lenses but didn't respond. 'And, lastly, Count Leonardo D'Angelo of Pontadera, who is our—'

'Miss Kirk, we are all friends and allies here so Signor D'Angelo, please,' he said, giving the woman to his left an entreating look.

A slight flush coloured Miss Kirk's downy cheek.

Signor D'Angelo turned his attention back to Francesca and gave her a charming smile. 'Welcome, Miss Fabrino.'

Francesca ventured a shy smile in response.

'Good,' said Miss Kirk. 'Now, perhaps you'd like to tell us why you're applying for this job, Miss Fabrino.'

'Well, when I saw your advertisement for a clerical assistant with some office experience and who speaks fluent Italian, I thought I would apply.'

'And what are you doing at the moment?' asked Mr Whyte, blowing a stream of smoke out of the side of his mouth.

'Factory war work,' Francesca replied. 'I can't say more.'

'You worked in an office before that?' asked Miss Kirk.

'No, I worked in a shop,' Francesca replied. 'But I—'

'So what office experience *do* you have, Miss Fabrino?' cut in Mr Carmichael.

'Well, I gained a distinction in my advanced Pitman's typing and a merit in shorthand,' Francesca replied.

'How many words per minute?' asked Miss Kirk.

'Forty,' Francesca replied. 'But it was difficult for me to get a job because of my father—'

'Is he sick?' asked Mr Whyte.

'No,' said Francesca, with a sigh. 'Just… Well, he's a bit of a traditionalist and believes that unmarried daughters should help their mothers in the home.'

'My father was the same,' said Miss Kirk, giving her a sympathetic look.

'So, you have no actual office experience,' said Mr Carmichael.

Francesca's heart sank.

'No,' she said in a small voice.

'Miss Fabrino,' the count said in a smooth voice, 'you say in your application that you are fluent in Italian?'

'I am,' Francesca replied firmly.

'Would you like to explain how that is?' he said, switching suddenly from English to rapid Italian.

Surprised to hear a question in her cradle language, Francesca paused for a moment then spoke.

'My grandfather came to England with his new wife about sixty years ago,' replied Francesca, her thoughts slipping easily into the familiar language. 'And although my father was born in this country, at home he spoke only Italian. My mother was a very distant cousin of his, and when my father saw a picture of her he fell in love.'

'*Che romantico*,' said Signor D'Angelo, looking Heavenward.

'*Si*.' Francesca laughed. 'He courted her by post for two years, then he asked her to marry him. She wrote back yes so, six months later, after he'd saved for her passage to England, he sent for her. They married three days after she arrived. Although she learnt enough English to talk to customers in the shop—'

Signor D'Angelo gave her a querying look. 'Shop?'

'My family owned a restaurant where people bought fish and sliced fried potatoes wrapped up in newspaper to eat at home,' Francesca explained. 'There's no equivalent in Italian.'

'*Non ce n'è*,' he agreed. 'Please continue, Miss Fabrino.'

'There's not much else to say except that my brother and I spoke only Italian until we went to school, then we'd switch back to our mother tongue at home. My brother is in the Pioneer Corps up north somewhere but we write to each other in Italian,' Francesca replied, at a speed to match his.

'Thank you, Miss Fabrino,' Signor D'Angelo replied, reverting to English and smiling broadly at her.

Holding her gaze with a warm look in his eyes, he addressed the man beside him. 'I'm sure you'll agree, Carmichael, that Miss Fabrino's command of her mother tongue is faultless.'

A tinge of colour lit the civil servant's sallow cheeks.

'Yes, faultless, indeed,' he said. 'But are you able to read and write in the language?'

Signor D'Angelo gave the man beside him a puzzled look. 'Miss Fabrino has just told us she writes to her brother in Italian.'

The faint colour on Mr Carmichael's cheeks darkened slightly. 'Oh, yes, yes, of course she did, I forgot.'

A wry smile lifted the corner of the count's mouth.

Looking past him, the civil servant addressed the woman sitting on the other side of Signor D'Angelo.

'Miss Kirk?'

'Thank you, Mr Carmichael.' She looked at Francesca. 'If you were successful you would be based at Bush House, which is near Fleet Street. In addition, as we work in the Overseas section and what we broadcast to occupied Europe is central to the war effort, you would be required to sign the Official Secrets Act. You would also be expected to be part of the fire watch rota and undertake fire-fighting training.'

'I used to be part of the auxiliary fire-fighting team at my previous job,' said Francesca.

'And I expect you looked very fetching in the uniform,' said Signor D'Angelo quietly, in rapid Italian.

'English, if you please,' said Miss Kirk.

'*Mi scusa*,' he replied. 'I said, that's good because she already knows the ropes.'

He caught Francesca's eye and winked.

Feeling her cheeks grow warm, Francesca lowered her eyes.

'Have you a question, Mr Whyte?' asked Miss Kirk.

Mr Whyte shook his head.

'Not as such,' he replied. 'I need someone who can make sure all the scripts are in the right place at the right time for our broadcasts and someone who also remembers not to talk when the studio red light is on.'

'I'm sure I'll remember,' Francesca replied, aware of Signor D'Angelo's molten gaze on her.

'Have you any questions?' asked Miss Kirk.

'How soon will I know if I've got the job?'

'We are hoping to get someone into post as soon as possible,' the older woman replied. 'How much notice do you have to give, Miss Fabrino?'

'A week,' Francesca replied.

Miss Kirk's professional smile returned. 'Well, if there's nothing else?'

She ran her gaze along her fellow panellists, who shook their heads.

'Very well.' She turned her attention back to Francesca. 'Thank you for coming and we'll let you know.'

Picking up her handbag from beside her chair, Francesca stood up. 'Thank you for your time.'

'It's been a pleasure, Miss Fabrino,' said Signor D'Angelo, giving her another dazzling smile.

Hooking her bag over her arm, Francesca turned to leave the room feeling Signor D'Angelo's gaze fixed on her every step of the way.

Chapter five

'FANCY COMING IN on the next game, Charlie boy?' asked Flight Lieutenant Keith White, looking at Charlie with his one remaining eye, as he dealt another round.

Charlie looked up from his book. 'Thanks, Chalky, but I'll pass if you don't mind.'

It was just about three on a lovely late March afternoon and almost four weeks since he'd been wounded, two days since he'd disembarked at New Haven Dock. He and half a dozen wounded had been transferred by ambulance to the grounds of Willington House just outside Eastbourne. He was now sitting beneath the branches of an elm tree in what had been the lady of the house's rose garden. However, where the cultivated blooms had once flourished there were now rows upon row of bean poles. The grand old ancestral pile, like so many others, had been requisitioned at the outbreak of war and turned into a military hospital, and its beautiful ornamental gardens dug up and turned into vegetable plots to feed the hungry convalescing men.

He was surrounded by soldiers, sailors and airmen, some of whom were burnt and maimed so severely and visibly it made him thankful he had only busted his shoulder.

As tea wouldn't be for another hour, nurses in their sky-blue uniforms, starched aprons and frilly caps were pushing wheelchair-bound servicemen along the sun-lit gravel paths so they could enjoy some fresh air and a change of scenery.

A few of the less injured men were playing croquet on what remained of the lawn while others, with bandaged stumps, were practising on their crutches. Over by the Victorian greenhouse a couple of men had set up easels and a few more were snoozing in deckchairs.

'He's just afraid we'll clean him out,' said Bomber Reginald Pye, picking his cards up awkwardly in his bandaged fingers.

'Never a truer word spoken, Porky,' said Pilot Officer Eric Smethurst, his wheelchair creaking as he sat forward to retrieve the cards he'd been dealt.

'These army types are all the same,' mumbled Co-pilot Rory Coats through burnt lips and missing teeth.

Charlie cast his gaze over the four airmen sitting across the patio from him. For all their bravado none of them could be older than twenty, as their juvenile moustaches and Brylcreem quiffs testified.

Charlie smiled. 'Sorry, lads, I don't want to take your money.'

The four airmen laughed and continued with their game.

Charlie returned to his book, but he'd only got halfway down the page when Staff Nurse Oliphant walked over, clutching a package to the square bib of her apron.

The young nurse was part of the team in charge of Wellington ward, where the walking wounded like Charlie were housed. Slightly built with light brown hair, a turned-up nose and ready smile, she always put Charlie in mind of his younger sister Cathy, the only one of the Brogan children who didn't have their mother's colouring.

'Afternoon, gentlemen,' she said, stopping just in front of them.

'Afternoon, Betty,' said Eric through the cigarette held in his lips. 'And how is our favourite nurse?'

'It's Staff Nurse Oliphant to you, Mr Smethurst,' she replied in her best matron voice. 'And I'm very well and thank you for asking.'

'Have I mentioned you are the prettiest nurse in the whole place?' said Reginald, resting his chin on his hand and gazing adoringly across at her.

Nurse Oliphant raised an eyebrow. 'Constantly.'

'And that I'm desperate to marry you,' added Chalky, matching his friend's doting expression.

'Perhaps you should ask your wife about that first,' Nurse Oliphant replied, struggling to suppress a smile.

'She's got you there, chum,' hooted Reginald, jabbing the stem of his pipe at the man opposite.

'So, divine creature from Heaven,' continued Eric, as he reshuffled the cards, 'which one of us are you bestowing your favours on?'

'Mr Brogan.'

The four airmen wolf-whistled and muttered 'lucky dog' and 'jammy bugger'.

'You'll have to forgive them, miss,' said Charlie, as she turned to him. 'They're not used to mixing with grown-ups.'

She smiled and handed him the package with a letter tucked behind it. 'These came in the afternoon post.'

'Thank you for bringing them out. I could have picked them up later.'

'Oh, I fancied a bit of fresh air,' she replied, shifting her weight onto her other foot. Her eyes flickered onto the brown paper package. 'Another book, I see.'

'From my sister Mattie,' Charlie replied. 'She sends me something new to read when she can.'

'That's good of her,' said Nurse Oliphant. 'You must be very close.'

'We are,' said Charlie.

It was true. Being the two eldest, he and Mattie had been the ones to help shoulder the burdens of the family. Mattie helped their mother care for the younger ones while he did his bit on their father's wagon. When the family could only eat each evening if there was a shilling or two in their father's pocket, as the eldest of the brood they had to pitch in.

Nurse Oliphant ran her eyes softly over Charlie's face with eager expectancy.

After a pause, Charlie smiled and held up the parcel. 'Thanks again for bringing it out.'

'It was no trouble.' She sighed. 'No trouble at all, Mr Brogan, but I'd best get on or matron will be after me.'

'Charlie,' he said. 'Mr Brogan makes me feel like me dad.'

She laughed and left.

'How in the blooming hell does he do it?' said Eric, slapping down a card as Nurse Oliphant headed across the lawn to the house.

Charlie grinned. 'Irish charm, boys. Irish charm.'

The airmen grumbled good-naturedly as Eric dealt another hand. Charlie opened his package and took out a copy of *The Case of the Empty Tin*.

'Is that a Perry Mason mystery?' asked Rory.

'Yes,' said Charlie, holding it up so he could see. 'I'll leave it for you when I ship out.'

'Old Skinflint signed you off?' asked Chalky.

Charlie shook his head. 'I saw him yesterday and he said if the shoulder's a bit more mobile by next Friday, I can go home to recuperate.'

'What did you have to say about that?'

'Nothing,' Charlie replied.

Actually, he did have something to say. A whole blooming lot but, as he didn't want to be up on a charge of insubordination for swearing at the man in charge, Major Flint, Charlie had kept schtum.

'Well, when you do finally get to the Smoke, you might want to take a gander at this,' said Eric, pulling a folded magazine out from the space between his leg and wheelchair arm. 'The Yanks have done a special edition of *Beauty Parade* for their GIs stationed in London.'

'God bless America,' said Reginald, giving an exaggerated salute with his bandaged right hand.

Eric threw it across and it landed on the ground in front of Charlie.

'It lists all the best strip clubs in Soho and has pictures of their top acts,' the airman continued. 'I tell you, a night with any one of those little sweethearts will do you more good than all the pills in the doc's medical chest put together.'

'I'm sure it would but all I need is some home-cooking and a bit of shut-eye to get me back on my feet,' said Charlie, thinking of the photo of his wife and son sitting on his bedside locker.

Leaning forward he picked up the periodical and was just about to throw it back to its owner when the wind caught the page and flipped it over.

As something like a fist smashed simultaneously into his head and guts, Charlie stared at the open page.

'Oi oi,' said Rory, from what seemed like a very long way off. 'Something's caught our solider-boy's interest.'

Focusing hard, Charlie closed the journal and stood up, tucking his book and the magazine under his sling.

'Sorry, chums,' he said, forcing a smile. 'I've just remembered I have to do something.'

Despite his heart crashing in his chest, Charlie managed to maintain his affable, unruffled expression as he strolled along the gravel path to the big house. However, as soon as the main door closed behind him, he collapsed like a puppet with its strings cut against the wall of the silent hallway.

His head spun. He locked his knees to stop himself sinking to the floor and took a couple of deep breaths. The dizziness receded a little as the floor settled back to its rightful place beneath his feet.

At the far end of the corridor that ran towards the kitchen at the back of the house a door opened, and the sound of women's voices drifted down.

Charlie forced himself upright and stumbled towards the sweeping central stairs that led to the wards on the first floor. Shoving the folded magazine in his back trouser pocket, he grasped the handrail with his good hand and hauled himself up to the top.

He steadied himself for a moment or two, then turned and headed for the toilets, halfway between his ward and the one opposite. Praying there was no one within, he stumbled in. Ignoring the four porcelain urinals, he pushed open one of the cubicle doors and went in. Locking it behind him, he took out the magazine and, with trembling hands, flipped the pages over until he reached the centrefold.

He studied the photo of his wife, wearing nothing but a smile, illustrating the full-page feature about the star stripper of the BonBon club for a long moment, then pitched forward. Dropping the periodical on the floor, Charlie grasped the black Bakelite lavatory seat and threw up down the bowl.

'As I said yesterday, Brogan,' said Major Flint, Willington House's senior orthopaedic doctor, 'you won't be fit for discharge until at least next week at the earliest.'

'I know, sir,' Charlie replied. 'But I have to go home.'

It had been some half an hour since he'd lost his lunch down the lavatory bowl and, after rinsing his mouth and sticking his head under the cold tap in the hand basin, it had taken him all of two minutes to reach the surgeon's consulting room where he'd had to kick his heels for a further quarter of an hour while he'd waited for the doctor to return from his ward rounds.

He was now standing at ease, in what had once been the lady of the house's morning room, with the late-afternoon sunlight streaming through the window. The consultant sat behind the desk surrounded by the tools of his trade, including a variety of different sized artificial legs, which, thank God, Charlie had no need of.

'But you said yourself my collarbone has mended,' Charlie persisted, forcing his right hand, pressed into his side, to remain still.

'Only *just* mended, I think I said,' the consultant replied. 'Which is remarkable enough given it had been broken in three places, but in the x-ray your shoulder blade still looks like an un-made jigsaw puzzle.'

'I really must go home,' said Charlie.

The consultant's pale eyes held his. 'What's the sudden urgency?'

'I'd rather not say,' Charlie replied. 'If you don't mind, sir.'

'I damn well do mind,' the medic replied. His eyes flickered on to the sling supporting Charlie's injured arm. 'Given the mess that lump of metal made of your shoulder, you're lucky to still have one. In fact, you're very lucky to be here at all.'

'Yes, sir,' said Charlie. 'And grateful so I am for you patching me—'

'For pity's sake, man. Won't it wait?' cut in Major Flint. 'A day or two at least. Let the bones mend some more before you go gadding about.'

'No, sir. Sorry, sir, I really have to go right away,' said Charlie. 'Please.'

Scrutinising Charlie's face, Major Flint's fulsome moustache shifted from side to side as he chewed the inside of his mouth. 'I suppose if I don't sign you off fit to travel, you'll go anyway.'

Looking at a point just above the officer's head, Charlie didn't reply.

He didn't want to go AWOL and lose his bombardier stripes, but…

With his pulse racing, Charlie waited for what seemed like an eternity.

Finally, Major Flint spoke again.

'It's against my better judgement, but very well.'

'Thank you, sir,' he said, letting out a breath he didn't know he was holding.

'I'm not discharging you as fit, but into the care of Sir Sidney Parkinson, the top man at the Middlesex. He's an old chum and owes me a favour.'

'Thank you, sir,' Charlie repeated.

'Yes, well.' The doctor's impressive moustache did another little dance. 'I know how hard it is for a chap to be away from the ones he loves for so long, but – ' he jabbed his index finger at Charlie '– you make sure you don't go doing something stupid and bust your shoulder open again.'

'No, sir,' said Charlie, wondering if confronting your wife about her change of profession constituted as 'something stupid'.

Taking a form from his stationery rack, the major picked up his fountain pen.

'I'll tell the bursar to issue you a travel warrant for tomorrow,' he said, unscrewing the top. 'And you might be able to cadge a lift to Eastbourne station from one of the chaps from the NAFFI picking up supplies.' He looked Charlie up and down again. 'Dismissed.'

Charlie snapped to attention and saluted the top of the doctor's head as his pen scratched across Charlie's discharge form. Then, piece of paper in hand, he marched out of the office.

Charlie jolted awake as the train ground to a halt. Wiping his hands over his face he forced his eyes open and looked out of the window. He could see the grey river sparkling in the mid-afternoon sunlight and, in the distance, the distinct shape of the Houses of Parliament and Big Ben but, given that there was no platform in sight, he guessed they were being held at a signal just outside the station.

He'd had to wait half the morning for the quartermaster to issue his travel warrant so instead of catching an early train, as he'd hoped, he'd ended up getting the eleven-thirty to London from Eastbourne. It meant he'd had to change at Croydon, but he should still have arrived in London just after two. Instead of which, because the down-line between Horsham and Uckfield had been put out of action by a bomb being dropped on it two days before, a delay of half an hour on the line meant Charlie had missed his connection and had had to wait another twenty minutes for the next train, which was why he was now pulling into the station at just before three.

'You look like you've been in the wars,' said a young woman opposite him, nodding towards the sling supporting his left arm.

'Just a bit of shrapnel,' he replied. 'I'll mend.'

'Well, you're very brave,' she continued, her eyes soft behind the round lenses of her metal-rimmed spectacles. 'You all are.'

The man in the tight grey suit and fedora, sitting at the other end of the seat from Charlie, put his paper aside.

'Africa?' he asked.

Charlie nodded.

'My lad's there,' said the man. 'What division were you in?'

Charlie smiled and tapped the side of his nose.

The man laughed. 'Of course, Son. Loose talk cost lives. You home long?'

'Until the docs say I can go back,' said Charlie.

'Well, even if it's a short stay,' said the woman, 'I'm sure your mother will be pleased to see you.'

'And your wife, too,' added the man.

Charlie forced a smile.

A billow of smoke obscured the view for a couple of seconds and then the train shunted forward and continued into the station.

As the engine pulling them ground and squeaked to a halt on platform five, Charlie rose to his feet. Pushing down the window, he reached out and twisted the door handle.

'After you, madam,' he said, standing back out of the woman's way.

She gathered up her things and stepped down from the train. Taking his case from the top rack, the man got off, too.

Reaching up, Charlie dragged his kit bag off the webbing of the luggage rack with his good arm and then stepped down onto the platform.

Breathing in the tangy smell of coal dust and oil, he strolled along the platform and showed his travel pass to the inspector at the barrier. The metal gables and glass of the Victorian railway station arched above him as Charlie surveyed the main concourse.

Before him was a sea of khaki and navy uniform. However, intermingled with the domestic colours of war, was a new shade of GI dark olive, while the familiar London accents that Charlie knew so well were now punctuated by the loud tones usually only heard from cowboys and gangsters on the silver screen.

The smell of fried fish and vinegar drifted across from the WVS canteen wagon next to the booking hall and Charlie's stomach rumbled.

Someone knocked into him and pain shot across his collarbone.

'Jeez! Sorry, pal,' said a bovine-faced GI as he brushed past him. Charlie grimaced.

'Bloody Yanks,' grumbled a station porter, stacking cases onto a trolley nearby.

Charlie smiled and adjusted his rucksack to ease his aching shoulder.

'Do us a favour, mate, and point me towards the nearest British Restaurant?'

An hour later, having polished off a plate of bangers and mash, a bowl of roly-poly pudding and two mugs of tea, Charlie stepped out of the door of the government feeding station on Vauxhall Bridge Road and into the dim light of early evening.

According to the chalked notice leaning against the ARP control hut outside the station, the blackout didn't start until seven thirty so there was enough time to take a leisurely stroll across Green Park and along Piccadilly.

Looping the straps of his kit bag over his good shoulder, Charlie crossed the road and headed towards Buckingham Palace.

By the time Charlie reached Green Park underground station there was already a stream of people making their way down the stairs to spend the night on the Piccadilly line platforms. Charlie watched the mothers with young babies, elderly men carrying blankets and baskets and young children disappearing into the underground station and wondered if his mum and Patrick were already settled for the night at the Tilbury shelter.

He forced his mind to focus on what his son might be up to so it wouldn't start wondering what he would encounter when he got to the strip club where his wife was billed as the star attraction.

Skirting around the crowds, Charlie continued down Piccadilly towards a Leicester Square that was chock-a-block with GIs of all shapes and sizes, many sporting a giggling girl, hair bobbing and skirt swinging, on his arm.

As the sun disappeared behind the Ritz and London shifted into the dark of the night, Charlie plunged into the melee and continued on towards Charing Cross Road and the BonBon club.

'You going in or what, pal?' asked one of the half a dozen American GIs shuffling impatiently in the queue behind him.

To be honest, he'd been asking himself the same question for the past hour as he'd sat nursing a pint in the George and Dragon around the corner. But now he was through the heavy blackout curtains and in the purple and gold foyer of the BonBon, surrounded by photos of scantily clad women, it seemed the decision had been made.

'Sure,' Charlie replied, sliding a shilling across to the redhead in the booth.

She was wearing heavy make-up and a sort of strapless satin swimsuit with white collar and cuffs and a stiff bow at her throat.

'I can't let you in with that,' she said, indicating his kit bag.

'Oh, but—'

'Quit stalling,' said the GI behind him again.

'Yeah! Come on, doll,' shouted another. 'We ain't got all night.'

They pushed forward and pain shot down Charlie's arm again. He pulled a face.

'Belt up, you lot, or I'll get the lot of ya banned,' shouted the girl, glaring at the men behind Charlie.

The Yank in the centre of the group held his hands up. 'All right, lady, we're just trying to have a little fun while we're in town.'

'Well then, wait your bloody turn!' She looked back at Charlie. 'You can leave it with me, luv,' she said, taking pity on him and pushing open the box office's narrow side door.

'Thanks,' said Charlie, swinging his kit bag off his shoulder and wincing as the wound reminded him of its presence. 'What time does the show start?'

'It already has, about ten minutes ago, but it's just the dancers. The main acts will be on later,' the girl replied. 'There's one every hour until midnight and you can stay as long as you like.'

Stowing his kit bag beneath the desk, Charlie took his ticket and, tucking his field cap through the epaulette on his right shoulder, made his way through the next set of heavy drapes.

By the time he'd reached the bottom of the half a dozen or so steps leading into the subterranean club, his vision had adjusted to the dim interior. The main area was roughly half the size of a dance hall with a bar along one wall and a small semi-circular stage on which a handful of scantily clad dancers in feathers cavorted.

Waitresses carrying trays of drinks and dressed in the same outfit as the ticket girl wove expertly in and out of the six-deep crowd of servicemen and civilians wedged up against the stage.

Hearing the group of Americans coming down the stairs behind him, Charlie moved aside. Spotting a couple of stools free at the far end of the bar, he made his way over.

The barman, a man of about his own age with light brown hair, spotted him and, throwing his tea towel over his shoulder, limped over.

'A pint of Guinness,' Charlie said, raising his voice to be heard.

Taking a glass from behind him, the barman held it under the tap.

As Charlie made himself comfortable, the barman's eyes flickered onto his sling

'You copped one?' he shouted, pulling on the pump handle.

'Shrapnel!' Charlie shouted back.

The barman placed the frothy black and cream pint in front of him. 'That'll be one and three.'

Rummaging in his pocket, Charlie handed over the appropriate coins.

'You want a chaser with that?' asked the barman. 'We've got Jameson's?'

'Not at those prices,' replied Charlie.

The barman gave him a rueful smile. 'Down here, mate, you ain't paying for beer.'

One of the waitresses returned to the bar and the barman limped off to take her order.

The dancers on stage were kicking high, wriggling their rears and swinging their tassels as they bounced around to whoops and whistles from the audience. Charlie watched, as any man who'd spent his last months in a tent in the desert would, and drank his pint.

The handful of Americans who followed him in pushed their way through and found a table in front of Charlie and closer to the stage. They spotted a waitress and the one who seemed to be the leader of the bunch flashed a couple of green pound notes in her direction. She hurried over and, after receiving a smack on the bottom for her trouble, went off to fetch their order.

The dancers trooped off, blowing kisses to the audience. The next act, a so-called comic, came on. He was given short shrift by the audience, so after a couple of jokes the cat-calls and boos were so loud that he disappeared backstage.

Despite the price being double what he paid in the pub around the corner, Charlie ordered another pint. The band struck up again and a fat man in a loud suit and lurid tie stepped onto the stage and announced the next act. Mademoiselle Fifi, a blonde wearing a parlour maid's costume, appeared on the stage. Flicking her feather duster first over the painted backdrop and then over the front line of the spectators, she stripped down to a small pair of knickers to wolf whistles and cheers before leaving the stage.

Lifting his pint to his lips, Charlie was just about to slurp the creamy foam off his fresh pint when the fat man returned.

'Now, fellas,' he shouted, casting his eyes across the packed club. 'This is what you've all been waiting for.'

A guttural male roar went up.

'Salome from the Mysterious East,' shouted the compère, stepping aside as the bass drum thumped out a primitive beat.

Charlie's mouth went dry as the blood pumping through his ears all but blotted out the sound of the cheers around him.

A single spotlight lit the stage as Stella, his wife and the mother of his child, appeared.

Heavily made up and dressed as a harem girl, Stella wore impossibly high heels, a sequined brassiere and skimpy matching briefs, into which were tucked a number of colourful transparent squares. In addition, she had a pill-box hat on her swept-up blonde hair from which a smaller piece of sheer fabric hung across her nose and mouth.

A low note from a trombone picked up the rhythm of the drum and Stella snaked her way round the edge of the stage as a trumpet joined in.

As his thumping heart matched the beat of drum, Charlie watched as his world shattered.

She was good, he'd give her that. She'd had the men on their feet from the word go, their eyes hard with lust, but just when he believed his heart couldn't be torn any further, Stella whipped off her sequinned briefs and ripped his soul from his body.

All but naked, and with outstretched arms, Stella cast her gaze slowly around the room, inviting the hundred or so men packed into the club to admire her.

In a room full of randy men Charlie was the only one who wanted to vomit.

Turning his back on the stage and leaving his expensive pint half-drunk, pain constricting his chest, Charlie stumbled back up the stairs to the lobby. Collecting his knapsack from the girl in the booth en route, he burst through the doors of the club into the dark street outside.

Dragging air into his lungs, he stared blindly ahead for a moment, then the raw wail of an air raid siren filled his ears.

Within a moment the searchlights started criss-crossing the sky, searching for enemy aircraft. The siren stopped and the low drone of approaching aircraft took its place. The ack-ack guns along the Thames started punching shells into the sky as somewhere to the south of him, probably London Bridge or Elephant and Castle, the first bombs started to fall.

Although people all around started rushing for shelter in nearby Leicester Square station, Charlie shouldered his kit bag and started to walk the six miles home.

Chapter six

'COME ON, SWEETHEART,' said Captain Hal Schaefer, as he captured Stella's hand. 'The sun isn't even up.'

'I know,' she replied, continuing to slide out from under the sheets. 'But I have to go.'

He relinquished his hold. Not bothering to cover herself, Stella stood up.

Going over to where she'd thrown her clothes, she picked up her silk knickers and stepped into them.

She didn't know what the time was, but she was in room 14 on the second floor of the Dover Square hotel, just a ten-minute cab ride from the BonBon club. Until six months ago the sedate Edwardian hotel, with its marble columns, mahogany furniture and Indian rugs, let its rooms to the good and great of the Home Counties who were in town attending the opera, charity galas or official functions.

However, the rounded vowels of well-to-do matrons and the strident tones of old generals reliving their youthful battles over a brandy had been replaced by Texan drawls and Appalachian Mountain lilts as the hotel was now the London billet for a hundred high-ranking American officers and the handful of privates who attended them.

Hal was one of them; a bulky, broad-faced blond with a crew-cut, blue eyes and a lot of energy.

Propping himself up on one elbow he reached across and took the pack of Lucky Strikes from the bedside table.

Taking out two, he lit them both and gave one to Stella.

Fastening the last suspender, she took it from him and inhaled.

Clenching his cigarette between his teeth, the American stretched across again and this time picked up his wallet.

'I don't think we set a price, did we?' he said, his blue eyes cool and assured as they studied her face.

'No, we didn't,' she replied, blowing a stream of smoke from the side of her mouth.

'Will this cover it?' he asked, taking out a fiver from the half a dozen notes squashed between the leather folds.

'I should think so,' said Stella. She took it and stood up. 'But a gentleman would see me home.'

He smiled and picked up the telephone beside the bed.

'Solomon. It's Captain Schaefer. Room fourteen,' he barked down the receiver. 'I have a young lady who needs a cab.'

'This will do!' Stella shouted through the cab driver's window as she spotted the sand-bagged frontage of Stepney town hall.

The cabbie stopped and flipped the meter flag down. 'Half a crown.'

'It was two bob last week,' Stella replied, slipping on her five-inch heels.

'That was last week,' said the cab driver, the roll-up stuck to his lower lips bobbing up and down as he spoke. 'Anyway, what's it to you? I saw that Yank bung you a quid.' His unshaved face lifted into a leer. 'Unless he was paying you for some'ink else.'

Stella gave him a withering look, hooked her handbag over her arm and climbed out of the taxi. Snapping her handbag open, she took out a silver coin and dropped it in the driver's outstretched hand.

'Wot about a tip?' he complained as he looked at the single half-crown that Stella had given him.

'I'll give you one,' Stella replied, slamming the door. 'Don't be so sodding cheeky.'

Closing her handbag, she turned on her heels and headed the hundred yards along Chapman Street towards the bottom end of Watney Street market.

Judging by the streaks of sunlight filtering over the block of flats at the end of the street, it was somewhere close to six in the morning.

The balls of her feet were burning. Hardly surprising really, seeing as how she'd been dancing around in them all night.

A little smile lifted the corners of her lips.

Well, not all night!

Usually she would have had the cab take her to her door but the letter from the army and the showdown with Ida and Queenie had unsettled her, so she had to be careful.

However, she was sure, as long as she got hold of Charlie before his bloody family spilt the beans, she'd be all right. She'd had a word with the BonBon club's owner, Tubbs, who'd reluctantly agreed to give her leave while Charlie was home so, with a bit of luck, he'd never know about Salome from the Mysterious East and she could go back to her very lucrative profession once he shipped out again.

Cursing her sore toes, and with the early-morning breeze humming through the metal cable of the barrage balloon bobbing over the town hall, Stella turned into Alma Terrace just as the milkman's horse stopped at the other end of the street.

A couple of her neighbours were already out and about, either going to an early shift or coming home from a night one, but, ignoring their disapproving glances, she carried on until she reached her front door.

Yearning to sink into her bed and snuggle under the blankets, Stella put the key in the lock and opened the door.

Throwing the keys back in her handbag, she put it on the shelf then kicked off her shoes, sighing with relief. However, just as she was about to amble down the hallway to the kitchen, she noticed the parlour door, which she had definitely closed before she left the house the night before, was now ajar.

Pushing it open, she stopped dead and her jaw dropped.

'Charlie,' she said, scrambling her tired wits about her.

He was wearing his uniform minus his battle jacket, which was slung over the chair behind him. The top two buttons of his shirt were unfastened, showing his dark chest hair. His army crop had grown out since she last saw him and the black curls she'd loved running her fingers through had sprung through again.

As her gaze ran over him, Stella remembered just why she'd been so keen to hook Charlie Brogan in the first place. The captivating smile she'd almost forgotten spread across her husband's chiselled features.

'Hello, Stella,' he said, rising to his feet.

After almost twenty-four hours without sleep, Charlie had been dozing in the fireside chair, but the key clicking in the lock had brought him back to the here and now. By the time Stella walked through the door, he was fully alert.

Dressed in a skin-tight black cocktail dress, with her make-up smudged and her hair swept up haphazardly on her head, she stared at him as if seeing a ghost for a second or two before her scarlet-red lips lifted in a joyful expression.

'Charlie!' She dashed across on stockinged feet and threw her arms around him.

The smell of stale perfume, cigarette smoke and a hint of something tangy he couldn't quite place wafted up.

He winced and took her hand from his left shoulder.

'Oh, Charlie, I'm so sorry, I forgot,' she said, smoothing her hand gently over his injured shoulder. 'Does it still hurt?'

'Now and again,' he replied.

'You are so, so brave.' She pouted. 'I'm so proud of you.'

She stood on tiptoes and pressed her mouth on his, her tongue inviting him to open his mouth. Charlie didn't respond.

'Are you?' he said, breaking free of her kiss.

She looked hurt. 'Of course I am. We all are.'

Slipping her arms around him, his wife pressed herself against him.

'I wish you'd told me you were coming home today, Charlie?' she said, adoration pouring out of her mascara-ed eyes. 'I would have meet you at the station with Patrick.'

Ignoring the ache in his chest at the mention of his son, Charlie forced a smile.

'I wanted to surprise you,' he replied, as her nails lightly raked his back. 'I suppose he's with my mum in the shelter?'

'It's the safest place for him while I'm working. He looks just like you, he does. He'll break some hearts when he gets older.' She gave him a lustful look. 'Just like his dad.'

A lump appeared in Charlie's throat. 'I can't wait to see him.'

'Although…' She pressed her pubic bone against his hip. 'Perhaps it's not a bad thing he's not here just at the moment.' Her hand ran down his back, over his rear, then around to the front. 'After all…' She unfastened his waistband and then started on the buttons of his flies. 'It's been a long time.'

Her fingers slipped through the front opening of his trousers but, just before she closed them around his hardening penis, he caught her wrist.

'How is work?'

Uncertainty flickered across her face for a split second before her smile returned. 'Oh, you know, dirty and noisy.'

She tried to twist her hand free, but Charlie held on.

'Bit overdressed for a night in a ball bearing factory, aren't you?' he asked.

'Er, I… I went out for a drink with a couple of the girls before—'

'Don't lie. I know where you've been. Prancing about on stage, naked,' he said, looking her square in the eye.

Alarm flashed across her face for a second, then fury replaced it.

'I suppose your precious bloody family told you,' she spat out, snatching her hand from his grip. 'I told them I'd—'

'You'd what?'

'Nothing,' she said, struggling to hold his blistering gaze.

Reaching down, he picked up the copy of *Beauty Parade* and flipped it to the centre page.

'This is how I found out my wife was the main attraction at the BonBon club,' he said, glaring at her. He thrust the magazine under her nose. 'And I went there to see for myself if it were true last night.'

She glanced at it, then looked back at him. 'It's just a job—'

'Driving a train is a job, Stella. Working in a factory is a job. Taking your clothes off on stage is stripping!'

He covered his eyes with his hands for a moment, then he raised his head.

'How could you?'

She tried to embrace him again, but he shrugged her off.

'I'm sorry, Charlie.'

'Sorry! You're sorry!' he shouted. 'For God's sake!'

'I am.'

He stared wordlessly at her for a long moment, then spoke again. 'What about Patrick?'

She looked puzzled. 'What about him?'

Charlie gave a mirthless laugh. 'If I have to explain to you how having a stripper for a mother will affect our son, then what's the point?'

She gave him a doe-eyed pout.

'Oh, Charlie,' she said, fluttering her heavily mascara-ed eyelashes at him. 'Let's not fight when we could be…' Her gaze roamed down to his crotch and back again. 'You know…'

She stepped closer and the heady aroma he smelt earlier wafted up again.

The void at Charlie's feet opened wider.

'Is fucking the customers just a job, too?' he asked, in a glacial tone.

She looked affronted. 'I don't know what you're tal—'

'Don't lie. I can smell him.'

'Who.'

'Whoever's bed you crawled out of an hour ago,' Charlie replied.

Guilt flashed across Stella's powdered face.

Charlie stared at his wife for a moment then, reaching down, he picked up his kit bag.

'Where are you going?' she asked, as he slung it across his good shoulder.

'Home.'

'But this is your home,' she replied.

Charlie cast his gaze around the parlour, knowing that the two-thirds of his wages he'd signed over to his wife could never have paid for such an expensively furnished room and shook his head.

'Not any more.'

She caught his arm. 'But, Charlie, I—'

'I knew you'd been with other men when I met you, Stella, but I believed you when you said you wanted to settle down and have a family—'

'I did,' said Stella. 'I do, it's just…just…the war. It's the war.'

Charlie looked at his wife for a long moment, then, without giving her a second glance, turned, strode across the room and out the door.

Chapter seven

'THERE YOU ARE, girls,' said Queenie Brogan as she scooped a handful of fresh worms out of the bucket and threw them into the chicken coop. 'You've got the bloody Hun to thank for that lot. Fair bombed the bejesus out of us they did last night, the shower of Godless heathens that they are.'

The hens, all eight of them, started pecking at the damp worms Queenie had gathered from King George's Park an hour or so ago.

After a night of heavy bombing, the worms, to avoid being squashed in compressed earth, all came to the surface. And was it any wonder there were dozens of them, all pink and shiny, wriggling around on the grey gravel, after the night they'd just lived through?

London had been hidden out of sight of the Luftwaffe, snug beneath a blanket of fog, for the past month, but two nights ago a stiff wind from the North Sea had stripped the capital of its camouflage and last night the Germans had returned to make up for lost time, sending a stream of anxious mothers and bleary-eyed children scurrying to the shelters when the siren went off, just as the ten o'clock news started on the wireless.

Not that she was among their number.

She didn't blame Ida for bedding those sweet boys, Billy and Michael and that darling little lad, Patrick, God love and bless them, in the Tilbury shelter each night. But if the good Lord wanted her, he'd find her in her own bed.

Oddly, Queenie had woken up just before the all-clear sounded at five with a very rare occurrence. A headache.

And not just any old headache but the sort of headache that would have you thinking the Devil had stolen in while you slept and cleaved your head in two.

Even a brisk walk to the baker's in the morning air hadn't sent it on its way, although mercifully it had gone from a saw cutting though the back of her eyeball to a dull thudding across her forehead.

The last time she could recall having such a brutal headache was the day before the police turned up on the doorstep to inform her that her Fergus had been found face-down in the London mud just below Wapping Stairs.

But she currently had no feeling of a departed spirit hovering nearby, so she was puzzled as to why it had come upon her.

Pushing the thought aside, Queenie turned her attention back to the hens. Having kept chickens as a girl back in Ireland, Queenie had taken over their charge after Jerimiah had brought them home just before Christmas. Although the eggs were a welcome addition to the family's diet and added a few pennies to the budget, Queenie had set her sights higher.

After chasing over half of Essex she'd acquired a cock and, having nurtured Winston and his ladies through the winter, the first three offspring had hatched six weeks before. They were putting on weight nicely and, with a bit of luck, they'd start laying soon.

Seeing the last of the worms had been eaten, Queenie opened the waxed paper bag full of chicken feed that she'd brought out with her and scattered it on the floor of the coop. Her parrot, Prince Albert, an African grey who had more brains on him than many she could mention, fluttered down from his favourite spot on top of the outside bog to perch on the chicken coop causing Winston to puff up his feathers in a display of bravado.

'There you are, girls,' she said, brushing her hands together. 'Eat up. I'll have some greens for you later.'

The hens clucked their appreciation and continued pecking

at the hard dirt while Albert cleaned up the seeds that had fallen outside the coop.

As she bent down to pick up the pail, a breeze swirled around her so laden with wretchedness that she staggered. Her head pounded again, and she wondered if it was her soul that was about to be taken up, then the back-gate latch clicked open.

For a split second her head didn't believe what her eyes were seeing.

'Charlie?'

He was wearing battle dress with his kit bag slung across him. His field cap was tucked through his right epaulette and he had a sling supporting his left arm. In the mellow light his morning bristles were clearly visible, as were the dark smudges of bone-weariness under his eyes.

'Hello, Gran,' he said in a tight voice, as moisture shimmered on his lower lashes.

Queenie stared at him. The pain in her head rose up to join the misery carried in the wind.

A single tear trickled down his cheek.

Leaving the pail where it was, she crossed the space between them. Standing on tiptoes, she stretched up and held her six-foot-one grandson as he sobbed his heart out on her shoulder.

'Can I fetch you another?' asked Queenie, picking up Charlie's empty plate from the occasional table at his knee.

'No, I'm grand.' Charlie smiled. 'I'd forgotten how good your eggy bread is.'

He glanced up at the clock on the mantelshelf.

'Don't fret, lad, your ma will be fetching him home soon,' she said softly, running her work-worn hands over his cropped curls. 'And it's good to have you home, lad.'

'It's good to be home,' he replied.

His grandmother's wrinkled face lifted in a tender smile, then, carrying the plate, she returned to the kitchen.

It was now almost half seven and, as the sun was fully up, the blackout curtains had been pulled right back, allowing the bright March sunlight to stream into the family's main parlour, where Charlie was now sitting.

The humiliation still lay like a lead weight in his gut, but being back in the familiar surroundings of his childhood soothed it a little.

Taking up his tea Charlie swallowed the last mouthful, then settled back into his father's old button-back chair.

As the sounds of his gran making breakfast and the smell of porridge drifted out from the kitchen, Charlie yawned. His eyelids were feeling heavy now, but, just as he felt them closing, the back door opened.

With his heart hammering in his chest, Charlie stood up.

His face soot-streaked from his night as a member of the auxiliary fire service's red watch in Poplar fire station, his father strode into the room.

Jerimiah Boniface Brogan had been hawking furniture on and off a horse-drawn wagon since he was ten years old and it showed. Although now in his mid-forties, he was still a force to be reckoned with.

A fraction under Charlie's height, his father had the physique of a prize fighter and a punch to match. However, although his temper was legendary and he was no stranger to a police cell, beneath his bear-like appearance beat a heart of pure gold.

'Hello, Dad,' said Charlie.

Jerimiah stood dumbfounded for a moment. He flung open his arms and Charlie accepted the invitation.

They hugged for a moment, then Charlie stepped out of his father's embrace.

'You look well, son,' said Jerimiah, looking him up and down. 'Stella didn't tell us you'd been discharge—'

'I know, Dad,' Charlie cut in. 'I know about the club.'

His father laid a beefy hand on Charlie's good shoulder.

'I'm truly sorry, lad,' he said quietly, his expression the same as when he'd explained to Charlie that, despite passing the entrance exam, his parents couldn't afford for him to go to Raynes grammar.

The back door opened again and, swallowing the lump that had returned to his throat, Charlie looked around as Billy, six months short of his twelfth birthday, burst through from the kitchen, closely followed by the other lad in the new family portrait.

'Charlie!' shrieked Billy, dashing across to Charlie.

'Mind your brother's arm,' bellowed their father, bringing the boy to a skidding halt just in front of Charlie. 'And where's your mum?'

'She's talking to someone,' Billy replied, hopping from one foot to the other.

'Hello, Billy,' Charlie said, ruffling his brother's sandy-coloured hair. 'You've grown.'

'Yeah.' Billy stood up straight. 'I'll be as big as you one day.'

'I bet you will,' Charlie replied.

He wouldn't, of course, because although no one, not even Aunt Pearl who'd given birth to him, knew who Billy's father was, judging by the boy's stocky build he hadn't been a tall man.

However, for the dark-haired boy standing behind Billy it was quite a different matter. Although almost ten months younger, he already topped his fairer playmate by a good inch.

'And this is your brother Michael,' Jerimiah said, his jaw firm as he held Charlie's gaze.

Gently placing his hands on the boy's still-slender shoulders, Jerimiah moved him forward.

Charlie extended his hand. 'Well, it's nice to meet you, Michael.'

His father's unease was understandable. After all, it wasn't every day you had to introduce your eldest child to their newest brother for the first time.

Still, who was he to judge?

Michael took Charlie's hand.

'Nice to meet you, too, Charlie. I've heard a lot about you,' the lad said, his eyes wide with hero-worship as he looked up at Charlie

'I told him you were shot,' chipped in Billy.

'I wasn't shot, I was hit by shrapnel.'

'Did it hurt much?' asked Michael, his eyes flickering onto Charlie's sling.

'Like hell,' Charlie replied.

Michael smiled and Charlie smiled back.

'Henry West's dad was hit by shrapnel,' said Billy, muscling in.

'Was he?' said Charlie.

'Yeah, killed him stone dead,' added Billy with relish. He cast a glance at the boy beside him. 'Michael's mum died.'

A bleak look flashed across Michael's young face.

'I'm sorry to hear about your mum, Michael,' said Charlie.

'Thanks.' The boy wiped his nose on the back of his hand. 'Auntie Ida says she's in Heaven with Jesus and we light a candle for her every Sunday.'

'Come on, you two,' said Queenie, coming through from the kitchen. 'You'd better get your skates on or you'll be late for school.'

'Yes, Gran,' said Michael, heading back into the kitchen.

'In a minute,' said Billy.

Queenie gave him a narrow-eyed look and he sloped off after Michael, muttering to himself while he brought up the rear.

Charlie glanced at the clock again.

'I don't know what's keeping your mum,' his father said. 'She's usually home by—'

The back door opened again, and Charlie's heart leapt into his throat.

With his thoughts and pulse racing, he strode across the room and into the kitchen.

The two boys were sitting at the table wolfing down their breakfast of porridge and toast while his mother, with her back to him, was hooking up her coat on the back-door peg. But all sights and sounds faded as Charlie's gaze rested on the dark-haired child, wrapped up against the morning chill, sitting in the pram.

'I thought I'd never get away from that Mrs—' His mother turned around. 'Charlie!'

Crossing the space between them, his mother enveloped him in a maternal embrace. 'Oh, Charlie,' she sobbed, hugging him tight.

'Hello, Mum,' he said, ignoring the pain in his injured shoulder and hugging her back.

She sobbed against his chest for a couple of moments, then held him from her. 'You look pale.'

'I'm tired.'

'He knows about Stella, Ida,' said his father, who had followed him in.

His mother hugged him again. 'I'm sorry. We would have said something, but—'

'It's all right, Mum.' Feeling his eyes tingling again, Charlie shifted his attention back to the child in the pram who was now sucking his thumb.

Untangling himself from his mother's arms, he hunkered down and smiled at the small boy.

Patrick studied him for a moment, then stretched two chubby hands up towards him.

Unfastening him from the reins anchoring him in the pram, Charlie tried to lift him but the pain in his shoulder was too much.

'Let me,' said his mother, seeing Charlie wince.

Gathering him up, she unwrapped Patrick's scarf and took off his hat, then settled him in Charlie's good arm.

'Hello, Patrick,' he said, enjoying the closeness of him. 'I'm your dad.'

'Give your dad a hug, Patrick,' said Ida.

Charlie's nine-month-old son stared solemnly at him out of the same dark eyes as his own.

'He's only just woken up,' his mother explained.

'That's all right,' Charlie replied, widening his smile. 'He's probably a bit puzzled to find a stranger hold—'

Patrick flung his arms around Charlie's neck and buried his face in his shoulder.

An emotion he'd never felt before rose up in Charlie's chest and filled his battered and torn heart. Tears crept out of the corners of his eyes again, so he closed them. Hugging his son to him, Charlie pressed his lips to Patrick's dark curls.

'It's good to have you home, son,' his father said softly.

Without opening his eyes and with his lips still pressed onto his son's head, Charlie nodded. Yes, he was home!

Chapter eight

'YOU LOOKED AS if you enjoyed that, Mr Green,' said Francesca as she reached David Green's table.

'I certainly did,' he replied, shifting his ARP tin helmet aside so she could put his mug of tea down. 'You can't beat a bit of bubble and squeak to set you up for the day.'

The signature tune for *Music While You Work* had just finished, which meant it was a few moments after nine on the first Thursday in April and two weeks since she'd had her interview for the clerical job in the Overseas department.

David Green was somewhere close to her father's age and when not about his duties as their local ARP warden, he and his wife ran a wholesale haberdashery business in New Road.

'You're late today for your breakfast,' said Francesca.

'I know,' he said, stirring a spoonful of sugar into his tea. 'Me and a dozen other ARP wardens have been giving the Heavy Rescue fellas a hand to shift rubble since four.'

'Where from?' asked Francesca.

'Cambridge Dwellings,' the warden replied. 'Jerry scored a direct hit and the old building blew down like a pack of cards.'

'Were many killed?' Francesca asked, thinking of the crumbling tenement at the corner of Balmy Park.

He swallowed a mouthful of tea. 'Ten for certain and another half a dozen missing.'

Francesca crossed herself. 'God bless and keep them.'

'Thankfully, most of the residents were safe and sound in Bethnal Green station,' he said. 'Or we'd have filled the morgue across the road.'

David nodded at the London hospital, which could be seen through the cafe window along with a stream of ambulances waiting to take those casualties who were fit to be moved to outlying hospitals away from London.

'Anyway, what are you doing here?' he asked. 'It's usually just your dad and Olive first thing.'

'I've got the day off so I'm letting Dad have a bit of a lie-in,' Francesca replied. She picked up his empty plate. 'Can I get you another cuppa?'

His grey moustache lifted in a friendly smile. 'Thanks, but I ought to get back and give a hand when I've finished me drink.'

'Right you are,' said Francesca. 'Just pop your money on the counter if I'm not there.'

Leaving the warden to finish his breakfast, Francesca cleared the last few tables from the morning rush and took the dirty crockery around to the business side of the counter.

After scraping the wiggly bacon rinds and crusts of toast into the pig swill bucket under the counter, she plunged the plates into the soapy water in the sink to let them soak.

Returning to the counter, she picked up the handful of coppers that David had left by the till and deposited them in the cash drawer. She then took the rag, which was in fact her father's old vest, and wiped down the marble counter.

'Any more for any more?' Olive shouted through the hatch from the kitchen.

'No, I don't think so,' Francesca called back as their last customer let the door shut behind them. 'That's it now until midday, I reckon.'

'I'll get these pots washed up then,' Olive replied, as she disappeared from the hatch.

Removing her apron, Francesca hooked it on the peg before taking two cups from the shelf and filling them with tea.

The bell hanging above the door tinkled and the postman walked in.

Well, post boy, really, because the slender-shouldered lad weighed down by a budging canvas bag looked no older than twelve.

'Post!' he shouted as he laid half a dozen envelopes on the counter.

'Thanks,' Francesca replied, as she picked up the letters.

Sifting through them she stopped when she reached one with her name on. It had a BBC frank mark obscuring the image of the king on the orange tuppenny stamp.

She stared at it for a moment then, with her heart thumping in her chest, carefully lifted the flap.

With the blood rushing through her ears and the letters jumping in her vision, Francesca scanned the page. When she reached the signature at the bottom she went back and read it again, then hurried through to the back room.

Her father was sitting in his dressing gown in the fireside chair with his slippered feet up on the pouffe. He was reading the morning edition of the *Mirror*. He looked up as she walked in.

'I've got it,' she said, bouncing on the balls of her feet. 'Blow me, Papa, I got it. I got the job at the BBC. I'll be based in Bush House, just off the Strand, so I can catch a number 15 from Aldgate straight there,' she continued. 'And my starting pay is three pounds two and six!'

Her father's thick eyebrows rose. 'That's a man's wage.'

She grinned. 'So no more drilling out aircraft pistons for me.'

Her father gave her a fond smile. 'Well done, my daughter.'

'Thank you, Papa.' She glanced at her watch. 'I've just got time before the midday rush.'

'Time for what?' he asked.

'To pop around to Mattie and tell her my good news,' Francesca replied.

Having not found Mattie at home, Francesca's next port of call was Mattie's mother's house, which is why, twenty minutes after leaving her friend's front door, she was taking the second left into Mafeking Terrace.

Picking up her pace, Francesca headed for the house in the middle of the street but, instead of using the freshly polished knocker, she slipped down the cool alleyway between the terraced houses. Opening the gate at the end of the passageway, she walked into the Brogans' rear yard to find Queenie Brogan, Mattie's grandmother, standing in the mist of her feathery charges.

Although it wasn't particularly cold, Queenie was dressed in a seaman's duffel coat that all but touched the floor and was tied at the waist with a Boy Scout's S-buckle belt. The whole ensemble was topped off with what looked like an airmen's leather helmet with the ear flaps tied on the top of her head. She looked up from the hens scratching at her feet and gave Francesca a gummy smile.

'Francesca, me darling,' she said, as she checked the nest boxes. 'Grand it is to be seeing you.'

'And you, Mrs B,' Francesca replied.

'So how is it with your father?' asked the old lady.

'Pa's fine, although busy with the cafe as always.'

'And that fine-looking brother of yours, how is he faring?' continued Queenie.

'He's doing well, too,' said Francesca. 'Is Mattie here?'

'She's not been near or by as yet.' The old woman gave her a querying look. 'Is it something in particular you're after her for?'

'Nothing that won't wait until I see her on Sunday,' Francesca replied.

'Well, seeing how you're here, you can pop in and say hello to Charlie,' continued the old woman.

Francesca's mouth went dry. 'Charlie!'

'To be sure, hasn't all six foot of him been sprawled in his father's chair since dawn,' said Queenie.

Leaving the old lady to her task, and with her heart pounding, Francesca pushed open the back door.

The homely aroma of the family's evening meal already cooking in the oven mingled with the tangy smell of starch from the washing which was hanging over the dryer.

Like the rest of the house, the Brogans' kitchen was furnished with items Jerimiah had acquired whilst on his rounds. None of the four chairs tucked under the square table or the crockery nearly stacked on the over-sized dresser at the far end of the room matched, but everything was spotlessly clean; as were the windows with the criss-crossed tape covering them.

Stopping just in front of the parlour door Francesca took a deep breath in an attempt to steady her galloping pulse, then, putting a happy smile on her face, she walked in.

She was just about to call a cheery hello when she stopped dead.

As Queenie had said, Charlie was sitting in the fireside chair. His feet were up on the pouffe and Patrick was snuggled into his uninjured arm. Both father and son were fast asleep.

Charlie had taken off his battle jacket, which was now draped over the back of his chair, and his boots sat together in the tiled hearth. The rolled-up sleeves and unfastened collar of his khaki shirt showed his hairy forearms and chest while his snug-fitting combat trousers drew attention to his long, muscular legs.

As Francesca's gaze ran slowly over the strong, angular face, he opened his eyes and the yearning she'd struggled so hard to conquer surged up again.

It took Charlie a moment or two to realise who the gorgeous woman smiling down at him was.

He knew Francesca, of course, and had done since she was in the first year and he was two classes above her in the third year. She was Mattie's best friend, practically part of the family, especially since she'd lived with them for nine months after her father and brother were interned. But now, seeing her standing there in a sky-blue dress with her large brown eyes warm and her smile wide, Charlie stared at Francesca as if seeing her for the first time.

'Sorry, Charlie,' she said, snapping his brain back to the here and now. 'I didn't mean to wake you, but I popped by to see Mattie and your gran said—'

'No, don't apologise, Fran.' He swung his feet off the pouffe and straightened up. 'I just didn't hear you come in, that's all.'

'I'm not surprised,' she replied, her dark eyes warm as they held his. 'You were sparko. When did you get back?'

'Yesterday,' he replied, noticing how her high heels emphasised her shapely legs. 'Late afternoon.'

'That's quick,' she replied. 'We weren't expecting you to be discharged for at least another couple of weeks.'

'I persuaded the doc that I needed to get home,' he replied.

'How's your arm?' she asked.

'Painful, but on the mend and—' Charlie looked down at his son and his heavy heart lifted a little '—although I could have done without having a lump of metal through my shoulder at least it's given me a chance to meet this little lad.'

He indicated Patrick with a nod of his head and Francesca's attention shifted onto his sleeping son.

'He's such a handsome boy.'

Charlie grinned. 'Like father like son, then.'

Something flared in her eyes, but then she laughed. 'Well, according to your mum and Mattie, he's certainly inherited your temper and stubbornness, Charlie. And, of course, now you'll be here for the wedding of the year.'

Charlie looked puzzled.

'Jo and Tommy Sweete?'

He rolled his eyes. 'How could I forget?'

She laughed and he joined in.

Her smile faltered a little. 'I bet Stella was happy to see—'

'I know about St…her,' he cut in, as tightness gripped his chest again. 'I found out a few days ago and that's the reason I got myself signed off. I'm moving back into my old bedroom until I'm fit to return to my regiment.'

Francesca large brown eyes grew soft again. 'I'm sorry.'

Charlie forced a weary smile but didn't reply.

They stared wordlessly at each other for a long moment, then the parlour door burst open.

'Charlie!'

Dragging his eyes from Francesca, Charlie turned to see his sister Jo streaking towards him with a heavily pregnant Mattie half a step behind.

Patrick woke up with a start.

Balancing his dazed son in his good arm, Charlie stood up.

Francesca stepped forward.

'Let me take him,' she said, holding her arms out to the child.

Charlie handed him over and was immediately surrounded by his sobbing sisters. Hugging them as best he could with one arm, Charlie looked across at Francesca, who had settled Patrick onto her hip.

She smiled and he smiled back.

After a moment or two of hugs and kisses, and with his shoulder protesting, Charlie disentangled himself from their embrace.

Mattie turned to her friend. 'This is a pleasant surprise, too.'

'Oh, I just popped by,' Francesca replied. 'Where's Alicia?'

'Helping Gran feed the chickens in the yard,' Mattie replied.

'How did you know Charlie was home?' asked Jo, perching on the arm of the chair he'd just vacated.

'I didn't,' Francesca said. 'I was after Mattie and when she wasn't at home, I thought she might be here.'

'As Jo's on late shift we caught the bus to Wentworth Street to buy her dress fabric,' Mattie said.

'It's a very pale blush pink and so beautiful,' said Jo, with a heavy sigh. 'I'll knock Tommy's eyes out when he sees me walking down the aisle.'

'I'm sure you will,' said Francesca with a smile. 'But the reason I was after Mattie was because…' Francesca grinned. 'I got the job.'

Mattie's eyes lit up. 'That's wonderful, Fran, although I didn't doubt it for a moment.'

'Job?' asked Charlie.

'With the BBC,' Francesca replied. 'In their Italian section.'

'Congratulations,' said Charlie with warmth. 'I couldn't think of anyone better and I'm so pleased for you.'

'I'm pretty pleased myself,' she replied. 'I start a week on Monday but I can tell you all about it after church.'

'You don't have to run away, do you, Fran?' asked Charlie. 'I mean, you've only just got here.'

An odd expression flitted across her face, then she gave him that lovely warm smile that he'd seen so often but that now inexplicably touched his soul.

'I know,' she said. 'But I have to get back and give Dad a hand with the lunchtime rush.'

Stepping close, she offered him Patrick. Charlie took his son from her, smelling a hint of violets as she moved against him.

'Good to see you, Charlie,' she said.

'Good to see you too,' he replied, captured in her lovely eyes.

For a second or two they stared wordlessly at each other, then Patrick started wriggling.

Francesca looked away as Charlie repositioned his son on his arm.

'See you all on Sunday,' she said as she headed towards the door.

'Congratulations again on your job, Fran,' he called after her. 'And that colour really suits you.'

Chapter nine

AS IDA BROGAN pulled out a pair of boys' shorts from the jumble of clothes in the sack, her daughter's jaw dropped.

'So he found out,' said Cathy.

Ida nodded. 'Saw her picture in some girly magazine. He jumped on the next train and confronted her with it as she got home this morning.'

It was just after three thirty and some eight hours since she'd walked into her kitchen and found Charlie grey with weariness and sorrow, waiting for her.

As usual at this time on a Thursday afternoon, Ida was dressed in her serviceable green drill WVS dress and was on duty at the rest centre in the Catholic club's main hall.

Helping with her task was her middle daughter, Cathy, who had the golden-brown hair and mid-blue eyes of Ida's mother and sister.

Although the rest centre was paid for by the council, it was run by the Stepney branch of the WVS. Most of the space in the hall was given over to rows of camp beds and because it had been a busy night the night before, every one of them was occupied by some poor soul who'd emerged from the night shelter to find all their worldly possessions blown to smithereens. The canteen and snack bar, had been flat-out since first light serving hot food and the ARP information desk at the far end was inundated with people seeking their missing relatives and friends. She and Cathy had been swamped by women and children who had been bombed out with only the clothes they stood up in. There had been so many in fact that they had had to limit the allocation of second-hand clothing to just two outfits per person and only four nappies for infants to make sure everyone had something.

As always, Ida had taken her WVS uniform to the yard that morning so she could change after her daily stint helping her husband book in house removals, schedule local traders' deliveries and sell the odd stick of furniture along the way. Jerimiah set off on his afternoon rounds at twelve, so she'd locked the yard gates and come straight to the hall to meet Cathy for lunch in the canteen.

Now they were unpacking the latest delivery of second-hand clothes from the Canadian Red Cross, while Peter, Cathy's eighteen-month-old son, was being cared for in the WVS nursery in the committee room. Cathy did her bit daily at the relief centre, obviously to help the war effort but mainly to get away from her impossible and mean-spirited mother-in-law, Violet Wheeler, who she lived with.

'Well, I'm not surprised,' continued Cathy. 'To be honest, I don't know how Stella thought she'd get away with it.'

'Me neither,' said Ida. 'But at least she can't blame us for letting the cat out of the bag.'

'How did he take it?' asked Cathy, as she put a smart-looking navy dress on a hanger and then hooked it on the rail.

'How do you think?'

'And did Stella come around and pick up Patrick later?'

Ida shook her head. 'Sent a kid around with a note saying she wasn't well and asked could I keep him for a bit?'

'I don't know why she doesn't just leave him with you and have done with it,' said Cathy.

'I would if I could, for Charlie's sake,' said Ida. 'But she's his mother and no court in the land would give me or even Charlie custody.'

'Poor little mite,' said Cathy. 'Being pushed from pillar to post. And what I can't understand is why on earth did he marry her?'

Ida gave her daughter a long-suffering look.

'I know she was up the duff,' said Cathy. 'But why did he get involved with her in the first place? After all, it wasn't as if Charlie didn't have the pick of girls. I tell you, Mum, with all the single and half the married women in the neighbourhood after him I can't understand why Charlie, who's supposed to be the brainbox of the family, ends up with Stella Miggles.'

'You'll have to ask Charlie that one,' Ida replied. 'Because it's a mystery to me, too.'

Bending down, she pulled out another pile of musky clothes from the hessian package and plonked it on the table.

You only had to look at the size of Stella's chest, thought Ida, to know why Charlie, who was sharp as a new razor, ended up getting her in the family way.

'So has he left Stella?' asked Cathy.

Ida nodded. 'Moved back into his old room. Of course, it's only until his shoulder's better and then he'll be sent back to his unit, but at least he can get to know Patrick.'

'And be around for Jo's wedding,' added Cathy.

Ida rolled her eyes. 'Oh, Jo's wedding! I had a full hour of it the other day talking about the food. Still, I can't blame her for being excited and happy.'

'Let's hope she stays that way once she's got a ring on her finger,' said Cathy, shaking out a pair of boy's trousers.

Looking at her lovely daughter's averted face, a lump formed in Ida's throat.

'I wish I'd known he was home,' Cathy continued. 'I would have come around.'

'Well, you can come tomorrow,' said Ida. 'To be honest, he was nearly asleep on his feet after Jo and Mattie went; he slept the rest of the day.'

'Trust Mattie to see him before me,' said Cathy, a sour look spoiling her pretty face.

'Don't you think this business with you and Mattie has gone on long enough?' said Ida.

'You know why I can't ever forgive her,' said Cathy.

Resting her hands on the top of the clothing pile, Ida gave Cathy a hard look 'You know, Cathy, whether you admit it or not, the truth of the matter is that it isn't Mattie or her husband's fault that your Stan got caught up with those Fascists.' Ida reached for an old wire hanger and slipped it into the shoulders of the man's jacket she'd just brushed down. Without returning her gaze to her daughter, she quietly continued, 'We might all go to our graves any day, isn't it high time that you move on?'

Pushing open her back door with her mother's words still ringing in her ears, Cathy manoeuvred the pushchair into her mother-in-law's furnished kitchen.

'Here we are, Peter,' she said, pulling a happy face at her son. 'Back home.'

'Is that you?' Violet Wheeler shouted from the front room.

'Home to the lair of the Wicked Witch of the West,' Cathy muttered under her breath, as she unwrapped Peter's scarf.

Unclipping Peter's harness, Cathy lifted him out and set him on his feet and took off his coat. As she would be putting it back on him in an hour or so when she went to the shelter, she left it draped over the handle.

Peter toddled off to see his granny as Cathy took off her coat and hung it on the back door.

Spotting the potatoes unpeeled in the rack, she went over to the oven. She opened the oven door to see the brown-and-cream dish she'd left there before she went out, uncooked on the middle shelf. Cathy's mouth pulled into a tight line as she slammed the oven door shut before resting her hand on the kettle. It was warm.

She marched into the lounge.

Violet Wheeler, who was hunched in her chair by the fire, looked up as she came in. Despite the fact it was a lovely spring day, her mother-in-law was dressed in one of her drab-coloured ankle-length dresses and swaddled in a mauve crochet shawl with a tartan blanket over her knees.

Digging her fist into her hips, Cathy gave her mother-in-law a hard look. 'I thought I asked you to put the dinner on at three.'

'The gas went off at lunchtime,' Mrs Wheeler replied.

'Well, it was on when you made yourself a hot drink an hour or so ago,' Cathy replied.

'I must have fallen asleep.' Looking down, Mrs Wheeler made a play of straightening her skirt. 'And anyway, if you were at home like you should be instead of gadding about all the time, you could have started the dinner yourself.' She shifted her attention to Peter, who was pulling the diecast soldiers out of the tomato punnet that served as his toy box.

'Poor little lad,' she said. 'Being left with strangers because his mother can't be bothered to look after him.'

Giving her mother-in-law a withering look, Cathy returned to the kitchen.

Taking hold of the solid-looking National loaf, which she'd bought on her way home, Cathy plonked it on the chopping board.

'It seems your family's the talk of every street corner again,' her mother-in-law shouted through from the front room.

Sawing off a slice and then a second, Cathy didn't reply.

'We've all heard about your brother and his slut of a wife,' Mrs Wheeler continued.

Jabbing her knife in the butter, Cathy spread the marge across the square of grey bread.

'Not that anyone would blame him for going back to his mother,' the old woman added. 'Taking her clothes off in front of a load of men! Disgusting!'

Cathy cut the sandwich into fingers and arranged them on her son's Bunnykins plate, which she then carried through to the lounge.

'Everyone knew Stella Miggles was no good,' Mrs Wheeler said as Cathy walked in. 'But your brother was too stupid to see it.' She spotted the plate in Cathy's hand. 'Don't put that on my sideboard or it'll take the polish off.'

Cathy gritted her teeth and put the plate on the sideboard before picking up her son.

'I said, don't put that—'

'Here we are, sweetheart,' Cathy cut in, placing Peter in the chair opposite the old woman. 'Have this while Mummy gets changed.'

'Changed for what?' asked Mrs Wheeler.

Cathy gave her a sweet smile. 'Well, I'm not going to the shelter dressed like this, am I, Vi?'

'What about supper?' asked her mother-in-law.

'Me and Peter will have it with my mum when we get there,' Cathy replied. 'It's only a bob for both of us, with pudding, and it's boiled beef and carrots tonight.'

'But what about me?' said Mrs Wheeler.

Cathy shrugged.

'There's some cheese in the pantry and half a loaf in the crock so you can make yourself a bit of Welsh rarebit if you like, Vi.' Irritation flashed across the old woman's face. 'Of course, you wouldn't have to,' Cathy continued, 'if instead of gossiping about my family you'd put the oven on when I asked you to. Now, if you'll excuse me.'

Without waiting for a reply, she turned and headed for the downstairs hallway.

'I don't see why you have to go to that shelter when my Stan spent two days digging out a shelter in the garden,' Mrs Wheeler shouted as Cathy started up the stairs.

Cathy ignored her.

In her bedroom, she quickly stripped off her WVS uniform and put on her navy siren suit, then added her thickest jumper over it. It might be spring up top but at twenty-five-feet below street level the Tilbury shelter was always damp and cold. Standing in front of the mirror hanging above the small cast-iron fireplace, Cathy brushed out her golden-brown hair.

Winding it in a scarf, she secured it with a knot in the front, then teased out the curls of her fringe. She looked at her reflection in the mirror quickly, before steeling herself for the inevitable tongue-lashing from Violet as she tried to leave the house.

Picking up the case containing her and her son's birth certificates, her marriage and insurance documents, she hooked her hand through the bundle of blankets and went back downstairs.

Peter had finished his bread and butter and, seeing her dressed for their nightly visit to the shelter, he turned and slid backwards off the chair.

'He's put his mucky hands all over my cushions,' said Mrs Wheeler, as Cathy walked back into the parlour.

'That's what children do, Vi,' said Cathy.

'It might not matter what you do at your mother's house,' continued Mrs Wheeler, 'but I have quality furniture in my home.'

'Come on, Peter,' said Cathy, giving him an encouraging smile. 'Let's go and see Nanna.'

Her son gurgled a reply and, clutching his teddy, toddled after her

'I'll be writing to my Stan,' said Mrs Wheeler.

'You do that,' said Cathy, as her mother-in-law's thin lips pressed together.

Taking her son's hand, she led him back into the kitchen and put on his coat and hat.

'He'll have something to say about the way you treat me,' Mrs Wheeler yelled from the parlour as Cathy wrapped the scarf around her son's neck.

'Sorry, did you say something, Vi?' Cathy called back as she settled her son into his pram.

'Don't try and pretend you can't hear me,' the old woman bellowed. 'And when my Stan gets home, he'll wipe that smile off your face. And don't call me Vi. You know I don't like it.'

Cathy smiled.

Grabbing the handle, she kicked off the pram's brake and opened the back door. She pushed the front wheel over the step.

'Bye, *Vi*!' she shouted back, slamming it behind her.

Chapter ten

'NICE TO SEE you, Charlie,' said his mother's old friend, Mrs Kennedy, as he stepped out of the pew with Patrick in his arms.

'Thanks,' he replied, smiling down at the middle-aged woman in her Sunday hat and coat. 'It's good to be back.'

'How's the shoulder?' she asked.

'On the mend,' Charlie replied.

He'd repeated the same three words at least a dozen times in the past twenty minutes.

It was the first Sunday in April, Easter Sunday in fact, and he was standing in the aisle of St Breda's and St Brendan's.

He'd been a choirboy in his family's place of worship and with choir practice on Tuesday and Friday, three masses on Sunday plus saint's day celebrations and weddings, he'd spent as much time in the church as at home when he was young. However, in the last few years he'd been a less frequent visitor, preferring to spend Sunday mornings in bed followed by a Guinness or two in the Catholic club with his mates.

That said, when he'd walked through the doors into the Gothic splendour of the Victorian church and saw it freshly dressed for the holy day, an odd feeling of comfort settled on him.

Mrs Kennedy's attention shifted to his son. 'And I bet this little chap is pleased to see his daddy.'

'Not as much as his dad is to see him,' said Charlie, giving his son a squeeze.

A sentimental look spread across the matron's face. 'Seems only yesterday your dad walked into church carrying you just like that. We were fighting the Germans then, too.'

Mrs Kennedy continued on towards the main doors.

Patrick started to fidget so Charlie repositioned his son in his arms and then gazed around.

Although the surroundings were as familiar to Charlie as his parents' parlour, the church had changed since he last walked in it. The railing outside had been taken for scrap, gummed paper criss-crossed the stained-glass windows and most of the statues of saints had been taken to the crypt for safety.

That wasn't the only thing signifying the old church was battle ready. Whereas once the women of the parish worshiped our lord in their best hats and Sunday clothes, they now knelt at the altar rail in black ARP helmets, navy ambulance jackets and green WVS coats. The older men, who'd served in the last war and were too old for this one, were also in uniform, mainly the khaki of the Home Guard, with the odd buff-brown boiler suit of the Heavy Rescue thrown in.

As the 10 o'clock Mass had finished a few minutes ago, so Billy and Michael were still in the chancery getting changed out of their cassocks and getting a severe telling-off from Father Mahon for sniggering when Old Pete Ryan farted as he bowed to the altar.

His father, Mattie and Jo had gone through to the hall where tea was being served while Queenie was having a heated discussion with Mrs Dunn, the rectory's housekeeper, on the chancery steps. But Charlie's attention was focused on the quiet of the side chapel where, by the ornate rack holding the votive candles, he could see Francesca.

She was wearing a raspberry dress with a white lace collar under a short navy blazer. Her abundant black hair was unbound and cascaded down to just above her waist. A small shallow-brimmed navy hat with white trim completed Francesca's Sunday outfit. He again noticed in passing her shapely legs, which of course he'd seen hundreds of times before but suddenly seemed to catch his attention.

She'd been sitting with Mattie at the end of the row in front when he'd slipped in the pew alongside his gran just as the service had started. She'd turned and smiled at him briefly but then the organ had struck the first chord and they'd both stood up.

However, instead of concentrating on the Mass liturgy, Charlie had found his attention and his eyes being drawn to her throughout the service.

Now Charlie walked over to her.

'Morning, Fran,' he said.

She turned and smiled up at him. 'Hello, Charlie.'

'Lovely day, isn't it?'

'It certainly is,' she replied, the warm spring light from the chapel window lighting her face.

Her gaze shifted down onto his son.

'And hello, Patrick,' she added as Charlie studied her long dark eyelashes.

Patrick waved his hands in greeting and Francesca laughed. Still smiling, she raised her head.

'For my mother,' she said, indicating the rack of flickering candles.

'I guessed,' he replied. 'How are your family?'

'Well enough,' she replied.

She gave him a brief run-down on her father's cafe as Charlie intently watched the shape of her mouth as she spoke.

'And we're really hoping Gio will get leave in a month or two,' she concluded.

'That'll be great. If I'm still here, we can have a couple of jars,' said Charlie.

'So you can moan about your sergeant majors,' Francesca said.

Charlie laughed. 'And the terrible food and hard beds.'

'Talking of family, where's your mum this morning?' she asked.

'Got up feeling a bit Tom and Dick, so she decided to have a lie-in,' he replied.

Francesca looked concerned. 'I hope it's nothing serious.'

'I shouldn't think so,' Charlie replied. 'She reckons the whelks she had on Friday were a bit dodgy. I'm sure she'll be as right as nine pence in a day or two.'

'Well, tell her I wish her better,' said Francesca. 'Mattie tells me you might be here through to the end of June.'

'Looks like it,' Charlie said. 'I'll be here for both Jo's wedding and this one's first birthday.' Looking at his son, he smiled. 'Won't I?'

Patrick gurgled and patted Charlie's face with a chubby hand.

A couple of the church's matrons who were shuffling towards the door shot him a pitying look as they went past and then started muttering.

The weight of Stella's betrayal pressed down on him again. 'I thought Mattie at least would have written to let me know what was going on.'

'And what could you have done if she had?' asked Francesca.

Charlie sighed. 'Nothing, I suppose.'

'Exactly,' said Francesca. 'Which is why she didn't. Your family figured you had enough to do to fighting Rommel without worrying about anything else and that you would deal with...'

She gave him a sympathetic look.

'My darling wife?' he said bitterly.

'The situation,' she corrected. 'When you got home.'

A lump formed in Charlie's throat.

'I suppose everyone thinks I'm a complete idiot,' he said flatly.

She didn't deny it.

Why would she? He bloody well was.

She took a step closer and placed her hand lightly on his injured arm. 'Don't take any notice.'

He studied her slender fingers with their neatly clipped nails resting on the coarse fabric of his sling for a moment, then looked up.

'Well, as my dad always says, if it wasn't for us Brogans, what would the neighbours have to talk about?'

Francesca laughed. 'Too true.'

Looking in her brown eyes, he smiled and she smiled back. Patrick let out a little cry and started wriggling in Charlie's arms.

'Well, I'd better be off home, or Dad will wonder where I am,' she said, adjusting her handbag over her arm. 'Bye, Charlie.'

'Bye.'

She gave him another little smile, then turned and walked away.

'And good luck for the new job tomorrow,' he called after her.

Running the tip of her Scarlet Kiss lipstick around her mouth, Stella pressed her lips together and then studied herself in the dressing-table mirror.

A satisfied smile crept across her face as she turned her head back and forth to admire her reflection.

Although she usually collected Patrick from her mother-in-law at one, today she wasn't in any hurry. In fact, she'd even considered giving one of next door's snotty-nosed kids a couple of coppers to pop around and say she wasn't well again, but decided against it as she didn't want them to think she was scared to face them.

Stella glanced at the clock. Two o'clock.

It was over a week since she'd walked into the parlour and found Charlie sitting there.

She hadn't pushed it all week so as to give him a bit of time to calm down, but enough was enough. People around here talked enough about her without Charlie giving them something else to gossip about.

Looking at her reflection, Stella adjusted the front of her summer-weight pink jumper. She'd selected it out of the other half a dozen in her wardrobe because it not only hugged her ample breasts, but the V-neck displayed her generous cleavage.

As it was Sunday the whole Brogan family would have finished bothering God a while back and would be shovelling up their last mouthfuls of pudding by now. The mad old woman had told her yesterday that Charlie would be returning Patrick to her after Sunday dinner, which suited Stella fine.

Although it wasn't ideal that Charlie had found out from that magazine that she was the top act at the BonBon club, as long as she was able to get her hands on him she was sure she could get around him and his interfering family. After all, Charlie had been stuck in the desert with only his right hand for company for over a year so he must be desperate for a bit of the other by now. And, all right, perhaps it wasn't bolting planes together or packing bombs with explosive, but keeping up troop morale was a sort of war work.

Giving herself a last admiring look she stood up, then, straightening her pencil skirt, stepped into her black court shoes and headed downstairs.

She'd just reached the bottom when there was a knock on the door.

Waiting on the doorstep was Charlie, standing with one arm in a sling and his other hand resting on the handle of her Silver Cross pram. Their son, sucking his thumb, was sitting happily in the shade of the raised hood.

Behind him, on the other side of the street, were Minnie Wallace and Elsie Griggs along with at least a dozen of Stella's neighbours, all of whom stood wide-eyed, anticipating a bit of drama to enliven their Sunday afternoon.

Charlie was dressed in his battle fatigues, as he had been when she'd come home that other morning, but his freshly shaven face and trimmed curls indicated he'd taken a trip to the barber's recently.

'Thanks, Charlie,' she said, giving him her warmest smile. 'But you didn't have to put yourself out, I'm always happy to collect him.'

Charlie cast his cool gaze over her again. 'Can I come in or do you want everyone to hear our business?'

'Course you can,' she said, standing back. 'It's your house.'

Pressing down on the handle to lift the front wheels over the step, Charlie wheeled the pram in.

She closed the door and followed him down to the kitchen. By the time she got there, Charlie had already unstrapped Patrick.

'Hello, my little sweetie,' said Stella, making a happy face.

Patrick turned away and reached for Charlie's neck.

'No kiss for Mummy, Patrick?' she said, stepping closer.

Under the pretence of tickling her son under the chin, she pressed her breasts against Charlie's arm.

Interest flashed across his face for an instant, then his stony expression returned, and he moved away. 'My mum's just changed him so you don't have to bother.'

'Has he had his afternoon nap?' asked Stella, looking adoringly up at him.

'Not yet,' Charlie replied.

'I'll take him up now then,' said Stella, reaching to take her son.

'I'll do it,' he replied, his large hand spread across his son's small back.

Turning from her, Charlie walked out of the kitchen. As she heard his footsteps on the stairs, Stella slipped her hands down the top of her jumper and after positioning her breasts higher in her brassiere cups, she pulled the front of her jumper down.

Hearing the stairs creak as he came back down, Stella pulled out a single blonde curl from behind her ear and twisted it to snake over the swell of her left breast.

She leant back seductively on the table and smiled at him as he walked back into the kitchen.

His eyes flickered down to her breasts and Stella suppressed a smile.

'Has he gone straight *down*?' she asked, flicking her eyes towards his crotch suggestively.

He nodded.

Giving him a smouldering look, she walked slowly across the room.

'He looks so much like you, Charlie,' she said, gazing adoringly up at him.

'Well, that at least answers one question,' he replied.

'Don't be like that!' Stella pouted. 'I thought you loved me.'

'Perhaps I did once,' he replied. 'But that died the moment you walked out on that stage.'

'You don't know what it's like here. How far do you think your bloody ten bob a week goes with prices double what they were a year ago?' she said. 'I had to do something to earn money, didn't I? I suppose you think I should have been working my fingers to the bone in some stinking factory.'

'Why not?' he asked. 'Other women do.'

'Well, I ain't other women,' she spat back. 'Queuing in the rain with their bloody food coupons. Chopping up curtains to make themselves a pair of drawers and knitting old wool into socks.'

'No, you're not like other women, Stella, you're a stripper,' Charlie said flatly.

She pouted. 'Come on, Charlie, I know you're angry with me, but—'

'I'm not angry with you, Stella,' Charlie cut in. 'I'm angry with myself for being such a fool.'

'I'm sorry, Charlie,' she said, trying to sound contrite. 'If you come home, I promise I'll leave the BonBon club and we can put all this behind us.' Reaching out again, she traced a pattern on his upper arm with her index finger. 'And, who knows, this time next year Patrick might have a little brother or sister.'

Charlie's implacable expression didn't falter so, after a moment or two, she stepped closer.

Reaching up, she went to run her fingers through his hair. 'You always were so handsome.'

Her hand left his face and smoothed along his shoulder and down his arm.

'So strong,' she murmured, lightly tracing the hard muscles beneath his army shirt.

'I'm not interested.'

'Don't lie, Charlie.' Reaching out, she cupped his erection with her hand. 'You were born interested.'

'But not with you.' Charlie removed her hand. 'It's over, Stella. As far as I'm concerned, you can do what you like with who you like. I don't care. All I care about is Patrick and when I come back for good, I want him, Stella. I want my son—'

'He's my son, too,' she interrupted. 'Don't forget that. It was me who was in agony for days and was almost ripped in half having him while you were miles away.'

'I want my son, Stella,' Charlie repeated. 'And I won't rest until I get him.'

His glacial gaze ran slowly over her face then he pulled himself away and strode out of the house.

Chapter eleven

AS THE 15 drew to a halt opposite St Clements's church in the Strand, Francesca, holding her basket with her lunch in it, stepped down from the platform.

It was a stop earlier than the one she wanted but as there was a crater in the westbound carriageway causing congestion on the eastbound side of the road, she'd guessed it would be quicker to walk.

Although it was just after eight and the sun was fully up, the Luftwaffe's visit to the capital was still occupying the city's ARP services. An ARP information booth by the Georgian church in the middle of the road was surrounded by a crowd of people scanning the list of casualties posted on its noticeboard while the WVS mobile canteen served tea and sandwiches to a collection of soot-stained and grey-faced Civil Defence personnel.

Since the German high command had turned its murderous attention on the historic towns of Britain a few weeks earlier, the nightly bombings in the capital had eased a little. However, if weather conditions prevented the Luftwaffe flying over Lincoln or York, then they returned to their old target – London – as they had done last night.

Crunching across the shards of glass from the shattered office windows still strewn across the pavement, Francesca crossed the road. The dirt-covered Heavy Rescue crew who were lolling around their truck smoking gave her the obligatory couple of wolf whistles as she passed them. Lifting her head and looking ahead, Francesca continued on towards Bush House.

With its two Doric columns topped by a couple of larger-than-life scantily clad heroic statues and vaulted entrance hall beyond, you'd be forgiven for thinking you were about to enter a Roman temple rather than the nerve centre of the BBC Overseas Broadcasting Service.

Mightily glad she'd decided on her businesslike mulberry-coloured suit and white shirt for her first day as an employee of the BBC, Francesca joined the stream of men and women hurrying through the imposing double doors.

Inside the marble-clad reception area, the BBC workers fanned out towards the lifts on either side of the entrance hall or headed for the stairs at the far end.

Feeling slightly overwhelmed, Francesca walked towards the reception desk just to the side of her and gave her name to the grey-haired woman behind it who directed her to one of the lifts, assuring her she couldn't miss the Italian section as it would be right in front of her when the doors opened.

The woman was right. Five minutes later, when Francesca stepped out onto the third floor of Bush House, she was relieved to see a door labelled Radio Roma right in front of her.

Straightening her skirt, Francesca grasped the brass handle and walked in.

The office was large, but what space there was looked smaller because of the half a dozen desks that had been placed almost end to end along each side of the room, leaving just a narrow passage down the middle. Behind each desk was an austere-looking chair while on the desks were various stacks of Shellac records in their buff paper sleeves. The two desks nearest the door each had a typewriter and a set of Bakelite earphones alongside it. The office's putty-coloured walls were barely visible as behind each desk was a pinboard covered with typed and scribbled notices.

There were two tall windows at the far end of the room, in front of which was a longer desk with three telephones on it. Beside the desk were three gun-metal-grey filing cabinets, each with a wire tray brimming with papers.

However, what Francesca noticed most about the place where she was about to work was that Miss Kirk, red-faced and her grey hair askew, was standing toe to toe and nose to nose with Mr Whyte, who was glaring back at her.

'Good morning, I'm—'

'What you don't seem to be able to understand, *Mr Whyte*,' shouted Miss Kirk, flailing her arms around, 'is that Professor Giulio is in Tooting hospital.'

'And what you fail to grasp, *Miss Kirk*,' the engineer yelled back, 'is that I have four BBC news bulletins– ' he jabbed a nicotine-stained finger at the round metal cannister sitting on one of the desks '–that I need translated into Italian and typed up so that Leo can broadcast them at six o'clock tonight.'

With a face like thunder, he turned and stormed towards Francesca who just managed to get out of the way before he barrelled into her.

Taking her handkerchief from her pocket, Miss Kirk blew her nose noisily.

'I'm sorry, Miss Kirk,' said Francesca. 'I didn't mean to interrupt, but my letter says to present myself at eight thirty.'

'And you have, Miss Fabrino,' Miss Kirk said, glancing at the wall clock, which showed twenty past eight. 'It's not your fault either that the professor stepped in front of a tram in the blackout and broke both legs.'

'Poor man,' said Francesca.

'Indeed,' said Miss Kirk. 'And poor us, too. He was supposed to have been in an hour ago to transcribe the reels the news department sent but instead I had a phone call from his wife telling me dear Bruno…' She fluttered her pale eyelashes. 'I mean, Professor Giulio, had had an accident.'

She blew her nose again, then her eyes fixed on Francesca. 'You can do it. You can transcribe the tapes and then type them up.'

'But I don't know how,' said Francesca.

'It's easy enough. You just write everything they say in the news report down in Italian, then type it up ready for Signor D'Angelo to read.' The supervisor's face brightened. 'It'll be a bit of a close-run thing but I'm sure if we put our shoulders to the wheel we can get it done.'

'Well,' said Francesca, placing her basket on the nearest desk and starting to unbutton her jacket, 'I suppose I might as well jump in at the deep end.'

'That's the spirit.' Miss Kirk wiped her nose again and pocketed her handkerchief. 'Now, you hang your jacket up and I'll take you through to our scribblers' den. Oh, I nearly forgot this.' She picked up a small card and handed it to Francesca. 'Your staff pass. Don't lose it.'

Francesca opened her handbag and proudly slipped her BBC credentials into her purse.

'Now,' said Miss Kirk, opening the door. 'Follow me.'

'Today our troops in North Africa withstood another unrelenting barrage of enemy fire as they stood their ground against Rommel's Afrika Korps at Mechilli, which was then captured by the 3rd Armoured Brigade,' said the plummy tones of the BBC war correspondent through Francesca's headset.

Reaching across, she flicked the switch and the disc on the turntable stopped. Francesca thought for a moment, then wrote down what she'd just heard in Italian on the notepad in front of her.

She was sitting, with a set of Bakelite earphones on her head, at a desk in a ten-by-ten windowless booth a few doors along from the Italian section's office. The wall behind her was one big set of shelves tightly packed with gramophone records. The desk where she was working had a lamp angled to illuminate the space in front of her and an industrial-looking record player with more dials, knobs and switches than you'd think possible. Thankfully, Francesca only had to worry about a couple of them.

It had been almost three hours since Miss Kirk quickly ran through how to use the machine and then disappeared to sort out some other crisis. Since then Francesca had steadily worked her way through a report from a mine sweeper somewhere in the North Atlantic, a very long report from a factory in the Midlands who had exceeded their production targets and were producing an extra dozen fighter planes each week and a dispatch from an RAF base in East Anglia.

Now she was just finishing translating the last of the discs she had been given from the BBC correspondent who was with the Eighth Army in North Africa.

Of course, the battle he was describing had happened some days before as the commentary had to be recorded onto a disc in a mobile radio van away from the front and then sent back to the BBC via army couriers.

Francesca turned the machine on again and, after listening to the final couple of sentences, pulled off the earphones and wrote in Italian: 'This is Richard Dimbleby signing off from somewhere in the North African desert.'

Putting her hands over her eyes, Francesca arched back in the chair to ease her aching back.

The door opened and Miss Kirk's round face appeared around the edge.

'How are you getting on?' she asked.

'I've just finished,' said Francesca, tapping her notes into order on the desk.

Her supervisor looked impressed. 'Good show. Did you have any problems?'

'Not really once I got into the swing of it,' she replied, placing her hand on the dog-eared book next to the record deck. 'Thankfully I brought my Italian dictionary with me this morning and now I'm dying for a cuppa.'

'Yes, I'm sorry about that,' said the older woman, giving Francesca a contrite look over her half-rimmed spectacles. 'It's been one of those mornings. But well done again.' Miss Kirk glanced at her watch. 'Did you bring lunch?'

'Yes,' said Francesca. 'Some sandwiches and a flask of tea.'

'Splendid,' said her supervisor. 'Why don't you have them now before you start typing up tonight's bulletins?'

'Yes, Miss Kirk,' Francesca replied.

The supervisor gave her a jolly smile, then disappeared back around the door.

Francesca stood up. Hooking her handbag over her arm and gathering her papers together, she left the room. Walking the short distance to the Radio Roma office, she opened the door. Finding it empty, she put her notes on the desk with the newest-looking typewriter, then sat down on the chair. Reaching into the basket at her feet, Francesca lifted out her Thermos flask and lunchbox from her basket on the floor and, having come to the conclusion that if she didn't work through lunch she wouldn't be done by five thirty, she began to type.

With the strip light above her reflecting off the black case of her Remington typewriter, Francesca pushed the release lever hard. The sheet of paper rolled up and the carriage returned to the left-hand side of the machine.

Glancing at the notes she'd made earlier that day, she returned her eyes to the page and then hammered on the keys.

It was now twenty to six and as the blackout came into force at the top of the hour, she intended to close the heavy office curtains as soon as she'd finished typing up her notes.

It was also five hours since she'd eaten the two rounds of pilchard sandwiches and drained the last drop from her flask. Truthfully, she really should have been sitting on a 15 bus trundling home through the city by now, but she'd phoned her father an hour ago to tell him that she'd be late. Miss Kirk had teetered on the edge of panic and tears all day and Francesca felt somewhat obliged to help her supervisor.

Other than the post boy popping in, an angry-looking chap asking for Mr Whyte and the tea lady who mercifully arrived with her trolley at three, Francesca had spent most of the afternoon alone in the office. And it was just as well because typing up thirty pages of notes required a great deal of concentration, especially when they were written in Italian. After all, she didn't want to get the sack on her first day for typing allied *dupes* instead of *troops*.

Reaching the end of the line, Francesca returned the carriage again and had just skimmed over the next line of her notes when the door opened and Miss Kirk came in.

'How are you getting on?' she asked.

'I should be done in a minute or two,' said Francesca.

'Thank goodness,' said the supervisor, heaving a sigh of relief. 'It's not usually like this but with poor Bru…Professor Giulio off sick…' Tears welled up in her eyes once more. 'He broadcasts weekly lectures on politics and historical themes for Radio Roma but he also translates the news bulletins ready for Signor D'Angelo's nightly broadcast, so you can understand why his absence today has left me in a panic.'

Francesca nodded.

'I've telephoned the hospital twice to see how he is, but they weren't very forthcoming,' the supervisor continued. 'Said I should contact his wife.'

'Do you have her number?'

'I do, but…' Miss Kirk's face darkened for a second, then she looked artlessly at Francesca. 'You have to understand, the professor is a genius. Like many men of high intelligence he is often unappreciated by those closest to him.'

'You mean his wife doesn't understand him?' said Francesca.

'Exactly,' said Miss Kirk pertly. She picked up the neat stack of papers next to Francesca's typewriter. 'Are these ready to go up to the studio?'

'Yes,' said Francesca. 'I just have these last two pages to type up.'

Miss Kirk's round face lifted into a jolly smile.

'Splendid, I'll take these up now,' she said, hugging the sheets Francesca had been typing all afternoon to her chest. 'And if you could bring the last couple up in a few moments before you go.'

'Up where?' asked Francesca.

'To studio three, where Leo does Radio Roma's evening news broadcast,' explained Miss Kirk. 'It's on the floor above, to the right.'

Turning, she opened the door but then looked back at Francesca. 'You've worked very hard today and I can't tell you how grateful I am, Miss Fabrino, for jumping into the breach like this. I'll see you tomorrow.'

Miss Kirk left and, with the last rays of the sun just dipping below the window sill, Francesca turned back to her task.

Five minutes later and just moments before the broadcast was due to begin, Francesca reached the floor above.

Spotting the door with a large 3 painted on it, she knocked.

'Come!'

She went in and found Mr Whyte sitting at a narrow metal desk in front of what looked like a wall of knobs, dials and switches. To his right was a metal cabinet with a record deck and a pile of records alongside while to his left was another door with a red light shining above it. A window separated him from the rest of the room.

'About time, too,' he said, glaring at her as she walked in.

'I'm sorry,' she said. 'I've done it as quickly as I could.'

He held her gaze for a moment, then looked back at the instruments. 'Well, you'd better take it in to him.'

'Him?'

'Count D'Angelo, of course. But we're on air in two minutes so as we can't have you clattering about trying to get out of the booth you'll have to stay until the end of the broadcast. Go on.' Mr Whyte indicated the door with the red light above it. 'And don't make a sound.'

Gingerly, Francesca turned the handle and entered the soundproofed broadcast studio.

Signor D'Angelo was perched on the edge of a desk reading the news bulletin she'd typed up earlier. Beside him was a microphone the size of Francesca's hand and a set of headphones.

Just as when he'd interviewed her, Radio Roma's main presenter and voice to occupied Italy was immaculately dressed in a sharply tailored grey three-piece suit with a contrasting berry-red waistcoat beneath. The gems on his cufflinks still twinkled at his wrists and on his tie pin.

He looked up as she walked in and smiled.

'Miss Fabrino,' he said, standing up to greet her.

'Signor D'Angelo,' she replied, her eyes flickering onto the tangle of hair visible between his unbuttoned collar. 'I've brought you the last couple of pages.'

She held them out.

'*Grazie*,' he said in Italian as he took them from her. 'I've just been skimming through the translations you did earlier, and they are *perfetto*.'

'*Prego*,' she replied, reverting to Italian and feeling a warm glow at his words.

'One minute to air,' Mr Whyte's disembodied voice said from the speaker above the window.

'Take a seat, Miss Fabrino,' he said, guiding her towards the chair beneath the large clock on the far wall.

Tucking her skirt under her, Francesca sat down and rested her hands on her lap while the count took his seat behind the desk, put in his earphones and picked up his script.

'Five, four…' said Mr Whyte from behind the glass partition.

The count smiled at Francesca, who smiled back.

'Three, two…'

On the unspoken 'one', the red light above the window went on.

'*Buona sera*, fellow countrymen and women of *Italia*,' said Count D'Angelo, his voice booming around the small space. 'Tonight…'

Feeling more than a little excited about being at the centre of Radio Roma's live broadcast into occupied Europe, Francesca sat very still and watched the count as he read through the news reports she'd spent all day translating and typing up.

Although he wasn't as tall or as broad, she had to admit Count D'Angelo could give Charlie Brogan a run for his money in the handsome stakes. He had a nice voice too, not as deep as Charlie's perhaps but, maybe because he was speaking her native tongue, still very appealing. His smile too, which he flashed at her as he spoke into the microphone, was relaxed and friendly.

After sitting motionless for what seemed to be an age but was in fact ten minutes, Count D'Angelo rounded off the bulletin with 'Goodnight, my fellow countrymen and women, from Radio Roma, and remember: together we will break the Nazi shackles chaining our glorious nation.'

From somewhere trumpets blazed out the opening bars of the *Marcia Reale Italiana* and the red light over the window went off.

Taking his headphone off the count let out a long sigh and lolled back in the chair.

'Well done,' said Francesca, standing up. 'I'm sure if I had to broadcast to a million people I'd be stumbling over every word.'

Rising from the chair he came around the desk and stood in front of her.

'You should take some of the credit, Miss Fabrino, for your faultless translation and accurate typing,' he said. The musky smell of his aftershave drifted up as he gazed down at her.

She glanced at the clock.

'I really should be going home…'

'Me too.'

'Good night.'

'Good night,' he replied.

Giving him an awkward half smile, Francesca turned and crossed the room towards the open door but, just as she was about to leave the studio, the count spoke again.

'And I very much look forward to seeing you again tomorrow, Miss Fabrino.'

Chapter twelve

'THAT'S YOU ALL booked in for next Thursday, Mrs Kemp,' said Charlie, closing the dog-eared diary and sticking the pencil back behind his ear. 'One bed and two wardrobes to 45 Jubilee Street.'

It was Tuesday, the week after Easter, and as the midday hooters in the docks had gone off a little while ago it was probably close to half-past twelve now. Charlie was standing in his father's rented scrap-metal yard beneath one of the arches in Chapman Street.

As always, the space under the arch was crammed with all manner of things but instead of the usual battered prams, iron bed frames and misshapen saucepans, now the yard was filled with double wardrobes, chests of drawers, rolled-up rugs and mismatched chairs, along with day-to-day items like scrubbing boards and zinc tubs.

With people donating their spare pots and pans to the war effort instead of selling them, his father's business would have gone under and taken the family with it had Jerimiah not had the foresight to start a removal and delivery business and switched to dealing in second-hand furniture.

Back then there had been a horse and cart too, both of which had now been replaced by a green Bedford lorry with Brogan & Sons Removals and House Clearance painted in smart bold gold lettering on the side.

'Thanks, Charlie,' said the middle-aged woman, who was wearing a headscarf and pushing a pram full of groceries. 'And good to see you back in one piece.'

Charlie smiled. 'Thanks. It's good to be back.'

Mrs Kemp placed her gnarled hand on his arm. 'And don't worry,' she said, glancing over her shoulder as she drew closer. 'No one round here blames you for walking out on her.'

Fixing a wooden smile to his face, Charlie didn't reply.

She released his arm as she kicked off the pram's brake and walked out through the yard's open gates.

Tucking the dog-eared diary under his bad arm he turned and made his way towards the boxed-off area at the very back of the yard which served as his father's office.

Well, he corrected himself, it was his parents' office now because his mother no longer spent her mornings on her knees cleaning various offices; she was his father's right-hand woman, working each morning in the yard, taking orders, selling second-hand furniture and keeping the books while his father was either attending the council auctions of unclaimed household effects left in the wake of bombing raids or moving people to their new houses.

In fact, that's where his father was now, moving a family to Manor Park although, to be honest, as he'd set out at seven and it was now almost two o'clock in the afternoon, Charlie had expected him back an hour ago.

Rolling his left shoulder to ease the stiffness, he headed back into the main part of the yard. Just then his father's Bedford van rolled through the gates.

Charlie strolled over as his father pulled on the handbrake.

'I thought you'd forgotten your way home,' Charlie said, as Jerimiah jumped down from the cab.

His father gave him an exasperated look. 'Bloody high-explosive bomb landed last night right by the Stratford Broadway and left a crater the size of West Ham football stadium in the middle of the road. It took me almost an hour to get past it on the way there and then another hour on the way back.'

'Well, at least you got back in time to get yourself to Cephas Street for the council auction,' Charlie said.

'Damn!' His father raked his fingers through his hair. 'I forgot.'

'Forgot what?'

'That I've to take half a dozen rolls of cloth from the wholesaler in Hackney to Fashion Mode's factory in Commercial Street this afternoon,' his father replied.

'I'll take them,' said Charlie.

'Are you up to driving the van yet?' Jerimiah said.

'Of course I am,' said Charlie, ignoring the ache. 'Give the joint a bit of exercise. Besides, I can drop you off on the way and then come and help you load up when I'm done.'

His father looked dubious for a moment, but then nodded. 'All right, as long as you get one of the fellas in the warehouse to load up for you or I'll have your mother after me.'

Charlie grinned, then slapped his father lightly on the arm. 'My stomach thinks me throat's been cut, and I expect you're the same so let's get some grub.'

'That's the last of them,' said Charlie as Fashion Mode's stockman, wearing a long tan-coloured overall, settled a roll of navy serge onto his shoulder and headed for the back door of the garment factory.

It was now just after three and he was parked behind the garment factory's back door and had just finished unloading the consignment of cloth he'd collected from the warehouse in Mare Street three-quarters of an hour ago.

The four-storey Victorian building with its dirt-encrusted windows and crumbling brickwork was situated in one of the alleys at the Shoreditch end of Commercial Street. It had been built to accommodate handcarts and so was only just wide enough for the Bedford to pass down. Although the April sunshine was warm, the chill in the narrow passageway raised goose bumps on his bare forearms.

His shoulder was acting up, too, from shifting the gear lever back and forth and turning the fifteen-hundred-weight lorry's steering wheel.

Jumping down from the tailgate of the Bedford, Charlie went round to the front and took out the receipt book, then walked back to the rear of the vehicle just as the warehouseman reappeared.

'Ta, mate,' he said to Charlie. 'Our girls get right stroppy if there ain't no work so that little lot should keep them 'appy for a bit.'

'I'm sure,' said Charlie.

As his sister Mattie had once earned a pittance on piecework as a machinist, Charlie understood very well why the women in Fashion Mode would be giving the foreman a hard time.

Taking the pencil from behind his ear, Charlie offered it to the other man and then held out the book. 'If you can give us your autograph.'

The warehouseman scribbled at the bottom of the page.

'And just call Stepney 279 if you need us again,' he said, giving his sister Mattie's telephone number.

The warehouseman waved his acknowledgement as he walked back through the door.

Going back to the driver's side, Charlie swung himself into the seat and felt his shoulder protest at the swift movement.

Giving it a quick rub, he stuck the key in the ignition and turned it on. The engine spluttered into life. Pressing down on the clutch and ignoring his injured shoulder's protest, Charlie grabbed the ball of the gearstick and shoved it into first.

Charlie inched along the passageway until he reached Goulston Street. Then, turning left, he headed past the public baths towards Aldgate High Street.

Turning left again, he swung out into the traffic, passing Whitechapel and the bombed-out remains of St Mary's church. Putting the lorry into third, Charlie drove down Whitechapel High Street.

Thinking nothing in particular, he trundled along the road until he reached the London hospital.

An auxiliary policewoman, in her navy uniform and peaked cap, was directing traffic. She stepped out into the road and raised her hand.

Charlie pulled on the brake.

With his idling engine vibrating through his seat, Charlie gazed across the road and spotted Alf's Cafe painted in bold black letters.

The image of Francesca in the side chapel at church wearing that pretty raspberry-coloured dress materialised in his mind and Charlie's pulse quickened.

Of course, now she had her new job she probably wouldn't be in anyway.

There was a flicker of movement and Francesca, holding a plate, appeared in the window of the cafe. She set the food down in front of someone sitting at the window table. The customer said something and she laughed in response.

Although he couldn't hear it, he knew exactly what it sounded like and this time it wasn't just his heart that responded.

A horn behind him blasted out.

Pulling himself back to the present, he realised that he was now holding up the traffic.

Raising his hand through the window to acknowledge his error, Charlie put the truck into first and moved off but, instead of continuing on towards the Cephas Street Depot, he signalled right and turned into Cavell Street.

Putting his foot on the middle pedal, he steered the Bedford alongside the kerb then brought it to a halt. Pulling up the brake, he switched off the engine.

Opening the door he jumped down, then looked at himself in the lorry's wing mirror. Smoothing down his hair with his hands and straightening his unfastened collar, Charlie strolled back to the main road.

*

Taking the cup and saucer back behind the counter, Francesca popped it onto the serving hatch. Olive, who was on the other side in the kitchen, picked the crockery up.

'I've got plenty of clean out here,' said Francesca. 'So leave them to soak with the others and I'll wash them when Papa comes down.'

'Right you are,' said Olive. 'Is he all right?'

'Yes,' Francesca replied. 'He'll be OK after a nap. I knew he'd start one of his headaches as soon as I saw Giovani's letter on the mat this morning.'

'How is your brother?' asked Olive, who was preparing for the evening onslaught of office staff streaming out of Whitechapel station and factory workers returning home on the buses and trams.

'Yes, fine,' said Francesca.

'I expect it's the relief of hearing from him that's set off your dad's 'ead,' Olive said, her beefy arms making light work of beating an egg into a bowl of National flour. 'He does worry so.'

'Don't we all,' Francesca replied.

It was just past four in the afternoon and after a long first week running up and down Bush House's stairs, she could have done with putting her feet up. But as her father was sleeping off a migraine, she was manning the shop for him.

Noticing one of their regulars, Mrs Munday, was now gathering her things together, Francesca dropped the damp cloth in the butler sink and, passing through the gap at the end of the counter, went over.

'Thanks, Mrs Munday,' she said, picking up the empty cup from the table. 'And see you next week.'

'God willing,' the matron replied, fastening her coat buttons. 'And that was a lovely bit of cake. Light as a feather.'

'Thank you,' said Francesca. 'Wag Merryman had a couple of lemons on his stall yesterday so I thought madeira would be a bit of a change from the usual currant cake.'

'Well, it was lovely,' the elderly woman replied.

'Now, you mind how you go,' said Francesca, handing the elderly woman her walking stick.

'You too, luv,' Mrs Munday replied. 'And you'll make some lucky young man a good wife one day.' Leaning heavily on her stick, the mother of four and grandmother of double that number waddled out of the cafe leaving only the two ARP wardens sitting in the corner.

Francesca had just finished wiping the table over when the bell hanging over the door tinkled.

She looked around and her heart did a little double step.

Dressed in his working clothes, with his cap at a jaunty angle, he looked just as handsome as he did when he appeared unbidden in her dreams.

Her heart tried to dance again, but Francesca cut it short.

'Charlie,' she said, smiling warmly at him. 'What are you doing here?'

'I could ask you the same,' he replied. 'I thought you'd still be hard at it you-know-where.'

'As I haven't been home before eight all last week Miss Kirk, my supervisor, let me have the afternoon off,' Francesca replied. 'Can I get you a cuppa?'

'That would be nice,' he replied.

Francesca returned to the business side of the counter and emptied the last brew's dregs into the bin.

'How's the new job going?' he asked.

'Busy,' she said, depositing five heaped spoons into the teapot. 'But very interesting. It's a small unit but at least that means it's easy to know who everyone is and what they do. It's been hard but it's better than factory work and I can use my office skills. Dad's happy, too.'

'I bet he is,' said Charlie. 'In fact, I'm surprised he let you sign up for the factory.'

'He didn't have much choice,' Francesca replied, putting milk in Charlie's mug. 'Not when the second National Service Act was passed. I told him if I didn't sign up for factory work, I could get called up for the ATS and end up on an army base with three hundred randy soldiers.'

'Oh, Fran.' Charlie laughed. 'Your poor dad.'

'I know, and I felt bad for him, but there's a war on and, like every other woman, I wanted to do my bit,' she replied, setting a mug of steaming tea on the counter. 'Do you fancy a bit of madeira?'

His dark eyes twinkled. 'Do you really need to ask?'

Francesca laughed again. 'Find yourself a seat and I'll bring it over.'

'Can you join me?' he asked.

Francesca glanced around. The cafe was quiet, so she nodded.

Taking his tea, Charlie strolled over to one of the tables against the wall and sat down, his long legs spread wide beneath it.

Francesca poured herself a cup. She cut a slice of the cake she'd baked the day before, put it on a tea plate, then went to join Charlie.

'So the job's going well,' he said as she sat down.

'I think so,' Francesca said. 'At least no one's complained yet and we're so busy the day whizzes by.'

Charlie broke off a piece of cake. 'Are there many of you in the office?'

Francesca gave him a brief rundown of Radio Roma's staff.

'And, of course, there's Count D'Angelo who is the cultural editor and main presenter. Unlike Mr Whyte, who barks at everyone, he's very friendly and helpful. Apparently he was living in London when war broke out because he'd been driven into exile in '37 when he spoke out against Mussolini.'

'I'm surprised they didn't throw him in prison like your dad and brother,' said Charlie.

'That's what I said when Miss Kirk told me but as he'd been at Oxford with half the government, he was made a Category A on the Alien Register. It's also the reason why when he approached someone he knew in the War Cabinet to start Radio Roma he was given a set of offices and a broadcasting studio in you-know-where.'

'Well, I suppose some crusty old aristocrat might as well do his bit too,' said Charlie.

'Oh no, he's not old,' said Francesca.

Charlie looked surprised. 'Isn't he?'

'No,' said Francesca, as an image of her new colleague flashed through her mind. 'In fact, I'd say he was only a few years older than you.'

An odd expression settled on Charlie's handsome face. 'Is he married?'

Francesca shook her head. 'At least, I don't think so.'

Lowering her eyes, Francesca took a sip of her drink.

Charlie broke off another piece of cake and they sat there together for a few moments, then Francesca broke the silence.

'I see the sling's gone,' she said

'When I saw the doc at the hospital last week, he said I had to exercise it,' he replied. 'So I'm helping Dad in the yard.'

'I bet your mum had something to say about that,' said Francesca.

He gave a short laugh. 'She and Gran would wrap me in cotton wool if they could, but they couldn't say too much as Mum's not all the ticket.'

'Has she still got that upset stomach?' Francesca asked, anxiously.

He shook his head, dislodging a dark curl onto his forehead. 'She's still a bit Tom and Dick first thing but it's just that whatever it is she caught off those whelks has whacked her out so she couldn't very well argue when I said I was going down the yard today.'

'Well, you be careful,' said Francesca. 'Does it hurt much?'

'To tell the truth, like buggery,' he replied, rolling his shoulder backwards.

Francesca laughed. However, the movement opened the front of his shirt and, before she could stop herself, her eyes shifted down to the dark curls on his chest.

'How's the cake?' she asked, forcing her gaze back to his face.

'Delicious and as light as a feather.' He popped the last morsel in his mouth.

'That's what Mrs Munday said.'

'Well, she's right,' said Charlie, washing it down with a mouthful of tea.

'She also said I'd make some lucky man a good wife one day,' said Francesca, remembering how often she'd prayed that the lucky man might be the one sitting opposite her.

The odd expression returned to Charlie's face.

'Perhaps to some Italian count,' he said.

Francesca laughed. 'Don't you dare say that when my dad's around.'

'Say what when I'm around?'

Francesca turned to see her father standing behind the counter looking a great deal more human than when he went upstairs three hours ago.

'Papa.' She rose to her feet. 'Are you better?'

'Much.' Her father's gaze flickered onto Charlie. 'Good to see you back in one piece, son.'

Charlie rose to his feet and crossed the room in two strides.

'It's good to be back, Mr Fabrino.' He offered his hand.

'So, what can't you say when I'm around, Charlie?' Francesca's father said, taking it.

'That Francesca makes the best cake in the world,' he replied.

'Because I don't want you to think I'm getting big-headed,' she added, feeling a little wave of pleasure at hearing Charlie say her full name.

'Well, you're entitled to, *mia cara*, because you do,' her father replied, stepping behind the counter and taking his apron from the hook.

She and her father exchanged a fond look, then his attention shifted back to Charlie, who gave Enrico a guarded smile.

'Well,' said Charlie, taking a set of keys from his pocket, 'I'm supposed to be picking my old man up at five, so I ought to get going.'

'Give my regards to your family,' said Enrico, his arms outstretched as his hands rested on the marble surface.

Charlie nodded, then his attention shifted. 'Bye, Francesca.'

'See you at church on Sunday?' she asked, gazing up into his dark eyes.

'Yes.' He smiled, then turned and left the shop, the bell over the door signalling his departure.

With the familiar ache in her heart Francesca gazed after him as he strode across the road.

'I hope you're not still holding a candle for him,' her father said quietly.

Francesca forced a laugh and turned. 'Don't be silly, Papa, that was ages ago when we were kids.'

'Good,' her father said. 'Better for your reputation that you leave Charlie Brogan to his wedded wife.'

'You're late tonight, son,' said Ted the ARP warden, as a high-explosive bomb landed somewhere to the east of them, shaking the ground under Charlie his feet.

'Pity Jerry isn't,' Charlie shouted over the boom of Tower Hill's ack-ack guns half a mile away.

'God rot 'em,' Ted replied, closing the Tilbury shelter's door as Charlie stepped in.

Tilbury Shelter, under the Tilbury warehouse on Cable Street, had been taken over by the council in order to offer refuge to the population of Stepney.

In the early days of the war, before he'd shipped out, Charlie had been down into its bowels a couple of times when it had been little better than a sewer. In fact, it was so squalid that it attracted wealthy sightseers from up West who came to gawp at those unable to afford to shelter from the murderous German onslaught in The Ritz's basement.

However, since he'd last seen the place, things had improved. Mainly thanks to no-nonsense women like his mother who spent each night in the shelter with their children. Working with the shelter's designated ARP wardens, Ida and some of the other women had become section marshals and made sure everyone behaved themselves and that people and possessions were safe. So much so that people now left things, like bedding, deckchairs or camping chairs, stacked by their regular berth instead of lugging them back each night. Even the rough brick walls of the old warehouse had had their starkness softened by the family photos pinned on them.

As a consequence, life underground was much more bearable, especially now most people didn't use the shelter every night. If the docks were covered with fog, people stayed in their own bed, safe in the almost certain knowledge that if they couldn't see to the end of the street, then the Luftwaffe bombers couldn't see their house from five hundred feet up in the air. The only ones who went to the shelter every night were women who had small children, joined only by their neighbours during periods of heavy bombing. However, after a week of nightly raids by the Luftwaffe, the shelter was filled to the gunnels.

Added to which, in the same way he'd got used to living under the constant barrage of enemy fire and knowing death could land on you at any moment, East Enders had too.

He'd had a couple of sideward looks and mutterings of cowardice when he'd first come down four weeks ago, but as he'd spent six days under German fire helping in the evacuation at Dunkirk, manned ack-ack guns on Hackney Marshes during the Blitz and had been fighting Rommel in North Africa for the past year, Charlie felt he'd earnt a bit of time off from making himself a target.

With the ground shaking as another bomb landed close by and grit pitter-pattering down from the rafters above, Charlie picked his way through the rows of neatly folded blankets towards the back of the shelter.

Pausing en route to collect three cups of tea from the jolly lady serving in the WVS canteen that had been set up between one of the archways, another improvement established by the women of the shelter, he continued on to where his mother and sister Cathy would be bedding down for the night.

He spotted his mother wrapped up in her old coat and, as she refused to wear trousers like most of the women in the shelter, thick knitted stockings. She was sitting on a folding garden chair by one of the loading bays. She and Cathy had tied a pair of old curtains up on either side of their patch to give them a bit of privacy. They'd also placed an old rug on the raised concrete platform on which were five sets of nearly folded blankets ready for Michael and Billy and the three adults in the family to snuggle under when the warden called 'lights out' at ten. In front of the platform were Patrick and Peter's, prams both of which were currently empty.

Pausing at the end of her row of knitting, his mother looked up and spotted him; relief flooded her face.

'Thank God,' she said as he reached them. 'I was beginning to worry.'

'Sorry, Mum,' he said, taking the empty chair beside her. 'We were late back to the yard, that's all. I bought you and Cathy a cuppa. Where's Patrick?'

'Thanks, luv,' his mother replied as he put her drink on the floor next to her. 'Cathy took him with her to story time with Peter.'

She nodded towards the small library that had been set up on the far side of the shelter where a young woman read from a large book on her lap surrounded by cross-legged children.

'Did your dad get off all right?' she asked.

'Yes,' said Charlie. 'He left for duty about an hour ago.' Another bomb found its target nearby and the ground shook beneath his chair. 'The cardboard box factory and United Cereal warehouse at the far end of the Highway were already ablaze when I set out, so it looks like he'll be in for a busy night.'

Another explosion shook the rafters and the strip lights swung back and forth sending chaotic beams of light across those huddled below.

Taking out her crucifix his mother closed her eyes and pressed it to her lips.

Reaching out, Charlie closed his hand over hers. 'Don't worry. He'll be all right.'

She forced a smile and they exchanged a fond look.

'Here's Daddy!'

Charlie looked around to see his sister coming towards them, carrying his son in one arm and holding her son's hand as he totted along beside her.

Seeing Charlie, Patrick's face lit up and he stretched his chubby hands towards him.

Love swelled Charlie fit to burst. He stood up and took his son from her.

'Have you had fun with Auntie Cathy?' he asked, as he settled the child in his arms.

Patrick kicked his legs and patted Charlie's face by way of reply.

'He was a good boy and sat nice and quiet all the way through the story,' said Cathy, making a happy face at her nephew.

'He's always a good boy,' said Ida, looking fondly at her grandson. Her gaze shifted up and onto Charlie face. 'Not like his father, who always had ants in his pants.'

Charlie laughed.

'I've just heard there's been a baby delivered in Ellen Conner's section,' Cathy continued, as she set her son down on her blanket roll. 'And some woman in Dolly's area is in labour.'

'Bless 'em,' said his mother. 'Once I've got the boys settled, I'll pop over to see if there's anything I can do.'

'Where are Billy and Michael?' asked Charlie.

'Well, they're supposed to be at homework club,' his mother replied. 'But if I know Billy, he's probably sloped off somewhere. Well, he'll have to pull his socks up when he starts at Parmiter's. A grammar school won't put up with all his skylarking around.'

'Has he got in?' asked Charlie.

'Both him and Michael have a place from September,' his mother replied. 'The letter arrived this morning.'

'Well, I hope they appreciate how lucky they are,' Charlie said.

Patrick started to grizzle.

'What's up?' Charlie asked his son.

'He'll be wanting his milk, I shouldn't wonder,' his mother replied, putting her knitting back in her patchwork bag and starting to get up.

'It's all right, Mum, I'll fetch it,' Charlie said.

His mother handed him a clean feeding bottle. Holding Patrick in his arms, and gathering more than a few admiring glances as he went, Charlie ambled across to the WVS wagon.

After waiting in the queue alongside a dozen or so mothers with infants in their arms, he returned to his family.

Cathy, who was wrestling her son into his night-time nappy, looked up as he got back.

'Thanks for the tea,' she said, through the safety pin gripped between her teeth. 'You'd better have yours before it's stone cold.'

'Give us it and I'll fix the teat,' said his mother, indicating the bottle in his hand. 'If you don't fix it on right, it'll be all over him and you.'

She expertly stretched the brown rubber teat over the top and handed it back to him.

Making sure he had the rug beneath him to keep his rear warm, Charlie sat on the concrete platform and offered Patrick his bedtime drink.

His son clasped the bottle in his chubby hands and Charlie tilted him backwards, a lump forming in his throat as his son's delicate eyelashes fluttered down.

Another almighty boom shook the earth and Charlie put his hand above his son's face to shield him from the falling grit.

The regular thump, thump, thump of the ack-ack guns along the river as they returned fire sent the lamps above dancing again. Somewhere behind Charlie a child started whimpering.

'Ruddy Germans,' said his mother under her breath, her voice joining with the low murmur of curses around them.

'Your boy's such a little darling,' said Cathy, looking fondly at the child in his arms as she rocked the pram she'd just tucked her son into.

'Pity he has such a terrible mother,' said Ida, taking a mouthful of her tea.

'Mum!' said his sister, glaring across at her.

'It's all right, Cath,' said Charlie wearily.

'The little lad deserves better,' Ida continued, ignoring her daughter's pointed looks. 'How many weeks did I have to ask before I got the milk coupon from Patrick's green ration book? Does she ever change his nappy? It fair breaks my heart to have to hand him over to *her* every day, but what can I do?'

'Perhaps I should just take him from her now,' said Charlie, as his son gulped down the last few drops of his milk.

Fear flashed across his mother's face. 'Don't.'

Charlie frowned. 'But I'm his dad and—'

'You might get away with it now, Charlie, while you're home,' said Cathy, as another bomb found its target close by. 'But as soon as you return to the front line, then what? She's already threatened to move away with Patrick and then he'll have no one to look out for him.' She stopped rocking the pram and sat on the concrete beside him. 'None of us like it, Charlie. But, like it or not, she's his mother and there's nothing any of us can do about it. No court in the land is going to take him from her.'

She patted his hand and Charlie forced a smile.

Patrick started to niggle again.

'Right, young man,' said Charlie, setting the empty feeding bottle down next to him. 'I think it's time for bed.'

The last chords of 'The White Cliffs of Dover' drifted across, signalling the end of the evening sing-song. Ida changed Patrick's nappy and Charlie swaddled him in knitted layers and a night cap to protect him against the damp chill of the underground shelter.

All around them children were being settled into the improvised beds, while babies, like Patrick and Peter, were tucked under their blankets like caterpillars in their cocoons with just the pink of their faces showing. Sleeping oblivious to the Luftwaffe bombers above doing their level best to send them all to kingdom come.

Charlie envied them their untroubled slumber as it looked like it was going to be a long, fitful night's sleep for all of East London.

Charlie sat down on his bed roll and propped himself against the pillar. He started reading C. S. Forester's *Plain Murder*, which he'd got from the shelter's library a few days before.

Ida had popped over to see the new arrival so, having settled her son, Cathy had gone to get them both another tea.

He'd just finished his chapter when Cathy returned, carrying two cups.

'Mum not back yet?' she asked, offering him one.

He smiled and took it. 'Probably giving the new mum some words of wisdom.'

Cathy laughed and sat back in her chair.

Setting her mug down, she reached into her bag but instead of pulling out her knitting she retrieved a book with *The History of America* stamped in gold letters across the front.

She saw the surprised look on his face.

'I suppose you were expecting a copy of *Picturegoer*,' she said.

'No… No… Of course not,' Charlie replied.

Cathy laughed. 'You're a terrible liar, Charlie Brogan.'

He smiled.

'Well, all right, Sis, I was a bit surprised,' he admitted.

'You're not the only one with brains, you know.' An amused look lifted the corner of his sister's mouth. 'It just took me a bit of time to discover mine.'

Charlie smiled at his sister then lowered his eyes back to his own book. He'd just managed a page and a half when their mother returned.

'How's the baby?' asked Cathy, looking up.

A doting expression lifted his mother's round face. 'She's a little darling of a child and a decent size too, for a first one. The mum had a bit of a rough time of it, so I said she should dab some witch-hazel on herself down below—'

'Mum!' interrupted Cathy, pointedly looking at Charlie, who discreetly returned his gaze to the page.

Ida looked around. 'Aren't the boys back yet?'

As if hearing her question, Michael came running over.

Leaving his younger brothers to get themselves ready for bed, Charlie opened his book but then Patrick gave a cry and burst into hiccupping tears.

Charlie stood up and by the time he'd got to the pram his son was having a full, red-faced scream.

Charlie picked him up.

'It's all right, Patrick, Dad's here,' he said softly, rocking him in his good arm.

'He's had a bad dream,' said Cathy as she tucked herself fully clothed into the bed roll next to her son's pram.

Cradling his son in his arms, Charlie resumed his position against the pillar. Leaning back, he rested Patrick against his chest.

Another bomb landed close by, shaking the dirt floor of the shelter and showering them with grit again.

The boys went off to brush their teeth at the communal washstands while his mother turned down their bedding and her own.

'I think he'll nod off again, Charlie,' said his mother. 'Do you want me to put him in his pram?'

Charlie shook his head. 'Me and Patrick are all right, Mum, you turn in.'

His family settled down around him. The lamps above flicked on and off, warning people it was time to get into bed. Five minutes later, as what sounded like a high-explosive bomb landed close by, the lights went out. Just a handful of torches and the yellow glow from the hurricane lamp in the WVS canteen illuminated the vast chasm of the shelter and the chattering ceased.

Charlie sat quietly with his sleeping son resting on his chest, listening to the bombs falling above them and the returning fire as the ack-ack guns sent a barrage of anti-aircraft shells into the air.

Patrick gave a little shudder in his sleep. Closing his eyes, Charlie pressed his lips to the baby's soft curls and his heart ached.

Perhaps it wouldn't be for a month or two, but soon he would have to return to the fight and leave the most precious thing in his world, Patrick, in the care of a woman he now loathed.

'Don't worry, Patrick,' he whispered in the petal-like ear of the sleeping baby. 'Nanny and your aunties will look after you until Daddy comes home and, when I do, you'll be living with me.'

Chapter thirteen

TAPPING THE RETURN bar a couple of times to raise the paper, Francesca read her work through carefully. Satisfied, she pulled it out of the typewriter, making the cogs on the carriage clatter as she did so.

Placing the piece of paper on top of the half a dozen sheets she'd already typed, she then picked them all up and tapped them into a neat pile.

It was almost twelve thirty on Wednesday and she was already in the middle of her second week as a clerical translator at Radio Roma. She had just finished typing up a translation of a talk entitled the 'Merits of Democracy', which the Home Service had broadcast the night before and which was due for a second outing in Italian sometime next week. Other than a quick cup of tea and a dry Rich Tea biscuit from the mid-morning tea trolley, she hadn't stopped since she'd arrived at eight o'clock that morning.

Everything had started well and even Mr Crozier, the beardless youthful junior programming assistant, who had been sent to assist until the professor recovered from his accident, was on time. Unfortunately, this was a brief moment of calm because at nine-sixteen precisely, the phone rang. Miss Kirk had promptly dashed out saying, 'It's going to be one of *those* days.' She needn't have bothered because Francesca was beginning to learn that at Radio Roma it was *always* one of those days.

It was also the day after Charlie had unexpectedly strolled into the cafe.

Taking one of the fawn folders from the bottom drawer of her desk, Francesca slipped the typed papers inside. She had just placed them in the out-tray to the left of her Remington typewriter when the door opened and a very red-faced Miss Kirk came in, clutching a half a dozen aluminium discs in brown paper sleeves.

'Sorry I was so long,' she said. 'How are you getting on?'

'Just finished,' said Francesca.

'Splendid,' beamed her supervisor.

'You look a bit flushed. Is everything all right?' asked Francesca.

'Oh, yes,' said Miss Kirk. 'I've just been up to see the old servants—'

'Old servants?'

'That's what we all call them,' her supervisor replied. 'The Corporation directors.' She laughed. 'Although, obviously, not to their faces.' She looked around. 'Where is Mr Whyte?'

'He came in earlier, muttering something about needing a recording of people talking and another one of furniture moving,' said Francesca.

'That must be the atmosphere recordings he requested from Broadcasting House last week,' said the supervisor. 'Haven't they arrived yet?'

'They did but were sent to the Dutch section,' Francesca explained. 'And when he went to get them, he found someone had put a hot cup of tea on the top and the heat had warped them.'

Miss Kirk looked alarmed.

'Don't worry,' said Francesca. 'He's in the men's lavatories now, soaking them in a basin of hot water to straighten them out. What are they for, anyway?'

'We have a theatre group coming in to record *Richard III*,' her supervisor replied.

'What, in Italian?' said Francesca, wondering if her translation skills would stretch to the Bard.

'Yes,' said Miss Kirk. 'But don't be alarmed. We managed to acquire a set of scripts in Italian from somewhere. Oh, and these are for you, Miss Fabrino.'

Her supervisor plonked the discs she was carrying in Francesca's in-tray.

'Bruno, I mean the professor, was allocated to translate them but, of course, he's still off sick after his unfortunate accident.'

'Any news of when he's coming back?' asked Francesca, looking at the half a dozen discs on the edge of her desk.

'Probably at the end of the month, according to his wife,' Miss Kirk replied. She spotted the clock. 'Perhaps you could make a start on them after you've had your lunch.'

'Yes, Miss Kirk.' Francesca reached into her basket, rummaged around for a moment, then looked down. 'Blast.'

'Miss Fabrino?'

'I've left my lunch at home.' Francesca stood up. 'Never mind, it won't hurt me to go to the canteen for once.'

Five minutes later, having walked down two floors and squeezed past a trolley stacked high with electrical equipment, she headed towards the pair of half-glazed doors at the far end of the first floor.

Pushing open the doors, which had Staff Canteen written on them, she walked into a large wood-panelled room. It had black and white tiles on the floor and globe lights fixed to the ceiling. There were at least three dozen tables set out in neat rows, all with white tablecloths, cutlery and glasses on them.

Although the women behind the counter at the other end of the room were only just taking the lids off the pots, there was already a sizeable queue snaking away from the serving area.

The meaty smell drifting across the room made Francesca's stomach rumble so she started towards the end of the queue, but she'd only taken a couple of steps when a short man with oiled hair, a pencil moustache and wearing a waiter's uniform stepped in front of her.

'Excuse me, miss,' he said, studying her closely. 'I hope you don't mind me enquiring, but may I ask what grade you are?'

Francesca looked confused. 'Grade?'

'Yes,' he said. 'Because this canteen is for senior grade two and above.' His beady eyes ran over her. 'And if you don't mind me saying, you don't look much higher than a level-two junior.'

Francesca bristled. 'I'm a clerical grade three, if you must know.'

The waiter gave her a smug look. 'Which means, miss, that you aren't—'

'Is there a problem, Mayhew?' asked a rich male voice behind Francesca.

The waiter's disdainful expression vanished.

Francesca turned to find Count D'Angelo standing behind her with an urbane smile on his face. As ever, he was impeccably dressed, this time in a tweed sports jacket with a mustard wainscot beneath and buff-coloured slacks. The diamond cufflinks he had worn before had been replaced with a gold pair with a heraldic crest.

'Sir,' said the waiter, a tinge of colour spreading up from his collar, 'I was just explaining to this young lady—'

'Who I invited to join me for lunch,' interrupted the count.

His attention shifted from the sniffy waiter onto Francesca. 'I'm sorry I'm late, Miss Fabrino.' Smiling, he took her elbow. 'Shall we find a table?'

Without waiting for a reply, he guided Francesca to an empty table by one of the long windows.

'Now, my dearest Miss Fabrino,' he said, switching to Italian, 'please, tell me what you would like and I – ' he placed a well-manicured hand on his chest – 'will fetch it for you.'

'That's very good of you, but—'

'I insist.'

Unsure, Francesca glanced across at the table closest to them.

'The pie looks good,' she said.

'If my lady wants pie, then pie I shall fetch her.' He pulled out a chair. '*Per favore.*'

Tucking her skirt under her, Francesca sat down, put her handbag by her feet. She rested her hands on the starched tablecloth and, feeling like a sparrow at a peacock ball, waited.

The count strolled over to the queue and started talking to a couple of young women near the front then, ignoring the hard looks from those behind, slipped in alongside them as the line moved forward.

Within a few moments he returned, carrying a tray with two plates and two cups on it, which he set it on the table.

'One pie,' he said, placing one of the plates before her. 'And I took the liberty of adding carrots and potato to your order.'

Francesca smiled. '*Grazie*, it looks delicious.'

'Indeed,' he replied, his eyes fixed on her face.

On the pretence of picking up her cutlery, Francesca lowered her gaze and the count took the seat opposite her.

Francesca frowned. 'Thank you for helping me out. I usually bring sandwiches, but I was awake half the night, then overslept and dashed out of my dad's cafe without them.'

He looked puzzled. 'Was there an air raid at your end of town last night?'

'There was but it wasn't Luftwaffe that kept me awake.' She gave a wan smile. 'It was just one of those nights.'

'Perhaps you were worrying about an absent sweetheart,' he said.

'I haven't got a sweetheart.'

The count's dark eyebrows rose. 'I am very surprised to hear that. Someone as beautiful as you, Miss Fabrino, should have at least a dozen hopeful young men vying for your hand.'

'Hardly!' Francesca laughed.

'Or perhaps just one,' the count continued.

The image of Charlie smiling at her as he strolled through the cafe door the day before flashed across her mind.

Francesca lowered her eyes again and speared a carrot.

The canteen door swung open and a tall man wearing a khaki uniform and a disdainful look entered the room, surrounded by a group of chattering people. Seeing them, the waiter sprang forward, hands clasped in front of him in supplication.

'*Che palle!*' muttered Leo, cutting through a potato.

Francesca studied the group for a moment, then looked back at the count.

'Isn't that…?'

'Yes,' he said, giving the group that had just entered a bitter look. 'De Gaulle. The self-styled "Leader of the Free French".'

The canteen manager indicated a table on the far side of the room and the party moved towards it. However, one of their number, a man with a clipped moustache and double-breasted suit, spotted them. Running his hand over his oiled hair, he peeled off from the group and sauntered across.

'Bonjour, Leo, *mon ami*,' he said, as he reached their table. 'Fancy seeing you 'ere?'

'I don't see why, Victor,' Leo replied. 'I work here.'

An exaggerated look of recollection spread across the other man's chubby face. 'Oh yes, I forgot. Radio Pisa! How's it going?'

'It's Radio Roma, Victor,' Leo replied. 'But I don't expect your petit pois French brain to retain such details.'

Irritation flashed across the other man's face for a second, then the cool smile returned.

'Still having trouble with the Italian jammers, are we?' he asked.

'A little,' Leo replied tersely. 'But I'm sure the boffins will sort it out any day now.'

'I hope so, for your sake, *mon ami*,' Victor replied. 'There's no point having a radio station that can't transmit to anyone, is there?'

Leo's expression changed from annoyance to fury and Victor's gaze shifted to Francesca.

'Aren't you going to introduce me to your delightful luncheon companion?' he asked.

'Miss Fabrino, this is Monsieur Victor Dubois, deputy head of programming at Radio Londres,' Leo said.

Victor smiled. 'Pleased to meet you, Miss Fabrino, but just a quick warning, *ma cherie*. Italian men are all romantic words, nothing more.'

Francesca gave him an innocent look. 'I thought that was Frenchmen, monsieur.'

His haughty smile slipped a little and a mauve flush coloured the Frenchman's throat.

'Good to see you, Victor,' said Count D'Angelo, not bothering to hide his enjoyment of the other man's discomfort. 'But you'd better run along now as your master's calling.'

He indicated to where de Gaulle, who was now standing behind the table at the other side of the room, was peering over the heads of the dinners.

Victor gave him a narrowed-eyed look, then turned and strode across the canteen.

'Bloody idiot,' muttered the count, when Victor was out of earshot. 'Pardon my language, Miss Fabrino, but you'd think the French are the only ones whose country is under the heel of a Nazi jackboot. It's only because de Gaulle made the prime minister feel guilty about Dunkirk that Churchill let him broadcast in the first place. Since then the general and his crew of oily Frenchmen have built themselves a nice little empire while we, the Italians, Poles and Greeks who are trying to broadcast to our fellow countrymen, are stuffed into a couple of rooms and have a handful of staff.'

He stared angrily at his half-eaten dinner for a long moment, then raised his eyes. 'I'm sorry, Miss Fabrino.'

'It's all right, Count,' she said softly. 'If I were in your position, I would feel just the same. But what did he mean about the jammers?'

'Unlike France, that is only a hop across the Channel or Norway on the other side of the North Sea,' Leo explained. 'Italy is much further away so the only way our broadcast can reach their audience is by routing the signals via Gibraltar and Malta. With the enemy's navy surrounding both it is very easy for their radio operators to jam our transmissions.'

'So the people can't hear them,' said Francesca.

'Exactly,' Leo replied. His urbane smile returned. 'But don't worry, as I said to that insufferable Frenchman. I'm sure the BBC boffins will sort it out.'

His warm gaze searched her face for a moment or two, then he stretched across and covered her hand with his.

'Miss Fabrino, I know those stuffed shirts on the fifth floor have a horror of employees of different ranks being on first-name terms but perhaps, when we are by ourselves, would you mind if I called you Francesca?'

'No, not at all,' she replied.

'*Splendido.*' A warm smile lifted the corner of his mouth. 'And you can call me Leo.'

A little fizz of excitement ran up her arm but, out of the corner of her eye, Francesca noticed people looking their way.

'I will,' she said, withdrawing her hand. 'If we can speak in English.'

He looked surprised. 'But your Italian is *perfetto.*'

'And so is your English,' she said, reverting to the language. 'And I know it sounds old fashioned, but people might think we are talking about something...something...'

He raised an eyebrow. 'Intimate?'

She gave a tight smile.

'Very well. English it is. And far from outdated, I find your regard for your reputation most commendable, Francesca.' He flashed her a brilliant white smile. 'How's the pie?'

*

149

'Only me, Papa,' Francesca called, as she closed the back door behind her.

'I'm just finishing off,' her father called back.

Although it was now almost eight in the evening, the introduction of double summer time at Easter meant that the blackout wouldn't come into effect for another half an hour so the blinds were still rolled up and the heavy curtains across the door drawn back.

She put her handbag on the sideboard, took off her coat and hung it up on the pegs behind the door. Kicking off her shoes and stepping into her slippers, Francesca padded through to the shop where her father, still in his horizontally striped apron, was wiping down the counter.

'You're late,' he said, depositing the dishcloth in the sink.

'Yes, sorry, had a last-minute job land in my in-tray,' she replied.

'Again?'

Francesca shrugged and gave him an apologetic smile.

'They work you too hard,' he said.

'No more than anyone else.' She glanced through the serving hatch at the kitchen's eight-burner stove. 'Is that my supper I see in the pot?'

'*Si*,' her father replied. 'You go through and I'll fetch it.'

Returning to the parlour Francesca sank into the fireside chair. Resting her head back on the antimacassar she'd embroidered to brightened up the dour brown chairs that were placed either side of the fireplace, Francesca closed her eyes and squeezed them tight. Having spent nine-plus hours typing, it was hardly surprising they were aching.

When Miss Kirk had arrived at four thirty with a copy of a programme about Francis of Assisi in the *Who They Were* series clutched to her chest, the task of translating it into Italian had seemed more than a bit daunting. However, fortified with a strong cup of tea from the trolley, Francesca had knuckled down and was more than a little proud of herself for being able to put the completed transcript on her supervisor's desk at five past seven as she'd left.

The door opened and her father walked in carrying a tray.

He'd swapped his apron for his old baggy cardigan and had loosened his tie.

'It's liver and mash,' he said, placing it on her lap. 'It's been in the pot for an hour so hope it's not too dry.'

'It's fine,' said Francesca as the meaty aroma set her stomach rumbling. 'Busy day?'

As her father ran through the various customers who'd been in and out of the cafe during the course of the day, Francesca ate her supper.

'But,' concluded her father as she scraped the last bit of potato onto her fork, 'the big news of the day is from Giovani.'

'You've had a letter?' asked Francesca.

'It arrived in the afternoon post.' Her father took an army-issue grey envelope from the top pocket of his shirt.

'Is he well?' asked Francesca. 'Is he still in Scotland? Is he coming home soon?'

'*Si*, to all you said, and probably in a month or two's time, plus,' her father's eyes lit up, 'he's bringing his friend *Sherry* home with him.'

'Gio's got a girlfriend!'

'He has,' said her father. 'And it seems they've been going to concerts and local art exhibitions together on their leave days.'

'Well, you could knock me down with a feather,' said Francesca.

'I don't know why you're so surprised, Francesca,' said her father. 'We always did double business on Friday evenings when he was serving up the fish and chips.'

'I know,' said Francesca. 'But although he's had the odd date or two, I can't remember him ever walking out with any girl seriously.'

'He's got plenty of time,' said her father. 'And he's sowing his wild oats before he settles down.'

'He's three years older than me,' said Francesca.

'It's different for women,' said her father. 'Young girls should stay with their mothers and marry young, to keep them safe.'

'Safe?'

'Safe from being foolish with young men,' said her father firmly.

'Sowing their wild oats, you mean?' asked Francesca.

A look of sheer horror flashed across her father's face.

'Don't worry, Papa,' laughed Francesca. 'I'm not about to start sowing mine.'

'This is why you should be married by now,' said her father, scowling across at her. 'If you had a house and family to keep you occupied, you wouldn't have time to worry about…'

'About?'

'About *things*, Francesca, your mother didn't even know about until her wedding night.'

Guilt tugged at Francesca again.

'Sorry, Papa,' she said softly.

'This modern way of women just going off with anyone they fancy is all wrong,' her father continued. 'In my day, a young woman looked to her parents to find her a suitable young man with a good trade and from a respectable family before she even started thinking about leaving her home. A young man who'd show respect to her parents.'

'But things are different now.'

'I know, I know,' he said with a sigh. His unhappy expression lifted a little. 'I only want you to meet a nice man and settle down.'

The image of Leo smiling across the canteen table tried to materialise in her mind, but Charlie's face supplanted it almost instantly.

'And I will,' she said, shoving the unhelpful thought aside. 'One day you'll be able to walk me down the aisle. Promise.'

He sighed and rose from the chair.

'I'll make us a cuppa,' he said, taking the tray back from her.

He left the room and Francesca rose to switch on the domed Bush wireless that sat on the sideboard.

As the valves warmed up, Francesca's gaze rested on the statue of the Madonna standing beside the wireless. It had been given to Francesca's mother by her mother as a wedding gift and had travelled all the way from Italy with her. It, along with a flask of tea and sandwiches, went with them to the basement whenever there was an air raid.

Because their old fish and chip shop on Commercial Road had been on the route of the yearly parade to honour the Holy Virgin in her blue cape with a circlet of gold pinned to the back of her head, she took pride of place ready for when the church procession and the priest passed by. However, as their cafe wasn't near to a Catholic church, no June parade passed them so, after they moved in, Francesca couldn't keep up her mother's tradition and the statue had remained in its place on the sideboard ever since.

As the signature tune of *Silver Screen Success* filled the room, her father returned with two cups of tea.

'Would you mind, Papa,' said Francesca, taking one of them and resuming her seat, 'if I asked Mrs Brogan if she would put Mama's statue of the Virgin on her family altar for St Breda and St Brendan's June parade, so it can be blessed.'

'Of course not,' said her father, sitting opposite. 'As long as it comes back in one piece.'

'Thanks, Papa. I'll pop it over when I have time,' said Francesca, the image of Charlie reappearing in her mind.

Chapter fourteen

RUBBING HIS DAMP hair with the towel, Charlie studied the four new additions to the family's food supply peck around their wire cage.

'Feeling more your old self, are you, lad?'

Charlie turned to see his grandmother, carrying out a basket of washing, stepping down from the back step.

'Much,' he replied, forcing a smile.

Physically he was on the mend, but inside he wouldn't be until he had Patrick with him for good.

When he'd woken up three hours ago in his iron-framed bed, with his old football posters still pinned to the wall, the knowledge that in a month or two he would have to leave his son in his wife's care caused a grey cloud of misery to press down on him.

The feeling hovered still, but with one of his gran's Saturday breakfasts under his belt, followed by a shave and a strip wash in the backyard, the cloud had lifted a little. His father had gone to the yard about an hour ago and Charlie would be meeting him later for a swift half at the Catholic club. As always, his mother was doing her Saturday-morning market shop along The Waste with Cathy. As the boys were at the Saturday club at St Breda and St Brendan's, it was just him and Queenie holding the Brogan fort.

As he stood there, shirtless, his grandmother's eyes shifted onto his shoulder for a second.

He'd taken the dressing off before his wash. Although the skin had closed over, the muscles beneath were only just beginning to heal. After a full week of helping his father at the yard, his damaged shoulder was more than thankful it was Saturday.

'How is it?'

'Well, let's just say I won't be bowling for England anytime soon,' Charlie replied. 'Your girls seem happy.' He nodded at the chicken coop.

'That they are,' said Queenie, giving the hens a fond look as she pegged one of his father's shirts on the line. 'And so will I be, if those eggs I left in each of their boxes last week hatch.'

Charlie reached for the clean vest that he'd draped over the handle of his mother's old 'hopping' pram that had been to Kent and back each autumn for twenty years.

'Looks like they've saved you from a life of crime,' he said, slipping it on.

His grandmother's face lifted in a cheeky grin. 'They have but really it wasn't fair on your dad. We had a bit of a set-to before Christmas and he's got enough on his plate without having to keep bailing me out of the nick. Fat Tony wasn't too happy, but he has other runners to collect his bets.' She nodded towards Patrick's pram parked at the end of the yard in the sun. 'I take it Patrick's still asleep.'

'Out for the count,' Charlie replied, looking over at his sleeping son.

The grey cloud of despondency descended again.

'I don't know why she doesn't just let me have him,' he said. 'After all, he practically lives here now.'

'Because that poor excuse of a mother is a dog in the manger,' his grandmother replied. 'She knows you want him and that's why she won't hand him over. God wither and rot her black soul. And I suspect she hopes that by hanging onto him, she can hang onto you, too.'

Charlie gave a hard laugh.

Pausing in her task, his grandmother looked across at him.

'And don't worry, boy, you'll be grand in time,' she said, her eyes soft with sympathy and love. 'Your tealeaves showed love and happiness this morning; possibly some children, too, although I can't be sure when.'

A memory of Francesca sitting opposite him while he tucked into her madeira cake flashed through Charlie's mind.

His grandmother shot him a querying look. 'What about cake?'

A chill ran up Charlie's spine.

While, like the rest of the family, he took his grandmother's so-called second sight with a bucketful of salt, he had to admit that hearing her echo his thoughts made hope flare in his chest – perhaps her predictions would come true and he would find love again.

Leaving her in the yard, he went back in the house and made his way upstairs.

Reaching the top of the stairs, Charlie pushed open the door of the six-by-ten box room that was his bedroom and walked in.

Taking one of his old work shirts out of the wardrobe he slipped it on. He was just easing the sleeve up his damaged arm when two pairs of feet thundered up the stairs and his door burst open.

'Leave the door on the hinges, you two,' he said, as Billy and Michael, wearing their school uniforms and socks at half-mast, shoved their way through the door frame.

'Sorry, Charlie,' said Michael, bending forwards and resting his hands on his knee as he caught his breath.

'I won!' shouted Billy, shoving the other boy sideways.

'No you didn't!' Michael replied, shoving him back.

Billy scowled. 'I did! I did! Tell him, Charlie.'

'I'd say it was a tie,' Charlie replied, finding the other shirtsleeve and pushing his good arm in. 'How was Saturday club?'

'Boring,' said Billy, scuffing his toe on the floorboards.

'Father Kennedy taught us about the Romans today,' Michael said. 'And how they were in charge of the whole world when Jesus was our age.'

'That's interesting,' said Charlie, straightening the collar and starting on the buttons.

'And did you know they used to live in London a long time ago?' Michael continued.

'Bo…ring,' said Billy.

'I did,' said Charlie, unbuttoning his waistband and tucking in his shirt.

'And there's a wall near the Tower that they built?' added Michael.

Charlie nodded. 'Perhaps we could take a stroll after lunch tomorrow and see it.'

Michael's eyes lit up. 'Could we?'

'I don't see why not,' said Charlie, closing his wardrobe door.

'Did you go to Saturday club, Charlie?' Michael asked.

'I did, although it was Father Mahon who taught me while your Aunties Mattie, Cathy and Jo had instruction from Sister Dorcas,' Charlie replied.

Billy spotted Charlie's haversack propped up on the floor at the end of the bed.

'Is that your kit?' he asked.

'Yes,' said Charlie.

'Can I see it?' asked Billy.

'If you like.'

Grabbing the khaki haversack with his good hand, Charlie plonked it in the middle of the floor.

Pulling open the drawstring, he dived in and pulled out a roll of rubberised canvas.

'This is my ground sheet,' he said.

He gave it to Billy who unrolled it and spread it on the floor.

One by one, Charlie removed his mess tin, water bottle, spare army-issue socks and leather laces and laid them out next to his gas mask and spare filter, rolled-up washing kit, empty ammunition and grenade pouch and, at the bottom of the sack, his tin hat covered with webbing.

'And you carry all that with you,' said Michael, looking wide-eyed at the collection of bags, tins and straps spread out on the floor.

'Along with my food rations, live grenades, and a shovel,' said Charlie. 'So I can dig in if we come under fire and I have to keep it all in tip-top condition.'

'There's a dent in your water bottle,' said Billy.

Charlie picked it up and turned the battered canister in his hand.

'That happened when we came under fire outside Sidi Barrani last year and in my haste to get the twenty-five pounder's barrel up to return fire, I stood too near the flywheel handle,' he said, as the chaos of the assault on the Italian stronghold flashed through his mind.

Casting his eye over Charlie's equipment, Billy looked puzzled. 'Where's your gun?'

'I don't have a rifle,' said Charlie.

His brother looked even more confused. 'Well, how can you shoot Germans then?'

'Charlie's in the Royal Artillery, Billy,' said Michael. 'And gun crew aren't issued with rifles.'

Billy swung around. 'How do you know?'

'Because I read it in *Boy's Own* last week,' Michael replied.

Billy's face screwed up and for a moment Charlie thought his brother was going to burst into tears, but then he shoved Michael again.

'Well, when I'm a solider I'll have a gun and I'll kill hundreds of Germans and get a medal from the king,' he said.

Charlie picked up his helmet.

'Well,' he said, repacking his kit bag, 'I hope this war is over before you two are old enough to fight.'

Queenie shouted up from the bottom of the stairs, 'If you want your bread and dripping, boys, you'd better get changed and come down now.'

'Coming, Gran,' Michael shouted back as Billy barged past him.

'And don't forget to bring your school shirts with you,' she added.

'I'll beat you down,' Billy shouted as he raced into the bedroom they shared at the front of the house.

Michael didn't follow.

'Thanks for showing us your kit, Charlie,' he said.

'That's all right,' said Charlie, pulling the drawstring tight. 'Take no notice of Billy.'

Michael smiled. 'I don't. He's just upset.'

'About what?'

Michael shrugged, then a smile lifted the corner of the boy's mouth.

'What are you grinning about?' asked Charlie, standing up.

'That I look like you,' Michael replied.

'Do you now?' said Charlie, dropping his haversack back at the end of the bed.

'Everyone says so.'

'Well, there might be a passing resemblance,' said Charlie, looking at the lad who was the image of himself at the same age. 'But you'll never be as handsome.'

Michael laughed and Charlie joined in.

Reaching out, he ruffled his half-brother's dark curls. 'Now, go and have your bread and scrape.'

Michael nodded and turned to leave but, as he reached the door, he looked back. 'I think you and me looking alike is one of the things that Billy's upset about.'

Although it was only just after midday, The Grave Maurice by Whitechapel station and the Blind Beggar, a few doors down from her father's cafe, were already filling with men enjoying their Sunday-lunchtime pint.

As Francesca turned down Brady Street towards the back entrance of the cafe, she did a double-take when she saw a two-seater sports car, with an Alfa Romeo badge on its front grill, parked outside with a dozen or so men gathered admiringly around it.

There were two reasons for her astonishment. Firstly, the scarcity of fuel meant private cars had practically vanished from the roads but the main reason for her surprise was that she had never actually seen the shiny red Italian sports car before other than in magazines and films.

Puzzled, she opened the door to the cafe's living quarters. The appetising smell of their Sunday roast drifted through from the kitchen.

It was a bit of a treat for them today as after weeks of sitting down to steamed pigs' hearts, braised liver and stewed neck of lamb, her father had managed to get half a leg of pork. So, for once, their Sunday roast was just that: a roast.

'Only me, Papa,' she called as she closed the door behind her and took off her jacket. Hanging it on the peg, she walked into the snug parlour at the back of the shop. 'Do you know there's a—'

She stopped dead.

'Count D'Angelo!' she said, staring incredulously at Leo sitting in one of the fireside chairs, a bouquet of flowers resting across his knee.

He was wearing a double-breasted charcoal-grey suit with a matching waistcoat beneath. A gold fob chain looped across his flat stomach and his shoes were so highly polished they could have been taken for patent instead of leather. There was a gold pin anchoring his tie, which was diagonally striped in the green, white and red of the imperial Italian flag and his cuffs were secured with the gold cufflinks with his family crest on them.

Freshly shaven and with his black hair swept back from his long, angular face, Leo D'Angelo looked every inch the aristocrat he was.

Certainly her father thought so as he'd got his prized bottle of Amarillo out and both men had a generous glass of it next to their respective fireside chairs.

There were also two bottles of ruby-coloured wine sitting on the sideboard next to the photo of Francesca's mother. There was a faint trace of dust and cobwebs around the bottles' shoulders and stamped on the gilded labels was a crest that matched Leo's cufflinks.

'At last, Francesca,' said her father, jumping up from his chair and giving her an exasperated look. 'The count has been here an hour.'

'A very pleasant hour in your company, Signor Fabrino,' said Leo smoothly. Unfolding his long legs, he stood up.

Crossing the space between them, he offered Francesca the flowers. 'Good afternoon, Miss Fabrino, these are for you with my deepest respect.'

Francesca took the collection of pink, red and white roses from him.

'Thank you,' she said, staring at the flowers that had all but vanished from market stalls or florists since the war started. 'They are beautiful.'

Clicking his heels together, Leo bowed.

'Your father has most generously permitted me to present them,' he replied, his eyes warm as they stared down at her.

Francesca smiled shyly. 'If you would excuse me, I'll put them in water.'

She hurried into the scullery and, after a bit of rooting around, found a wide-neck vase large enough to accommodate the dozen or so thorny stems.

After carefully stripping off some of the lower leaves, crushing the ends and adding a spoonful of sugar and salt to the water, Francesca carried the arrangement back through to where her father and their unexpected visitor were sitting.

They were sitting in silence but, as she entered the room, Leo stood up again.

Acutely aware of his eyes on her, Francesca set the blooms next to the photo of her mother and the statue, which she had cleaned ready to take to Charlie's mother so it could be placed in Ida's family shrine.

Tucking her skirt beneath her, she sat down and Leo did the same.

Resting her hands lightly on her knees, Francesca waited.

There was a long silence, then Leo cleared his throat. 'Your father tells me you've been to Mass.'

'Yes,' said Francesca. 'I go most Sunday mornings.'

'And where is that?' he asked.

'At St Breda and St Brendan's,' she replied. 'I would have been home an hour ago, but I called in on my friend Mattie. She wasn't at church and I was worried.'

'Is she ill?' he asked.

'No, just six months' pregnant and she has a lively two year old,' said Francesca. 'But she's all right.' She smiled. 'Well, actually more than all right because her husband had returned that morning, which was why she wasn't at church.'

'Returned from where?' Leo asked.

'Where he's been,' Francesca replied.

He smiled. 'Of course, loose talk cost lives.' He changed the subject. 'I go to the eight o'clock at St Peter's in Clerkenwell. It's a bit of a walk from my suite at Claridge's, but favoured by our countrymen in exile.'

'Mayfair's a fair way from Whitechapel, too,' Francesca replied. 'And I can't remember telling you our address.'

'I apologise for my presumption but after hearing you talk so fondly of your father, I felt it only right and proper that I present myself to him out of regard for you, Miss Fabrino,' Leo replied.

'A tradition too many young men overlook,' her father chipped in.

'And as for finding you,' Leo continued. 'I surmised, Miss Fabrino, there couldn't be too many cafes called Alf's on Whitechapel High Street.'

Francesca smiled. 'I take it that's your car outside.'

'Yes,' he replied. 'I drove her out of Italy five years ago to escape Mussolini's thugs, sent to arrest me.'

'You must have been heartbroken to leave our beloved country,' said her father.

Francesca raised an eyebrow. Although he always referred to England as his adopted home, her father had been born in the East London lying-in hospital and was as much a Cockney as any of the costermongers on the market.

'I was inconsolable,' Leo agreed. 'Which is why as soon as I reached London, I moved heaven and earth to set up Radio Roma to continue the fight against those who would destroy Italy.' He placed a hand over his heart. 'Viva Italia!'

'Er…Viva Italia,' repeated her father, with a little less certainty.

'And I may say, Signor Fabrino, since your daughter, Miss Fabrino, joined our small team at Radio Roma, the bleakness of my exile has all but evaporated,' Leo added, gazing adoringly at Francesca.

Feeling her cheeks grow hot, Francesca lowered her eyes and studied the tips of her shoes.

'But I see you have a little piece of our beloved country in your very own front room,' Leo continued.

Francesca looked up to see his gaze resting on her mother's statue of the Madonna.

'My dear Rosa was given it by her mother on her marriage,' her father explained. 'In the same way as her mother before her. It has been passed down from mother to daughter for generations. She brought it with her to England when we married.' Rising, he went over to the heavily carved oak cabinet and gazed at the sepia photo.

163

'Your daughter looks exactly like her,' Leo said.

'She does and, like her mother, Francesca will make the best of wives to some very fortunate young man,' her father replied, looking squarely at the affluent young man sitting in front of him.

Leo's gaze shifted from her father to Francesca.

'I'm certain she will.'

Despite the handsome Italian count filling her vision, an image of Charlie carrying Patrick effortlessly in his arms flashed across Francesca's mind.

Her father put the photo back where it had been. 'I'm honoured you called, Signor D'Angelo.'

Leo rose to his feet.

'The honour is all mine,' he replied. 'And I wonder if you would do me an even greater honour and permit me to take your most charming daughter to dinner one evening.'

Francesca's father pulled himself up to his full five foot nine and squared his shoulders. 'Signor D'Angelo, you may take Francesca out to supper with my blessing.'

'What could I say,' Francesca replied, as she smoothed the last few creases from the fabric spread before her. 'I didn't want to be rude.'

'Well, you wouldn't catch me going on a date just to be polite,' said Jo, who was standing in her knickers and brassiere on the other side of the table.

It was nearly seven thirty on Monday evening, and she had just finished telling Jo and Mattie about Leo's visit to her father's cafe the day before.

They were standing in Mattie's dining room with the solid oak table fully extended to accommodate the eleven yards of blush ivory satin laid along its length. The fabric was anchored with an iron at one end and a pair of shears at the other.

'Neither would I,' Francesca replied. 'But to be honest, Leo—'

'Leo, is it?' said Mattie, giving her a knowing look.

'Yes, it is,' said Francesca. 'And, what's more, he's very nice.'

'Raise your arms, Jo,' said Mattie.

Her sister did as she was instructed.

'What's he look like?' asked Jo as her sister ran the tape measure around her bustline and back to the front.

'He's about five-ten, five-eleven,' said Francesca. 'Slim with black hair and dark brown eyes. He dresses well, too.'

'Handsome, I hope?' asked Mattie, measuring her sister's waist. She looped the tape measure around her neck. 'I'm done, Jo. You can get dressed.'

'Very,' said Francesca. 'Papa likes him, too. In fact, Leo's visit has been his sole topic of conversation ever since.'

'I bet,' said Jo, stepping into her dress.

'So, when are you going out with this rich Italian aristocrat?' asked Mattie.

Francesca raised an eyebrow.

'Well, he is a rich Italian aristocrat, isn't he?' Her friend laughed.

'Next Friday,' Francesca said.

'It's so lovely,' said Jo, her eyes soft as she looked over the shimmering fabric.

Mattie, who before the start of the war had been a machinist in a local sweatshop, had an expert eye when it came to fabric and could be justly proud of herself for spotting the material now smoothed out and ready to cut. Firstly, because it was a beautiful colour, which would enhance Jo's brunette hair and dark brown eyes, and secondly because the bolt of fabric was the trade-sized forty-five-inch width rather than the thirty-six-inch width usually available for home dressmakers.

'And you'll look lovely wearing it,' said Francesca.

Jo frowned, then looked at the discoloured fabric at the folded edge. 'I'm a bit worried about that stain.'

'Well don't,' said Mattie, picking up the Simplicity pattern Jo had chosen. 'With a little bit of jiggery-pokery the bodice sections should fit across without trouble and I've already worked out that if I give the skirt eight panels instead of six, I'll be able to lay the pieces both ways and avoid the damaged area. In fact, I might even have enough material to make a frilly underslip for Alicia's bridesmaid dress to match yours.'

'That would be so pretty,' said Jo.

'And you want to be glad it has that dirty streak down the middle or else it would have cost you at least half a dozen clothing coupons.'

'What colour is Alicia's dress?' Francesca asked.

'Apple-green,' said Jo. 'Mattie's making it out of the bridesmaid's dress she wore for Cathy's wedding. Do you remember?'

'Yes, I do. It's hard to believe that was just two and a half years ago.'

'I'm not surprised,' said Mattie. 'We've been fighting the Germans ever since.'

Jo's happy expression gave way to a sad one.

'I wish you and Cathy weren't still at odds, Mattie,' she said.

'So do I, Jo,' said Mattie. 'But what can I do? I've tried to talk to her dozens of times over the past year but she either ignores me completely or gives me a one-word answer.'

'It must be hard for you being stuck in the middle,' said Francesca.

'It is, and I know Mattie's tried, but…' Jo gave a deep sigh and her despondent expression deepened. 'I just wish we were all happy together like we've always been.'

'And we will be one day, I'm sure. Sisters fall out all the time.' Mattie put her arms around her younger sister and gave her a squeeze. 'Even we did last year for a time, remember.'

'I know, but…'

'Don't worry.' Mattie gave her an affectionate squeeze. 'Cathy and my quarrel won't make one little cloud on your special day. Promise.'

Jo forced a smile.

'That's better, we can't have an unhappy bride.' Mattie hugged her again. 'Now, I tell you what, Jo, why don't you make us another cuppa while me and Francesca lay out the pieces?'

Jo nodded and left the room.

'Poor Jo,' said Francesca as Mattie carefully unfolded printed tissue paper. 'But it's not your fault Cathy's husband was sent to prison.'

'I know,' said Mattie. 'But if the truth were told, I reckon Cathy's refusal to speak to me is less to do with what I'm supposed to have done and more to do being stuck with Stan and his miserable old mother.'

'You're probably right, Matt,' Francesca replied.

'I can't imagine how miserable it must be to be married to someone you loathe and despise and have no way out,' her friend added.

'Yes, it must be awful,' Francesca agreed as the image of Charlie walking into her father's cafe the week before materialised in her mind again.

'But I don't like Jo being upset,' continued Mattie, cutting across her disturbing thoughts, 'not on her wedding day, so I'm going to go round to see Cathy next week and ask her if we can call a truce for the sake of our little sister on what should be the happiest day of her life.'

'Do you think she will?' asked Francesca.

Mattie gave her a forlorn look. 'I can but try.'

Chapter fifteen

TILTING HER FACE to lift the brim of her forest-green WVS hat enough to allow the mid-April sunshine to warm her cheeks, Cathy emerged from the Catholic club rest centre carrying Peter in her arms.

It was close to five now and, as usual for a Tuesday afternoon, she'd been up to her elbows separating second-hand clothes into sizes, sex and seasons.

London had enjoyed a brief respite from the Luftwaffe when it had turned its attention to other towns and cities in England, but since the spring equinox, heralding the return of lighter evenings, the Germans had once again decided to grace the capital with its presence and the neighbourhoods that followed the contours of the Thames, from Wapping to Barking on the north and Bermondsey to Belvedere on the south, had been showered nightly with high-explosives and incendiary devices.

Cathy had just collected Peter from Auntie Muriel and Auntie Pat, the motherly women who ran the nursery where her son had been playing while she undertook her regular stint in the centre.

Usually she and her mother manned the second-hand clothing section together but although Ida had recovered from her brush with the dodgy whelks a few weeks before, she seemed to have overdone it recently, most likely by chasing around after things for Jo's wedding. Therefore, just for once, Ida had decided to have an afternoon with her feet up listening to *Afternoon Playhouse* on the wireless. And Cathy didn't blame her.

To be honest, what with helping Dad in the yard each day, trudging around half the market in East London trying to find something for tea and constantly having to see Billy's teacher to discuss his latest shenanigans, Cathy wasn't surprised her mother was fast asleep the minute the shelter warden called lights out.

The Catholic club was as familiar to Cathy as her parents' front room as all of the major family and neighbourhood events were celebrated within its walls including the annual St Patrick's Day dance, where her parents had met over twenty-five years ago, and the Sunday school that all the Brogan children had attended since they had been able to sit up. Queenie had held the wake for her husband, Fergus Brogan, in the bar above when he went to meet his maker after ending up face-down in the river mud after a three-day pub crawl. In fact, it was the same bar where her own wedding reception had been held on the day before war broke out. Although it was just over two and a half years ago, to Cathy it felt like another lifetime, so much so she could hardly recognise herself as the blushing bride when she looked at the photos of the so-called happiest day of her life.

Adjusting her son in her arms, Cathy headed across the small gravelled area at the back of the club towards the line of prams parked by the back wall.

'There we are, Peter,' she said, plonking him in his pram. 'Let's go and see what the miserable old witch is going to moan about today.'

She pulled a happy face and her son laughed.

Grasping the handle, Cathy kicked off the brakes and pivoted the pram out of the line on its back wheels. She pushed it towards the exit.

She'd left an oxtail stew in the oven on a very low light with a couple of large spuds so they should be just about ready by the time she got home.

Within ten minutes of leaving the rest centre, Cathy turned into Senrab Street.

As always when she looked along the row of houses, a feeling of despondency at the prospect of eating yet another evening meal across the table from her whining mother-in-law pressed down her.

She forced it away and focused on the fact that by the time she'd eaten and got herself and Peter ready for their night in the shelter, she would be walking out of the back door precisely an hour and a half after she entered it.

Reaching her mother-in-law's house, Cathy guided the pram down the narrow alleyway between the houses and, stretching across Peter, she clicked open the back gate. She crossed the paved yard and did the same with the back door, then, pressing her foot on the pram's back axle, she raised the front wheels over the doorstep and pushed the pram into the kitchen.

The delicious smell of the stew hit her immediately but, instead of being in the oven where she'd left it, the ceramic pot was in the middle of the kitchen table with its lid off and its contents emptied. On one side of it was one of Vi's best plates covered with gravy smears and dirty cutlery.

'Is that you, Cathy?' her mother-in-law called from the parlour in an oddly cheerful voice.

'Of course,' she replied, taking off her jacket and hooking it on the door. 'Who else are you expecting, Jack the Ripper?' Unclipping Peter from his pram reins, she lifted him out. 'And,' she continued, settling her son on her hip and marching towards the parlour door, 'what in God's name has happened to our—'

'Surprise!' said Violet, spite turning her watery grey eyes into pinpoints of flint.

Cathy stopped dead. Her brain couldn't believe what her eyes were seeing. 'Stan!'

At thirty, Stanley Kitchener Wheeler was eight years older than Cathy. She'd last seen him just before Christmas through the grilles that separated the inmates from their visitors in Bedford prison. It had been a week before he was paroled into the army and sent north to the wilds of Perthshire to guard the bleak coast facing occupied Norway.

The slight curl in his light brown hair had returned now the prison crop had been allowed to grow and three square meals a day had added some flesh to his bones.

Standing there in his khaki battle dress with his field cap tucked in his epaulette, he looked like any other solider.

Except there were many hereabouts who believed he should have been strung up, not imprisoned for a couple of years then sent to fight alongside those men who he would have betrayed to his Nazi friends.

What Stan did was supposed to be a state secret under the War Powers Act but no vote in Parliament could stop East Enders from knowing what's what.

'Who were you expecting?' her husband asked. 'Jack the Ripper?'

Cathy stood in stunned silence for a moment, then forced her brain to work.

'Stan.' Crossing the room, she gave him an awkward hug and a peck on the cheek.

'When did you get back?' she asked, as a combination of tobacco and stale body odour wafted up.

'A couple of hours ago,' he replied, his arms still hanging at his side.

'While you were out enjoying yourself,' said his mother.

'I was working at the ARP rest centre not dancing at the Lyceum, Vi,' Cathy replied, stepping away from her husband.

'See how she talks to me, son,' Violet said. 'No respect. And after all I've done for her.'

'Why didn't you write and let us know you were coming?' asked Cathy.

'I wrote and told Mum last week,' he replied.

An innocent look settled on Violet's wrinkled face. 'Didn't I mention it?'

Cathy gave her mother-in-law a hateful look and received the same in return.

Peter, who had been studying his father solemnly, tucked his head into his mum's collarbone and started crying.

'See, I told you,' said Violet, clawing at her son's arm. 'She's turning that lad into a right mummy's boy.'

'He wants his supper,' said Cathy. 'I don't suppose you left any for him.'

'Sorry,' said Violet. 'Stan was hungry after his journey. It's his money that bought it and you can't expect a man to make do with half rations, so I gave him the lot.'

'Well, if you'll excuse me, I'll have to find Peter something for supper,' said Cathy.

Without waiting for their reply, she turned and carried Peter back through to the kitchen. By the time she'd clipped Peter into his highchair and cut a slice of bread, Stan had joined her.

Pulling one of the chairs out from the kitchen table, he sat down. It creaked as it took his weight.

'I have to say I didn't expect you to run up the flag,' he said, 'but I thought you'd be a bit more pleased to see me.'

'Of course I'm pleased,' said Cathy, hoping she sounded it. 'It's a bit of a shock, that's all, walking in and seeing you. How long you here for?'

'We're shipping out to North Africa soon, so I've got a thirty-six-hour pass,' he replied.

Cathy cracked one of the half a dozen eggs her gran had given her into the saucepan.

'It's just as well I tell you straight, Cath, I ain't happy about the way you've been treating Mum while I've been gone,' he said.

'And how exactly is that?' asked Cathy, whisking a knob of marge and a splash of milk into the beaten egg.

'Giving her a load of backchat all the time,' Stan said. 'Leaving her alone without a cup of tea or a crust to eat. Ruining her furniture by bringing the pram through the house.'

He glanced meaningfully at the light-blue Marmot Cathy had wheeled in moments ago.

'I'm not leaving it outside in the yard to be rained on just to save a bit of polish,' retorted Cathy.

She scraped the scrambled egg onto the bread and butter soldiers, then carried the plate to the table.

She pulled a kitchen chair next to her son's highchair and sat down.

'And abandoning her in the shelter when there's an air raid on,' said Stan.

'You spend a couple of nights listening to her whinging and whining,' said Cathy, tucking a tea towel round Peter's neck before scooping up a spoonful of scrambled egg and offering it to her son. 'Then see if you don't want to sleep somewhere else. She screams like a bloody banshee at the slightest tremor and, honestly, it would be easier to sleep next to the air raid siren than your mother.'

His mouth twisted into an ugly line and he stood up. 'Mum!'

Violet, who had obviously been lurking just outside the door, appeared almost immediately.

'Look after the boy while I have a word with Cathy, will you?' he said, grabbing Cathy's arm and hauling her to her feet.

Peter screamed and reached for his mother as Violet took her place at the table.

'It's all right, Peter,' said Violet, picking up the spoon. 'Nanny's here.'

With the sound of their son's sobbing ringing through the house, Stan dragged Cathy down the hallway to the stairs, his fingers biting painfully into her flesh all the way.

'Let go of me,' Cathy yelled, trying to wrench her arm free.

He answered by shoving her against the wall.

Staggering to regain her balance, Cathy's hip struck the corner of the banister as Stan hauled her up the stairs. Stumbling, she caught her free hand on the carpet runner as she attempted to stay upright. She finally gained a firm footing as they reached the upstairs landing.

Without pausing, Stan stomped the couple of steps to their bedroom and, kicking open the door, threw her in.

She fell against the footboard of the bed but swung around immediately to face him.

'What the bloody hell—'

The back of his hand swiped her face, his signet ring slicing her cheekbone.

She staggered as small lights popped in the corner of her vision. As the floor swayed under her feet, Cathy forced the blackness at the corner of her vision away and raised her head.

'Now, you shut your trap and listen to me.' Leaning across, Stan jabbed his finger in her face. 'She's my mother, do you hear? My mother and you're living under her roof so, from now on, I want you to show her some proper respect.'

'Do you?' she replied, feeling blood trickling down her cheek.

His other hand smacked against her ear, setting off a clamour of bells in her head.

'Yes, I do,' he snarled. 'And you'd better, if you know what's good for you.'

Several retorts sprang into Cathy's mind but she judged it sensible to bite them back.

Wondering why on earth she had ever been keen to marry him, she lowered her eyes.

'That's better,' he said, interpreting her diffident demeanour as capitulation.

Without looking at him, Cathy walked over to her wardrobe and took out her navy siren suit and school satchel.

'Where do you think you're going?' he asked, stepping in her path.

Cathy raised her eyes. 'To the Tilbury with Peter.'

'Not when we've got a shelter in the garden you're not and, besides…' A leer spread across his heavy features as he ripped off his belt. 'I've not finished with you yet.'

Something akin to ice water ran through Cathy. 'No!'

'Yes,' he snarled, as he unbuttoned his shirt. 'I've been banged up in poxy prison or confined to barracks on parole for six months and why? I'll tell you why.' He dropped his shirt on the floor. 'Because of your bastard sister who shopped me to the bloody Jew-loving authorities, so you can shut up with your bleeding complaining and get your knickers off.'

Cathy stared at him for a long moment and then, although her knees were on the point of buckling, she forced her legs to work.

As his hands went to his waistband, she tried to dodge past, but his arms shot out and he caught her around the throat.

The smell of body odour and bad breath wafted up as Stan thrust his face into hers.

'I said…' Shoving his hand up her skirt, Stan tore the flimsy fabric from her body. 'Take your knickers off.'

He threw her on the bed.

Cathy tried to roll sideways but Stan was on her instantly, his heavy body pinning her to the bed. He forced his knees between hers and pushed her legs apart.

Pressing the air from her, he frantically freed himself from his trousers and pants, then thrust into her.

Cathy lay on the very edge of the mattress, staring blindly at the evening light playing on the dressing-table mirror. Stan was sprawled across the bed behind her, snoring quietly after his ten minutes' exertion.

Tears pressed at the back of Cathy's eyes, but she bit her lower lip hard to keep them at bay. Her gaze shifted to her underwear, lying in tatters on the rug beside the bed.

She listened to Stan's nasal whistle for the count of six then, trying to keep her weight from shifting too much, she stretched out and hooked them up with her finger.

A spring beneath her boing-ed and Stan spluttered and shifted position.

Cathy froze.

With her heart thumping in her chest, she waited until his breathing returned to a steady rhythm. Using what remained of her knickers, she reached under her skirt and wiped between her legs to clean away the deposits of her husband's ejaculation, wrapping the cloth over her finger to remove as much as she could from inside her.

Dropping the semen-soaked rag on the floor, Cathy returned to her contemplation of the fading spring sunlight in the mirror.

An image of her sister Mattie, giving Peggy Rippon a roasting for putting a cockroach down Cathy's back in the playground, flashed through her mind. Then she remembered how, when the sisters shared the big double bed as children, she would snuggle into her older sister's embrace after a bad dream, and tears of a different kind gathered in Cathy's eyes.

It had been Mattie who had come to her a day after she given birth to Peter and told her that Stan had been arrested for treason and that she would have to give evidence against his involvement in the plot to smuggle Nazi spies into London.

Since that day she had blamed Mattie for everything that was wrong in her life and marriage but now the scales had fallen from her eyes. None of it was Mattie's fault. It was hers. Hers for being stupid and blind enough to marry a traitorous thug.

Chapter sixteen

'THERE YOU ARE, Mattie,' said Ray, offering her a package wrapped in a couple of sheets of yesterday's *Mirror*. 'Three-quarters of best lambs' liver.'

Mattie took it.

It was late morning and, as always at this time of day, she, like all the other housewives in the area, were scouring the shops and stalls for something for supper.

Having skirted the stalls outside, she was now at her last call: Harris the butcher next to the Lord Nelson. There were butchers closer to where she lived in Belgrade Street, but as she'd queued with one or other of her sisters outside Harris & Sons, with a list from her mother and a few coppers in her hand, since she was six or seven, she'd decided, despite the extra walk, to register her meat rations at Harris.

As it happened, she'd had quite a successful morning and not just for herself. Her mother, having now gathered together enough dried fruit, flour and marge for Jo's wedding cake, was now turning her attention to the spread after.

To this end, Mattie had snapped up three tins of peaches, which would go well in a trifle, plus two tins of pressed tongue, which were only three points each this week. She'd also got tins of something called barracuda, which the grocer assured her was fish and tasted just like mackerel.

To be honest, the Brogans did have a bit of a bonus in that, thanks to Queenie's care and attention, not only were all of the six chickens now laying an egg apiece most days, but she'd successfully hatched another three chicks. Of course, they wouldn't know for a few weeks if they were cocks or hens but either way they were a welcome supplement to the family's supplies, especially with two growing boys in the house.

'Anything else?' asked Ray as Mattie tucked her supper into the shopping basket propped at the end of Alicia's Silver Cross pram.

'Bacon?'

He shook his head.

'Sorry. I have trotters and half a pig's head,' he said, 'if your old man's after a bit of a change. Fresh in.'

Mattie eyed the row of meat hanging from a hook at the side of the window display and the tray of pigs' trotters below.

'No, I'll pass thanks.' As offal was off rations and she wouldn't need her ration book, Mattie delved into her handbag and pulled out her purse. 'What do I owe you?'

'Just a tanner,' he replied.

Mattie handed over a shilling and Ray pulled out the cash drawer below the counter.

'Not long now,' he said, indicating her bulging stomach.

'No, I'm just hoping I last out until after my sister's wedding in June,' Mattie replied, as he handed her two threepenny pieces.

'Your mum was talking about that yesterday when she popped in,' said Ray. 'She looked a bit peaky. Is she all right?'

Mattie nodded. 'Just tired like the rest of us.'

'Too right there,' Ray replied. 'You done for today?'

'Just about.' Grasping the pram's handle, Mattie kicked off the brake. 'See you Thursday.'

Stepping out of the queue and scattering the sawdust on the butcher's floor, Mattie left the shop.

Outside, the queue she'd joined twenty minutes earlier was still stretching along the front of the butcher's window. Standing amongst the women was a little girl of about six or seven, clutching her mother's hand and peering through the widow at the display.

An image of Cathy at about the same age, with her nose pressed up against the glass window, eyeing a tray of sausages, flashed through her mind, causing a familiar ache of unhappiness to make itself known.

Setting her mouth into a firm line, Mattie turned towards Commercial Road. She was almost ready to go home, but she'd had one more thing she had to do.

Cathy let the cup half fill with water before turning off the tap. Resting the two Anadin on her tongue, she took a mouthful of water, hoping that the painkillers would have more effect on her throbbing face than the two she'd taken in the middle of the night.

But to be honest, even if the two little white pills took the edge off the pulsing pain in her jaw, cheek, black eyes and battered sex, they would do nothing to dull the agony cutting through her soul. Nor the fear that Stan's forced coupling would bear fruit.

Pushing the black cloud threatening to engulf her away, Cathy turned and looked across at her son who was playing with a couple of wooden spoons by the back door.

He raised his head and his soft cheeks bunched up in a smile.

Cathy's heart ached but she smiled back, causing the wound on her cheek to protest at the movement.

Picking up the teapot she swilled the hot liquid around, then put the strainer across the first cup then the next as she poured two cups of tea. She added three spoonfuls of sugar to one cup and two to the other before picking them up.

Discarding his improvised toys, Peter stood up and toddled across the room. He grabbed her skirt.

'Let's take Nanny and Daddy their tea,' she said, in as light a tone as she could manage through her busted top lip.

With Peter gripping tight to her, Cathy walked out of the kitchen carrying the two cups of tea.

'I thought you had a thirty-six-hour pass, Stanley,' Cathy heard her mother-in-law say as she got halfway down the hall.

'I have, Mum,' he replied. 'But it's from when I left camp until I return, which is why I have to catch the mail train back tonight.'

'But you've only just arrived,' protested his mother.

'That's the bloody army for you,' Stan replied. 'If only Mosley was prime mini—'

Cathy entered the room.

Stan was dressed in his uniform, as he had been the day before. His canvas kit bag was already packed and had been stowed in the corner. Violet, on the other hand, in celebration of her hero son's return, had put on an old rose-coloured, low-waisted dress that must have been the height of fashion two decades ago.

Both of them gave her a hateful look but lapsed into silence as she placed their drinks in front of them.

'I hope you remembered to let it brew properly,' said Violet, as Cathy straightened up.

Cathy didn't reply. As she turned, she caught sight of herself in the over mantle mirror.

'What time have you got to go, son?' asked Violet.

'Seven-ish, if I want to catch the nine o'clock from Waterloo,' Stan replied. 'It arrives in Portsmouth at four a.m. so even if I have to walk five miles back to camp, I'll be back by six, ready to ship out.'

Violet extracted a none-too-clean handkerchief from her sleeve. 'It's so unfair. I haven't seen you for almost two years and...' She dabbed her dry eyes.

Stan comforted his mother for a moment, then his deep-set eyes fixed on Cathy and, if looks could kill, she'd have been singing in the celestial choir in an instant.

Sticking his thumb firmly in his mouth, Peter curled into Cathy's leg, pressing his face into the folds of her skirt.

'See what I mean about him being clingy, Stan,' said Violet, her wrinkled face twisted into a hateful expression that matched her son's.

Stan's gaze shifted to his son for a second, then back to Cathy.

A smug smile lifted the corners of his lips as he surveyed his handiwork.

'Don't worry, Mum. When I'm back for good I'll sort him out, too.'

Panic rose up in Cathy's chest, but she pushed it away. Reaching down, she scooped her son into her arms.

'I've got to pick the meat up from Harris,' she said.

'I don't know why you have to go traipsing all the way to Watney Street when Hartman's in Stepney High Street is just around the corner,' said Violet.

Cathy didn't reply but went back into the kitchen.

'Well, wherever you're going, don't be long,' said Stan as, with shaking hands, Cathy threaded Peter's arms through the harness. 'There'll be trouble if my dinner's not on the table when I get back from the Feathers in a couple of hours.'

Putting Peter into his pram, Cathy didn't reply.

Grabbing the handle, she pushed it across the room and out into the hall.

'Mind my paintwork with those wheels,' Violet shouted after her.

With tears gathering along her lower lids, Cathy snatched the scarf her mother had bought her for Christmas off the coat rack. She folded it into a triangle and flipped it over her head. Turning towards the hall mirror she tied it under her chin, pulling it around her battered face.

Picking up her handbag, she opened the back door and escaped into the yard.

Thankfully, as it was now coming up to lunchtime, most of her neighbours were inside their houses busily preparing their midday meal.

Enjoying the feel of the warm sunlight and the freedom from critical eyes upon her, Cathy started walking towards Commercial Road, which ran along the bottom of her road.

Her already crushed heart ached even more. Squaring her shoulders, Cathy strode down the street but, just as she was about to wheel Peter's pram around the corner, it collided with another pram turning into the street.

Raising her gaze, Cathy looked up to see the face of her sister.

They stared at each other for a couple of heartbeats then, when she could hold the tears and unhappiness inside no longer, Cathy covered her face with her hands and wept.

A pair of familiar arms enclosed her.

'Oh, Mattie,' Cathy sobbed, shaking uncontrollably.

'It's all right, luv,' whispered Mattie softly.

Cathy laid her head on her sister's shoulder and felt her elder sister's lips press onto her forehead.

'Let's go and see Mum.'

Charlie's father brought the lorry to a halt outside their front door at just after twelve thirty, an hour later than they intended.

The reason for their delay was an unstable building by the gasworks in Ben Johnson Road, forcing them to loop around via Mile End Road to get home from their delivery in Devons Road.

Although it was the time when most of their neighbours would be sitting around their kitchen tables tucking into their dinner, there seemed to be a great number milling around outside their houses. As he and his father got out of the van and headed for the side alley to their backyard, many pairs of eyes followed them.

'You'd better be getting your tin hat on, son,' said his father, as they entered the paved area at the back of the house.

Charlie knew what he meant as Mattie's Silver Cross and Cathy's Marmot were parked alongside Patrick's light blue and silver pram. Charlie smiled to see his son tucked up inside and having his afternoon nap in the fresh air.

Hoping he wouldn't have to eat his dinner with his two sisters glaring across the table at each other, Charlie followed his father into the house.

Oddly, despite there being a delicious smell of hotpot filling the room and the table laid with cutlery, the kitchen, usually a hive of activity at this time of day, was empty.

'Anyone at home?' shouted Jerimiah.

His mother dashed though the parlour door. She grabbed her husband's arm.

'Now, I want you to promise me you won't go off alarming, Jerry. You neither, Charlie,' she added, turning her fearful eyes on him. 'It's Cathy.'

A deep frown creased Jerimiah's brow and, removing his arm from his wife's grip, he marched into the parlour, with Charlie just half a step behind. As they entered the family's main living room, they both stopped dead.

Mattie, with Alicia playing at her feet, was cradling Cathy in her arms as they sat on the sofa. Charlie was pleased to see his sisters reunited at last, but as his gaze reached Cathy's face, fury swept over him.

Along with a florid purple discolouration along the right side of her jaw, she had a matching black eye so swollen the left one was all but closed.

Charlie clenched his fist. 'Who did this?'

'Stan,' Mattie replied. 'He came home on thirty-six-hour leave yesterday and…'

She gave him a meaningful look, which told him everything he needed to know.

'Where is he now?'

'Now, Charlie,' said his mother. 'Your shoulder's only just healing and—'

'Where?'

The door flew open and Charlie's gran marched into the room, with a sack marked Chicken Feed over her shoulder.

As it was a warmish day outside, Queenie had dispensed with her over-sized fur coat. She was dressed in her dark-green day dress over which was a knitted waistcoat that could have served Joseph as his coat of many colours. On her head was a straw boater with a red-and-white-striped Petersham band around the crown.

She, too, stopped for a second as she took in the scene and fury contorted her wrinkled face.

'Jesus, Mary and Joseph,' she pronounced, dropping the sack on the floor and shooting over to her granddaughter's side. 'What cursed devil did this?'

'Stan,' said Charlie.

'I swear by all the saints above,' Queenie shouted, her bony hands clenched in fists as she shook them Heavenward, 'I'll dance on that man's grave for this, so I will.' Her coal-black eyes shifted to Charlie and his father. 'Why are you two still stood standing here?'

'We won't be, Ma,' he replied. 'As soon as—'

'He's in the Feathers,' said Cathy.

Charlie and his father turned on the balls of their feet, but Ida caught her husband's arm.

'Jerry,' she said, looking up at him with anxiety written all over her face.

Charlie's parents stared at each other for a long moment, then his mother let go of his father's arm and stood aside.

Jerimiah strode out.

'Don't worry, Mum,' said Charlie. 'I'll keep him out of trouble.'

'Mind your shoulder,' she called after him as he followed his father out of the house.

Charlie caught up with his father by the time he'd reached the end of the alley, so they were shoulder to shoulder as they emerged back into the early-afternoon sunlight. The neighbours who had been milling around when they'd arrived home ten minutes earlier all stopped talking and looked in their direction.

The Feathers, or the Prince of Wales to give the public house on the corner of Portman Street its proper title, was just a ten-minute walk away and as there was almost certainly going to be an almighty punch-up, by the time he and his father pushed open the public bar door, they had a sizable crowd bringing up the rear.

The lunchtime drinkers propping up the bar froze, drinks halfway to their lips, dominos poised to be laid, as Charlie and his father walked into the bar.

Stan was standing alone at the far end of the counter, pint in hand, and his right foot resting on the brass runner that skirted around the lower edge of the wooden bar.

'We want a word with you outside, Stan,' said Jerimiah.

Without looking at them, Stan took a sip of beer.

'Are you going to step out or do we have to drag you?' asked Charlie.

Stan took another mouthful of beer, then turned to look at them.

Charlie hadn't seen Stan for over two years and, on the surface, with his light brown hair, sunken eyes and slack mouth, he appeared to be the same slow-witted individual he'd always been.

However, as Stan looked back at him, Charlie could see that two years in prison had changed the boy who'd enjoyed pulling the legs off daddy-long-legs into a man who would enjoy doing the same to anyone who crossed him.

Stan studied Charlie and his father for a moment. Putting his pint on the bar's polished surface, he turned to face them.

Gripping the empty bottle of pale ale beside him, he smashed the bottom off against the bar.

'You can try,' he said, pointing the jagged edges of the razor-sharp glass at them.

The muscles in Charlie's jaw tightened as his father rolled his shoulders in preparation.

Although he didn't relish the feel of the razor-sharp edges of the broken bottle slicing his skin, Charlie was going to teach Stan a lesson. Even with an injured shoulder and his father in his mid-forties, Charlie was confident that they could take Stan, eventually.

The landlord pulled out his till drawer and hurried through to the pub's back room. Drinkers downed their pints and started to disappear through the side door while those who wanted to watch the upcoming fight edged their way to safe areas of the public bar.

Clenching their fists, and as if they knew what the other was thinking, Charlie and his father stepped off together but, just then, the door behind them swung open.

As his father was watching Stan, Charlie glanced around just in time to see his grandmother march into the bar. She was carrying something in her right hand and it took Charlie a moment to recognise it as his long-dead grandfather's shillelagh. It had been propped up in his parents' umbrella stand for as long as Charlie could remember.

Roughly two feet long, Grampa Brogan's cudgel was made from a section of gnarled branch stripped of its bark and was smooth from years of polishing. With a knob about the size of Charlie's fist at one end, it tapered down to a circumference of no more than a couple of inches at the other. It had been the weapon his grandfather had carried with him as a warehouse night watchman.

Although it probably weighed more than both her arms glued together, Queenie carried it with ease.

Dumbfounded by her appearance, Stan's jaw dropped as she marched across the bare floorboards towards him.

As she reached within a foot or so of the splintered bottle end, Queenie adjusted her grip on the club, then, with a lightning twist of her hand, brought the bulky end down against Stan's wrist bone with a crack.

He yelped and dropped the bottle, which shattered as it hit the floor.

As Stan held his injured wrist, she turned the Irish fighting weapon in her hands and jammed the narrow end into Stan's crotch with such force there was a collective intake of breath from every man in the bar.

With his eyes out on stalks and gasping for breath, Stan pitched forward and cradled his injured cods.

'Use your fists on my darling girl, would you, you great ugly savage?' Queenie shouted, bobbing up and down on her spindly legs like a demented sparrow.

Swirling the cudgel again, Charlie's gran took hold of the narrow end then, adjusting her stance, swung it in a high arc and smashed into the side of Stan's head.

He tried to grab the bar to stay upright but his eyes rolled up into his head. With a vacant look on his face he staggered a couple of paces then crashed into the beer, mud and sawdust on the pub's floor.

Having felled her quarry, Queenie turned to face Charlie and his father, who were both staring at her opened-mouthed.

'Now Stan knows our mind on the matter,' she said, tucking the shillelagh under her arm, 'perhaps we can be about our victuals.'

Chapter seventeen

AS THE SEVEN o'clock pips sounded from the kitchen wireless, Charlie strolled into the kitchen, looping his khaki tie around itself.

'Are those boys anywhere close to being dressed?' asked his mother as she slipped a sizzling square of fried bread next to a pile of scrambled egg.

'They were both in their uniforms when I walked past,' he replied.

It was true; they were. However, while Michael was packing his satchel, Billy was sitting cross-legged on the bed reading a comic.

It was the 24th and the last Friday in April. The spring sunlight was streaming over the rooftops, turning the barrage balloons hovering over the docks and visible through the Brogans' back window a cheery shade of pink.

The previous night had been clear with a full moon but enemy action had been light as the Luftwaffe had been concentrating their efforts to the east of London in Essex where fields were being Tarmacked over and turned into airfields for the Americans.

It had been so quiet in fact that when the all-clear had sounded just before eleven, Charlie had come up top from the Tilbury shhelter to enjoy the cool evening and star-filled sky.

He'd spent a good hour above ground, taking in the enormity of the universe and thinking about the hopelessness of his situation before returning to his son's side. He'd lain staring at the dirty ceiling above for another hour, with images of a life that could not be dancing in his head. He'd finally drifted off to sleep a few hours before people started packing away and going to work.

Seeing his father appear, Patrick, who was sitting in the highchair eating his bread soldiers, smiled and started kicking his legs.

As always, Charlie's heavy heart lifted a little at the sight of his son. Careful to keep his freshly pressed khaki shirt way from his son's buttery fingers, he kissed him on the head.

Patrick held up a piece of bread to him.

'Thanks, son,' said Charlie, ruffling his son's dark curls. 'I think Nanny's making mine.'

Skirting around the back of his own father, who was just finishing off the last of his breakfast, Charlie pulled out the seat next to his son but, as he went to sit down, Michael walked in with his satchel slung over his shoulder. Dumping it beside the dresser, he slid onto the seat the other side of his brother.

Charlie's mother put a plate of scrambled egg and toast in front of Charlie and did the same for his younger brother. They both thanked her.

'Billy not with you?' she asked.

'He's just coming, Auntie Ida,' Michael replied.

She gave him a dubious look. 'So's Christmas.'

She returned to the hob and, taking the steaming kettle off the heat, topped up the teapot.

Billy came storming into the room with his shirt misbuttoned and school tie askew.

'About time,' said their mother as Billy squeezed into the chair alongside his younger brother.

Pulling out the grill, she flipped the two slices of toast, which were just at the point of singeing, onto a plate. She added a mountain of scrambled egg and placed it in front of the boy. 'Ta,' said Billy.

Charlie stuck his fork into another square of bread. 'Have you got much on today, Dad?'

'A couple of local deliveries this morning, then a drive out to Stratford to drop off some furniture this afternoon,' Jerimiah replied.

Patrick had finished his soldiers so Charlie picked up a teaspoon and scooped up a small amount of his scrambled egg, then offered it to his son.

'With a bit of luck,' he said, as Patrick took it, 'I'll be back in time to give you a hand, Dad.'

'Where you off to, Charlie?' asked Michael, sawing through his toast.

'The outpatients' department at the Middlesex again, so the doc can check my shoulder,' Charlie replied.

'Does that mean you're going back to the army soon?' asked Michael.

Charlie shook his head. 'I hope not.'

Billy's sandy eyebrows pulled together. 'Don't you want to?'

Charlie's gaze rested on Patrick for a heartbeat then he returned his attention to his brother.

'Not just yet,' he replied.

Ida placed a cup of tea in front of both boys and everyone got on with their breakfast. She took a cup of tea out to Queenie, who was feeding the chickens in the yard and returned as the boys devoured the last scraps off their plates.

After their mother had straightened them both out and told them twice not to dawdle on their way home, the boys dashed out the back door with their satchels over their shoulders. Having safely packed her two younger sons off to school, Ida dished up her own breakfast and sat in the seat Michael had just vacated.

She picked up her knife and fork.

'I thought Ma bought two loaves this morning,' said Charlie's father as he spotted his wife's single round of toast under a spoonful of scrambled egg.

'She did,' Ida replied. 'But I'm trying to cut down before my middle-aged spread – ' she patted her stomach – 'spreads any further.'

Jerimiah grinned.

'Don't be daft, woman. You're neither middle-aged nor fat,' he said, slipping his arm around her waist. 'Just a bit mature like myself and a pleasing armful.'

Charlie's mother gave his father a playful slap and then his parents exchanged a fond look.

Feeling it was time to leave, Charlie swallowed the last mouthful of his tea.

'I should make tracks, too,' he said, rising to his feet.

'If you're catching a twenty-five, I'll give you a lift to Mile End Road if you like,' said his father.

'No, it's all right, Dad, I'll catch the bus to Aldgate garage and pick one up there.' Charlie shrugged on his combat jacket.

As the 15 sped up Commercial Road and past Gardiner's Corner, Charlie waited until he spotted Aldgate station on his right, then, rising from his seat on the top deck, he made his way towards the stairs at the back of the bus. Looking through the rear window he spotted a 25 passing Whitechapel library no more than three or four minutes behind them.

Perfect!

However, as he reached the platform and was about to jump off, he noticed Francesca waiting in the queue to get on and, although it took him a mile out of his way, he decided to stay on the bus.

The vehicle stopped and, stepping aside, Charlie tucked himself next to the luggage rack to let those who had followed him down the curved stairs get off.

People pressed on, the men going upstairs while women found seats downstairs. Charlie moved down the aisle of the lower deck and made his way to the front of the bus.

A couple of shop girls got on and made themselves comfortable in the last available double seat just as Francesca stepped up onto the platform behind a short man in a bowler hat. Charlie found himself wedged against the driver's glass partition next to a woman carrying a shopping bag.

The conductor rang the bell and then went upstairs as the bus pulled away from the kerb. Holding onto the handrail, Charlie looked over the woman's shoulder at Francesca, who was looking exceptionally smart in a forest-green suit with a perky red hat.

With three people between them she hadn't noticed him, which allowed Charlie the luxury of studying her averted face. He marvelled again at just how beautiful she was. After a few moments and perhaps sensing someone's eyes on her, Francesca looked up.

Their eyes met and Charlie's soul took flight.

As she raised her gaze and found herself looking into Charlie's eyes, Francesca thought for a moment she was still dreaming.

She'd woken up before the alarm with him vividly in her mind. Seeing him now, dressed in his khaki shirt and snuggly fitting combat trousers, with his field cap tucked into his epaulettes, he looked exactly the same as he had in her dream.

Well, perhaps not exactly the same as he was wearing clothes, but the grey-green eyes and tousled dark curls were the same.

'Charlie,' she said, her heart fluttering in her chest.

'Hello, Francesca,' he said.

He took half a step towards her but must have bashed his legs into the bag of the woman standing in front of him as she gave him a cross look.

He apologised, then raised his eyebrows and pulled a comical expression. Francesca smiled as the bus jolted forward again.

The conductor came down to collect fares and Francesca handed over her sixpence and got a ticket in return.

The vehicle whizzed on past the Tower of London, its ancient moat now sprouting bean canes and rows of cabbages, heading towards Custom House and Billingsgate instead of through the City.

After squeezing up a side street to avoid a bomb crater in front of St Peter ad Vincula, the bus stopped by the sandbag-encased Monument.

'Your family all right?' Charlie asked across the shoulders of the women between them, as they started off again.

'Dad's back's playing him up again but other than that he's fine,' she replied, as the fishy smell from Billingsgate filled the lower deck.

'Any news from Gio?'

Francesca shook her head. 'Not yet but, fingers crossed, he said in last week's letter he'll be home before the end of July.'

The vehicle stopped then set off again. After bouncing over the cobbles of Lower Thames Street it drew to a halt outside Cannon Street station. Several people stood up to get off and the woman with the bag sank into a vacated seat.

Francesca moved down the bus to where Charlie was standing.

'Hello again,' he said, in a low voice that resonated through her.

'Hello to yourself,' she replied.

'I guess you're on your way to work,' he said.

She nodded. 'What about you?'

'Just on my way to see the bone quack in the Middlesex,' he replied. 'Got anything special on today?'

'Just finishing off translating a report from a correspondent based on a merchant ship in the North Atlantic convoy,' she replied, wondering why he was on a 15 bus when a 25 from Aldgate would take him to the hospital's door. 'After which I've got to make a start on translating some short stories that are being broadcast next week.'

'I'm impressed,' he said. 'But then you always were the brightest girl in the class.'

The memory of watching Charlie play football through the gaps in the fence that divided the girls' small playground from the boys' larger one flashed through her mind.

'I didn't think you noticed me at school,' she said.

'Of course I did,' he replied. 'I remember your long black plaits for a start.'

'Only because you used to pull them,' Francesca replied.

Charlie laughed that rumbling laugh again, then his eyes flicked onto the snood encasing her hair.

'I'm glad you haven't followed the fashion for short hair,' he said, his eyes warm as they looked into hers.

The bus started its convoluted journey through the shattered buildings around St Paul's before drawing to a halt outside Blackfriars station where more people piled on.

'Move down!' bellowed the conductor over the heads of the half a dozen or so passengers standing between the seats on the lower deck.

Charlie grabbed the upright handrail to steady himself and Francesca stepped into the space next to him. The faint smell of fresh male body and aftershave drifted up, setting Francesca's heart fluttering.

The bus set off again, but it had only gone a few yards when the driver slammed on the brakes, sending those standing on the lower deck flying forward.

Francesca was thrown squarely into Charlie's chest; she could feel the hard muscles beneath his battle jacket.

'Sorry!'

He winced a little, his shoulder protesting slightly. But, as his gaze ran slowly over her face, the odd notion that he was about to kiss her sprang from nowhere into Francesca's thoughts.

They stared wordlessly at each other for a moment then, as the bus rolled forward again, Charlie looked away.

'I suppose as it's Friday you'll be round Matt's later to help with Jo's dress,' he said, clearing his throat as he studied something through the bus's window.

This time Francesca's heart fluttered; for a different reason.

'Well, no, actually,' she said, losing all moisture in her mouth. 'I'm going out.'

'Out?'

'Yes. With a friend.'

'Oh.'

'From work.' Holding his dark gaze with her own, she forced a smile. 'Signor D'Angelo. I think I told you about him.'

A peculiar expression flitted across his face. 'The count chap?'

'Yes.'

'That's nice.'

'It's not a date or anything,' she added, before she could stop herself.

'No?'

'No.' She forced a laugh. 'Of course not.'

The peculiar expression shot across Charlie's face again, then he gave her his widest smile.

Someone rang the bell as the bus trundled over Ludgate Circus and into Fleet Street, drawing to a halt opposite the *Daily Express* building.

'This looks like my stop,' he said, squeezing around her.

'Is it?' Francesca asked. The heady smell of his aftershave drifted over her again.

'Yes, a brisk walk up Shoe Lane and I'm almost at Tottenham Court Road and the Middlesex,' he replied. 'Nice to see you, Francesca, and good luck with the translating.'

Side-stepping past the other passengers he headed for the exit but, as he reached the open platform at the back of the bus, he turned.

'Oh, and have a lovely evening,' he called over his shoulder as he jumped off.

A few hours later, rolling his shoulder to ease the soreness caused by contorting his arm into unnatural positions so it could be X-rayed, Charlie started weaving his way between groups of women gossiping and mothers pushing prams, as he walked down Sidney Street towards his house.

There was the usual dozen or so women, in wraparound aprons and scarf turbans, standing on their doorsteps. They stopped talking as Charlie walked towards Stella's house, and all eyes turned in his direction.

Ignoring them, he continued to his front door; the only one in the street without a scrubbed circle on the pavement. Stopping in front of it, he raised the knocker and brought it down, hearing the echo through the house.

He waited a few moments for Stella to come down the stairs but when there was no answer, he knocked again. Another length of time passed, but still no response.

'She ain't in,' called a voice from across the road.

Charlie turned to see two women standing on the other side of the street. Both had their arms crossed and smug expressions on their middle-aged faces.

'No,' said the first one who was so thin she'd have to run around in the rain to get wet. 'Went out about an hour ago, all tarted up like a dog's dinner.'

'As usual,' added her squat companion. 'And by herself.'

Charlie turned back to the door. Bending down, he lifted the flap of the letterbox. Patrick's pram was parked at the bottom on the stairs.

And then he heard it. His son sobbing.

Straightening up, he raked his fingers through his hair. Unlike most people in the area, Stella didn't leave her spare key dangling on a string behind the letterbox. His eyes darted around the door frame looking for where she might have stashed it.

'Third brick up from the window sill,' Stella's spare-framed neighbour shouted across.

'Thanks,' he called back.

Prising out the loose brick, Charlie retrieved the key. He unlocked the door and dashed in.

'Daddy's coming, Patrick,' he shouted, as he took the stairs two at a time.

Grasping the knob at the top of the banister, he swung around and was in his son's room in two strides.

Patrick was standing up and clinging to the top rail of his cot, red, snotty-faced and sobbing his heart out, the old teddy Charlie had given him on the floor. When he saw Charlie, he stretched over the top of the cot and screamed louder.

Charlie picked up his son's lost toy, scooped Patrick into his arms and kissed his hot forehead.

'Here's Mr Blue, Patrick,' he said, handing the fabric bear to his son.

Patrick took it and his sobbing eventually subsided. Finally calm, Patrick snuggled against Charlie and rested his hot head on his collarbone.

Love swelled Charlie's heart as he held his son. Pressing his lips onto Patrick's damp curls, Charlie closed his eyes.

The front door slammed.

Charlie kissed Patrick again then, settling his son in his arms, walked out of the bedroom.

Making his way downstairs, Charlie walked through to the kitchen at the back of the house. Stella, who was holding a bottle of Beefeater gin and pouring herself a little afternoon snifter, looked up as he walked in.

She was, as her neighbour had said, done up like a dog's dinner in a short pencil skirt, a blouse with the top five buttons unfastened, a patent belt and high heels.

'Where have you been?'

'I just popped out,' she replied, taking a packet of Chesterfield from her handbag.

'Where?'

'Just out.' She flicked a flame from her lighter.

'Where?'

Stella blew a stream of smoke out the side of her mouth. 'To the hairdresser's, if you must know. And what are you doing here, anyway?'

'Doing what you should have been doing; looking after Patrick,' he replied. 'You should have taken him with you.'

'He was asleep in his cot, and I didn't like to wake him,' she replied. 'And you're early.'

'Just as well I am,' Charlie replied. 'He was screaming his head off. You shouldn't leave him alone, Stella. He could climb out or get his leg twisted in the bars. It's too dangerous.'

She rolled her eyes.

Charlie's simmering temper boiled over. 'Now, you listen to me, Stella—'

'You don't know what it's like having a baby crawling around your feet all day,' she shouted. 'Getting into everything and messing up the house.'

'Well, if you don't want to have the bother of it, give him to me,' Charlie replied in as near-to-normal voice as he could muster.

'Never!' she screamed. 'He's mine.'

Patrick buried his face in Charlie's chest and started crying.

'It's all right, Patrick,' said Charlie, in a light, sunny tone despite his fury. 'See, Mr Blue is all happy.'

He tickled his son with the soft toy a couple of times and Patrick laughed.

'Shall we go and see Nanny and Granny?'

'Nanna,' his son babbled.

He looked across his son's head at Stella. 'You're never to leave him alone again. Do you hear? Never.'

She gave him a belligerent look but didn't reply.

Shifting his son onto the other arm, Charlie kissed Patrick's soft curls again, then, turning his back on his loathsome wife, walked out of the kitchen.

'After you,' said Leo as a doorman, in the black livery of Claridge's hotel, sprang out from under the art deco canopy and opened one of the iron and glass doors.

Francesca walked into the plush interior of the hotel situated in the heart of Mayfair.

She'd promised herself she wouldn't act like a complete idiot but as she surveyed the marble columns, gold leaf, crystal-laden chandeliers and mythological fresco on the hotel's soaring, arched ceiling, she couldn't stop her mouth dropping open.

They'd met at Marble Arch station earlier that evening, at eight, and had strolled down Park Lane just as the sun sank and the blackout came into force. They weren't the only ones enjoying the mild spring evening as the main thoroughfare was awash with boisterous GIs who, like over-sized puppies, bumped and jostled each other whilst whistling and calling to passing women.

However, although the streets outside were awash with olive and green, in the hotel's lobby there was barely a uniform in sight. Apart from a couple of generals tucked in the corner and an admiral checking in, the atrium was almost devoid of military personnel.

'So, what do you think?' asked Leo, as he slipped the doorman a couple of coins.

'I wish I'd worn a different dress,' she replied.

Leo laughed.

'Nonsense. You look *bellissima*,' he said, the look in his eyes confirming his words.

Actually, to be truthful, even if she did say it herself – swathed in Mattie's midnight-blue cocktail dress, with her hair swept up into a thick coil – she didn't look half bad. Which was just as well because Leo, in his perfectly fitting lounge suit and club tie, was positively dashing.

Of course, she couldn't match the twinkling jewels dangling from the ears and draped around the necks of the other dozen or so women gliding around the foyer, but her mother's strand of cultured pearls and matching earrings were respectable enough.

'It's wonderful,' she said, casting her gaze around the sumptuous surroundings again.

He offered his arm. 'Shall we go through?'

Francesca smiled and took it.

He tucked her hand into the crook of his arm and led her through.

The maître d', wearing white tie and tails, hurried to meet them as they walked in.

'Good evening, Count,' he said, scraping a bow. 'How delightful to see you again and with such a lovely companion.'

'Thank you, Gilpin,' said Leo. 'My usual table, if you please.'

'Naturally, sir,' the restaurant manager replied, scraping another bow.

He snapped his fingers.

A boy sprang forward and took Francesca's coat, then a waiter led them to a table at the far end.

Stepping in before the waiter could, Leo pulled out the chair and, tucking her skirt beneath her, Francesca sat down.

Leo took the seat opposite as the string quartet on the small stage in the corner started to play.

The waiter shook out the stiff white napkin folded on the small plate to her left, then draped it across her lap. He handed the menu to Leo.

He studied it for a moment, then handed it back.

'We'll start with chicken consommé,' Leo told him. 'Followed by the breaded cutlet of veal with dauphinoise potatoes, buttered garden peas and glazed carrots. And a bottle of barbaresco.'

The waiter bowed and left.

Thinking it would be impolite to ask why he'd ordered three vegetable dishes when, under Ministry of Food regulation, restaurants could only serve a maximum of two, Francesca placed her hands together in her lap and smiled across at Leo.

'It's very busy tonight,' she said, looking around at the sea of faces bent over their plates.

'It always is,' he replied. 'Most of the occupied governments and half the crowned heads of Europe are billeted at Claridge's.'

Francesca's eyes stretched wide.

'Really?' she said, looking around at her fellow diners with renewed interest.

He smiled. 'See that tall man with the dark hair and hooked nose?'

Francesca nodded.

'That's King Zog of Albania,' said Leo. 'And the man and woman in the corner?'

Francesca followed his gaze to where a young couple huddled over a table just to the left of the musicians.

'King Peter II of Yugoslavia and his wife,' Leo said. 'And that chap with the long face and receding hairline over there, sitting alone?'

Francesca looked at the table near the main door.

'King George II of Greece.'

The monarch of the Hellenes, sensing someone's gaze on him, turned and looked across.

Francesca lowered her eyes and studied her gold-rimmed side plate with the hotel's blue crest on it.

A waiter arrived carrying a bottle of red wine.

He uncorked it and, after Leo had tasted it, the waiter filled their glasses.

'Now, while we wait,' he said, 'perhaps we could get to know each other a little better.'

Francesca picked up her drink and took a sip. 'All right, you first.'

By the time the soup arrived, Leo had run through the last two hundred years of his ancestors. As she worked her way through her starter, Leo then told her about his immediate family, which, as his father had died a decade before, comprised of his mother and three sisters, all of whom had escaped and were now still living in a villa in Lucerne.

As the waiter laid their main course before them, it was Francesca's turn so, after giving Leo a brief rundown of her parents and brother, she told him about her time at St Breda and St Brendan's, her achievements at secretarial college and then onto the night her family's business had been torched and how Ida had taken her in.

'It must have been a bit of a squash,' he said, when she finished.

'It would have been if Jo and Billy hadn't been evacuated, and Michael wasn't living with them then, so it wasn't too bad,' she said. 'And, of course, Charlie was in the army.'

Interest flickered across Leo's well-constructed face. 'Charlie?'

The memory of standing so close to him on the bus that morning flashed through Francesca's mind.

'Mattie's older brother,' she said, hoping only she could hear the tightness in her voice. 'He's married with a little boy.'

Leo scrutinised her face for a second, then smiled. 'How's the veal?'

'Absolutely delicious,' said Francesca.

'I know,' he relied. 'Albert in the kitchen isn't so much a chef as a magician.'

Francesca laughed and they ate the rest of their meal.

'Can I get you or the young lady a dessert of some kind, Count?' asked the waiter when he came and took their plates away.

'What do you have?' asked Leo.

The waiter reeled off a list of puddings that Francesca hadn't tasted for years.

'Not that you're not sweet enough,' Leo said, bringing a blush to Francesca's cheeks. 'But what would you like, my dear?'

'Chocolate custard pie,' she said.

'And I'll have gorgonzola and a few grapes plus coffee for two,' said Leo.

The waiter bowed. 'Very good, sir.'

He left, then returned and placed their desserts in front of them.

Francesca relished the sweetness of her pudding as it dissolved on her tongue.

'My goodness,' she said, as she broke off another piece. 'I'd almost forgotten how good chocolate tasted.'

Leo cut off a lump of cheese and speared it with his knife. 'I'm glad you're enjoying it.'

'It's lovely,' she said. 'As is the music.'

'Vivaldi,' he said, stabbing a square of blue-veined cheese with his knife. '"Spring Allegro pastorale". It's part of his work known as *The Four Seasons*.'

'I know,' said Francesca. 'My father had them on record.'

He looked surprised.

'He was Italian, wasn't he?' she added, with a wry smile.

Leo chuckled and the coffee arrived.

'I like your father,' he said, as the waiter left.

'And he likes you,' she replied, stirring two spoonfuls of sugar into the tiny cup. 'Which I guess was your plan when you paid your respects to him, then asked his permission to take me out.'

'It is the way it's done in the old country,' he replied.

'I know,' said Francesca. 'And my father did appreciate you asking but, in case you haven't noticed, it's 1942 and women are driving buses and building aeroplanes.'

Leo smiled but didn't reply.

Listening to the string quartet they drank their coffee. Swallowing the last drop, Francesca smiled.

'I've had a lovely evening, Leo,' she said, placing her cup back on the saucer. 'But I really should go home.'

'Of course.' Leo rose from his seat. Going round to the back of her chair, he pulled it out as she stood up.

He clicked his fingers and the waiter hovering nearby dashed over.

'Miss Fabrino's coat, if you please,' Leo said.

The waiter hurried off and returned a few moments later with Francesca's coat.

Leo took it and held it out for Francesca to put on.

The bill arrived and he signed it. Taking Francesca's elbow, he guided her out of the restaurant and through the lobby to the front entrance.

The doorman sprang into action again.

'Can I get you a taxi, sir?' he asked, as they walked into the chilly evening air.

Leo nodded.

Taking his torch out of his pocket, the doorman stepped out into the dark to hail a passing cab.

Francesca turned.

'I can just as easily catch the night bus from Marble Arch,' she said, looking up at him.

'I wouldn't dream of it,' he replied. 'I would drive you myself, but I've used this week's petrol ration.'

A taxi, its front headlights covered so just slits of illumination remained, pulled up alongside them.

The doorman opened the cab's door.

'Goodnight, and I'll see you on Monday.' Taking her hand, Leo raised it to his lips.

Francesca smiled. 'Promptly, at eight thirty as always. And would you mind, Leo, if we didn't say anything in the office about tonight?'

'Of course.' He winked. 'It's our little secret.'

Francesca climbed into the back of the taxi and the doorman closed the door.

Leo spoke to the driver, then tapped on the window.

Francesca wound it down.

'Just so you know, Francesca,' he said, his dark eyes holding hers, 'I wasn't just asking your father's permission to take you to dinner, but to pay court to you as well.'

Chapter eighteen

'LOOK AT THAT little one over there, Patrick,' Charlie said, pointing through the mesh at one of the newly hatched chicks hopping around beside its mother.

Patrick bobbed up and down in excitement and Charlie put a steadying hand on his back to stopping his son falling backwards.

It was the last Saturday in April and the day after he'd met Francesca on the bus. He was in his rough cords and old collarless shirt because, although it was Saturday, he and his father had been up early on a delivery to Mare Street. They'd got back just as his grandmother was dishing up the midday meal. His parents were now both out, as were Michael and Billy. His gran had also nipped out for a 'few minutes' about an hour ago, leaving him and Patrick home alone.

'Shall we count them?' Charlie asked.

Gripping the edge of the chicken coop, Patrick jogged about again.

'One, two three,' Charlie said slowly. 'Four, five—'

The side door creaked open.

Charlie looked around to see Francesca standing in the back-yard. She was wearing a very fetching flowery dress with her abundant black hair gathered into a figure-of-eight bun at the nape of her neck.

Her eyes flickered down onto his unbuttoned shirt then back to his face. She smiled.

'Look, Patrick, Auntie Francesca's come to see us,' he said, his heart swelling at the sight.

Looking around, Patrick wriggled a chubby hand by way of a greeting.

'Actually,' said Francesca, waving back, 'I've come to see your mum. Is she in?'

Charlie shook his head. 'She gone with Cathy to a Ministry of Food cookery demonstration at the rest centre.'

'That's a shame. She kindly said she'd put my mother's statue of the Virgin on her shrine for a blessing in the June church parade, so I've brought it over,' Francesca replied. 'And it's blooming heavy, I can tell you.'

Charlie stood up.

'Let me take that,' he said, leaving his son side-stepping around the chicken coop.

As he took the shopping bag from Francesca, his hand brushed against hers, sending a pleasant sensation up his arm.

'Have you got time for a cuppa?'

Francesca shook her head. 'Not really. Olive's gone to see her sister so I promised Dad I'd be back in time for the afternoon teas.' An amused smile played on her lips.

'What?'

'Charlie Brogan making tea,' she laughed. 'I didn't think you could boil a kettle.'

'Well, two and a half years in the army has taught me a thing or two,' he replied.

'I bet,' she said.

He raised an eyebrow. 'Like... How to tell when a fig's ripe or how to joint a rabbit with a bayonet on a seven-pounder's breach block, oh, and how to milk a camel.'

'Milk a camel!'

'Well, perhaps not actually milk one,' he admitted, 'but certainly how to drink the stuff without throwing up. I'll just pop this inside.'

Dashing into the kitchen, Charlie carefully placed the bag in the middle of the table. He hurried out again but when he got to the back step he stopped.

Francesca was leaning over talking to Patrick but, as he took a step sideward, he lost his balance. However, before his bottom met the flagstone, Francesca scooped him up in her arms and kissed his soft curls before setting him back on his feet.

Swallowing the lump in his throat, Charlie stepped out.

'I've learnt a few things while I've been home, too,' he said. 'Like how to attach a teat to a bottle so it doesn't pop off, or if a toddler's quiet they're probably up to something and, don't laugh, how to change a nappy.'

'Really?' She smiled, straightening up.

'Yes, really. My dad used to change ours,' he continued. 'Although he threatened us with no treats for a month if we breathed a word of it. After all, you can't have it known that Jerimiah Brogan, who carried a donkey on his back the length of Cable Street for a bet, was a dab hand at changing bums.' Sadness suddenly caught him in the chest. 'If I was only half as good a dad as my dad, I'd...'

'You are a very good dad, Charlie,' she said, closing her small hand over his bare forearm.

Charlie felt her soft touch in every part of his body.

His gaze rested on her fingers for a moment, then he looked up and their eyes met.

It would have been so easy to slip his arm around her slender waist and draw her to him. He wanted to so much it was like a physical ache. But he couldn't.

Although he'd given her hundreds of fraternal hugs over the years, if he put his arms around her now, he would be doing it as a man with more on his mind than brotherly affection.

Francesca withdrew her hand. 'How did you get on at the doctor's yesterday?'

'He's pleased with the way the shoulder blade's fusing together, but reckons it'll be another couple of months before I'm fit to return,' he replied. 'How was your date?'

She raised an eyebrow. 'I told you, it wasn't a date.'

'All right, your meal out with your friend,' he said. 'How was it?'

'Nice.'

Charlie forced a laugh. 'Nice!'

'Actually, it was very nice,' she said, looking him in the eye.

'I hope he took you somewhere special,' he said.

'Claridge's.'

Bloody hell! thought Charlie

'He's got a room there,' she continued.

A cold hand gripped Charlie's innards.

Her gaze flickered over his face. 'Not that I went up to it or anything, you understand.'

'Of course not,' he said. 'I didn't think that for a moment.'

'In fact, he was a perfect gentleman,' she added. 'Even insisted on paying for a taxi as he'd used up his petrol ration.'

'He's got a car?'

'Yes, an Alfa Romeo,' she said, quickly realising her mistake.

'Oh.'

Grabbing a handful of sawdust that had spilled through the mesh of the cage, Patrick threw it at the birds.

The hens, sensing there might be some grub coming their way, fluttered over.

Propping his son against the coop, Charlie went over to the chickens' feed bucket and plunged his hand in.

'Here, Patrick,' he said, dropping a small amount of grain into his son's hand. 'Throw it in.'

Patrick threw it overarm through the wire mesh and the chicks hopped around.

The little boy laughed and so did Francesca.

Oblivious of the dusty yard beneath her feet, she crouched down beside his son.

'That one there.' She pointed at one of the chicks. 'He's a big boy, Patrick, just like you.'

She wriggled her finger into his side.

Patrick giggled and squirmed.

'Just like you,' she repeated, tickling him again.

Charlie laughed. Striding over to the bucket, he grabbed another handful of feed. He turned just in time to see Patrick let go of his support and totter three steps before falling back on his bottom.

'Did you see that, Charlie?' laughed Francesca.

'I did,' he replied, staring incredulously at his son.

Francesca lifted him back onto his feet.

Squatting, Charlie held out his arms. 'Come to Daddy.'

'Go on, Patrick, walk to Daddy,' said Francesca, gently letting go of him.

Looking at Charlie, Patrick wobbled unsteadily for a moment or two then, reaching for his father, he took a couple of steps before thumping down on his nappy-ed rump again.

With pride swelling his chest, Charlie scooped him up.

'Clever boy,' he said, swinging his son in a high arc.

Patrick laughed and so did Francesca.

Then he started wriggling, so Charlie lowered him to the floor.

Francesca stood up and, straightening her crumpled skirt, came to stand beside him.

'His first steps,' she said, as they watched Patrick bouncing on his knees in front of the chickens.

'You'll have to tell Stella,' she said softly.

Charlie's attention shifted from his son to the woman beside him.

Tell her what? he thought. *Tell her I love you and wish you were Patrick's mother?*

Her beautiful brown eyes captured Charlie's soul and time stood still for a moment, then her gaze shifted onto something behind him. Her face filled with anxiety.

Tearing his eyes from her, Charlie turned to see Stella standing in the open back gate.

Although it was only just after mid-afternoon, she was fully made up with bright-red lipstick, which matched her long, pointed nails. Her platinum-blonde hair was swept up into two massive rolls on the top of her head and she held a cork-tipped cigarette between the first two fingers of her right hand. As always, the tartan pencil skirt and black short-sleeved jumper were too short, too low and too tight.

Stella's hard, heavily mascara-ed eyes slid from Charlie to Francesca and back again, instantly evaporating the happiness of the last hour.

Blowing a stream of smoke out of the corner of her mouth, Stella's scarlet lips twisted into a sneer. 'Sorry. Am I interrupting something?'

Charlie studied his faithless wife coolly. 'I thought you said people who came round the back of houses were common.'

'They are but, as no one answered the ruddy door, I had to.' She took another long drag of her cigarette. 'And what are you meant to tell me?'

'That Patrick took his first steps,' he replied flatly.

'I ought to be off,' Francesca said.

'Perhaps you should,' said Stella.

Francesca turned to face him. 'Will I see you and Patrick at Mass tomorrow?'

Unable to speak, Charlie nodded.

Francesca gave him a little smile then, without looking at Stella, she walked across the yard and through the back gate, taking his heart with her.

As the gate banged closed, Stella's hard gaze fixed on him.

'It didn't take long for her to start sniffing around you, did it?' she sneered.

'Not that it's any of your business, but Francesca dropped off a statue for my mum,' he replied.

'Statue for your mum!' Stella gave him a mocking look. 'Pull the other one, it's got bells on. She's fancied you since you started shaving.'

Charlie stared wordlessly at her.

Stella's top lip curled. 'For God's sake, Charlie. Don't tell me you didn't know.'

He couldn't answer. Something like ice water washed over him.

Stella gave him a pitying look, then her eyes shifted to Patrick, who was still watching the hens scratching around.

'Baby,' she called across. 'Mummy's here.'

On hearing his mother's voice, Patrick dropped to the floor and crawled over to his father, who gathered him into his arms.

Realising what was happening, Patrick threw his arms around Charlie's neck.

'It's all right, lad,' he whispered in his son's ear as he hugged him. 'I'll be there soon and we can see Auntie Cathy and the boys.'

Gripping her cigarette between her lips, Stella wrenched Patrick out of Charlie's arms and, carrying him across to his pram by the side wall, plonked him in it.

Patrick twisted around and looked beseechingly at his father as Stella kicked off the brake and pushed him out into the alleyway.

The gate banged shut behind her.

Leaving the chickens scratching around, Charlie turned and went back into the house. As he entered the kitchen, his gaze rested on the bag on the table.

He opened it, unwrapping the silky baby's quilt that was wound around the statue.

As Charlie stared at the effigy, he didn't see the lord's mother dressed in her blue and white robes with a painted halo behind her head, but instead he saw Francesca, smiling as she cuddled and kissed his son. Staring at the foot-high figurine, Charlie's stupid male brain came to a long-overdue conclusion.

Francesca Rosa Fabrino was an exquisite diamond. An exquisite diamond whose beauty had been sparkling at him for as long as he could remember and he, blind, dim-witted fool that he was, had overlooked her in favour of a brash paste gem of no worth.

*

'There you are, Mrs Jolly, a nice cup of rosy lee and a piece of cake,' said Francesca, placing a mug of steaming tea and a plate with a slice of chocolate cake on it in front of her.

'Ta, luv,' said the middle-aged women. 'Just what I need after traipsing up and down The Waste all afternoon.'

It was just after three and the cafe was packed with shoppers having a well-earned cuppa before catching their buses and trams home. Along with women like Ivy Jolly, their heavy bags crammed full of vegetables and groceries, there were a few ARP personnel in their navy uniforms and Home Guards in their khaki sitting at tables enjoying a hot drink at the end of a long shift.

In fact, looking around, there was hardly a table spare, which is why Francesca had been rushing back and forth getting customers' orders and clearing away used crockery since she'd got back from Charlie's house.

'Lovely,' said Mrs Jolly, through a mouthful of cake crumbs. 'I suppose you made this.'

'Yesterday, when I got in from work,' said Francesca. 'I'm glad you like it.'

Leaving her father's regular to enjoy her afternoon refreshment, Francesca collected two cups from the table behind her and took them back to the kitchen.

'Any more?' she asked her father, who was on the business side of the counter refilling the half-gallon teapot.

'I'm just brewing a fresh pot,' he said, as the boiling water from the water urn sent billows of steam upwards. 'If you could cut another couple of slices of cake ready, then—'

The bell over the door tinkled.

Francesca glanced around and her heart lurched as Stella strode into the cafe, thrusting Patrick's pram with the hood down through the door in front of her.

In the cafe full of modestly dressed women, with her overly made-up face, brash clothing and six-inch heels, Stella looked like a carousel horse amongst a herd of pit ponies.

Patrick, who had his thumb stuck in his mouth, spotted Francesca and his eyes lit up. Francesca gave him a little smile. However, as the door closed behind his mother and the room fell silent, he drew his crocheted blanket around him and huddled down under the canvas canopy.

Taking a long drag on her cigarette, Stella scanned the room. As she spotted Francesca, her mouth pulled into an ugly line.

'Oi, you,' she shouted, pointing at Francesca with the two nicotine-stained fingers holding her cigarette. 'I want a word.'

Using the pram to barge through the people sitting at the tables, she marched up to the counter. Shoving the pram to one side, she stood in front of Francesca, filling Francesca's nose with cheap perfume.

'You listen to me, you bloody Eyetie,' she shouted. 'I know your game but I'm here to tell you to keep your Dago hands off my husband.' She shoved her left hand into Francesca's face. 'Charlie Brogan is mine. Do you understand? Mine.' She tapped her wedding ring with a nail-vanished finger. 'And I don't want the likes of you sniffing around him like a bitch in heat, so stay away.'

'I didn't go to see Charlie, I went to see his mum,' said Francesca, squaring her shoulders as she faced her.

'To give her some statue,' said Stella.

'That's right,' said Francesca, scowling at her.

'Don't give me that load of old twaddle,' spat Stella. 'I know you'll try any trick to take Charlie away from me.'

'I don't need to do that,' said Francesca. 'You seem to be managing to turn him against you all by yourself. I don't suppose many men would be keen to have their wives prance around naked each night on a stage.'

Stella's eyes flickered onto Francesca's father, who was standing white-faced behind the counter.

She smiled. 'I wonder if your father knows that his darling daughter, his so-called respectable unmarried daughter, is having it off with a married man?'

'Don't judge everyone by your own standards,' Francesca replied.

Under her powdered face, a crimson flush coloured Stella's cheeks.

'And I think you had better leave,' Francesca added. 'Unless, that is, you want me to call the police.'

'Don't worry, I'm going,' Stella replied. 'The foreign stink in here is turning my stomach, but if you – ' she jabbed her finger in Francesca's face – 'want a man between your legs, find your own because Charlie Brogan is taken.'

Inhaling a lung full of cigarette smoke, she turned to leave, then spotted Francesca's chocolate cake sitting on the counter.

'I suppose you made that, didn't you?' she said.

Francesca didn't reply.

Stella snickered. 'Quite the little housewife, aren't we?'

Taking another drag on her cigarette, she tapped the ash from her cigarette over the cake. Kicking off the brake, and with all eyes on her, Stella shoved the pram towards the exit.

Someone sprang up to open the door and she stomped out.

There was complete silence for a moment before everyone turned back to what they had been doing before Stella marched in.

Francesca turned and looked at her father who, with a downturned mouth and his eyebrows pulled tightly together, scowled at her.

'Papa, I'm sorry—'

His angry eyes stopped her words. He picked up the ash-covered cake and scraped it into the pig swill bucket under the counter.

Francesca reached into the oven and lifted out the steak and kidney pie from the middle rack and placed it on the counter beside her.

Her father was just putting the shutters over the windows and locking the cafe for the night.

As she heard the top and bottom bolts on the door being slammed into place, Francesca cut the pie in two. She put a portion on each plate, added the potatoes and carrots and then carried them through to the back parlour.

She'd already laid their drop-leaf table and, as she placed each plate between the knife and fork, her father walked in.

She gave him a cheery smile. 'That's good timing, Pa—'

'What was all that about you and Charlie Brogan?' he shouted, striding across to her.

'Well, firstly, Papa, I'm hurt you even have to ask,' she said, matching his furious gaze. 'But, seeing as you are, just so you know, I'm not carrying on with Charlie Brogan.'

'Then why did his slut of a wife come into the cafe screaming and shouting that you were?' he asked.

'Look, Papa, when I got round to Ida's to drop the statue off earlier, I found Charlie with Patrick in the yard. Stella arrived as we were playing with Patrick, that's all,' she said, her heart fluttering at the memory.

'So she found you alone with her husband?' asked her father, looking incredulously at her.

'I wasn't *alone* with Charlie, like that,' said Francesca. 'We were in the backyard with his son.'

Her father stared open-mouthed at her, then his face screwed up into an angry expression.

'This!' He jabbed his finger at her. 'This is why the proper place for unmarried young women is at home. I know you think I'm old fashioned but, to my way of thinking, it's best innocent young women stay close to the home, so they aren't lured into bringing disgrace on their families.'

Francesca rolled her eyes. 'Honestly, Papa. We're not living in the Dark Ages.'

'Perhaps not. But men are men and ever have been, and Charlie Brogan always was one for the women,' her father said.

The familiar pain of watching Charlie with a succession of young women on his arm surged again in Francesca's chest.

She sighed. 'Papa, I'm not involved with Charlie Brogan and that's the truth.'

'The truth hardly matters after Charlie Brogan's slut of a wife announced to the whole world that you are carrying on with her husband. And what if Leo hears about it? I can't imagine he'd be so keen to wed you if he heard about you and Charlie.'

'For the last time, Papa, there is no me and Charlie,' she shouted, as the ache for just that squeezed her chest. 'And if Leo is put off by a baseless rumour, then he's not a man I'd consider marrying in any case. And, while we're on the subject, why are you talking about me marrying Leo? I've only been out with him once.'

'No reason. I'm just saying,' he replied airily.

Francesca raised an eyebrow. 'Well then, perhaps we should eat our supper before it goes stone cold?'

She sat down and, after a moment or two, her father took the chair opposite.

Francesca picked up her cutlery and started on her supper. Her father sprinkled salt on his potatoes then tucked into his meal, too.

They ate in silence for a moment, then Francesca spoke again.

'How's the pie, Papa?'

'Very good,' he replied, stabbing his fork into a piece of carrot. 'You've got a light hand with pastry just like your mother.'

He munched his way through another few mouthfuls, then raised his head.

'Even though there's nothing between you and Charlie, perhaps it would be better, Francesca, if you didn't visit the Brogans too often until he goes back to the army,' he said.

Gripping her knife and fork, Francesca rested her wrists on the table and looked across at her father.

'I've known the whole Brogan family since I was five,' she said, firmly. 'And, in case you've forgotten, Papa, it was Ida who took me in when I was homeless. The Brogans are like family to me so, no matter what Stella Miggles or anyone else says, nothing is going to stop me popping in on them any time I feel like it.'

Chapter nineteen

DRESSED IN A diaphanous pink gown and nothing else, Stella studied herself in her dressing-table mirror. Blowing a stream of smoke towards the ceiling, a lazy smile spread across her powdered face.

See if you can say no now, Charlie boy, she thought.

Despite not getting home until six thirty earlier that morning, she'd still managed to collect Patrick from Ida and get back home before one. Having bunged Hettie across the road a couple of bob to mind him, she set about getting herself ready. After a good strip wash in the kitchen, she'd shaved her legs and underarms before applying her make-up and doing her hair.

The floating see-through gown was one she'd used when she'd started out at the BonBon club before she became Salome. She'd brought it home with her and it had been hanging up all day so the creases could drop out.

She toyed with slipping on a pair of her shimmery stage briefs but dismissed the idea. When Charlie's starved cock finally persuaded the rest of him to overlook her new profession, they'd be off in an instant, so there was no point. Plus, she was sure hitting him with everything on offer up front, so to speak, would blow away any remaining hesitation he might be hanging onto.

Perhaps she should have showed him what he'd been missing a bit sooner, but she'd been convinced that hanging on to Patrick would have brought Charlie around.

That Fabrino girl had been casting adoring glances at Charlie for as long as Stella could remember, and it had always given Stella no end of pleasure to see the stricken expression on the foreign

219

girl's face every time she saw her arm in arm with Charlie.

So, although she'd planned to leave it until his pent-up balls were ready to burst, after finding him playing Happy Families with that skinny Eyetie four days previously, she'd decided she ought to act sooner rather than later. Having warned her off good and proper it was now time to rein Charlie in.

Inhaling another lungful of smoke, Stella glanced at the alarm clock sitting on the bedside table. Almost four thirty. Good, just enough time to get herself sorted out.

Balancing her half-smoked Benson & Hedges on the crystal ashtray beside her make-up bag, she stood up.

She stomped downstairs, flipped the latch up, then headed back to her bedroom. Picking up what was left of her cigarette, she clamped it between her lips and, opening the wardrobe, pulled out her red six-inch high heels. They were almost impossible to walk in but, with a bit of luck, she wouldn't be on her feet for very long.

She heard the front door click open.

'Hello?' Charlie shouted, his voice echoing up the stairwell from below.

Stubbing out her cigarette, Stella draped herself seductively across the bed. Rolling onto her hip and supporting her head with her hand, she arranged the fabric of her see-through gown so her nipples, which she'd enhanced with a dab of Winter Berry lipstick, were clearly visible.

'Anyone in?' Charlie called again.

'Up here,' Stella called back.

As Charlie pushed open the bedroom door, his jaw dropped and a lazy smile spread across Stella's face.

'Still not interested, Charlie?' she asked.

Actually, he really wasn't and never would be again and, although he couldn't explain it, this blatant appeal to his carnal instincts just increased his loathing of her.

He loved Francesca. He had been a blind fool before, but his eyes were wide open now.

'Where's Patrick?' he asked, looking at her face.

The indolent smile widened. 'Don't worry about him.'

Sliding off the bed, and with the sheer robe billowing behind her, she swayed over to him.

'Where is he?' Charlie repeated. She stopped in front of him.

'Somewhere where he won't disturb us.' Winding her arms around his neck, she moulded herself into him.

Charlie reached up and removed her arms.

'Where is he?' he asked again, hoping she could see the abhorrence in his eyes.

Her languid expression slipped a little. 'But, Charlie—'

'Where?'

'Across the road at number six,' she replied.

Charlie turned, but she caught his arm.

He pulled it free of her grip. 'Get off me.'

'Don't be like that, Charlie,' she whined, giving him her little-girl-hurt look.

He started for the door, but she stepped in front of him and slammed it shut, blocking his path.

Charlie's mouth pulled into a hard line. 'Move aside, Stella.'

She laughed. 'As a special treat you can do anything you fancy and—'

Grabbing her shoulders, Charlie pulled her away from the door. Her high heels caught on the bedside rug and she fell back onto the counterpane in a heap.

He ripped open the door.

'Don't you dare walk out on me!' she screamed, as he strode out.

Taking the stairs two at a time, he hurried down to the hall, but before he reached the door, he heard the sound of Stella coming after him.

'Charlie!'

Without breaking his stride, he opened the front door. The mothers of the street, who were calling their offspring in for tea, stood in wide-eyed astonishment as he stepped out but their jaws all but hit the pavement when Stella, who'd grabbed a coat in passing, stumbled out after him.

'I'm your wife, Charlie!' she shrieked, as he crossed the road. 'Do you hear? Until death do us part, Charlie, I'll be your wife.'

As the stage curtain fell across in front of her, muffling the roaring crowd in the club, the smile on Stella's face disappeared.

Turning on her high heels, she stomped to the back of the stage. She'd just snatched her robe from the props man when the orchestra played the opening bars of the next number.

In a flutter of feathers, sequins and a waft of stale sweat, Evette, the lead dancer who came from Streatham but who made out she was French, burst out from the wings.

Behind her, wearing their costumes of glittering G-strings and glued-on nipple tassels, scurried the half a dozen girls who made up the club's chorus line.

'Watch where you're going,' Stella snapped as an ostrich feather from Evette's headdress swiped her round the face.

'Well, get out of the way, fat arse,' Evette replied, as she ushered her dancers past her onto the small stage.

'Who you calling—'

The band struck up again, drowning out Stella's words.

Giving her the sweetest smile, the lead dancer blew her a kiss and then skipped onto the stage to take her position.

Cow! thought Stella, glaring after her.

Tugging the flimsy material around her, she continued off stage. Stella stormed into her dressing room, then slammed the door behind her.

Although the BonBon club had anything up to five strippers to entertain the customers each night, most were circuit girls who rushed from one venue to another to perform at their allotted time. However, as the headline act at the BonBon club, Stella had the only single dressing room in the place.

Even Bernie Bronski, the Jewish comic who was forever boasting about how he'd worked with all the music hall greats, had to share with Mysterino, the club's permanently sozzled magician.

The small dressing room, which was just nine by five, was below street level so Stella could see people's feet walking past the narrow windows high up on the wall. There was an ancient dressing table, which had a light fixed above it. Running water came from the single tap fixed to the brickwork and although there was no sink, Tubbs had squeezed in a washstand with a flowery china bowl beneath it for her to use.

To be honest, it wasn't the Palladium, that was for sure, but it confirmed Stella's status as the number-one attraction in the BonBon club.

Sitting down on the chair in front of her dressing table, Stella studied herself in the silvering mirror.

There were men, lords and generals amongst them, who'd give their eye teeth to get between her legs and yet Charlie sodding Brogan, even though he'd had a full view of what was on offer, had just turned and walked away. Bloody cheek.

The humiliation of Charlie's rejection pressed down on Stella for a second or two. She took the lid off her face powder and pulled out the puff.

There was a knock on the door.

'Come,' she called, dabbing the powder over her nose.

The door opened, and Tubbs stepped in.

Tubbs Walker was the wrong side of forty and, at just five foot six and weighing in at fifteen stone, gave the impression of being as wide as he was tall. He still had a full head of slicked-back hair, but its reddish–chestnut colour was down to regular application from a bottle rather than nature. That, along with his heavy black eyebrows, rosy cheeks and extravagant taste in chequered suits and garish ties, reminded Stella of a brightly painted child's whipping top.

His gaze flickered down to the open front of her gown, then back to her face.

Smiling, he closed the door behind him.

'You brought the house down tonight,' he said, crossing the space between them and standing over her.

Turning back to the mirror, Stella resumed her powdering.

'Did I?' she asked, regarding him coolly in the mirror's reflection.

Her movement had loosened the tie holding the front of her dressing gown together and Tubbs' eyes flickered down to her breasts.

'You did,' he replied, forcing his gaze back onto her face. 'I bet there wasn't a limp old man in the house.'

Stella gave him a lazy smile. 'That's what you pay me for.'

His gaze wandered downwards again. 'You're the best in the business.'

'I know,' said Stella.

A lustful expression crept across his fleshy face.

Reaching out, he slipped his hand down the front of her gown and cupped her left breast.

'You certainly are,' he replied, in a thick voice as he toyed with her nipple.

Stella let him enjoy himself for a moment or two longer, then she knocked his hand away.

'Apart from the obvious, Tubbs, what are you after?' she asked, pulling the front of her gown across.

He straightened up and adjusted the front of his trousers.

'I've had a request from someone who wants me to put on a special show in a couple of weeks to keep the top-brass Yanks happy while they're billeted in London,' he replied.

Stella laughed. 'The American Red Cross want you to put on a tea dance?'

'It ain't the Red Cross and it ain't the usual rest and recreation show. I met this fella who runs a burlesque theatre in New York, and he told me what he had in mind as entertainment for our brave allies. I thought of you straight away as the star of the show.'

'I should think so too,' Stella replied.

In the mirror's reflection he gave her a steely look. 'But they want something a bit out of the usual.'

'Like what?' asked Stella, holding his gaze in the reflection.

'All girls in the buff,' he replied.

Popping the powder puff back in the tub, Stella turned to face him. 'What, like The Windmill?'

'Yes, just like The Windmill,' said Tubbs. 'Except this is a private function. Officers only, by invitation. He wants it livelier. You know, high kicks, swivelling about on a chair, rolling about on the stage, the odd cartwheel or—'

'Cartwheels! I haven't done a bloody cartwheel since I was—'

'You'll get paid a pony.'

Stella's eyes flew open.

Twenty-five pounds! More than half of what she earned in a year even with after-show extras.

'It's just what you do now, Stella, but in the nuddy,' Tubbs continued, as thoughts of dozens of green pound notes floated around Stella's head. 'Just flash them a bit of this and that, and…' A sly expression replaced his lustful one. 'Who knows, it might be the start of big things.'

The image of money faded in Stella's mind and was replaced by one of her dancing on a New York stage.

Stella smiled. 'All right, count me in but no cartwheels!'

'That's me girl, and no cartwheels,' he replied, beaming at her. 'Now, I'd better leave you to get ready for your next spot.'

Stella turned back to the mirror and picked up her lipstick.

'Oh, and by the way, as I said this is a private event, invitation only, for the GI top brass, if you get my drift,' he said, giving her a meaningful look as he opened the door. 'Make sure you have a close shave downstairs.'

Yanking the wheel of his father's Bedford lorry, Charlie turned across the traffic and into Darling Row. Guiding the vehicle to a stop alongside the high walls of the Albion Brewery, he pulled on the brake and switched off the engine.

It was Wednesday afternoon and he had just finished delivering a double bed and table plus four chairs to a family in Old Ford Road and was on his way back to the yard. However, there was no rush. It was only just after three and he had plenty of time to fill in the order book and pick up any messages slipped under the gate before he picked Patrick up from Stella at five, so he had time to do what he had to.

Locking the cab, Charlie straightened the knot of his neckerchief. He sauntered to the end of the short passageway, then turned into Brady Street.

The awnings of Alf's cafe were fully extended to shade the patrons within from the very bright May sunlight. He walked into their shadow and ventured a glance through the window.

There were a few customers sitting at the window tables and a young girl was clearing away dirty crockery. Francesca's father was behind the counter.

Pulling down his waistcoat, Charlie pushed open the door, setting the bell above tinkling as it opened.

Enrico looked up.

Hostility tightened the older man's sallow features as he watched Charlie walk to the end of the counter, furthest away from the handful of customers.

The girl wiping the table moved forward to serve Charlie.

'You carry on,' said Enrico, drying his hands on a tea towel.

She returned to her task.

Flipping the tea towel over his shoulder, Francesca's father moved slowly towards Charlie and stopped on the other side of the polished wood. Spreading his hands on the counter, he leant forward and waited.

'Afternoon, Mr Fabrino,' said Charlie.

Maintaining his unfriendly expression, Francesca's father didn't reply.

'I've come to apologise for what happened last Saturday,' Charlie said.

'Well, you've taken your time,' Enrico replied. 'That was four days ago.'

'I only heard about it last night at the Catholic club,' said Charlie.

Enrico snorted. 'Did you?'

Charlie looked him square in the eye. 'Yes, I did, which is why I'm here now to assure you that what my wife said about myself and your daughter is a lie.'

'Of course it is,' Enrico replied. 'My daughter has too much self-respect to throw away her good name and reputation with a married man.'

'She has,' said Charlie. 'And quite rightly so. I would never do anything to harm her.'

'Well then, stay away from her,' Enrico replied. 'Francesca has met a young man, a nice respectable Italian young man. An aristocrat, in fact, with a profession and money in the bank who can give her a home, a family, a secure future and, most importantly, a wedding ring. Everything that any father would want for his daughter, so I don't want you or that cheap tart you're married to mucking up Francesca's chance of taking a step up in the world and being happy. Do you understand?'

Although every part of him wanted to yell at the top of his voice: *No! I won't! I can't! I love her!* Charlie just nodded.

'Good.' Enrico's face lost some of its belligerence. 'I'll always be grateful to your family for what they did for Francesca, but I won't stand by and see her life ruined.'

'I understand,' said Charlie.

Turning, he retraced his steps to the door. Leaving the bell tinkling behind him, he stepped back out into the street.

He returned to his parked lorry, opened the door and swung himself into the driver's seat. Grasping the steering wheel with both hands until his knuckles were white, he stared blindly ahead.

He was tortured by the thought of this Leo, or any man, holding and kissing the woman he loved more than he ever knew he could love. Images of her laughing and smiling danced in his head day and night. He wanted her as a man wanted a woman and only her. He wanted her to be a mother to Patrick and any other children God might bless him with. He wanted all and everything of Francesca, now and for ever, but her father was right. He couldn't.

He couldn't because he was married and there was no way out.

All she could be was his common-law wife and their children bastards. A life with him would make her the subject of whispers on street corners and she would be reviled as a woman living in sin with another woman's husband. And he wouldn't do that to her because he loved her.

And, because he loved her, he had to let her go, so she could have all the things he couldn't give her.

His heart ached. Resting his head on the steering wheel, Charlie closed his eyes as hopelessness and despair engulfed him for several heartbeats, then he forced his head up and thought of Patrick.

In the gloom of his misery a little light shone through, easing his painful emotions.

He might have to suffer because he had been a brainless idiot with Stella, but at least he had his precious boy.

Chapter twenty

'WELL, HERE WE are,' said Leo, turning to face her as they reached the back door of her father's cafe.

Francesca smiled. 'Thank you again for a lovely evening.'

'The pleasure was all mine,' he replied. 'And you dance like an angel.'

It was the first Saturday in May and just after ten thirty in the evening. Although the blackout had started half an hour ago, the night was clear and there was still enough light in the sky for her to see the admiration in Leo's eyes.

Truthfully, it was hard to miss as his intense gaze had been on her all night, making her feel quite special.

'Well, perhaps an angel who needs to practise her quickstep,' she replied, fishing her key out of her handbag.

Taking her hand, he bowed over it and then pressed his lips to her fingers.

'I know this is only our *terzo* evening out,' he said, slipping into Italian. 'But I have to confess that I feel as if I've known you for far longer. And I hope you might feel likewise.'

'It does seem like I've known you for much than four weeks,' she replied.

Reaching out, he slipped his arm around her waist. 'In that case, could I come in and say goodnight?'

Francesca studied Leo's finely etched features in the fading light for a moment, then smiled. 'Of course you can, Leo, but only for a moment or two.'

Francesca opened the door and led him into the family parlour at the back of the cafe. Pulling the blackout curtain across, she switched on the light. The forty-watt bulb fizzed for a moment, then illuminated the room. Well, as much as it could given that the electric board had cut the domestic supply to half power during the hours of the blackout.

She hung her coat on the coat stand next to the door and Leo put his hat alongside. She turned around.

'Would you like a coff—'

Her words were cut short by his arms closing around her. His lips pressed on hers.

She stood unmoved for a second or two but, as his kiss deepened, the image of Charlie in his backyard, smiling at her as she held Patrick, flashed through her mind.

Francesca forced it away and slid her hands up Leo's chest and around his neck.

His embrace tightened for a moment, then he released her lips and looked down at her, his eyes black in the dim light.

'I've wanted to do that from the first moment I saw you,' he whispered breathlessly. 'At that moment,' he continued, planting feathery kisses across her cheeks, 'I knew how Antony felt when he saw Cleopatra, or Romeo when he spied Juliet on her balcony and why Napoleon couldn't leave Josephine alone.'

'Didn't he divorce her to marry a princess?' asked Francesca.

Leo answered by kissing her again.

'What man could resist your beauty?' he whispered, as his mouth closed over hers again. 'You are perfection.'

Charlie's image tried to force itself into her mind, but she shoved it aside and tightened her hold around his neck.

He gave a low moan and his kiss deepened, sending Francesca's senses reeling.

The handle on the door rattled and they sprang apart.

Her father, wearing his tartan dressing gown and slippers, opened the door.

'Good evening, *Signor Fabrino*,' Leo said, reverting to English as he stepped back.

Francesca's father's eyes flickered from Francesca to Leo and back again.

'I was just saying goodnight to Leo, Papa,' she explained.

'I thought it would safeguard your daughter's reputation if I came in to say my farewells,' Leo added.

Francesca's father gaze shifted between them again.

'Very well,' he said after a moment or two. 'But five minutes and no longer.'

'Thank you, sir,' continued Leo.

'My daughter is a respectable young woman,' her father continued.

'Indeed she is,' said Leo. 'And can I assure you, *Signor Fabrino*, my intentions towards her are strictly honourable.'

Francesca's father gave them another considered look, then left. Leaving the door open, he ascended the stairs back to his bedroom above.

'I'm sorry,' whispered Francesca as she heard her father's footsteps above her head. 'As I said, Papa's a little old fashioned about these sorts of things.'

Leo took her hands.

'*Mi dispace*,' he said, slipping back into Italian. 'I'm sure if I had a daughter, I'd be just as protective of her chastity.'

Slipping his arm around her again, Leo drew her to him. He pressed his lips onto hers for a second, then released her. He retrieved his hat from the peg.

'A woman's purity is her crowning glory,' he said softly, his eyes warm as they looked across at her. 'A gift for her husband on their wedding night.'

He smiled, then slipped behind the blackout curtain and left.

Francesca stared after him for a moment then, switching off the light, made her way upstairs to her bedroom. Without turning on the light, she crossed to the window and pulled back the curtains.

The very last pink rays of the sunset were just visible in the sky. It had been a quiet couple of weeks as the Luftwaffe had been targeting the newly constructed American Air Force bases across East Anglia, giving Londoners the luxury of enjoying their own beds for a night or two.

That said, the ARP were still on alert and although the air raid siren hadn't gone off, the searchlights were already criss-crossing each other in the navy-blue sky.

Watching the beams of light high above her, Francesca ran her fingers lightly over her lips. A little thrill ran through her and she smiled.

She turned her head and looked at the photo on her bedside cabinet. As always, her gaze was drawn to Charlie, standing on the other side of Mattie.

Francesca studied it for a long moment then, reaching out, she turned it face down.

Shifting her weight on her knees, Francesca gently tugged on the hem of Jo's wedding dress. Satisfied that it was straight, she took a pin from her mouth and stuck it through the fabric.

'I think that's the last one,' she said, her gaze skimming over her work just to check.

'I've done this edge, too,' said Mattie, who was kneeling on the other side of the bride-to-be.

Francesca was in Mattie's front parlour and, as the signature tune for *Monday Night with the Classics* had just finished playing on the polished Murphy's radiogram in the corner, she guessed it must now be just after seven in the evening.

For the first time since she'd started at Radio Roma, she'd walked out of Bush House on time after she'd told Miss Kirk she had an important appointment which she couldn't be late for.

That important appointment was what they had been working on for the past hour; Jo's wedding dress.

Sticking the unused pins back in the pin cushion on the floor beside her, Francesca rocked back on her heels and stood up. Going around to her friend, Francesca offered her a hand.

'Thanks,' said Mattie, taking it as she struggled to her feet.

Mattie gasped, then put her hands into the small of her back.

'You all right, Mattie?' asked Francesca, taking her elbow as well.

'Yes.' Mattie gave her a weary smile. 'I just don't think I'm made for crawling around on the floor at the moment.'

That was certainly true.

Although you couldn't be absolutely certain about these things, it was clear that Mattie had only a matter of weeks before she and Daniel welcomed their next little McCarthy into the world. Fingers crossed it would be after Jo's wedding in two and a half weeks' time.

Mattie's gaze shifted to her sister. 'It's worth it, though.'

Francesca followed her friend's gaze to where Jo was standing on the kitchen stool in her wedding dress, like a ballerina in a jewellery box.

Mattie was right. It was worth all the aching knees and pricked fingers because Jo looked absolutely beautiful in her eight-panelled wedding dress with fitted sleeves and sweetheart neckline.

Francesca smiled. 'You look absolutely lovely, Jo.'

'Thank you, Fran.' Jo blew a kiss to Mattie. 'And thank you too, my clever big sister.'

'My pleasure,' said Mattie. Pulling one of the dining-room chairs out from the table, she sat down.

'Let me help you get it off without scratching yourself to bits, Jo,' said Francesca.

Going around to the back of the bride-to-be, she unfastened the hooks and eyes then, as Jo raised her arms high, Francesca scooped her hand under the skirts and lifted the dress off, leaving Jo in her underwear.

Carefully, to ensure none of the pins around the hem fell out, Francesca laid it on the dining-room table. Jo left the room to put her uniform back on.

'She's right you know,' said Francesca, smoothing her hands over the satin. 'You are very clever.'

'Perhaps I'll be making your wedding dress soon, too,' said Mattie, giving her a knowing look. 'Although I don't think eleven yards of satin from Petticoat Lane would be good enough for a countess.'

Slipping Jo's dress onto a hanger, Francesca raised an eyebrow. 'I know you're a hopeless romantic, Mattie, but I've only been on a couple of dates with Leo.'

'You have to start somewhere.' Mattie gave her a hesitant look. 'You know, Fran, I hope you don't mind me saying it but when you first told me about Leo, I did wonder if perhaps he was just after one thing.'

'To be honest, Mattie, the thought crossed my mind, too,' Francesca replied. 'You know, rich aristocrat dazzles lowly maiden to have his wicked way with her, but I have to say he's been a perfect gentleman. Of course, my dad thinks he's absolutely wonderful and he's forever telling customers I'm walking out with a count.'

'Well, it certainly sounds as if Leo is really keen, what with those flowers and everything.'

Francesca hung the gown from the picture rail.

'He is a bit,' she said, brushing the creases out of the dress and thinking of the latest massive bouquet that had arrived for her on Saturday morning.

'Good,' Mattie said, behind her. 'I'm sure he's already wildly in love with you.'

'Of course he's not!' Francesca laughed.

'Well, he should be.' Mattie's face lit up. 'I know. Why don't you bring Leo to Jo's wedding?'

Francesca blinked. 'No, I couldn't. I mean, I hardly know him and what would Jo say?'

'What would Jo say about what?' asked Jo, buttoning up her shirt as she walked back into the room.

'Bringing Leo to the wedding,' said Mattie.

'Oh yes, what a great idea,' said Jo, looking as excited as her sister.

'I wouldn't want to impose,' said Francesca.

'You're not,' said Jo. 'We're having a spread so we don't need to squeeze in an extra seat, and I'd love you to bring him so we can get a proper look at him.' She winked at her sister. 'Eh, sis?'

Mattie grinned. 'And give him the once-over.'

Francesca looked from Mattie to Jo and back again and then gave a big sigh.

'All right, I'll ask him,' she said. 'But I'm not promising, as he might be busy.'

'Jo, do us a favour and put the kettle on, I'm gasping,' said Mattie, rising to her feet.

'Righty-ho.'

'I'm glad you've met Leo, Fran,' said Mattie, as her sister left. 'Because it's about time you started to have some fun and stop…'

She pressed her lips together.

The thought of Charlie's grey-blue eyes looking into hers and his hard muscles under her fingertips flashed through Francesca's mind.

'Pining for something I can't have?' asked Francesca, as the yearning for him squeezed her chest again.

Mattie nodded. 'You deserve to be happy, Fran.'

Francesca summoned up a little smile.

Did she? Did she deserve to be happy? Probably no more than anyone else, but she wanted to be. She wanted to be happy with a man who loved her and to have children of her own. For years she'd dreamt and prayed that that man would be Charlie and that he'd be the father of her children, but she had to face the facts. Even though her heart still ached for that future, it could never, ever come true so perhaps it *was* time to look to someone else to fulfil her dreams.

Chapter twenty-one

DABBING THE POINT of the eyeliner pencil on her tongue, Stella leant forward and traced it along the top of her lashes. She studied her reflection in her mottled dressing-room mirror for a moment, then repeated the curve on her other eye.

Satisfied the green shadow on her lids and the sweep of the thick jet-black lines around her eyes were even, she dropped the pencil back in her jumbled make-up bag and picked up her mascara.

There was a knock at the door.

Opening the lid of the mascara, Stella spat on the block. 'Come.'

The door opened and Tubbs, looking like an over-fed penguin in his dinner suit, walked in.

'Ready?' he asked.

'Almost,' Stella replied, running the kohl-loaded brush along her eyelashes.

He walked across and stood behind her.

'You look a bit tasty,' he said, his eyes hot as they looked at her in the reflection.

He wasn't wrong.

She usually got old Sadie in Wentworth Street to knock up her costumes, after all you didn't need to be Norman Hartnell to stick bits of satin and net together, but as tonight she was giving a special performance, she wanted something a bit classier.

In keeping with her stage name of Salome, she'd told the elderly tailor in Berwick Street she wanted something exotic, like a harem girl in *The Thief of Bagdad*, and the costumier had done her proud.

Her new outfit was a bit different from usual as, instead of a brassiere, she had a waistcoat, which didn't meet in the middle and only just covered her nipples. The knickers, encrusted with paste jewels, were even skimpier than the skin-coloured stockinette ones she usually wore. Tucked into their waistband was a rainbow of gossamer scarves while at her wrists and ankles she wore bands of jingling bells. A small veil covered her nose and mouth. All in all, it looked the cat's whiskers and well worth the seven quid she'd forked out for it.

Closing her mascara, Stella gave a smug smile. 'I do, don't I?'

Reaching over her shoulder, Tubbs' hand started to make its way towards her left breast.

'Will you make sure that lazy bugger Harry has put my stool in the right place?' she said, fixing him with a steely gaze.

The proprietor withdrew his hand. 'I'll go check.'

Giving her another lascivious look, he turned and left.

Stella picked up her lipstick and applied it, then pressed her lips together and fluffed up her hair.

There was another knock.

'Two minutes,' one of the stage hands called through the door.

Standing up, Stella stepped into her scarlet high heels and then headed towards the stage.

A bevy of naked dancers, red-faced and giggling, all scurried past her as she took up her position in the wings.

The orchestra played a bit of incidental music as the stage hands shifted the props. Stella pulled the curtain open an inch and looked out at the club.

As always, the BonBon was packed to the rafters with service personnel but whereas it was usually a sea of British khaki and navy, tonight the place was bursting at the seams with US taupe.

Tubbs waddled out from the other side of the stage and stopped at the edge of the footlights.

'I hope the Dance of the Nymphs met with your approval, gentlemen,' he bellowed over the racket from the floor.

A howl of approval from the all-male American audience indicated that it had.

'And now, for your further delight, we have something even more tantalising,' he shouted, 'something exotic, something altogether more uninhibited, gentlemen, if you get my meaning.'

Another throaty roar signalled they most certainly did.

'Then I give you Salome of the Mysterious East!' Tubbs yelled, exiting backwards off the stage.

There was a pause and then the band's clarinet player stood up. After capturing the audience's attention with a single long note, he started playing pretend Arab music; the sort snake-charmers did in films. The crowd started to settle, then the drums joined in.

The curtain swished back.

Taking a deep breath and with her heart pounding in time with the beat, Stella sashayed out into the spotlight.

A roar of approval went up and a wall of voices and wolf whistles surrounded her.

Putting her hands together above her head, she stood motionless in the centre of the stage, enjoying the crowd's adoration. Then, on the down beat of the fourth bar, Stella started her routine. Eager hands lunged at her ankles as she shimmied to the front of the stage and then wriggled back to the centre.

Taking a gossamer scarf from either side of her hips, she pulled them free and let them flutter to the floor behind her.

The tempo increased. Stella did another circuit of shaking and bouncing before returning to the middle of the stage.

Turning away from the audience, and to hollers of approval, Stella removed the two lengths of sheer fabric covering her bottom. She paused to enjoy the shouts before turning back to face her audience. With a lazy smile, she pulled the final two gossamer scarves free but instead of dropping both to the floor, she kept one of each in her hand.

She turned to face the back of the stage again and shrugged her arm out of one side of the waistcoat and then the other. Letting it slide off her arm, she threw it to the side.

The shouts behind her grew even louder. Waiting for the beat of the drum, she turned.

She paused again to let her audience have a full eyeful and then slowly shimmied around the footlights, dipping to blow a kiss or wave at any American who caught her eye.

Returning to the centre of the stage, she smiled and turned from the audience again.

Placing her feet a shoulder's width apart, Stella reached around and snapped open the clip at the back of her jewelled knickers.

As they hit the deck, Stella took a deep breath. Closing her feet together and raising her arms, she turned to face the men in the room, wearing just her high heels and the bracelets on her ankles and wrists. Beneath the half-veil stretched across her lower face, Stella smiled.

A deafening roar filled the club as the men strained forward.

Usually at this stage of the proceedings the curtain would fall and she'd be done, but tonight was different.

Stella stood for a moment, waiting for the musicians to slide into the next tune.

Pirouetting on her high heels with the remaining square of diaphanous fabric in her hand, Stella sat on the edge of the stool.

Bestowing a lavish smile on the crowd of men in front of her, she went through a series of gymnastic-like moves, swinging her legs, bending over and arching her back, designed to bring the audience to a frenzy of anticipation.

As the small orchestra started the final chorus, Stella stood with her back to the audience and draped the semi-transparent square across her hips.

She waited for a couple of beats, then turned and, placing her high heels a shoulder-width apart, faced her baying, screaming audience.

The cat-calls and whistles reached a crescendo until, on the fifth and final beat of the drum, Stella whipped the fabric away.

The place went wild as the men continued yelling and jostling for a better view. Stella looked out over the sea of hungry faces.

Across the heads, she saw a GI perched on a bar stool with a glass.

She noticed him for two reasons.

Firstly, amongst the chest ribbons, gilded epaulettes and star-studded lapels of the commissioned officers in the room, he was the only man who sported the three-bar chevron of a lowly sergeant on his sleeve and, secondly, he was the only man in the room looking at her face.

Blowing a long stream of smoke towards the brown-stained ceiling, Stella leant back in the chair and put her feet up on the edge of the dressing table.

It had been some fifteen minutes since she left the stage to rapturous applause and her heart had only just returned to its normal rhythm.

She still had her stilettos on but had swapped her ankle bracelets and face veil for her pink silk dressing gown, which she'd wrapped loosely around her.

Usually, she would have been tidying herself up, ready to mingle with the customers, and she should be doing that right now.

She glanced at her red cocktail dress hanging on the painted screen and was just about to get up to search out her underwear when there was a knock on the door.

Taking another long draw on her cigarette, Stella flicked the ash on the floor.

'Come.'

The door opened and the GI who'd been perched on the bar stool stood in the doorway.

Although a good three to four inches shorter than Charlie, he

240

was just as broad, with a dark blond crew-cut and a nose that, by the shape of it, had been broken more than once. His face was saved from being too hard and brutal by his clear blue eyes. His well-fitted uniform jacket, which hugged his hefty frame, had the three-chevron emblem she'd spotted as she'd looked across at him from the stage.

He'd tucked his peaked cap under his arm, and his highly polished black boots were planted slightly apart. Although his huge hands were relaxed, as they hung at his side, if balled into fists, they could do some damage.

His gaze flickered down onto her unfastened gown for a second, then back to her face.

'Good evening, ma'am,' he said, his expression respectful as he looked at her. 'Staff Sergeant Donald J. Muller at your service.'

He saluted.

'Who let you back stage?' she asked.

'The doorman,' he replied.

'Well, he shouldn't have,' said Stella, stubbing out her cigarette.

A lazy smile spread across the GI's broad face. 'That's what he said until I gave him one of your ten-shilling notes.'

Ten bob!

'I just wanted to drop by and tell you what a great performance you gave tonight, ma'am,' the sergeant continued. 'Truly outstanding.'

'Thank you, Staff Sergeant Donald J. Muller,' said Stella.

'And I was wondering if you might let me take you to dinner,' he added.

'I don't think so,' Stella replied. 'I only—'

'Keep company with the top brass?' he cut in, raising a sandy eyebrow. 'Why wouldn't you? I mean, a classy broad like you deserves nothing less.'

Stella gave a smug smile and reached for her pack of Benson & Hedges.

'Here, have one of mine,' said Sergeant Muller.

Stepping closer, he took a packet of Lucky Strikes from his pocket and handed it to her.

Reaching into his pocket he retrieved his Ronson lighter, with DJM inscribed on one side, and offered her a light.

Stella lit the cigarette and then went to hand the box back.

'Keep 'em,' he said. 'I've got plenty.'

Stella put the packet in her handbag.

'As staff sergeant in charge of the Curzon Street PX, I—'

'What's a PX when it's at home?' asked Stella.

'Wherever Uncle Sam's army goes in the world, the PX follows to give us poor doughboys all the comforts of home, right down to Mom's apple pie. I tell you, we have everything by the dozen and more. Nylons, candy, coffee, Scotch. You name it, lady, I have it.' His heavy features lifted in an oddly boyish smile. 'So what about that supper? I thought perhaps The Rosewood.'

Stella's eyes opened in surprise.

His smile widened. 'A classy joint for a classy lady.'

Taking a drag on her cigarette, she rose to her feet.

His eyes flickered down to the open front of her robe and then back to her face.

'All right, I suppose I can make an exception,' she said, half-heartedly tying the sash. 'But you'll have to wait while I get ready.'

'Yes, ma'am.' Taking the chair she'd just vacated, the GI turned it round and sat astride it, then beamed at her. 'I'll just wait here while you wriggle yourself into that pretty little red dress and then we'll hit the town.'

With the wail of the all-clear siren filling her ears, Stella opened her eyes. Sergeant Donald J. Muller or Donny, as he had insisted she call him, was standing with his back to her looking out the long sash window. Despite the curtains being drawn back and the morning light filtering in, he didn't seem bothered that, apart from the dog tag around his neck, he was completely naked.

She was naked, too, but lying under a crisp white sheet in a double bed in the Hibernian Hotel just off Piccadilly, which was doing its bit for the war by billeting two hundred GIs, one of whom was Donny.

Raking her hair off her face with her fingers, Stella propped herself up on one elbow.

'What time is it?'

'Just after five,' he replied. 'By the look of the sky, the East End had a rough time of it last night.'

'Don't we always,' Stella replied.

He turned. 'You live there?'

Her eyes flicked over his hairy chest and then onto his equally hairy crotch. He might lack Charlie's inches in a couple of places, but he wasn't hard to look at.

'All my life,' she replied, as her eyes returned to his face.

His eyebrows rose. 'So you're not from Old Bagdad?'

Stella laughed. 'Where are you from?'

'New York,' he replied. 'Coffee?'

'I wouldn't mind,' Stella replied, sitting up and resting against the headboard.

He strolled over to the telephone and picked up the receiver. 'Coffee for two and a plate of pastries.'

He put down the receiver and returned to the bed.

Propping himself up against the headboard, he reached across to the pack of Lucky Strikes that were lying next to the carton of French letters on the bedside table.

'New York sounds so glamorous,' she said as he lit two.

'Not in the Lower East Side it isn't,' he replied. 'Just dirt, squalor and hunger.'

'Sounds like East London,' Stella replied, as he gave her a cigarette.

He gave a mirthless laugh.

She shifted over and snuggled into him, smelling the sweat and sex of their coupling.

'I had a really great time last night,' she said, stroking her hand across his chest.

It certainly had been. She hadn't believed he could get them through the front door of The Rosewood, one of the most exclusive and expensive restaurants in Mayfair. However, to her utter amazement, not only were they ushered straight in but the waiter had shown them to one of the best tables by the dance floor. And that wasn't all. Donny had ordered prime steak for them, something she'd not set eyes on, let alone tasted, for three years, which when it arrived had almost filled the plate. Added to which, in addition to the bottle of champagne he'd ordered, another had appeared, compliments of the manager.

Blowing a series of smoke rings towards the decorative plasterwork ceiling, Donny turned and studied her for a moment, then put his arm around her. Stella snuggled closer and inhaled another lungful of the strong American cigarette.

There was a knock at the door.

'Come,' Donny shouted.

It opened and an elderly man, with sparse white hair, rheumy eyes and dressed in an oversized butler's uniform, came in carrying a silver tray.

He looked as if he should have been wearing a shroud rather than the hotel's livery, but Stella guessed he'd probably been re-employed by the owners when other staff were called up.

He caught sight of Donny lying starkers on the bed and averted his eyes.

'About time,' Donny barked. The cups rattled in their saucers as he shuffled across.

'Sorry, sir,' the old man mumbled as he set their breakfast down on the coffee table in front of the window.

'What's your name?' Donny asked.

'W…W…Widdicombe, sir,' the old man replied, setting out the crockery.

'Well, W…W…Widdicombe,' continued Donny. 'Let me warn you, if that coffee is cold, I'll be having a word with the manager about you.'

'Yes, sir.' Without raising his eyes, the elderly man turned and clasped his hands in front of him. 'Will there be anything else, sir?'

'Not just now,' Donny replied. 'But make sure you jump to it next time I ring down for something.'

'Yes, sir,' Widdicombe replied, his eyes glued to the floor.

'And don't they teach you manners over here?' Donny barked. 'Look at me when I'm talking to you.'

The elderly man raised his eyes from the floor and his gaze flitted over Donny's muscular body for an instant before fixing on a point just above his head.

'Goddamn it, Widdicombe old bean,' Donny continued in an upper-class English accent. 'You're acting like you've never seen a cock before.'

Mottled patches coloured the old man's quivering jowls.

'Perhaps he has, Donny,' said Stella, giving him a sly look. 'And liked it.'

Amusement rippled across Donny's face, then he looked back at the old man standing awkwardly at the foot of the bed.

'Get out!' shouted Donny. The elderly retainer turned. Stumbling over their discarded clothes in his haste, he fled the room.

'Silly old fart,' giggled Stella.

Donny gave her an approving look. 'That's a new one. I'll have to remember it.'

His eyes roamed over her body for a second, then he stretched across and captured her sex in his large, hairy hand.

'I like fanny myself,' he said.

Stella raised a pencilled eyebrow. 'So I noticed.'

Swinging his leg over hers, he rolled between her legs.

'Your coffee will get cold,' she said, as his weight pressed her into the mattress.

He smiled. 'I'll get W…W…Widdicombe to fetch us some more.'

She gave a low laugh.

He stubbed out his Lucky Strike and reached for the opened packet of condoms.

While he sorted himself out, Stella took a last drag on her cigarette and ground it into the ashtray just as he rolled on her, forcing her legs wider with his body.

Putting her arms around his shoulders, Stella closed her eyes.

He hadn't mentioned money and, even though she'd seen the wodge of white and black five-pound notes in his wallet, neither had she.

She hadn't because there was more than money to be gained from Sergeant Donald J. Muller.

Chapter twenty-two

ADJUSTING HER HEADPHONES, Francesca flipped the switch and the modulated tones of the BBC reporter in Gibraltar started a blow-by-blow account of how the British forces had withstood the recent Italian bombardment.

After two sentences she switched it off and wrote what had just been said in Italian.

It was Monday and the start of another week in Bush House and, although it wasn't yet lunchtime, Radio Roma had already had more than its fair share of drama.

It had started off when Miss Kirk arrived at work weeping after a heated early-morning telephone conversation with Professor Giulio's wife.

She had just dried her eyes when one of the sound technicians arrived. Someone had tried to plug two double adaptors together and had blown all the fuses on the floor below meaning that there was no recording studio available. The electrician had only just surmounted that obstacle to the day's work when the Doncaster & District Co-operative Society brass band turned up a day early. To top it all, Broadcasting House's Atmospheric Recording department had sent Mr Whyte a disc with the background sound of people drinking *tea* in a Lyons teashop instead of the *sea* recording he'd requested for the dramatisation of *Moby Dick*.

Quite frankly, by ten thirty, when Miss Kirk plonked the half a dozen wax recording discs on her desk, Francesca was pleased to escape into the solitude of a soundproof booth.

She went to play the next section of the news report when the door behind her opened.

She turned just as Leo closed it behind him.

'I thought you were having a meeting with the overseas controller about them cutting our studio hours,' she said, slipping her earphones off.

Leo's face darkened.

'I did,' he replied. 'Much good it did me as the stupid old fossils still won't budge.'

'So we are going to lose a third of our studio time?' said Francesca.

'We are until the Corporation's technical staff find a way to get our broadcasts past the German jammers blocking our transmission.' A smile replaced Leo's frown. 'But at least not having to spend hours arguing with the short-sighted fools upstairs has allowed me to hurry back to you.'

Bending down, he kissed her.

'Leo!' she said, pushing him off. 'What if someone sees us? You know what the fifth floor is like about employees fraternising.'

He planted his hands on the arms of her chair, boxing her in.

'*Cara mia, non siamo fraternizzare,*' he replied, slipping into Italian as he always did when they were alone. 'But they are going to find out sooner or later that we are courting.'

'I know, but not yet. And what if Miss Kirk catches us?' said Francesca.

'She won't.' He brushed her lips on hers. 'I've locked the door.'

'Leo!'

'And if she does, then I shall just tell her I have every right to kiss my girlfriend and ask her to join me for dinner later,' he added.

'But we went out three times last week,' she replied.

'Who's counting?' he replied.

He tried to capture her lips again, but she held him off. 'I'm not really dressed for a restaurant.'

'You look perfect to me,' he replied. 'And I had in mind a little place I know in Soho, so no ballgown required.'

Francesca suppressed a smile. 'But my father is expecting me home after work.'

'Ring him,' Leo replied. 'He won't mind.'

Her father certainly wouldn't. In fact, if she telephoned to say she was eloping with Leo, he wouldn't mind that either.

'I suppose I could,' she conceded.

A triumphant smile spread across Leo's fine features. Taking her hands, he drew her up from the chair.

She rose to her feet and his arms wound around her. Their lips met and Francesca gave herself up to his embrace.

After a heady moment she put her hands on his chest and held him off again.

'Leo?'

'Yes, my darling.'

Francesca caught her bottom lip with her teeth.

'What is it, my sweetheart?' he asked, his gaze flickering over her face.

'Well, it's a bit short notice and you don't have to say yes if you don't want to,' she blurted out breathlessly. 'And I'd quite understand if you had a prior engagement somewhere or something, but…' She took a deep breath. 'Would you like to come to Jo's wedding next Saturday?'

'Your friend Mattie's sister?' he asked.

'Yes, I'm very close to her and Jo,' Francesca explained. 'And they are more like sisters than friends. In fact, all the Brogans are like family to me, because—'

'I'd be delighted to accompany you.' Leo's arm snaked around her waist again. 'I do love a wedding.'

He pressed his lips on hers again.

'Reluctant though I am to let you out of my arms, I should let you get on,' he said, releasing her.

Leo blew her a kiss as he opened the door but as Francesca picked up her headphones to put them on, he spoke.

'They have a brother; Charlie, if I remember correctly,' he said, casually.

'Yes, that's right,' said Francesca. 'Fancy you remembering.'

'I'll collect you later at six.'

'So did you ask him?' said Mattie, cutting up her potato.

'Yes I did,' said Francesca.

'And?'

It was the Monday before Jo's big day and they were squashed in the corner of the British Restaurant in Stepney Green, which had been set up in the main hall of Redcoat School.

The council had taken the old school buildings over the year before and set up the communal feeding hall after the Luftwaffe's nightly visits during the autumn of '40 had left thousands homeless. Although the food was plain, just a portion of meat, potatoes and vegetables, usually carrots or swede, it was nourishing enough. However, more importantly, what with the weekly housekeeping budget being squeezed by shortages and rising prices, a main meal and pudding was pegged at nine pence and was coupon free.

To be honest, because of her father's cafe, it wasn't often she ate in one of the handful of British Restaurants in the area, but the gas had been off at Mattie's all day so when she'd arrived at her friend's house an hour ago at six to help with the finishing touches on Jo's wedding dress, they'd decided to take the short walk round to Stepney Green for their evening meal.

'He said yes,' said Francesca. 'But I'm not sure.'

'About what?' asked Mattie.

'Him coming,' said Francesca. 'I mean, inviting him to a wedding, especially a close family wedding like Jo's, is more or less saying we're a proper couple.'

'Well, you are, aren't you?' said Mattie.

'I suppose,' said Francesca. 'My dad certainly thinks so. Leo is very passionate and attentive, but it's all so quick.'

'There's a war on and people haven't got time for long courtships,' said Mattie. 'The local registrar and churches are inundated with couples tying the knot while the groom's on leave.'

A couple of girls from one of the nearby factories squeezed behind Mattie, heading for a free table under the window.

Even though it was now almost six and many of the locals would be heading off to the shelters, the feeding centre was still doing a roaring trade. This was mainly because, after a week or so of respite, the Germans had returned the night before and dropped a high-explosive bomb between Shady Street and the gasworks, not only rupturing the mains but destroying three streets of houses close by.

Despite working all day, there were still Heavy Rescue crews from the surrounding area digging out the debris alongside a dozen fitters from the gas company trying to restore the supply. Some of their number were taking their evening break in the feeding station and sat, covered in brick dust and goodness knows what else, at one of the long tables in front of the school stage.

Wiping her daughter's mouth with her handkerchief, Mattie looked around.

'I thought Jo would be here by now. I hope she saw the note we left her.'

As if hearing her name, Jo, dressed in her ambulance uniform and looking like she was about to burst into tears, appeared in the door at the top of the stairs.

She spotted them and hurried over.

'Jo,' said Mattie as her sister reached them. 'What on earth is the matter?'

'The Memorial Hall,' Jo replied, tears gathering in her eyes. 'It's gone.'

'Gone?' said Francesca and Mattie together.

'Yes,' said Jo. 'A direct hit last night. I've just been round there and it's a pile of rubble. In fact, the whole of Swede Street has been flattened, including the bakery.'

'Many injured?' asked Francesca.

Jo shook her head. 'A few taken to the London with shock and the odd scrape, but most of them went to the shelter when the siren went off.'

Francesca and Mattie crossed themselves.

'Thank God there were no fatalities,' said Francesca.

'Other than my wedding reception,' said Jo. Her face crumpled and she burst into tears. 'I'm getting married in five days and I'll never find another hall at such short notice.'

'Well, we'll have to have your do at home,' said Mattie.

'But we've got fifty people coming, they'll never all fit into the back parlour,' said Jo.

'We'll lay up the buffet in the street on a couple of trestles and Dad can set up the drinks alongside,' Mattie replied. 'That's what people used to do years ago.'

'What if it rains?' said Jo.

'We'll worry about that *if* it happens.' Mattie placed her hand over her sister's.

'And, Jo,' said Francesca, 'even if it snows and we all have to huddle together to keep warm, you'll be marrying Tommy and surely that's all that matters.'

'And you will still look stunning when you walk down the aisle on Dad's arm,' added Mattie.

Jo looked at them for a long moment, then sighed. 'You're right. But I want both of you on your knees every day between now and Saturday praying to St Medardus for fine weather.'

'Promise.' Francesca laughed.

'Mum wants me to let out the waist of her skirt so she's coming around about seven, and she wants to see you in your dress, too. We can talk about it all then,' added Mattie.

'Is she bringing the boys?' asked Jo.

Mattie shook her head. 'Charlie's taken them to the shelter and she's going to join them when we're done. Now, you'd better get yourself some grub before it's all gone, Jo.'

Jo stood up and went to join the queue.

'How's Charlie's shoulder?' asked Francesca.

'Fine, I think,' Mattie replied. 'Why do you ask?'

'Oh, it's just that he said yesterday at Mass that it had been aching a bit, that's all,' Francesca replied nonchalantly.

Mattie's perceptive gaze scanned her face for a couple of seconds, then Alicia wriggled on her lap and she grimaced.

Francesca stood up.

'Let me have her,' she said, taking the lively toddler from her mother.

'Thanks,' said Mattie, running her hands over her bulging stomach. 'This baby's not stopped shifting about all day.'

'Not long now,' said Francesca, settling her goddaughter on her lap and giving her a spoon to play with.

'Thank goodness,' said her friend with feeling. 'But I'm hoping he or she will stay put until Jo walks out of the church as Mrs Sweete.'

'A bit longer maybe or we'll have to eat your sandwiches,' said Francesca.

Jo returned with a plate loaded with stew and potatoes.

'Well,' said Mattie, as her sister took the chair next to her, 'I've got a bit of news that will cheer you up. Francesca's bringing Leo on Saturday!'

'Is she?' said Jo.

'She is,' said Mattie, her eyes dancing with merriment as she looked across at her. 'So we'll get to meet this aristocrat who's smitten by our Fran.'

'Indeed.' Jo winked. 'Might even put him in the mood to go down on one knee and whisk Fran down the aisle, too.'

A little flutter started in Francesca's stomach as an image of Leo looking down St Breda and St Brendan's aisle as she walked towards him materialised in her mind. However, before it was fully formed, it was replaced by the image of Charlie in his shirtsleeves with his collar open. The flutter turned into a full-blown storm.

Stepping from the bus's platform as it drew to a halt by St Paul's Cathedral, Charlie pulled down the front of his battle dress and straightened his field cap.

The area around him, which had been a mismatch of Victorian and Edwardian office blocks with the odd Georgian structure mingled in, was now little more than a collection of broken walls and charred beams. A few shops and workplaces had somehow survived the closing days of 1940 when the City's ancient place of worship had been relentlessly targeted by the Luftwaffe, but those buildings still intact around the cathedral's courtyard and Paternoster Row were few and far between.

As it was a Friday the smell of fried fish and vinegar drifted across from the WVS canteen wagon that was parked in the shadow of the great dome.

'*News* and *Standard*!' yelled a newspaper seller standing beside a pile of midday editions.

Taking a couple of coppers out of his pocket, Charlie handed over the money in exchange for a folded early edition of the *Evening News*.

'Ta,' he said, tucking it under his arm. 'Do us a favour, mate, and point me in the direction for Creed Lane.'

A few moments later, Charlie was standing in front of a solid-looking six-panelled door. To the left of it was a brass plate with Stratton, Briggs, Wilberforce and Associates, Solicitors, Commissioners of Oaths etched into it.

He pushed open the door and stepped in.

He found himself in a high-ceilinged hallway lined with watercolour landscapes. Behind the desk was a young woman at a typewriter. Taking off his cap and tucking it in his epaulette, he walked over.

As he stopped in front of her, she looked up.

'I've an appointment with Mr Briggs,' Charlie said.

She gave him a professional smile. 'Name?'

'Mr Charles Brogan.'

She scanned the diary next to the typewriter. 'Ah, yes.' She picked up the telephone receiver. 'Please take a seat and I'll let him know you're here.'

Choosing one of the three comfortable chairs that had been arranged around a low coffee table, Charlie sat down, but no sooner had he scanned the front page of his newspaper than one of the doors opened and a well-fed middle-aged man in a pinstriped suit and red bow tie stepped out.

'Mr Brogan?'

Charlie stood up.

The solicitor offered his hand and Charlie took it.

'Please come this way.'

Mr Briggs ushered Charlie along the corridor and into the last office on the left. As he entered the room, the smell of dusty books and old cigar smoke filled his nose. The room itself wasn't large but it felt even smaller due to the fact that all four walls were filled floor to ceiling with loaded bookcases. The courtyard garden could be seen through the solitary window, and a long bureau covered with files sat on the Persian rug.

'Sit, sit,' he said, indicating the leather-buttoned armchair in front of the desk.

Charlie did and the solicitor resumed his seat. He scanned the file lying open on his leather-bound blotting paper, then looked up.

'So you've come to see me about a marital issue,' he said.

'I have,' Charlie replied.

'And you were given my name by the…'

'The workers' welfare office in Toynbee Hall,' Charlie replied. 'As having a great deal of experience in such matters.'

Flipping open the box on his desk, the solicitor took a cork-tipped cigarette out. 'Well then, young man, perhaps you could enlighten me as to your predicament.'

'The long and the short of it, Mr Briggs, is that while I've been serving with the army in North Africa …'

As Mr Briggs puffed away at his cigarette, Charlie ran through the events of his marriage and everything that had occurred since his return.

'So now all I care about is my son and I fear for his safety when I have to return to active service in a few months,' he concluded.

'Understandably,' said the solicitor, tapping cigar ash into the cut-glass ashtray at his elbow.

'I've been to the police, but they won't touch it,' said Charlie. 'And while the council welfare officer was sympathetic, she said her hands were tied too, unless I got a court order giving me custody of Patrick.'

'Which I imagine is why you're sitting across from me now,' said Mr Briggs.

Charlie nodded.

The portly solicitor sucked on his teeth. 'Fathers have got custody of their children but only in the rarest of cases. In fact, to be honest with you, Mr Brogan, I can't remember the last time it happened.'

'But what about my son being left alone in the house?' asked Charlie.

Mr Briggs shook his head. 'I still think it very unlikely in this case. I've been in court where the police have stood up and testified to finding an iron burn on a child's back and the magistrates still refused to take the child from its mother. And what your wife does

256

for a living, Mr Brogan, is of no consequence. Even if she were soliciting it would make no difference. Most of the prostitutes who are brought up before a magistrate are mothers to one of two children, often more, and no one turns a hair.'

'What about if I divorced her? Would I have a better chance of getting custody then?'

'Possibly,' Mr Briggs replied. 'But on what grounds?'

'Well, adultery, of course,' said Charlie. 'After all, she's sleeping with any Tom, Dick or Harry that takes her fancy.'

'But you'd have to name Tom, Dick or Harry as correspondent,' explained the solicitor. 'And to do that you'd need witnesses to testify that they've seen your wife having sexual relations with another man. You'd have to have the means to pay a private investigator.'

Charlie sagged in the chair.

'I'm sorry,' said the solicitor. 'I truly am but, as the law stands at the moment, I'm afraid if you take your wife to court for custody of your son, you would be throwing hundreds of pounds down the drain. In my opinion, the best way you can ensure your son's welfare, Mr Brogan, is to make sure you come home from the war in one piece.'

A black cloud of hopelessness pressed down on Charlie's shoulders.

Taking a deep breath, Charlie ran his hands over his face and stood up.

'Thank you for your time, Mr Briggs,' he said, offering the man on the other side of the desk his hand.

The solicitor rose from his seat and shook it.

Turning, Charlie left the room.

The receptionist looked up as he came out and Charlie went over to her desk.

She handed him a bill. 'That will be three guineas, Mr Brogan.'

Charlie balked. 'I thought I was seeing Mr Briggs under the Workers' Concessionary scheme.'

She gave him a long-nosed look. 'That is the concessionary rate, Mr Brogan.'

Charlie took out his wallet and removed his two pound notes and the one his father had pressed into his hand that morning and placed them on her desk then, diving in his pocket, he counted out three shillings in change.

Taking the bill from him, she scribbled paid across the bottom in red, then handed it back to him.

'Thank you,' she said, gracing him with her professional smile again.

Having handed over what most men earned in a week for the half-hour consultation, Charlie headed for the door. Feeling like his heart had turned to solid lead in his chest, he left the building.

Chapter twenty-three

AS THE BRASS section of the black jazz band, dressed in morning suits with red bow ties, blasted out the last chord of 'Chattanooga Choo Choo', Donny swirled Stella to a stop.

The dancers around them applauded the seven-piece band on the stage. The trombone player, who led the group, bowed and then turned back to his fellow musicians and counted in the next tune.

As the first notes of 'Lullaby of Broadway' drifted across the dancefloor, Donny's arm slipped around Stella's waist.

'Shall we sit this one out?'

Stella smiled her agreement and he led her off the dance floor to their table.

As he pulled out the chair for her to resume her seat, a waiter, dressed in gold-trimmed livery, hurried over.

'Can I get you anything, Sergeant Muller?'

'Another one of these for the lady,' Donny replied, grabbing the empty bottle of champagne from the chrome bucket in the middle of their table. 'And a double bourbon.'

'Very good, sir,' said the waiter, making a deep bow before shooting off towards the bar.

It was a little over a week since the night of the private show and the third time Donny had taken Stella out to dinner.

Tonight they were in the underground club at the Mayfair Castle Hotel, just off Shepherd Market. It had been the Dorchester Hotel, with Lew Stone's orchestra, three nights ago and The Ritz two nights before that.

Of course, Donny wasn't the only US soldier enjoying an evening out with his date by any means as the place was awash with US olive green. However, while men wearing squares or pips on their epaulettes were seated a few rows back from the dance floor, Donny, with the upended chevron on his sleeve, had been shown to the best table in the house.

'It's a good band,' said Stella, as the drummer thumped out the beat.

'That's about all darkies are good for, leaping about on stage.' He grinned and drained the last drop of champagne into her glass. 'Well, that and scrubbing the latrines.'

Stella laughed.

He took out his gold cigarette case and flipped it open. Stella took one and he retrieved the lighter from his pocket.

He flicked it into flame and their eyes met as she lit her cigarette.

The waiter appeared carrying another bucket of ice with a fresh bottle of champagne in it.

'Compliments of the house, Sergeant Muller,' said the waiter, twisting off the cork. After replenishing their glasses, he set the bottle into the ice.

Picking up his glass, Donny raised it towards a stout man in a dinner suit who was tucked into the shadows at the far corner of the room. The man raised his glass of bourbon in acknowledgement.

Taking a long drag on his cigarette, Donny leant back in his chair and studied Stella for a moment, then spoke again.

'Babe, you look like a million dollars tonight,' he said, blowing a stream of smoke towards the crystal chandeliers above.

Stella smiled.

He was right, of course. The blood-red satin cocktail dress with its tight bodice, plunging neckline and pencil skirt fitted her like a second skin; as the heads turning as she walked from the club door to their table testified.

Leaning forward to give him the full benefit of her cleavage, she gave him a lazy smile. 'You don't look too bad yourself.'

Of course, although his uniform was the standard US design,

the one Donny was wearing wasn't off a rail from the General Issue Supply store. No, Donny's uniforms, all three sets of them, were from an enterprising tailor in Soho who had turned his workshop over to making made-to-measure uniforms for US officers.

Stella raised her glass but, before it reached her lips, a young girl dressed in a skimpier version of the club's livery stopped beside their table.

'For Sergeant Muller?' she said, holding a white cardboard box tied with a pink ribbon.

'For my enchanting dinner companion,' he said, raising his glass to Stella.

The young woman placed the box in front of Stella.

Donny reached into his trouser pocket.

'For your trouble, miss,' he said, handing the girl a florin.

She stared wide-eyed at it for a moment, then her fingers closed around it and she left.

'Open it then,' he said.

Stella stared at the book-sized white cardboard box for a moment then, plucking the pink ribbon loose, she lifted off the lid.

Her eyes opened wide with astonishment.

'Like it?' asked Donny.

'It's beautiful,' said Stella, reaching in and lifting out the white orchid corsage from its tissue paper nest. 'But where on earth did you get it?'

He smiled, but didn't reply.

Stella's gaze returned to the flower.

With every scrap of spare land in the country turned over to food production, you couldn't get cut flowers for love nor money so how on earth…?

Stella placed the lid back on the box. She shoved it across the table.

'Why me?'

'Why you, what?' he replied, holding her gaze.

261

'All this,' she said, indicating the champagne and flowers. 'There are prettier girls you could have on your arm and in your bed. So why me and don't say because I'm special or you're in love with me or any other old codswallop. I want the truth.'

A smile lifted the corner of Donny's hard mouth. 'Codswallop. Huh?'

'Yeah, codswallop, flannel, soft-soap,' said Stella. 'Whatever you want to call it.'

Donny studied her for a long moment, then he clicked his fingers and a waiter appeared.

'The bill!' he said, holding Stella's gaze.

The waiter dashed away and returned a few moments later. He placed a silver salver beside Donny's hand.

Taking his wallet from his inside pocket, Donny pulled out a five-pound note. Without looking at the bill, he threw the money on top of the receipt.

'Keep the change,' he said, his eyes still fixed on Stella.

The waiter scooped up the money and hurried away.

Donny stood up. 'Let's go.'

Downing her drink, Stella rose to her feet. 'Where?'

Taking her mink-coloured Coney wrap from the back of her chair, he draped it around her shoulders.

'To answer your question,' he replied.

Grabbing the neck of the champagne bottle in one hand and her in the other, he led her towards the door.

Stepping out of the sweltering atmosphere of the club, Stella shivered. The clear night above had let the heat of the spring day escape and there was a definite chill in the air.

'It's just a short walk,' Donny assured her, as she pulled her stole a little closer.

Taking his torch from his pocket he switched it on then, pointing the light downwards, he gave her the bottle and offered Stella his arm.

She took it.

With her high heels echoing around the narrow Mayfair Mews and holding the half-drunk bottle of champagne, she and Donny headed south towards Piccadilly.

Although it was close to one in the morning, the road that ran between St James and Piccadilly Circus was brimming with people. Well, specifically GIs, many with laughing young women hanging off their arms.

The dark thoroughfare was lit by little beams of light from the pencil torches being used to illuminate the pavement so people could see where they were walking but sometimes the dim lights were shone on the faces of women in doorways so that servicemen looking to buy a bit of company could see what they were paying for.

Taxis pulled up, disgorging gangs of GIs onto the pavement and into the clutches of pimps in long overcoats, their fedoras pulled low over their face as they negotiated terms.

'It's not far,' said Donny, as he guided her past an unconscious private sprawled drunk across their path.

'I hope not,' Stella replied. 'These shoes aren't made for a blooming hike.'

Donny laughed and strode on, thrusting drunken soldiers out of their path as they went. Within a few moments they left the hustle and bustle and turned up Half Moon Street and then into Shepherd Street. The wires of the barrage balloons floating above sang as they bobbed in their moorings.

'Follow me,' said Donny, shining his torch down a passageway.

Letting go of his arm, Stella did, finding herself in a cobbled courtyard at the back of a tall building.

Stopping in front of a door with a bar bolted across it, Donny took a set of keys from his pocket. He unlocked it and threw the door open.

Clutching the champagne, Stella stepped in.

Donny stepped in behind her. He shut the door and switched on the light.

As the fluorescent strip light flickered on, Stella found herself in a cavernous room with a high ceiling. There were iron grilles at the window and brighter-coloured rectangles on the faded walls showed where pictures had been removed.

However, what really stopped her in her tracks and made her jaw drop was what was stacked in the room. Not truly believing what she was seeing, Stella ran her gaze over crates labelled coffee, candy, beer, cookies, soap, shampoo. There were cardboard boxes marked singlets, shorts and nylons, plus rows upon rows of men's jumpers and trousers. Things that most people in England hadn't set eyes on for over two years.

Stunned by what was stacked high around her, she looked incredulously at Donny.

'What is this place?'

'Mayfair's Exchange Post,' he replied, taking the bottle from her and placing it on a crate marked Wild Turkey Bourbon. 'And I'm the sergeant in charge.'

'You're in charge of all this?' said Stella, unable to believe what she was seeing.

'Yes, ma'am,' said Donny. 'Come.'

He beckoned for her to follow him again.

Stella did as he asked and wove her way through the crates of treasures to a door. Donny switched on the light.

She found herself behind a long counter which stretched between the two walls of what had been the house's grand hallway. There was a cast-iron till at one end and boxes of sweets, gum and different brands of cigarettes in a row beside it. Behind her were floor-to-ceiling shelves crammed full of clothing, writing paper and pencils along with shoe polish, aftershave, comics and rows upon rows of books with pristine dust covers.

At the far end of the counter was a box with the words 'Saxon: the Best Grip-tight Prophylactics You Can Buy' on the folded-up display lid. Inside were packets of condoms lined up in two neat rows. Pinned to the wall above them was a poster showing a woman in a frilly apron baking a cake watched by two eager-eyed children, on it was the message, 'They are Waiting at Home. Protect yourself from VD.'

Beyond the black and white tiled hallway was a door through which she could see easy chairs and a coffee table with drafts, chess and playing cards on it.

She spotted a pile of crates in the corner.

'Is that Coca-Cola?' she asked, staring incredulously at the new drink everyone was talking about.

'Yep,' he replied. 'You want some?'

Without waiting for her reply, he reached in and pulled one of the stylised glass bottles out. Popping off the top against the counter edge, he handed it to her.

'Take this too.' He grabbed a chocolate bar from the top of one of the displays. 'Take it for your kid.'

He tossed it at her, and Stella caught it.

'How did you know—'

'You've got a kid?' he asked, taking a packet of cigarettes from the stack on the counter and opening it.

She nodded as he offered her one.

'I didn't until now.' Taking the lighter from his pocket, he flicked it into a flame. 'Husband?'

'Still around.' She drew on her cigarette, enjoying the tingle as the nicotine filled her lungs. 'But not so I'm bothered,' she added, blowing a stream of smoke from the side of her mouth. 'You?'

'A wife and a couple of weaners, none of whom I'm exactly eager to get back to,' he replied. 'In fact, if what I have in mind comes off, I won't have to.'

Stella took a swig of Coca-Cola, and felt her tastebuds explode with pleasure. 'And what do you have in mind, Donny?'

Grinning, he pulled out a stool from under the counter.

Stella perched on it, tucking her heels behind the cross bar.

'You see this.' He swept his arm around, indicating the shelves piled high with unimaginable luxuries. 'It's just a drop in the ocean. There are some ten thousand GIs in England at the moment but there're dozens of ships steaming their way across the Atlantic bringing more. The American Red Cross has just taken over the Eagle Club around the corner as a home from home for GIs and rumour has it that they've got their eye on the Washington Hotel in Curzon Street to set up another. There'll be half a dozen more billets for GIs opening around and about before the end of the year. All filled to the roof with my fellow countrymen, all with time on their hands and money in their pockets. As I said, where the army goes, American merchandise goes too. However, it seems to me a real crying shame that our dear friends and allies in this swell town can't enjoy these most excellent provisions, especially as they seem to be in such short supply hereabouts.'

'At a price, I'm guessing,' said Stella.

He nodded.

'You've already got a flourishing black market in London so I'm going to get my share. I'm in a position to supply what the average British Joe demands, which, if I play it right, will make a fortune, and that's exactly what I'm going to do.' A slow smile spread across Donny's square face. 'You asked me: why you? And, while it's true I could have younger girls, and by the pair if I wanted, I need someone with *moxie*, guts and that's what you've got. When I saw you on that stage buck naked and proud of it, I guessed you might be someone who could help me with my business arrangements. From what I hear, East London is like my neighbourhood in New York.'

'Is it?'

He nodded. 'So let me ask you, Stella, who controls the streets and pubs? Who do the knocking shops and bookmakers pay for protection? Who has their finger in every pie, takes a cut from every racket and can get you anything at a price?'

There was a metal ashtray on the counter with New York World Fair 1940 stamped around the rim. Stella tapped the stack of ash at the tip of her cigarette into it.

'And what do I get out of this?' she asked.

Donny smiled. 'Twenty pounds for the introduction, then a straight five per cent on everything I shift.'

Stella inhaled another lungful of cigarette smoke. 'Thirty. And ten per cent.'

'Twenty-five,' said Donny. 'And seven per cent on the net profit after expenses.'

'Expenses?'

'Backhanders,' he replied. 'Now, Stella, is it a deal?'

Stubbing out her cigarette, Stella slid off the stool and stood up.

Placing her hands on Donny's chest, Stella ran them up and around his neck.

'Twenty-five quid and seven per cent it is then,' she said, smiling up at him and pressing her pubic bone into his crotch. 'And I know exactly who might be interested.'

Looking in the corner-shop window, Stella checked her new felt hat, with its feather pointing skywards and a small veil around the brim, was still in place.

Satisfied it hadn't shifted during her thirty-minute train journey from Mile End to Forest Gate, she took out her compact and checked her make-up, too. Snapping it closed, she popped it back in her handbag, then, adjusting Donny's latest gift, a musquash stole, around her shoulders she turned and walked down Woodgrange Road towards the Princess Alice.

Acknowledging the wolf whistles from a group of Heavy Rescue lads loitering around the WVS mobile canteen, Stella crossed into Claremont Road.

When they were first built, the double-fronted Victorian villas had been home to bankers and city traders, who would jump on the Great Eastern train that collected the capital's workers as it puffed through the Essex countryside to Liverpool Street station each day. However, now all of the grand dwellings, which once would have housed a family, a handful of servants and a carriage and pair, were home to at least half a dozen families and sometimes more. All except the house she was heading for, which sat halfway down the street on its north side.

Instead of cracked glass, missing tiles and loose stonework, the dwelling she was heading for had curtains and nets behind polished window panes and its facade shone in the late May morning sunlight.

Reaching the house, Stella stepped through the stone pillared gate and started walking towards the lacquered front door with its massive brass knocker. However, she'd only got halfway along the black and white mosaic pathway when a thick-set man wearing a single-breasted suit and black tie, who was standing to the right of the entrance, stepped into her path.

'Can I 'elp, miss?' he asked, studying her from under his heavy brow.

'I've come to see Mrs Stamp,' said Stella.

'Have you?' he asked, clasping his huge hands in front of him.

'Yes,' said Stella. 'About a family matter. I'm married to her nephew.'

His deep-set eyes flickered down to her breasts for a second, then returned to her face. He thumped on the door with his fist.

It was opened by another man in an identical suit with a cauliflower ear and a deep scar down his right cheek.

'Visitor for Mrs Stamp,' said the first heavy.

The second heavy gave Stella the once-over, then stood back to let her into the hallway, the red flock-wallpapered walls were all but obscured by crystal-edged mirrors and old-fashioned paintings of country scenes.

Shutting the door behind her, the heavy held out his hand.

'Bag!' he said, as they stood beside a coat stand made of antlers.

Stella gave him her handbag.

He rummaged around amongst her lipstick, purse, keys and handkerchief for a moment, then pulled out half a dozen pairs of nylons. He turned them over in his hand then shoved them back where they came from and handed the bag back.

'This way.'

Hooking it over her arm and adjusting her fur again, she followed him down the hallway until they reached a door at the far end.

Knocking, her escort waited for a second then opened the door and stepped in.

'A visitor for you, Mrs Stamp,' he said, and ushered Stella in.

Ida Brogan's younger sister, Pearl, was reclining on a chaise longue with her stockinged feet up, a copy of *Vogue* in one hand and a cut-crystal whiskey glass in the other. She was, as the locals described her, well preserved.

Although she was only four years younger than Stella's mother-in-law, she looked a good decade her junior, thanks mainly to regular trips to the hairdresser to keep her hair barley-corn blonde and her long fingernails crimson red. Unlike her sister's broadening hips, Pearl still had a trim figure, mainly because after Billy her waist had never had to stretch to accommodate another growing child.

Although it was just after eleven, Pearl was dressed in a petrol-blue satin dress with a pencil skirt and sweeping shawl collar more suitable for tea at The Ritz than idling away the morning in Forest Gate. In addition, she had a thick choker of paste gems around her throat and a charm bracelet with so many trinkets hanging from it, Stella wondered how she managed to raise her arm.

'Morning,' said Stella.

Pearl stared at her for a moment, then recognition sparked in her eyes and she signalled for the flunky to leave.

He did and closed the door behind him.

'This is a bit of a surprise,' she said, swinging her legs around and sitting up.

Stella smiled and sat down on the easy chair opposite, putting her handbag on the floor.

'Nice place you've got here,' she said, crossing her legs and casting her eyes around.

Crowded might have been a better description of the room Stella was now in. Pearl obviously had a thing for dark colours as the walls of the lounge were covered with a purple and silver wallpaper. The imperial theme was continued with elaborate mauve drapes at the casement windows. The fireplace was in the style of a Greek temple with columns at each side, and an onyx clock sat in the middle of the mantelshelf between two classical plaster statues.

The chandelier in the centre of the room was just a little too low for most men to pass under comfortably but, as Lenny Stamp only just skimmed five foot five, it didn't matter.

'I like it,' said Pearl. She flicked her ash into the glass ashtray on the marble coffee table in front of her. 'So, to what do I owe this unexpected visit?'

Reaching down, Stella unsnapped her handbag and took out the nylons Donny had given her the night before.

'Business.' She threw the cellophane packets on the table between them.

Pearl's eyes lit up as she looked at the items that were rarer than hen's teeth, strewn across her table.

She picked up the nearest packet. 'Fifteen denier, American Tan with a fashioned heel. Where did you get them?'

'May I?' asked Stella, indicating the inlaid cigarette box on the table with lighter alongside.

Pearl nodded.

Stretching across, Stella opened the box and took one.

'I've got a friend. An American friend,' she continued, drawing on the cork-tipped Benson & Hedges. 'He's got chocolate, coffee and tons of other stuff people around here haven't clapped eyes on for years, not to mention Lucky Strikes, Camel and A1 fags by the carton load.'

'So why tell me?' said Pearl, the flash of eagerness in her eyes belying her disinterested tone.

'My friend's a sergeant in the US Army and he's the man in charge of the main US Post Exchange in London, but he has a problem.'

'What sort of problem?' asked Pearl, blowing a stream of smoke up towards the plaster cherub on the decorated ceiling.

'He's got so much stuff being delivered from the States each day, he's having a problem storing it. He asked me if I knew of someone with contacts who might like to help him offload some of it. I thought of your husband, Len.'

Of course, technically speaking Pearl and Len weren't married. Well, they couldn't be seeing how he had a wife and a couple of snotty kids who lived somewhere down Southend way.

'Did you?' said Pearl.

Stella smiled. 'You know, keep it in the family, like.'

The older woman studied her for a moment, then ground out the stub. 'I heard my nephew Charlie moved out.'

'So?'

Pearl took another cigarette. 'So does he know about your friend?'

'Charlie's got nothing to do with this,' said Stella. 'Let's cut the shit, Pearl. Your Len runs the best part of East London, everyone knows it. My friend's putting together an operation that promises to rake in a fortune, but he needs a partner who knows the lay of the land and can keep others from muscling in on the action, but if you don't think Len would be interested, then—'

'Now I didn't say that,' Pearl cut in.

Stella smiled. She stubbed out her half-smoked cigarette and rose to her feet. 'Good. My friend wants you and Len to join us at The Ritz for dinner next Saturday. Can you make it?'

Pearl looked surprised. 'The Ritz! You mean in Piccadilly?'

'That's the one. Say about nine? Oh, Pearl?' Stella paused. 'It's on us.'

Chapter twenty-four

AS CHARLIE REPOSITIONED Patrick on his lap, Cathy sighed.

'Doesn't she look lovely?' said Cathy, gazing across at her sister Jo.

Jo was sitting next to her new husband on the dais while Fr Mahon tidied away the Communion silver at the altar. The altar boys, Billy and Michael, were stationed either side of him with their hands together and an unconvincing innocent expression on their faces.

'She does,' agreed Mattie, sitting on the other side of her. 'Every inch the blushing bride.'

Charlie was sitting with his two sisters in the row behind their parents and Queenie on the left-hand side of St Breda and St Brendan's church, watching their youngest sister marry Tommy Sweete.

His father was dressed in his best suit with a Donegal tartan waistcoat beneath and a matching green neckerchief at his throat. Thanks to clothes rationing, instead of a smart new outfit for her youngest daughter's wedding, Charlie's mother was dressed in the same navy suit and pink blouse she'd worn to Cathy's wedding almost three years previously. However, as befits the mother of the bride, she'd gone to town hat-wise with an extravagant felt creation with a massive pink peony on the side. His gran, in contrast, had dug out a low-waisted black dress which she'd matched with a sleeveless yellow cardigan so long it practically scraped the floor. She'd swapped her lace-up boots for patent dancing pumps and had finished off the ensemble with a fox-fur stole complete with head, tail and feet. She also wore a hat with a brim so wide she wouldn't need an umbrella if it rained. Charlie, in contrast to his family's colourful appearance, was dressed in his battle dress, which had been damp-sponged and brushed down for the occasion.

Having returned to their seat after receiving the nuptial Communion, he was sitting on one side of his two sisters while Mattie's husband Daniel, also wearing his dress uniform, was sitting on the other side. Charlie had Patrick on his knee while Cathy's Peter was sitting on a tapestry kneeler at her feet turning the pages of a rag book. Alicia, who'd managed to have nearly every woman in the congregation dabbing their eyes with a handkerchief as she tottered down the aisle as her aunt's bridesmaid, was sitting on her father's knee.

The bride's side of the church was packed with distant cousins from the Brogan side of the family with a sprinkling of Jo's ambulance colleagues amongst them, while the groom's side was a sea of khaki from his signal corps regiment.

'So beautiful,' added Cathy, with another deep sigh.

Charlie smiled. 'Yes, she is.'

Patrick started fidgeting so Charlie set his son down on the tiled floor of the aisle. He caught a glimpse of red out of the corner of his eye.

Resisting the urge to look over, Charlie returned his gaze to the front.

St Breda and St Brendan's ancient organ wheezed into action as old Mr Byrne struck up the opening chords of the 'Wedding March' and the congregation rose to its feet.

Scooping up Patrick, Charlie turned with the congregation to watch the newly married couple make their way down the aisle to the door.

Francesca, in her cherry-coloured suit and black hat, was standing three rows behind him. He could see her smiling profile as Jo and Tommy glided past on their way out of the church.

Free to look at the vision of loveliness, he allowed himself the sheer pleasure of studying Francesca for a long moment before his gaze slid onto the man standing beside her, who made Fred Astaire look dishevelled.

Dressed in a lounge suit that was clearly made for him, Francesca's count was obviously rich, handsome and, by the way he was looking at Francesca, totally besotted. He was, in short, everything Charlie had dreaded he would be.

Daniel and his sisters shuffled out of the pew. Settling his son on his hip, Charlie side-stepped out to join the rest of his family.

Their fervent prayers had been answered and Charlie, with Patrick in his arms, stepped from the cool of the stone porch into warm late-spring sunshine.

Leaving his sisters and friends to cluster around the happy couple, Charlie went over to join Daniel, who was standing by a lichen-covered memorial a little way off.

'Glad to see you made it,' said Charlie, lowering Patrick to the floor.

'It was touch and go,' Daniel replied. 'But we've got a lot brewing so I wouldn't be surprised if I don't get called back later. What about you?'

'Almost as good as new,' Charlie replied. 'I'm back to the docs in three weeks and I reckon he'll mark me fit.'

'Then you'll be off.'

Charlie nodded and looked down at his son, who was practising walking around his father's legs.

'It's hard leaving them, isn't it?' said Daniel.

Mastering his fear of leaving Patrick with Stella, Charlie looked up.

'Yes, it is,' he said, with a heavy sigh. 'But we've all got to do our bit.'

Charlie's attention returned to his sister and her new husband.

Although there was no rice to be thrown, other traditions were being upheld and well-wishers pressed wooden spoons, sprigs of

275

heather, cardboard black cats and horseshoes tied with ribbons into the hands of the happy couple.

After a moment or two his gaze shifted from the couple at the centre of the attention to another couple, standing a little way away in the shade of the crab apple tree.

Pain and longing gripped Charlie's heart as his gaze rested on Francesca. He marvelled again at how utterly stupid he had been not to notice her loveliness before. And it was too late.

Someone jostled them and, under the pretext of protecting her, the man beside her slipped his arm around her waist.

Charlie pressed his lips together.

Thankfully, Mattie and Cathy beckoned her over and Francesca slipped out of his embrace to join the bevy of womenfolk clustered around Jo and Tommy.

The count's eyes followed after her for a moment then, sensing someone's gaze upon him, he turned and looked at Charlie.

They stared at each other for a long moment then, picking up his son from the floor, Charlie smiled and strolled across.

Standing Patrick back down on the grass, he extended his hand.

'You must be Count D'Angelo.'

'And you must be Charlie,' the count replied, giving him a flash of white teeth as he took it. 'And Leo. Please.'

'And this is Patrick,' Charlie added, gratified that although the count's grip was firm, his was firmer.

'Unmistakably your son,' said the count, looking down at Patrick as he practised a few steps.

He bent down and offered the child a well-manicured finger in greeting.

Patrick regarded the aristocrat for a moment, then buried his face in his father's legs.

The count's smile slipped a little.

'It's his age,' said Charlie, pleased at his son's egalitarian sentiments.

Behind Leo the photographer was setting Jo and Tommy up in front of the church doorway as the rest of the family and their friends waited to be called forward.

The count's attention shifted back to Charlie and his refined smile returned. 'Francesca tells me you were injured in North Africa.'

'Yes, back in February,' Charlie replied, hating the sound of her name on the other man's lips. 'Although I expect to be returning to my regiment soon.'

'I'm sure your wife will be sad to say goodbye,' said the count. 'Is she here?'

'She couldn't come,' Charlie replied flatly.

He and the count stared at each other for a moment, then the aristocrat's refined smile returned.

'I know Francesca will be sad to see you go too,' added Leo.

Before he could stop it, hope flared in Charlie's chest.

'Will she?'

The count's smile extended. 'I'm sure of it. She has often told me you're like her second brother.'

Charlie's heart turned to lead in his chest.

A flash of red caught his eye and, looking past Leo, he saw Francesca weaving her way through the gravestones towards them.

'Sorry to have abandoned you for so long, Leo, but—'

She spotted him and stopped dead in her tracks.

Something was clearly wrong with her brain as, seeing the man who'd held her in a spell beside the man who might free her, Francesca lost every thought in her head.

For what could have been ten seconds or an eternity, she stared wordlessly at Charlie, then Leo's arm around her waist brought her back to the here and now.

'I forgive you, my angel,' he said.

Drawing her to him, he pressed his lips to her cheek. An odd emotion Francesca couldn't interpret flitted across the back of Charlie's eyes for a second, then he smiled.

'Me and Patrick were just saying hello to your—'

'Devoted admirer,' Leo cut in, giving her another affectionate squeeze.

Francesca's brain stopped working again but, before she could kick it into action, a voice cut between them.

'Charlie. Fran!' Cathy shouted through her cupped hand. 'You're needed for the photos.'

Gathering together her ragged wits, Francesca smiled at Leo. 'I'm afraid I'm going to have to abandon you again for a little while.'

He placed a hand dramatically over his heart and said something in Italian.

Francesca forced a smile and started off between the gravestones towards the wedding party.

'I'll see you later, Leo,' said Charlie, as he scooped his son into his arms and fell into step beside Francesca.

'Leo seems a nice chap,' he said, as they skirted a scrubby patch of dandelions.

'He is.'

They reached the flagstone pathway and joined the rest of the family as they milled around with the other guests in front of the church.

'Now, if I can have the family,' called the photographer.

'That's us, Mattie,' said Cathy, taking her son's hand and moving forward. 'You too, Charlie. And you, Fran.'

Francesca shook her head. 'He said family.'

'Well, you are family,' said Mattie, grabbing her hand. 'Isn't she, Jo?'

'Isn't she what?' Jo called back.

'Family,' Mattie replied, dragging Francesca into the line-up.

'Of course you are, Fran,' Jo replied.

Francesca admitted defeat.

'If the parents and grandmother could stay where they are,' called the photographer, 'and if the two gentlemen could stand at each end and the rest of the family…'

Having located Billy and Michael kicking stones about down the side of the church, the photographer lined the family up.

'It's not fair,' Billy whined, as his mother shepherded him into place beside her. 'I'm the oldest so I should be standing next to Dad, not Michael.'

'That's enough, Billy!' Jerimiah barked.

Billy subsided into sullen silence and everyone breathed easy.

Charlie took Francesca's elbow and she looked up into his blue-grey eyes.

'Come and stand with me and Patrick, Francesca,' he said in a low voice that vibrated through her.

She stepped in beside Queenie and Charlie took up position behind her.

Crouching behind his camera, the photographer threw the black square of fabric over his head then, after a few seconds, reappeared.

'If you could all budge up together a little,' he said, waving them towards the middle.

They all shuffled in.

'And perhaps you, sir—' he pointed at Charlie – 'could stand a little closer to your wife?'

Francesca's heart thumped in her chest as all the little domestic daydreams she'd harboured for so many years dashed across her mind.

Charlie's chest skimmed her shoulders, setting her heart galloping. Instinctively, she wanted to rock back to feel the hardness of his body but, instead, she schooled herself to remain still.

The photographer reappeared from under his fabric screen and held up his hand.

'Now, everyone, hold!'

With her senses reeling, Francesca held her breath. Finally, after what seemed like an eternity, the photographer's hand fell and everyone relaxed.

The photographer ushered the bride and groom away for the last few photos. Children started running about again as their parents resumed their conversations while making their way out of the churchyard. Patrick wriggled in Charlie's arms, so he lowered him to the ground, and he grasped his father's trousers.

Francesca turned to make her way back to Leo, but, as she did, she came face to face with Charlie.

Their eyes meet.

Captured in his gaze, Francesca's mouth opened.

Just one step. That was all. That's all and she could have pressed her lips onto his, run her hands over his chest and shoulders and felt the hard contours of his body.

Without thinking, her left heel lifted but, as she leant forward, Patrick shuffled between her and Charlie.

She looked down at the little boy enjoying the feel of his legs beneath him.

Taking a firm step back, Francesca raised her head and looked at Charlie.

'I'm just popping in to light a candle,' she said, giving him her brightest smile. 'I'll see you back at the house.'

Somehow her legs managed to get her into the church and to Our Lady's side chapel. Grabbing the altar rail she all but collapsed onto the padded kneeler. Placing her hands together on the hard wood she rested her forehead on them and closed her eyes. Tears pressed at the back of her eyes.

Footsteps echoed around the empty church behind her.

Raising her head, Francesca looked around to find Leo standing in the entrance to the chapel.

Blinking away her tears, she got to her feet.

'I'm sorry,' she said, straightening her skirt. 'I was just...'

'Praying,' he said. 'For your mother, no doubt.'

Francesca didn't correct him.

Dropping his hat on one of the chairs, he crossed the tiled space to join her.

'Actually,' he said, his eyes warm as they gazed at her. 'Perhaps this is the perfect place.'

'For what?'

'For what I have to say, *amore*,' he said, slipping into Italian. He took her hands. 'Dangerous times such as these makes a man think of what is important to him. Like love.'

A little tremble ran through Francesca.

'I know we have not known each other for very long, my darling, but I have loved you from almost the first moment I set eyes on you—'

'Have you?'

'From the first second, I believe, and therefore...'

Still holding her hands, he lowered himself onto one knee. 'Francesca, will you make me the happiest man on earth by consenting to become my wife?'

Francesca's mouth dropped open and she stared down at him.

'Ideally I would have spoken to your father first, but –' His well-formed features lifted in an indulgent smile – 'being at a wedding has put me in a romantic mood.'

Francesca put her hand on her chest. 'Leo, I don't know what to—'

'I know, perhaps it's unexpected,' he interrupted. 'And I am prepared to wait for your answer, my love.' Taking her hand, he raised it to his lips then rose to his feet.

He offered her his arm. 'Shall we?'

'Would you mind if I had a moment or two longer in the chapel?' Francesca asked, feeling more than a little lightheaded.

'Of course,' he replied. 'Your piety is one of the qualities I admire most in you, my angel. I'll wait outside.'

He bowed and then strode out of the church.

Francesca stared after him for a moment, then turned and sank back onto the kneeler at the altar rail.

She looked up at the painted stature of the Virgin Mary.

However, although her gaze was on the serene face of the Queen of Heaven, none of the thoughts racing around in her head were remotely holy.

Leaning against the wall, Charlie took a sip of his beer as the Catholic club's fiddle band, or the three of the six who hadn't been called up, struck up another tune.

They'd started playing after the speeches had finished and the assembled wedding guests had toasted the happy couple.

Thanks to the Luftwaffe, Jo and Tommy were having an old-style wedding celebration; that was to say it was in the street outside the house. In the old days this would have entailed borrowing all the neighbours' chairs so the guests could sit down. However, one of the advantages of his father's profession was that he had plenty of spare chairs so, along with every seat in the house, Jerimiah had brought a further dozen or more from the yard for guests to sit on.

These had been set out in a large square outside the front of their house while a long table, also from his father's store, had been covered with a couple of sheets to serve as a bar. There was a hotch-potch of glasses, from tumblers to dimpled pint mugs, lined up at one end of the bar with gin, port and a crate of stout for the female guests and beer with Jameson chasers for the men.

Jerimiah had just tapped the second barrel of beer, a pint of which, having put Patrick down for his afternoon nap, Charlie was supping on as he watched the festivities.

Now, at four o'clock, most of the buffet his family had set out had been demolished and, having completed the formal part of the proceedings, the guests were bobbing about on the street cobbles. The fiddlers had started with 'When Irish Eyes are Smiling' and followed up with a couple of old favourites before shifting onto more modern tunes such as 'The White Cliffs of Dover' and 'I'll be With You in Apple Blossom Time'. People sang as they danced: these tunes and the songs' sentiments were now part of everyone's daily lives.

The sun in the cornflower sky above was bathing the whole area in a mellow warmth. The couple, arm in arm as they chatted to well-wishers, looked even happier, if that were possible, and, with their stomachs full and a few drinks inside them, everyone was having a marvellous time. Everyone that was except him because, across the street, not a hundred yards from him, Leo took Francesca into his arms again.

As they joined the dozen or so dancing couples on the cobbles, it took all Charlie's willpower not to stride across and snatch her from the other man's arms.

Especially now. After that look she gave him outside the church. The look that made his heart sing and almost made him believe she might still love him. Added to which, although it was quite possible he'd imagined it, for one giddy, heart-stopping moment he'd had the impression she was about to throw herself into his arms.

'This is supposed to be a wedding not a wake,' said Mattie's voice, cutting through his miserable thoughts.

Tearing his eyes from Francesca in Leo's arms, he turned to his sister.

'Shouldn't you be taking the weight off your feet?'

'I was until I spotted your miserable mosh,' she said. 'What are you playing at, Charlie?'

Charlie took a large mouthful of beer. 'I don't know what you mean?'

'Yes you do,' she replied, fixing him with a steely gaze unsettlingly like their grandmother's.

Charlie forced a laugh. 'I'm watching the dancing like everyone else.'

'Watching Francesca and Leo like a blooming hawk, don't you mean?' Mattie replied. 'Like you've done since the moment they walked into church this morning.'

He opened his mouth to deny it, but let out a long sigh instead.

'I was such a fool,' he said, studying Francesca's shapely legs as Leo swirled her around.

'Well, you won't get any argument from me on that score,' Mattie replied. 'But Fran's my friend, Charlie, I love her like I love Jo and Cathy and I don't want you to hurt her any more.'

'Why didn't I realise before I...?' He buried his nose in the glass and took another gulp of beer.

'Acted like a brainless loon with Stella?' suggested Mattie.

Despite his heavy heart, Charlie gave her a wry smile. 'Don't spare me, Matt.'

'Well, you did,' she said. 'And now you've missed your chance and—'

'But I love her,' he cut in. 'I can't tell you, Mattie, how much I love her. I love her so much it hurts. Francesca is all I think about, day and night.'

'Well, I'm sorry, Charlie, really I am,' his sister replied. 'But now she's met someone who can offer her what you can't. Marriage and a family.'

Charlie's shoulders slumped.

'As I say, I'm sorry,' Mattie said in a softer tone. 'But it's too late...'

The dancers whirled around at the closing bars of the tune and Leo spun Francesca around him as they came to a stop.

Madge Turner, who lived three doors down from them, had kindly offered her upright piano so, earlier in the day, Charlie and his father had heaved it out of Madge's front room and into the street. As the fiddlers, who had been playing for an hour, indicated they were taking a break, Manny Cotton from number 7 opened the lid and struck up the opening bars of 'I'll be Loving You'.

The dancers took their place. As they stepped off, Leo slipped his arm around Francesca, ready to lead her into the waltz. Charlie swallowed the last of his pint.

'Too late, is it?' he said. 'Perhaps we should let Francesca decide.'

He handed his sister his empty glass and strode across the street.

Leo saw him coming and tried to guide Francesca away, but Charlie beat him to it and blocked him.

'You don't mind if I cut in, do you, Leo?' he said, taking Francesca's hand before the other man could answer.

Francesca's lovely dark eyes opened wide with surprise as his arm slipped around her. Savouring the feeling of her in his arms and the faint smell of lavender from her hair, Charlie stepped off and she followed his lead.

Over her head, he saw a couple of Tommy's chums walk up to Leo and point to his car, parked at the far end of the street out of the way of the festivities.

'Your Jo looks lovely,' she said, as he guided her over the cobbles.

'And happy,' said Charlie.

'And happy,' she agreed, as he guided her away from another couple.

'Plus, the sun came out,' she added. 'And all the spread was eaten.'

'A successful day,' Charlie agreed.

Seeing that Leo and half a dozen men were clustered around his vehicle in deep discussion, Charlie drew her closer.

He allowed himself the exquisite pleasure of holding Francesca against him unobserved for a couple more steps, then he spoke.

'Red always was your colour, Francesca,' he said softly, as they moved through a side-step.

'Thank you,' she replied.

'And you look absolutely beautiful,' he continued. 'You always have been beautiful, so beautiful.'

She turned and looked at him.

Gazing into her eyes, he drew her even closer. 'But stupid fool that I was, I didn't realise how beautiful you actually are, until now.'

Her eyes opened even wider as her lips parted. 'Charlie, what are you saying?'

'I'm saying I love you, Francesca,' he said. 'I love you so much—'

'Stop it.' She stopped dancing. 'Just stop it.'

'But, Francesca—'

She pushed herself away from him and walked quickly into the alleyway between his house and the one next door.

He dashed into the cool, dark passage after her.

'Francesca!' he called, his voice echoing around the space.

She carried on.

'Francesca. Please!'

She stopped. Pulling her shoulders back, she turned to face him.

He strode towards her and stopped.

She raised her head. Tears were shimmering on her lower lids as she gazed up at him.

They stared wordlessly at each other for a long moment, then, taking half a step nearer, Charlie took her into his arms.

She raised her hands and rested them lightly on his upper arms, sending love and desire pulsing through him. With his gaze locked with hers, Charlie drew her closer then, closing his eyes, he lowered his mouth onto hers.

There was a moment of hesitation then, with a small cry, Francesca's hands slid up and around his neck as she moulded herself into him.

As his lips touched hers, all the hundreds of dreams Francesca had ever had about this exact moment flooded into her mind.

He loved her. Charlie Brogan loved her. The man she'd loved, and whose children she ached to bear for so many years now, actually loved her.

With his strong arms tight around her and his hard chest pressing against her breasts, she gave herself up to the exquisite pleasure of the moment.

However, as his kiss deepened, and a new craving started to hum within her, another emotion burst through.

Tearing her lips from his, she shoved him away.

'You love me, do you?' she managed to utter.

'So much.'

He tried to take her in his arms again, but she moved aside.

'Why now? Why after all this time?'

He spread his hands.

'I don't know. I can't explain it,' he replied, giving her that quirky smile of his. 'I just do. I love you.'

Francesca balled her fists.

'Do you know how long I've loved you? Dreamt of you? Wanted you, Charlie Brogan?' she forced out between gritted teeth.

Staring blankly at her with his arms dangling at his side, Charlie didn't reply.

'For years, do you hear? Years,' she said, answering her own question. 'For as long as I can remember, I've loved you, Charlie. Loved you and had to watch you walk out with dozens of other girls on your arm while never giving me a second glance.'

He opened his mouth to speak.

'And then there was Stella,' Francesca cut in before he could. 'Stella! Who played you false from the first but who caught you with the oldest trick in the book.'

Anguish shot across Charlie's handsome face.

For a second Francesca's anger abated but then she thought of the countless nights she'd sobbed into her pillow over him marrying Stella and her eyes narrowed.

'And after all the pain and heartache, you have the bloody nerve to stand there and tell me you love me,' she said.

'I do,' Charlie replied, raking his fingers through his hair. 'I can't change the past but we—'

'There's no we, Charlie,' she cut in. Pain and fury boiled in her chest. 'There never can be, not now.'

'But, Francesca, I can't live without you,' he said.

'You'll learn to,' she replied. 'Like I did.'

Anguish distorted his handsome features for a moment, then he looked across the space between them for a long moment.

'Don't you love me any more, Francesca?' he asked softly, love blazing from his eyes.

The word yes burst up in her, but she bit it back.

He saw her hesitation and strode forward but, as he reached out for her, she raised the flat of her hand.

'Don't, Charlie,' she said, half hoping he would. 'You're married to Stella and I've met someone else and that's the end of it.' She squared her shoulders. 'Now, please let me pass so I can go and rejoin Leo.'

Charlie held her gaze for several heartbeats, then stepped back against the wall.

Raising her chin, Francesca walked back along the alleyway but, as she reached him, Charlie spoke again.

'I love you,' he whispered.

Before she could stop herself, Francesca turned and looked into Charlie's dark blue-grey eyes.

Captured in his gaze, the love for him that was almost part of her very being surged up in Francesca but, just as it threatened to overwhelm her, the ear-piercing wail of the air raid sirens sliced between them.

Their heads snapped around in the direction of the street party but, just as they moved forward, an explosion shook the ground. A pulse of air, carrying stones and grit, surged down the narrow alleyway.

Grabbing her, Charlie pressed her against the wall and, with his head tucked into her shoulder, he shielded her from the blast. There was a pause of absolute silence, then screaming filled the air.

Staggering to her feet, her hearing muffled by the blast, Francesca, with Charlie a step behind, dashed back into the street.

The scene before them was devastation. Chairs had been blasted the length of the street and nearly all the windows now lay shattered on the pavements, leaving only transparent nets floating in the gaping holes. The piano had been upended onto its back, its brass pedals pointing skyward.

The barrel of beer had been blown off the trestle table and was spouting frothy streams of amber upwards. Dogs were dashing up and down between the injured guests, barking in panic and confusion as people scrambled slowly to their feet.

Francesca's eyes went to Mattie, who was sitting on the kerb, puffed cheeks and blowing hard as Queenie held her hand, leaving Cathy to care for a frightened-looking Peter and Alicia. Tommy and Daniel, along with the groom's army chums, were helping people to their feet while Jo, still in her bridal gown, and her ambulance colleagues were assessing the casualties.

However, although the street was littered with shattered glass and crockery and some people were holding their heads in a daze, mercifully, the houses on both sides of the street were still standing. Behind the corner shop at the end of the street an ominous pool of black smoke spiralled upwards, showing them just how lucky they'd been.

'Francesca!'

She looked around to see Leo racing towards her. He smothered her in his embrace. 'I was so afraid—'

'I'm fine,' shouted Francesca over the incessant wailing of the siren as she disentangled herself from him.

Her eyes met Charlie's briefly before she looked away. 'We ought to—'

'Charlie! Charlie! Quick.'

Francesca looked around as Michael skidded to a halt in front of them.

'Come quick,' he said, grabbing Charlie's arm. 'Auntie Ida's been hit and won't get up.'

His father, who'd been sitting with his elbows on his knees and his head in his hands for the past thirty minutes, raised his head as the door to St George's children's hospital's outpatient department opened.

A nurse wearing a candy-striped pink uniform, starched apron and frilly hat walked out and sped along the corridor towards the main part of the hospital.

Jerimiah slumped back in the chair, as did those in the waiting area around him.

'Don't worry, Dad,' Charlie said, placing a hand on his father's beefy forearm. 'I'm sure Mum'll be fine.'

Jerimiah gave him a weary smile. 'I hope to God she is, son.'

Charlie had found his mother cradled in his father's arms at the other end of the street. A plywood board advertising *Brimo* that had been ripped from the shop's wall by the blast had landed on her, knocking her to the ground.

By the time he'd reached them, his mother had regained consciousness but she'd looked so deathly white that the ambulance crew, who'd arrived a few minutes after the all-clear sounded, felt she should go with the other casualties to be checked out by the doctors. Mattie, too, was taken to see the doctor; not because she was injured but because her waters had broken with the force of the explosion. She'd gone off with Daniel to the lying-in hospital, leaving Alicia with Queenie and Cathy.

Thankfully, other than a couple of perforated ear drums, Mafeking Terrace's casualties were mainly bumps, bruises and cuts from flying glass. That's why they'd been shipped off to the dressing station at the children's hospital half a mile away and not to the London where the survivors of the direct hit in Elm Row had been ferried off to.

The bomb that had brought an abrupt end to Jo and Tommy's party had been dropped by a Luftwaffe bomber squadron who, having dumped most of their load over the west of London, were returning to their base.

After checking that the rest of the family were more or less whole, Charlie had left Patrick with his grandmother and accompanied his father to hospital.

That was an hour and a half ago and they'd been waiting for news about Ida's condition impatiently ever since.

With a heavy sigh, his father resumed his position.

Stretching out his legs and crossing them at the ankle, Charlie put his hands behind his head and rested back in the chair, staring at the wall opposite. Its grubby grey colour almost perfectly reflected his life.

A squeaky trolley rolled past with an elderly porter behind it and then a couple of nurses walked by in the opposite direction. The large clock above the door ticked off the minutes but, as the red second hand started another pass, the door opened and a doctor walked out.

'Mr Brogan,' he enquired, looking over the collection of people dotted around the waiting area.

Jerimiah sprung up and Charlie also rose to his feet.

The doctor smiled and walked over.

'Good afternoon, Mr Brogan. I'm Dr Collins. I've just examined your wife and I'm happy to tell you that other than a bruise the size of your hand on her buttock where she landed on the kerb and despite having the wind knocked out of her by the flying board, she will be perfectly fine in a couple of days.'

'Praise Mary.' His father crossed himself and Charlie did the same.

'I'm going to keep her in overnight, just to be sure, but I see no reason why you won't be able to collect her tomorrow at midday after I've done my morning rounds and – ' the doctor beamed at them – 'I'm delighted to tell you that the baby she's carrying is fine.'

Chapter twenty-five

REACHING UP ONTO tiptoes, Francesca put the last pile of plates on the top shelf of the dresser.

'Is that the lot?' she asked, turning to Cathy, who was still at the sink.

'I think so,' she replied, wringing out the pair of Jerimiah's old underpants that served as a dishcloth. 'And thank you for staying to help tidy up.'

'That's all right,' Francesca replied. 'You'd have been a bit short-handed if I hadn't.'

It was now just before seven and three hours since the bomb had gone off and, as always, people had pitched in to get things straight. Tommy and his mates from the unit had helped hammer temporary boards up at the windows to keep the houses secure until the glaziers could fix them. They'd now gone around to Elm Row to give a hand, leaving the neighbours to wield their yard brooms to clear splintered glass from the footpath.

As always, following in the wake of an explosion, the Heavy Rescue service came with the WVS, bringing one of their mobile canteens, this time in the back of a converted Morris van complete with a fold-out counter, a five-quart urn and a tray of sticky buns. So, neighbours and wedding guests alike were soon supping mugs of hot sweet tea while they cleared up the street.

Queenie had taken charge of the three toddlers while Fran and Cathy had divided the leftover food into what could go to the hens and what needed to go into the pigs' bucket for collection. After which they'd gathered together any crockery and glasses that hadn't been smashed to smithereens and had spent the last three-quarters of an hour washing everything up.

Tucking the ragged cloth behind the tap, Cathy frowned. 'I hope Mum's all right.'

Crossing the kitchen, Francesca put her arm around her shoulders. 'I'm sure she is.'

Cathy gave her a tight smile and looked up at the clock on the dresser. 'I thought Charlie would be back by now.'

Francesca's heart started to do a little dance, but she cut it short.

'I ought to go and see if Leo's all right,' she said.

Leaving Cathy to put away the last few things, Francesca walked through to the parlour.

Leo was sitting in one of the chairs by the fire with Queenie opposite him in the other. Prince Albert was perched on the back of Queenie's chair, and Patrick, Alicia and Peter were playing on the hearth with some of Billy and Michael's wooden soldiers.

Putting down the cup of tea she'd fetched him half an hour ago, Leo stood up as Francesca walked in.

'I'm sorry I've been so long,' she said.

'That's all right,' he said, relief flooding across his face. 'Mrs Brogan Senior has been keeping me entertained with her wonderful stories of when she was a girl in Ireland.'

The hall door opened, and Jo walked in. Cathy had helped her out of her wedding dress a little while back and she was now wearing her royal-blue going-away suit. Behind her was Tommy, who, as it was his wedding day, had been sent home by his mates and was carrying a suitcase.

'All ready for the off then?' said Cathy, walking in from the kitchen and sitting on the sofa under the window.

'We are,' said Jo. 'But we can't go until I know Mum's all right. I thought Charlie might have been back by—'

The kitchen door opened.

Francesca turned and found Charlie had come into the room right behind her.

Her heart crashed in her chest as she gazed wordlessly up at him, his words and kiss filling her mind.

Love and longing flickered in his eyes for an instant, then Jo's voice cut between them.

'How's Mum?'

'She's all right, isn't she?' added Cathy.

Charlie's love-filled eyes shifted from Francesca to his sisters behind her.

'Yes, she's fine,' he said, giving them a reassuring smile. 'Just winded and battered and bruised, that'll all. They're keeping her in overnight, but doc said she can come home tomorrow.'

Seeing his father, Patrick shoved his bottom in the air, stood up and toddled over.

'Thank God,' said Cathy, with a heavy sigh.

'Dad's staying with her for a bit and he'll tell you about…he'll tell you the rest when he gets back,' said Charlie, lifting his son up. 'Any news on Mattie?'

'Not yet,' said Queenie. 'Sure but won't Daniel be hot-footing it around to us the moment the hospital calls.'

Jo slipped her arm through her new husband's. 'Well, this will be a wedding to remember, won't it?'

'I'll say.' Tommy kissed her on the head. 'Perhaps now we know your mum's fine and dandy we can go on our honeymoon?'

Jo laughed. Snatching up her bouquet of artificial flowers from the sideboard, she let Tommy lead her towards the front door. Queenie and Cathy moved after them.

Leo sidled over. Putting himself between her and Charlie, he slipped his arm around Francesca's waist.

'Perhaps once we've seen the happy couple off we should go too, *mia cara*,' he said.

Francesca looked up at him and, with Charlie's face in the edge of her vision, she nodded.

'Yes, let's,' she replied, forcing a bright smile.

He squeezed her and they too followed the newly married couple out into the street. The neighbours were still hard at it sweeping up glass, removing broken chairs and boarding windows, but they stopped mid-task as Jo and Tommy emerged from the house.

After kissing her sister and gran, Jo, clutching her bouquet, turned to Francesca.

'Congratulations, Jo,' said Francesca, hugging her.

'Thanks, Fran,' the new bride replied, giving her a peck on the cheek. 'And who knows? It might be you next.'

Francesca felt her cheeks grow warm.

Her eyes darted to Leo, who was shaking Tommy's hand.

Jo hurried past her and threw herself in her brother's arms as he stepped out of the house.

'Charlie!'

He hugged her. She gave Patrick a kiss, then broke free and hurried to Tommy's side.

Arm in arm, and waving to their family and neighbours, they set off up the street. Taking her hand, Leo led Fran forward to join the procession but, after a few steps, Jo stopped and held up her bouquet.

Several young girls from neighbouring houses rushed forward.

'Throw it!' they shouted.

Letting go of Tommy's arm, Jo scanned the crowd of women. Spotting Francesca, a grin spread across her face.

She turned. Swinging the bunch of flowers in her hand, she pitched the bouquet over her head but, seconds before she released it, the heel of her shoe caught between the cobbles and she slipped sideward.

The bouquet went sailing over the outstretched arms of the eager young women and straight towards Charlie. He grabbed it with his free hand.

Everyone laughed except Charlie who, with love and longing in his eyes, stared across at Francesca, who held his gaze for a couple of heartbeats before Charlie tossed the bouquet back into the bevy of girls.

Francesca turned away and hugged Leo's arm.

'Yes,' she said, looking up at him.

'Yes?'

'Yes, Leo,' Francesca said, giving him her brightest smile. 'I will marry you.'

His brown eyes studied her face for a moment, then he threw his arms around her. Francesca pressed her face against his shoulder.

Unable to stop herself, her gaze returned to Charlie, standing with Patrick in his arms.

His eyes, filled with grief, locked with hers for a moment then he turned and went back into the house.

'*Mia cara*,' Leo whispered. 'You have made me the happiest of men.'

He released her and frowned.

'Don't weep, my angel,' he said, pulling a pristine handkerchief from his pocket and offering it to her. 'You're supposed to be happy.'

'I am, Leo,' she sobbed, as tears gushed down her cheeks. 'I am.'

'So, Mr Fabrino,' said Leo, holding Francesca's hand tightly in his as they stood side by side facing her father. 'I know I should have asked your permission before asking your daughter to marry me, but I just couldn't help myself.' He turned and looked down at her. 'And she has made me the happiest man in the world by saying yes.'

Francesca gave him her brightest smile then looked across the cafe's back parlour at her father.

Enrico, who was dressed in his pyjamas, dressing gown and slippers, had been, until five minutes ago, drinking his evening cocoa and listening to the Halle Orchestra on the wireless. Now he stared across at them.

'I know it's rather sudden, Papa, but—'

'Never mind about that,' her father said.

Springing to his feet, Enrico rushed over. He threw his arms around her and kissed her on both cheeks.

'You're getting married, that's all that matters. And to Leo.' Holding her face between his work-roughened hands, his eyes danced with happiness. 'My clever little girl.'

He kissed her again, then turned to Leo. Her father offered his hand. 'Congratulations, son.'

'Thank you,' said Leo, shaking her father's hand. 'As I said, I would have asked you but—'

'This is 1942 not 1842,' her father said.

Leo slipped his arm around Francesca's waist and drew her to him.

'I just couldn't let so perfect a prize get away,' said Leo.

He pressed his lips onto her forehead and, although not sure she liked to be regarded as some sort of trophy, Francesca smiled up at him.

'Well, this calls for something a little stronger than cocoa,' said her father, striding over to the sideboard. He picked up his prized bottle of Fernet-Branca.

Pouring a generous measure into three glasses, he returned to where they were standing and handed one to each of them.

'To marriage,' he said, raising his glass.

'To love,' said Leo, looking adoringly at her as he held his drink high.

Francesca took a sip while Leo and her father swallowed a full mouthful.

'So when?' said her father, indicating the sofa as he resumed his seat by the fire.

'Leo only asked me this evening, Papa,' said Francesca, tucking her skirt under her as she sat down. 'So we haven't had time to think—'

'I thought the end of July,' Leo cut in.

'So soon?' said Francesca.

Leo gave her an indulgent smile and then turned back to her father. 'Unless your son is home on leave before? In which case, we could make it sooner.'

Sooner? How soon?

An image of Leo slipping a ring on her finger loomed into Francesca's mind, setting panic fluttering in her chest.

She damped it down and smiled brightly. 'I'll write to Giovanni tomorrow with the good news.'

Swilling his liquor around in his glass, her father gulped the last of it down and then rose to his feet.

After finishing the last of his drink, Leo did the same.

'It's getting late, Mr Fabrino,' he said, setting his glass on the occasional table. 'And I should be on my way before the Hun come calling.'

'I hope you will come to dinner tomorrow,' said her father, as he got out of his chair.

'It will be my pleasure,' said Leo, putting put his arm around Fran's waist.

Her father's gaze shifted from Leo to her and back again.

'I'll say goodnight then,' he said, placing his empty glass back on the sideboard.

'And to you,' said Leo.

Her father nodded and, as the Luftwaffe had visited them almost nightly for the past three weeks, he made his way towards their basement shelter beneath the cafe.

As her father disappeared through the door, Leo's arms wound around her.

'Oh, Francesca, my love,' he whispered.

She slid her arms around him but, as she did, the memory of running her fingers over the hard contours of Charlie's body filled her senses. Forcing it away, she tilted her face up to Leo's, inviting him to kiss her.

He accepted and pressed his lips onto hers.

Holding him close, Francesca concentrated on the man in her arms. Leo. The man she'd agreed to marry not two hours before. She willed him to blot out the feel, taste and yearning for Charlie that his kiss had ignited.

Sensing her heightened emotions, Leo's hands ran up and down her back as he crushed her to him.

'Say you love me, Francesca,' he murmured, between kisses. 'Say you love me as much as I love you.'

'Leo, I…' she whispered, gathering the words into her throat. 'I—'

The shriek of the air raid siren situated on top of the East London district sorting office opposite filled Francesca's ears.

'Francesca!' her father shouted up from their shelter below.

Leo released her.

'Coming, Papa,' she shouted back.

The nerve-jangling wail of the siren stopped.

They waited for a moment. The all-clear didn't sound so Francesca took Leo's hand to guide him to safety below, but he held back.

'It's all right,' he said. 'It's the first warning. If I put my foot down, I can get through the city before they hit my end of town.'

Taking his car keys out of his pocket, he strode across to the door. Francesca followed.

Francesca opened the rear entrance to the cafe as the last few rays of the mid-summer's evening streaked across the sky.

Stepping out, Leo paused on the step.

'Good night, *mia cara*,' he said. 'My darling fiancée.'

Kissing her lightly on the lips, Leo dashed to his car and jumped in. It roared into life and he sped away as the second warning pierced the still evening.

'Francesca! Quick!' bellowed her father.

'Coming!'

Shutting the door, Francesca dashed across the room. She reached the stairs to the cellar as the first explosion rocked the floor and sent the cups in the cafe jingling in their trays.

Closing the door behind her, she hurried down the stone steps to their refuge beneath the cafe. Her father was already tucked into his truckle bed on his side of the curtain that they'd draped over a washing line down the middle of the cellar. Next to him on an orange crate was a hurricane lamp, a Thermos flask and an alarm clock and he cradled a steaming enamel mug between his hands.

'Where's Leo?' he asked, as she stepped off the last step.

'He decided to drive back to the Dorchester,' Francesca replied.

'I've put your Ovaltine beside your bed,' he said.

'Thanks, Papa.'

Francesca went behind the curtain into her section of the shelter. As she drank her milky drink, she changed out of her best suit and, after hanging her outfit on a nail in an overhead beam, put on her loose-fitting pale-blue siren suit. Francesca drained her mug then climbed into her two-foot-wide camp bed just as another bomb landed somewhere close by, sending grit pitter-pattering down onto the candlewick cover.

'Are you in?' asked her father.

'As snug as a bug in a rug,' she replied.

She heard her father shuffle about, then the light went out as another explosion rocked their underground dormitory.

Snuggling under the cover, Francesca stared up into the pitch black of the cellar.

The faint pop, pop, pop of the ack-ack guns in Barmy Park half a mile away sounded for a second or two before another collection of German munitions struck the ground.

In the dark, her father chuckled. 'You know, in all the excitement I forgot to ask you how the wedding went.'

'It was a lovely day,' said Francesca, as she thought of the laughing bride and proud groom in the midst of their happy family. 'And...'

With the Luftwaffe dropping death from the sky all around them, Francesca told her father about Jo and Tommy's ceremony, Jerimiah's speech, what the spread was like, the bomb cutting short the proceedings, Mattie going into labour.

'And on top of that,' he said, when she'd finished, 'you and Leo got engaged.'

'We did.'

Her father gave another chuckle. 'Well, it's a day you'll never forget, that's for sure.'

'You're right, Papa,' Francesca replied, as the earth around her shuddered again.

Reaching up, Francesca ran her fingers lightly over her lips.

No, she would never forget the day that Charlie Brogan at long last told her he loved her, and she agreed to marry another man.

Chapter twenty-six

THE CRYSTAL CHANDELIERS of The Ritz's dining room jangled above her as another bomb found its target somewhere close by. Stella swallowed the last portion of her pudding and then placed her spoon on the dessert plate.

Opening her evening bag, she took out a gold cigarette case.

'Pearl?' she asked, opening it and offering it to the woman sitting beside her.

'Ta,' Pearl replied, taking a cigarette.

'A Chesterfield,' she said.

'Naturally,' said Donny, who was sitting on the other side of Stella. 'Only the best is good enough for my gal.'

He squeezed Stella's knee. She gave him a wrinkled-nosed smile then, leaning across the empty plates and half-drunk glasses, she offered the open cigarette case to the man opposite.

'What about you, Mr Stamp?' she asked.

'I think Mr Stamp might prefer one of these, babe,' said Donny.

Reaching inside his jacket, he pulled out a leather cigar case. Flipping back the flap, he took one for himself then offered Lenny Stamp one of the remaining six-inch Corona Havanas.

It was close to midnight and they were sitting in a booth in The Ritz's downstairs dining room and had just finished eating. Well she, Pearl and Donny had, but as Lenny had ordered both ice cream and trifle, he was still munching his way noisily through his double portion.

Despite the air raid that had been going since they'd arrived an hour ago, the restaurant was crammed with women in shimmering evening gowns and men in tuxedos, along with a goodly portion of American brigades, major colonels and five-star generals. There was also the odd flash of royal blue, the colour of the US Airforce.

Donny was also in uniform and, not to be outdone by service personnel, Lenny had put on his best bib and tucker, which comprised of a satin-lapelled dinner suit and red waistcoat with a massive gold fob chain strung across his paunch.

In his middle to late forties, Lenny Stamp was the undisputed top guv'nor of East London and his territory ran from Whitechapel in the west to the leafy suburbs of East Ham and Manor Park in the east.

Like everyone else east of the Aldgate pump, Stella knew Lenny by sight but had never sat across the table from him socially before and, given the way he shovelled food in his gob, she wouldn't be keen to do so again anytime soon. But this was business.

'Don't mind if I do,' said Lenny, taking the case from Donny.

After selecting a fat cigar, he went to hand it back, but Donny held up his hand. 'Keep it, Mr Stamp. I've got crates of them back at the store.'

Although he tried not to look it, Lenny was obviously impressed.

Biting off the end, he spat it on the floor. Donny offered him a light from his personalised Ronson, then lit his own.

Lenny shoved the case of cigars into his inside pocket and smiled, revealing a set of widely spaced, tobacco-stained teeth.

'We're all friends here,' he said, puffing out smoke. 'So it's Lenny.'

'Well, Lenny,' drawled Donny, 'what say we get these charming young ladies here another bottle of bubbly to enjoy while I buy you a double shot of brandy at the bar?'

Pushing their chairs back, Donny and Lenny stood up.

A waiter hovering nearby shot over.

'Another one of these,' Donny said, indicating the upturned bottle in the chrome bucket beside him.

The waiter bowed and hurried away.

'Ladies,' said Donny, giving a little bow before he and Lenny, both puffing cigars, strolled across the floor to the sleek ebony bar on the other side of the dancefloor.

The waiter returned and popped the cork. He refreshed their glasses as another waiter cleared away the empty bottle, used plates and dirty glasses.

The band finished the number with a brass fanfare and the dancers clapped as they milled around the floor waiting for the next number. The conductor raised his baton and the dancers took their places again as the strains of a long violin chord sounded out.

Pearl flicked her ash into the fresh ashtray that had just been placed there.

'Nice colour,' said Stella, indicating the other woman's nail vanish.

'Hot Tango. Had them done to match my dress,' Pearl said, placing them on the skirt of her beaded orange cocktail dress to illustrate the point.

'Nice.' Stella held up her hand. 'Wicked Red.'

'Suits you,' said Pearl. 'And the frock.'

'A present from Donny,' Stella said, smoothing her fingers across the boned bodice of her strapless black velvet evening dress.

Pearl smirked. 'Did you wear it to Ida's girl's wedding last week?'

'I wish I had,' said Stella. 'Just to see that doddery old fart Father Mahon's face but, oddly, I wasn't invited.'

'Me neither,' said Pearl. 'Not that I would have gone if I had. I've got better things to do than waste my Saturday watching a bunch of bloody bog-trotters jigging about to a fiddle.'

'Too right,' agreed Stella.

Pearl gave her a speculative look. 'What about you and Charlie?'

'What about me and Charlie?'

'I know he's my own flesh and blood, Stella, but he can't just walk out on you. You're his wife when all's said and done,' said Pearl.

'Well, he seems to have forgotten that,' Stella replied. 'And it's not my fault. I've tried to talk him around, but he just keeps telling me it's over.' She took a sip of drink. 'Anyway, Charlie's lost his chance now cos I'm with Donny.'

'He seems like he's got his head screwed on the right way,' said Pearl.

'He has,' agreed Stella. 'And that's why, unlike Charlie who went on something alarming when he found out, Donny isn't bothered a jot that men ogle me because I'm an exotic dancer.' Picking up her glass, she swallowed a mouthful of champagne. 'It's just a job.'

'And part of the war effort,' added Pearl. 'To cheer up the troops.'

'Exactly,' Stella agreed. She raised her glass. 'To the war effort.'

'To the war effort,' Pearl repeated.

She took a swig of her drink and Stella did the same.

'Oh, by the way,' said Stella, as the champagne bubbles tingled down her throat. 'You've heard about Ida, haven't you?'

'What about Ida?'

'That she's up the duff again,' Stella replied.

Pearl's mascara-ed eyes stretched wide. 'What, at 'er age?'

'Apparently, she thought she was going through the change,' said Stella. 'But instead she's five months' gone.'

Pearl rolled her eyes.

'Ain't that bloody typical.' She stubbed her cigarette out in the crystal ashtray. 'She and that old he-goat of hers ought to be ashamed of themselves, and at their age, too.'

Taking a fresh cigarette from the pack, she lit it then glanced across at the bar where Donny and Len were deep in conversation.

Her eyes returned to Stella and a sweet smile lifted the corner of her painted lips.

'Never mind about my sister and her bloody Paddy husband.' Picking up her glass of champagne. 'To better days.'

Stella raised her drink.

'And rich ones,' she replied, tapping Pearl's glass with hers.

Chapter twenty-seven

TAKING HIS PENCIL from behind his ear, Donny ticked off the consignment of Lucky Strike cigarettes from the list on his clipboard.

'Stack them next to the crate of candies over there,' he said, pointing to the only free space in the warehouse.

'Yes, Sergeant,' the private from the US transport corps replied.

Putting his foot on the axle to get the trolley rolling again, the regular, a thick-set individual with no visible neck, wheeled the four boxes across the storeroom.

'It's a bit of a tight squeeze, Sergeant,' he called across as he offloaded the boxes. 'I ain't too sure I'll be able to get them all in.'

'Don't worry,' shouted Donny, ticking off the box of biscuits. 'Just move those two boxes of nylons and slide them beside the candies.'

The guy was right.

With truckloads of goods from the central PX depot arriving every other day, the storage area was full to bursting but it wouldn't be for long as Lenny's crew would be dropping by tomorrow after the blackout.

'Beats me what GIs want with so many pairs of stockings,' said the private as he heaved a box marked fifteen denier size seven American Tan onto a box of shoe polish.

Donny laughed. 'Then you're in the wrong army, fella. And don't stomp your army-issue size tens over the vanilla wafer cookies. The grunts want to dunk them in their coffee not sprinkle them.'

The private touched his fatigue cap again, then rolled his empty trolley towards the loading bay, passing his mate who was bringing in six crates of Coca-Cola, bottles jingling as the wheels rolled over the flagstone yard.

Leaving them to unload the rest of the order, Donny returned to his office to get on with the paperwork. Taking a cigar from the box on the desk, he bit off the end and lit one, but just as he inhaled his first lungful of sweet Havana, he spotted a stout individual strolling through the back gate. A peaked cap with a yellow badge was balanced on his head and there were three striped chevrons on the upper arm of the uniform jacket he was squeezed into.

Goddamn it!

Resting his cigar on the New York Yankees ashtray at his elbow, Donny stood up and, pulling down the front of his uniform, walked back into the storage room.

'Well, as I live and breathe,' he said, sticking a friendly smile on his face. 'Eli Moffit.'

Master Sergeant Elijah Forrester Lee Moffit III was somewhere around Donny's height but probably weighed double his one hundred and forty pounds. With a full head of corn-coloured hair and over-large lips, you could be forgiven for thinking he was some big, dumb hick. Woe betide you if you did.

Eli came from an old Southern family. It was rumoured that the Moffits went from share-croppers to mill owners in two generations and, if Eli was cut from the same cloth as his ancestors, Donny could believe it.

He had first met him some five years before and had been trying to avoid him ever since. However, thanks to the damn Japs, that was now impossible as Eli was master sergeant in charge of The Army Exchange Service Overseas Central Stores in Hampshire, through which all the goods for the GIs were distributed.

'Well now, if it isn't my old pal Donny Muller,' Eli replied, a sardonic look in his pale-grey eyes.

'Come,' said Donny, indicating his office.

Eli waddled in and Donny followed him, shutting the door behind him.

'Make yourself at home,' said Donny, picking up the bottle of bourbon and two glasses from the filing cabinet.

'Don't mind if I do,' Eli replied, the chair creaking as it took his weight.

Donny placed the glasses on the desk and half-filled them.

Taking off his cap, Eli dropped it on the desk, then clasped one of the glasses in his sausage-like fingers.

Donny offered him a cigar, which Eli declined, so Donny picked up his and took a long drag, hoping it would steady his nerves.

'Nice little place you've got for yourself here,' Eli said, scanning his piggy eyes over the Regency architraves above. 'Bit olde-worlde, but nice.'

'I can't complain,' said Donny, blowing a thick cloud of cigar smoke upwards.

'I heard tell that the king and queen live just a stroll away,' continued the master sergeant.

'Across the park,' Donny said, as he resumed his seat. 'But they ain't come calling yet.' He took a sip of his drink. 'So, Eli, what brings you to this neck of the woods?'

Gulping down a mouthful of bourbon, the master sergeant smacked his loose lips.

'Well now, I'd like to say I just dropped by to say howdy, but you know the top brass have been reorganising the whole damn PX,' Eli said, swilling the amber liquid around.

'I have heard.'

'Well, now the good-for-nothing bean-counters at Central have asked me to get the books straight before the new system gets going, just to make sure everything is as it should be.' Eli chuckled. 'Do you know, Donny, the dandiest thing is, I found that the GIs who get their home comforts at your PX here are buying twice as much as at any of the other public exchanges in the whole country.'

Donny forced a nonchalant smile.

'Well, that's hardly a surprise given we've got half of the US Army billeted here in Piccadilly,' he replied. 'I tell you, those boys spend their dough as fast as old Uncle Sam puts it in their pocket.'

'And that is the most likely explanation and I might just tell the top brass that, too,' said Eli, swilling his drink around some more.

Donny's mouth pulled into a straight line. 'Might?'

'Yes, might! Because, see here, I weren't found under the briar patch yesterday and I can smell a fiddle a mile off, and phewy...' He drew a noisy breath through his nose. 'Am I smelling one now.'

Stifling the urge to reach across the desk and rip Eli's fat throat out with his bare hands, Donny chewed his lip for a moment.

'How much?'

'Twenty per cent.'

'Ten,' Donny said, more out of principle than any real hope.

'Twenty.' A sly smile lifted Eli's fleshy face. 'And the way I see it, you ain't got no choice, pal. It's pay me or it's the army's ice house.'

Donny glared at him for a moment, then gave a sharp nod.

The fat master sergeant sat back. 'Good. I'll let you know when and how.'

Knocking back his drink, Donny stood up. 'If we're done—'

'Now hold up there, there's one other thing,' interrupted Eli. 'Just to seal our little understanding, I'd like you to do me a favour.'

'What?'

A venal expression spread across Eli's pudgy face.

'That little stripper gal of yours,' he drawled.

'What about her?'

'I saw her on stage a few weeks back and it's given me a bit of a hankering for her,' Eli replied. 'I want you to persuade your little dolly with the big bazooms to be friendly to me. Just for a night, that's all, and you can have her back after.'

'And if she won't?'

A brutal expression replaced Eli's congenial one. 'Then she'll find herself having to look for some other GI to get her nylons from, won't she?'

Knocking back the last of his drinks, the master sergeant heaved himself out of the chair and stood up.

'Good doing business with you, Donny,' he said, putting the empty glass on the desk. 'I'll be seeing you around.' And with a mocking look, Eli lumbered out.

Raging at having nigh on a third of his hard-earned profits skimmed by that shyster lump of lard, Donny watched him go. He swallowed what remained of his drink and then, scoring the polished wood with the force, slammed his glass on the desk.

Letting out a long groan, Donny thrust into her, then his head flopped onto Stella's shoulder. She lay there for a moment under his sweaty body before shifting slightly to ease his weight.

Donny rolled off her and stood up.

A bomb landed somewhere to the north of them, setting the glass ceiling light in Donny's room jumping on its plaited flex.

The warning sirens had gone off as she'd joined Donny at the bar after her last slot some two hours ago and had been going ever since. Although she didn't read the papers as they were just full of war stuff, she couldn't help but catch whispers of how the Germans, having been sent packing by the Russians, were turning their attention back to Britain.

Stella guessed they were right as, since Whitsun week, there had been an air raid almost every night, which played havoc with her act: it wasn't easy to dance with the stage shifting about under your feet.

Taking the packet of cigarettes from the bedside table, Donny pulled one out with his teeth and, after lighting it, threw the packet on the bed. He ambled over to the window.

Resting his arm on the window frame, he stared out at the searchlights criss-crossing the cloudless sky as ack-ack shells exploded in little dots of light in the ink-black sky.

Holding the sheet around her breasts, Stella wriggled up the bed and rested back against the padded headboard.

Another bomb found its target a few streets over, illuminating the eastern sky and Donny's naked body with a yellow and orange glow.

Taking the discarded pack of Lucky Strikes, she lit one. Inhaling deeply, she studied his muscular back for a moment. A fire engine, bell clanging wildly, screeched by.

'Are you going to tell me what's been eating you all night or what?' she asked, blowing smoke out of the side of her mouth.

He didn't answer but went to the dresser, poured them both a bourbon, then walked back to the bed.

He handed her one. First taking a large slug, Donny then gulped it down.

'I've got a problem,' he said.

'What sort of problem?'

'A problem called Eli Moffit,' Donny replied. 'Elijah Forrester Lee Moffit III, to be precise.'

'And who's he when he's at home?' Stella asked, as Donny perched on the window sill.

'Master sergeant in charge of Stores at the main depot in Hampshire,' he replied. 'And a right piece of shit, too. Strolled in today…'

He filled her in about Moffit's visit to the Curzon Street PX that morning.

Stella looked at him in utter disbelief.

'And you're going to give the bugger twenty per cent!' Stella said, hardly believing her ears. 'Twenty pigging per cent?'

'I don't like it but what Goddamn choice do I have?' shouted Donny. 'He only has to whisper in the colonel's ear and it'll be goodbye to my swell Manhattan club when I get back State-side and hello to a twenty-year stretch in Fort Leavenworth.'

Stella took another drag of her cigarette. 'I suppose we should be grateful he didn't want anything more.'

Donny gave her a shifty look.

'What?'

'He wants you for a night,' he said.

'Well, I hope you told him to go whistle for it,' Stella said, tapping her ash into the ashtray.

Donny didn't reply.

Stella glared at him but, with the ack-ack guns in Green Park peppering the sky behind him, Donny's pale-blue eyes held her gaze.

'You haven't got a choice either, not if you –' he jabbed his finger at her – 'want to keep getting your cut each week.'

'And what if I don't?' she asked.

'Then I'm in the slammer and you're back to turning tricks with punters from the club to earn an extra few quid each week,' Donny told her. 'Now, don't take on like you're some virgin or something. I know you've done it with others for less.'

Stella gave him a filthy look. Hugging her sheet around her, she fixed her eyes on the wall opposite.

Another bomb rocked the building. When the noise died away, Donny spoke again.

'Look, babe, if he fancied me, I'd have to get in the sack with him but he doesn't, it's you he has a hankering for. And what red-blooded man wouldn't?'

Stella looked at Donny. His lips lifted on one side and he gave her an ingratiating smile.

Her mouth softened slightly.

'This is business,' he added, giving her a pleading look. 'Pure and simple.'

'One night?' she asked.

'Just the one,' Donny assured her. 'And I'll tell you what, to show my appreciation, what say I take you down to one of those fancy jewellers off St James's and treat you to some earrings or something.'

Stella studied him for a second or two. Taking out a Lucky Strike, she lit it from her spent cigarette butt.

'All right,' said Stella, grinding the stub into the ashtray.

Donny's shoulders relaxed as relief flashed across his face.

Leaving his perch on the window sill, Donny crossed the floor to sit on the bed next to her. He went to take her in his arms, but she held him off.

'One night and make sure he's got a pack of French letters with him.'

'I will, babe.'

Donny took her in his arms and Stella didn't resist. Ripping away the sheet, his eyes roamed over her for a moment or two, then he pressed her back onto the bed. Arching over her on his elbow, he kissed her. He spread her legs with his, then rolled between them.

Stella slid her hands up his arms and around his neck, feeling the soft hair under her fingers as they ran over his shoulders.

In the red glow of the burning buildings on the horizon, she looked up at him.

He smiled. 'You haven't asked me what he looks like.'

As another bomb sent a flash of red and yellow across the sky, Stella shrugged. 'What does it matter? It's just business.'

With the first spots of rain leaving dark splodges on the pram's cover, Cathy pushed open the back door and guided the front wheels through it.

The kitchen was exactly how she'd left it except that her mother-in-law's used cup was on the draining board and the biscuit tin was on the table instead of the shelf above.

Manoeuvring the pram parallel to the kitchen dresser, Cathy snapped off the canvas cover and, unfastening her son, lifted him out.

'You're back then,' said Violet, walking through from the lounge as Cathy set Peter on the floor.

'Go and play with teddy, Peter, while Mummy makes some sarnies,' said Cathy, placing her basket on the table.

Her son toddled off into the lounge. Cathy took off her jacket and hooked it on the back door, then started unpacking her shopping bag. She pulled out a pack of powdered milk with the American flag on the packet, two tins of soup and half a pound of Mazawattee special blend, the family's two-weekly tea ration.

'You know I don't like that,' her mother-in-law moaned as she set a tin of corned beef on the table.

Cathy didn't reply.

In the weeks since Stan left with a black eye, split lip and throbbing headache courtesy of her gran, Cathy had kept her responses to her mother-in-law to the minimum. In fact, when she joined her mother in the shelter some nights, she gave herself a little pat on the back for not having exchanged one word with the hateful woman all day long.

Diving back in the wicket basket, Cathy pulled out a still-warm loaf she'd just bought from the baker's. However, as she did, a pink-striped paper bag fell out, open, on the table.

Her mother-in-law's gaze shifted to the packet of Dr White's for a second, then back to Cathy.

'You having your monthlies?' asked Violet.

'Yes,' said Cathy. 'Not that it's any of your business, but I came on this morning.'

Her mother-in-law's expression soured further.

'I thought perhaps my Stan left you in the family way,' said Violet.

'Well, he didn't,' Cathy replied.

Thank God, she thought.

She had been, in fact, two weeks overdue and had all but wept with relief when she'd found blood on her knickers after an early-morning visit to the shelter's bogs. As much as she'd always dreamt of a large family, the thought of having one of Stan's seeds take root in her made Cathy want to vomit.

'It seems even at her age, your mother can do her duty by her husband, but you're too selfish,' continued Violet, her thin mouth turned down.

Ignoring her, Cathy pulled out the breadboard and knife. Unwrapping the bread, she cut off the crust.

'I never wanted my Stan to marry you,' said Violet, as Cathy cut a thin slice for Peter. 'I told him, time and time again, "You're too good for the likes of her."' Her mother-in-law continued, warming to her favourite topic. '"Bloody tinkers, that's what 'er family are" and "Marry her and you'll regret it", I said to him…'

Humming 'Deep in the Heart of Texas' to herself, Cathy let her mother-in-law rant on about her deficiencies, as she made her son's fish paste sandwich.

Placing it on a tea plate, she then picked up the bread knife again. She cut another two slices, then re-wrapped the bread and placed it in the crock on the back of the table.

'I'd rather have a hot midday meal,' said Violet, as Cathy spread a knob of marge across the first slice.

Scraping a smear of paste from the glass Shippam's jar onto her knife, Cathy didn't answer.

'Still, if all there is on offer is a sandwich, I'll have one, too,' added Violet.

Cutting her sandwich in half, Cathy placed it on another plate.

She gave her mother-in-law a sweet smile and picked up hers and Peter's plate. 'I'll get out of your way then so you can make it.'

Loathing narrowed her mother-in-law's eyes.

'I wish my Stan had never married you,' said Violet as Cathy swept past her.

'So do I,' muttered Cathy as she left the room.

Chapter twenty-eight

'ROBERT IS JUST such an adorable baby,' said Francesca, gazing down at the baby asleep in her arms.

'Yes he is, isn't he?' Mattie replied, sitting on the fireside chair opposite with her feet up on the pouffe.

'Your husband must be very pleased to have a son,' said Leo, sitting beside Francesca on the sofa.

It was two weeks after Jo's wedding, and they were sitting in her friend's front room. The BBC Northern Orchestra were just tuning up for the Saturday evening slot, meaning it was just after six thirty.

'To be honest, neither of us were bothered what we had as long as we had a healthy baby,' said Mattie. 'Especially as he was born in the basement of the lying-in hospital in the middle of an air raid.'

'I'm sorry we haven't been able to pop around sooner but it's been frantic at work this week,' Francesca said, studying the baby's tiny hand wrapped around her finger.

'Yes, what with all the to-ing and fro-ing in North Africa between Rommel and Montgomery, my poor darling has been snowed under with news reports all week,' said Leo. 'Not that it matters. With our studio time cut to the bone there's not much chance of transmitting them.'

'I quite understand,' said Mattie. 'Daniel's supposed to have had a few days off after I got home last Saturday, but he's been back and forward to Whitehall all week.'

Daniel walked in through the open lounge door.

'Is Alicia asleep?' asked Mattie.

'Soundo,' said Daniel. 'Mind you, it took three chapters of *Booboo the Barrage Balloon* before she was. Anyone for a cuppa?'

There was a knock at the front door.

'I'll see who that is, then put the kettle on,' said Daniel.

He went to the front door and the latch clicked as he opened it.

'Hello, mate,' he said. 'Come in.'

'Thanks, Daniel,' said Charlie's voice from the hallway. 'How you doing?'

'Oh, you know,' said Daniel. 'I was just putting the kettle on, so go through.'

Francesca's heart thumped uncomfortably in her chest a couple of times then raced off at a gallop as Charlie, dressed in worn cords and open-necked shirt, walked into the room.

'Hello, sis, I thought I'd—'

He stopped dead.

Francesca's mouth opened and she tried to speak but no words came out.

With their gazes locked together, she and Charlie stared at each other for a couple of heartbeats, then Mattie's voice cut between them.

'Hello, Big Brother,' she said loudly.

Charlie blinked and his attention shifted to his sister.

He smiled and, with Francesca unable to take her eyes from him, he strolled across the room.

He kissed Mattie on the forehead. 'Hello, sis, how are you?'

'Very well,' she replied.

Leo rose to his feet.

'Nice to see you again,' he said, offering his hand.

'And you, Leo,' Charlie replied, taking it.

They shook, then Charlie's gaze returned to Francesca.

'I didn't know you'd be here, Francesca,' he said, the warmth in his eyes as they rested on her setting her pulse racing again.

'We just popped in,' she replied. 'To see this little lad.'

She shifted the child in her arms so Charlie could see him better.

An unreadable expression flashed over the angular panes of Charlie's face for a second, then he smiled.

Bending down, he ran his work-worn index finger lightly down the baby's soft cheek.

'So gorgeous,' said Francesca, enjoying the feel of the child in her arms.

'Absolutely,' said Charlie, in a low voice that vibrated through her.

Knowing he was looking at her, Francesca forced her gaze to stay on the baby in her arms and not the man whose lips were just inches from hers.

A heartbeat or two passed again, then Charlie straightened up. 'And a chip off the old block.'

'Devastatingly handsome then,' said Daniel as he walked in, carrying a tray of tea.

Everyone laughed.

Taking one of the upright chairs, Charlie placed it alongside Mattie's chair and sat down.

Daniel put the tray on the table, then, having added the required sugar, handed around the drinks.

They chatted a bit about the weather and then Mattie gave them a rundown on how many times Robert woke up each night and how Alicia was helping with her new brother.

'So how have you enjoyed your time off with the family, Daniel?' asked Charlie, when she'd finished.

'When I have some, I'll let you know,' Daniel replied. 'I've been called in three times so far since I brought Mattie home from the lying-in hospital last Saturday and I wouldn't be surprised if I don't get a phone call later.'

'And Mum coming in each day to help has been an absolute lifesaver,' added Mattie.

'Well, she needs to get in some practice,' said Charlie.

Everyone laughed again.

'When's your parents' blessed event due?' asked Leo.

'The midwives at Munroe House think Mum's due late October,' Charlie replied.

'Honestly, what a day that was,' said Mattie, rolling her eyes. 'Jo gets married, I go into labour and we find out we've another brother or sister on the way.'

'And my angel – ' Leo took Francesca's hand – 'made me the happiest man alive by accepting my proposal of marriage.'

Charlie's eyes locked with hers. 'You're getting married?'

Francesca tried to speak but, with the memory of his arms around her, his lips on hers and his words of love filling her mind, she could only nod.

'Have you picked a ring yet?' asked Mattie, from what seemed like a long way away.

'Not yet,' said Francesca, tearing her gaze from Charlie's. 'As Leo said, I've been flat-out at work all week.'

'I was hoping to take Francesca to a little place I know in Hatton Garden this morning, but—'

'Dad was short-handed in the cafe so needed me to help.' Francesca laughed. 'And there's no rush.'

Charlie cleared his throat. 'Have you set a date?'

'I thought fourth of July,' Leo replied.

'So soon?' said Charlie.

'There's a war on so there's no point hanging around,' said Leo. 'But Francesca wants to wait until then as we're hoping her brother might get leave then.'

'But we'll put it back a few weeks or even a month if necessary,' said Francesca hastily.

Leo squeezed her hand. 'I can't wait to see everyone's faces at Radio Roma when we tell them we're getting married.'

'No,' Francesca replied hollowly.

'Shall I take him?' asked Daniel.

Francesca handed the baby over and picked up her tea.

Leo gave her an adoring look. 'Holding a baby suits you. You're such a natural mother.' His gaze shifted to the man sitting opposite them. 'Don't you think, Charlie?'

Something flickered in Charlie's eyes for a split second, then he smiled.

'Indeed.' He downed the last of his tea and stood up, putting his empty cup back on the tray. 'I ought to be off to the Tilbury. Depending on what deliveries Dad's got in the book, I'll pop down later in the week with Patrick, Matt.' He looked across to Leo. 'Nice to see you again, Leo.'

Leo put his arms on the back of the sofa, behind Francesca.

'You, too,' he replied. 'And look out for your wedding invitation.'

Charlie gave a tight smile.

'I'm afraid I'm not likely to be around,' he said. 'I'm seeing the doc on Friday and I expect he'll be signing me off, so I'll probably be shipped out in a week or so.'

'So soon?' said Francesca, as a black chasm opened at her feet.

'As your fiancé said, Francesca, there's no point hanging around,' he replied.

His blue-grey eyes held hers for a moment, then he turned and left the room. The front door latch clicked as he shut the door behind him.

The urge to dash after him and throw herself into his arms, then kiss every inch of his face before locking her mouth over his, rose up in Francesca and almost overwhelmed her, but thankfully she held it back. Instead, she looked at Leo's dark, refined features.

She was fond of him, very fond of him, and she was sure in time, when they had a home and children, she would come to love him in the same way she loved Charlie now. All she and her broken heart had to do was carry on without Charlie until that day.

Chapter twenty-nine

'NOW, WITH YOUR arm straight, rotate it forward all the way around,' said Sir Sidney Parkinson.

Glancing at the clock above the door which now showed five-fifteen, Charlie did as he was asked, feeling just a slight pull on the still-raw scar as he completed the motion.

Looking over his half-rimmed spectacles, the consultant gave a grim smile. 'Good, good.'

Sir Sidney, a stout man who was seventy if he was a day, wearing a morning suit with a red-and-yellow bow tie at his throat, stepped back a few paces.

'Now backwards,' he said, his eyes fixed on Charlie's shoulder.

It was Friday evening and, having been kicking his heels for almost three hours in the waiting room, he had finally been shown into Middlesex hospital's number-one orthopaedic consultant some fifteen minutes ago.

He was now standing, stripped to the waist in his combat trousers, in a ten-by-twelve consultation room on the second floor of the late Georgian building, which was located to the north of Oxford Street behind the bomb-pummelled Bourne & Hollingsworth.

There was the usual paraphernalia you'd expect to find in an examination room – a metal and glass cabinet containing some painful-looking instruments, a couple of gruesome anatomical wall charts and a sink with flipper-handled taps. There were also some items you wouldn't expect to see, like a Civil Defence volunteer's tin hat hanging from the coat hook and an Enfield rifle propped up in the corner.

However, even the warm sunlight streaming through the gummed tape criss-crossing the windows could do nothing to lift the grey cloud of misery gripping Charlie. He loved Francesca. Totally loved her and would until the day he died. Although his shattered heart kept trying to tell him otherwise, there was no hope.

For all their learning and wisdom, he had a much clearer understanding of purgatory than any priest. After all, he'd been living in it since he'd walked into his sister's house the previous Saturday and discovered Francesca was going to marry Leo.

Looking straight ahead at the skeleton dangling from a metal stand in the corner and trying to keep a hold on his impatience, Charlie reversed the motion.

'Very good,' said the consultant. 'Now, pick up that weight.' He indicated a dumbbell on his examination couch. 'And repeat the movement.'

Grasping the ten-pound weight, Charlie did as he asked, making the recently healed bones of his chest and shoulder protest a little.

'Excellent,' said Sir Sidney. 'Right, get dressed and take a seat, Bombardier Brogan.'

Slipping on his khaki vest, Charlie picked up his shirt and glanced at the clock again. Unsurprisingly, it had only moved on a couple of minutes.

Sir Sidney tottered back behind the desk and resumed his seat, almost disappearing behind the files piled high on it.

Adjusting his glasses, he studied Charlie's medical records, open on his ink blotter.

'I see here it was back in February you were injured,' said the consultant, looking up from the scribbled notes.

'Yes, sir,' Charlie replied.

'Well, I have to say you've made a remarkably quick recovery,' Sir Sidney said.

'Thank you, sir,' said Charlie, glancing at the clock again as he finished buttoning up his shirt. 'Although I reckon my mum and gran should really get the credit for that as they seemed to have been in competition to see who can feed me the most each day.'

The consultant's moustache lifted at the ends a little.

'Well, whatever the reason,' he said, 'I'm happy to say you're now fit to return to active duty.'

'When?' asked Charlie, as he tucked his shirt in his trousers.

'Well, it'll take a few days for your notes to get to London district headquarters so I'll sign you fit from next Tuesday, which will give you a couple of days at home to say your goodbyes before presenting yourself for duty at Leconfield House, 0-six hundred hours. Take a seat outside while I record my findings and write your certificate.'

Charlie saluted. 'Thank you.'

Sir Sidney searched in his inside jacket pocket for a moment, then started patting the papers strewn across his desk.

He frowned. 'I don't seem to be able to find my pen—'

'Here, sir,' said Charlie, retrieving the consultant's tortoiseshell fountain pen from under a stack of letters.

The consultant took it and, at what seem like half speed, unscrewed the end.

'Sorry to ask, sir,' said Charlie. 'Will it take long?'

Sir Sidney looked up.

'Have you got a date, Bombardier?' he asked, over his spectacles.

'Only with my son,' Charlie replied. 'My wife works nights and I have to be home before she leaves at six.'

'Well, in that case, I'll write your certificate first,' the consultant replied.

'Thank you, sir.'

Taking a sheet of headed writing paper, the consultant lowered his head and started scribbling Charlie's certificate. After signing it and rubber stamping the hospital's crest in purple ink at the bottom, he handed it to Charlie.

'Thank you, sir,' he repeated, saluting the elderly consultant again.

'And try not to let Jerry take a pop at you again, son,' said Sir Sidney.

Charlie laughed. 'No.'

He left the examination room and hurried down the corridor to the central staircase.

Dodging between nurses in frilly caps, white-coated doctors and khaki-clad army personnel, Charlie dashed down the stone stairs two at a time. Crossing the foyer in a handful of strides, he pushed open the main door and walked out into the street.

He glanced at his watch. Five-thirty.

He'd be a little bit late, but it couldn't be helped and he didn't have to worry. Not after the row they'd had when he discovered she'd left Patrick alone in the house a few weeks back. He'd told her clearly that if he hadn't arrived by six thirty, she was to take their son to Ida before she flitted off to the BonBon club and God help her if she didn't.

He made it to Tottenham Court Station in five minutes flat and was standing on the platform when an eastbound Central line train rattled to a stop. A 25 bus would have dropped him off nearer to his home but catching the tube to the end of the line at Liverpool Street would be faster and then he could catch the 100 bus to Wapping or walk the mile or so back to Alma Terrace.

Charlie waited until the passengers got off, then, ducking to avoid braining himself on the low doorway, he stepped inside the third coach from the front.

As it was now the end of the working day, the carriage was packed with businessmen in serious pinstripes and bowler hats, secretaries in twinsets and pearls, and giggly shop girls in colourful dresses, bright lips and victory roll curls high on their heads. Amongst them were the usual selection of Army and Air Force personnel. In addition, as with everywhere you went in London, there were several small groups of Yanks skylarking about like overgrown schoolboys at a funfair. Smoking expensive cork-tipped cigarettes while everyone else in the carriage was puffing on lean roll-ups.

Tucking himself into a space, Charlie spread his legs to balance and leant back against the glass panel at the end of a row of seats.

The door rolled shut and the train lurched forward into the tunnel towards Holborn.

As much as he hated leaving Patrick, perhaps it was just as well he was returning to active service. It was torture enough to know he could never marry the woman he loved without having to stand in a church and watch her become another man's wife.

The train shuddered on to its next stop and arrived some four minutes later. The doors opened and passengers got off the train only to be immediately replaced by more getting on.

Charlie shuffled over to let a tired-looking middle-aged woman in a tweed suit grab the upright handrail to steady herself as people piled into the carriage. Sweat sprung out between his shoulder blades and the combination of cigarette smoke and bodies packed tightly together turned the atmosphere in the carriage from sweltering to stifling.

Charlie loosened his tie as the door rolled closed again. The train shunted forwards into the black of the tunnel, the internal lights glowing dimly as it sped towards Chancery Lane. The train clattered and squealed along for a few moments, then Charlie felt it slow as it approached the station. People around him were just folding away newspapers and gathering their bags together in readiness when the train lurched to one side and stopped. Women screamed and men bellowed their protest as they were thrown forward onto each other and the floor. There was a moment of utter silence, then the carriage was plunged into darkness as the strip lighting above them flickered once and then went out.

Standing in her front lounge, Stella glanced at the clock in the centre of the mantelshelf.

A quarter to seven!

Tapping the column of ash at the end of her cigarette into the ashtray, her eyes slid from her stylish new timepiece onto the child sitting on the tufted rug in front of the three-bar electric fire in the hearth.

'Where's your fucking father?' she barked at him.

Dropping the old wooden soldiers Charlie had left for him to play with, Patrick picked up his father's tatty old teddy and stuck his thumb in his mouth.

Grinding her cigarette into the collection of butts already in the ashtray, Stella took a fresh one from her case, placed it between her scarlet lips and lit it.

Drawing in a lungful of smoke, she looked at the smooth gold-plated object in her hand and a smile crept across her face.

Donny had given it to her a few days ago, along with a slimline Dunhill lighter of the same design. He'd bought her other things too, including a pair of drop diamond earrings, a huge bottle of Guerlain's Vol de Nuit and the gold charm bracelet with a dozen jewelled trinkets that was now hanging from her wrist. He'd given her money too, lots of it. All of which was stashed in the tin beneath the metal fire grate in her bedroom. A partner's bonus, he'd called it. She called it keeping her sweet. Sweet so she'd play her part with this bastard Moffit, which is why she was fully made up and dressed in her plunge-neck, strapless red velvet cocktail dress, six-inch stilettos and silky underwear.

Most days Charlie was knocking on her door long before the six o'clock pips but it was sod's law that tonight, of all nights, he'd be bloody late. Despite the nicotine flowing around her veins, fury gripped her.

She glanced at the clock again.

Where in God's name was Charlie?

Donny was bringing this Moffit to the club at eight.

If she'd known Charlie was going to be this blooming late, she would have taken Patrick around to Ida's before she left for the shelter. She was now cutting it fine so she didn't have time to traipse all the way to the Tilbury with him.

Clamping her cigarette between her lips, Stella picked up her son. Patrick, seeing his mother advancing on him, had gripped his teddy tight.

Holding him away from her so he didn't dribble on her, Stella marched him upstairs and plonked him and his motley toy into his cot.

She went back downstairs to the lounge. Dropping her cigarette case and lighter in her handbag, she hooked it over her arm and walked into the hallway.

Checking that she hadn't smudged her blusher or mascara carrying her son upstairs, she took the fox fur elbow-length cape Donny had also given her and draped it around her shoulders. She opened the door.

However, as she stepped out into the street, the blazing row they'd had few weeks before, when Charlie had found out she'd left Patrick alone in the house while she'd popped out to get her hair done, loomed into her mind.

Stella paused for a moment and then, gripping the knob, pulled the door firmly shut.

Well, don't blame me, Charlie Brogan, because this time it's your fault Patrick's been left in his cot. You're blooming well late.

'Take my hand and I'll help you down,' Charlie said, reaching up to the young girl standing hesitantly at the train driver's open door.

'Thanks, Charlie,' she said, taking it and stepping down from the train onto the rough ballast between the railway tracks. 'And for, you know…'

He gave her a little smile. 'That's all right.'

Her 'you know' referred to the fact that for the past half an hour, Charlie had quizzed the pale-haired fifteen-year-old canteen assistant about her family and pets to keep her from dissolving into a quivering wreck as they waited for the rescue party to reach their carriage.

After the lights had gone out there had been a moment of complete silence, then pandemonium broke out. Thankfully, before people started stampeding towards the door at the end, Charlie and most of the other servicemen in the carriage had switched on their torches.

This had calmed things a little and allowed them to take control of the situation. Most of the injuries were just minor bumps and scrapes, except for one woman who had fallen badly and broken her leg and a man at the front of the carriage who had headbutted the door and was unconscious. Charlie, along with a couple of the Americans, had moved them towards the front of the carriage ready to be evacuated as soon as help arrived. A couple of ATS girls and three squaddies from the Royal Corps of Transport had patched up the walking wounded and the GIs had handed around their cigarettes, which had helped calm everyone's nerves while they waited in the half-light to be rescued.

One of the Chancery Lane's rescue crew had reached them half an hour after the system went dead. He'd informed them that an unexploded bomb had detonated at Shepherd's Bush, knocking out the power to the entire line, and they were starting to evacuate the front carriage. They'd been told to sit tight as they would be out in a jiffy.

That was two and three-quarter hours ago and now, having helped the last woman in his carriage to safety, he felt he could, with good conscience, leave the men remaining in the train to fend for themselves and make his own escape to the surface.

Picking his way between the inert rails, Charlie walked towards the station lights a couple of hundred yards ahead of him. He then clambered up the ramp onto the platform.

Joining the stream of people heading for the exit, Charlie climbed up the two sets of stationery escalators. He skirted around the first-aid post set up by a St John's Ambulance on the concourse, then trotted up the short flight of stairs to the surface.

He emerged as the sun behind the building to the west streaked the sky with pink and yellow.

Free from the claustrophobic atmosphere of the underground, Charlie drew in a deep breath to clear his head but, as he exhaled, the wail of the air raid siren cut through the cool evening air. It called out in a single voice for a moment or two before the distinct boom of German bombs and the pop-pop-pop of the capital's ack-ack guns joined in with their nerve-jangling song.

With the tube lines down and knowing no buses would be running and the streets would soon be filled with fire engines, ambulances and Heavy Rescue trucks dashing along them, Charlie decided walking the three or so miles home was his best option. Crossing Gray's Inn Road, and noting, as he passed, that Gamages' clock was showing nine-fifteen, Charlie headed east in double-quick time to join his family in the Tilbury shelter.

Chapter thirty

THE LOW BOOM of the bomb that had just found its target somewhere around Aldgate pulsed through the air as Charlie hurried past Leman Street police station three-quarters of an hour later.

The first Luftwaffe squadron of Messerschmitt 264 that had triggered the initial warning sirens and set the ARP teams into action had flown right over London, probably heading for the industrial areas to the west of the capital. But why wouldn't they?

Not only was it a completely cloudless night, there was almost a full bomber's moon. With such perfect conditions for killing the population of London, the Luftwaffe had a whole night of flying to do just that.

Predictably, the second wave of enemy aircraft that had followed the first, just over half an hour ago, had been raining down death and destruction on North and West London. Judging by the low hum vibrating through the still night air, the next wave of bombers were just passing Barking Creek and would be with them soon, probably to give the east of London their fair share of the night's carnage. Knowing he was just five minutes from safety, Charlie quickened his pace and turned left under the arches into Hooper Street. As the entrance to the Tilbury shelter came into view, a line of orange and red flames burnt upward like Roman candles on bonfire night as the Nazi armaments destroyed East Enders' homes and businesses in quick succession. The ack-ack guns joined in and soon the velvet-blue night sky was ablaze with spent weaponry.

Quickening his pace, Charlie ducked inside the shelter, just as the tell-tale whistle of a bomb's tail fin plummeting to earth screeched overhead.

'Evening, Charlie,' said Ted, the head ARP warden. 'Bit lively out there tonight.'

'You're not wrong, Ted,' said Charlie, closing the door as, bell clanging frantically, a fire engine streaked by.

Leaving Ted to do his rounds, Charlie went down the half a dozen steps into the main part of the shelter. Lights out had been called some fifteen minutes or so ago and the shelter was in darkness. Picking his way carefully between the rows of people curled up in blankets, Charlie made his way towards the alcove at the back where his family would be.

Drawing close, he saw the familiar shapes of his mother and sister tucked up under the covers with Peter between them and Michael and Billy alongside. He looked for his son but, when he saw only his sister's Marmot pram, ice replaced the blood in Charlie's veins.

Crossing the space in two strides, he shook his mother.

'Mum.' He shook her again and she raised her head. 'Where's Patrick?'

'Patrick?' she said, shuffling onto her elbow and looking up at him with bleary eyes.

'Yes,' Charlie replied, as fear twisted his gut.

She looked puzzled. 'Isn't he with you?'

'No, the Central line went down and I've only just got back,' Charlie replied. 'Didn't Stella bring him around?'

His mother was fully awake now and so was Cathy.

'No,' she said, sitting up. 'We thought you must have gone round to Mattie's after you collected him and bedded down in her basement when the siren went off, like you did last week.' In the half-light of his torch, he could see the blood drain from his mother's face. 'She wouldn't have?'

Charlie's mouth pulled into a hard line. 'I'll kill her if she has.'

With the blood pumping through his ears, he turned and tore between the huddled figures to the entrance.

Taking the stairs two at a time, he burst through the door and onto the pavement. The street was illuminated red by the burning warehouses on either side, and the rotten-egg smell of sulphur and ammonia hung heavy in the hot air.

Pulling his neckerchief from his top pocket and folding it into a triangle, Charlie tied it over his nose and mouth then, turning his collar up and anchoring his field cap firmly on his head, he turned and raced down the blazing street towards his house in Alma Street.

With his heart pounding in his chest, Charlie tore along Cable Street, jumping piles of rubble in his path and crunching shards of glass underfoot. As he reached Stepney town hall, a bomb crashed to earth a few streets behind it, sending a plume of earth and flames high into the air. The vacuum of the burnt air sucked at his clothes for a moment before the grit-laden gust whooshed between the buildings towards him, fragments of metal sending up sparks as they struck the cobbles.

Turning into a shop doorway, Charlie covered his face with his arm and pressed himself into the corner until it passed, then he dashed off again. With his lungs burning with exertion and acerbic fumes, he pelted past Shadwell station. He turned under the railway into Alma Terrace and skidded to a halt.

With his heart crashing in his chest, Charlie stared in horror. What had been a modest street of two-up, two-down terraced houses was now little more than a pile of rubble. Although the dwellings at the south end of the street were completely destroyed, his house – which stood at the far end – was still standing but, with flames engulfing the house next to it, for how much longer was anyone's bet.

Charlie paused.

Although she'd never done it before, Stella could, of course, have left Patrick with a neighbour who had taken him to another shelter or, perhaps, knowing Ida would already be in the Tilbury, to Mattie's where he would be tucked up safe alongside his two cousins. Surely no mother, not even Stella, would leave their child in such danger.

A creak, like an unoiled door, echoed across the space then the central beam of the house next to his split in two and crashed into the inferno within, sending sparks flying upwards to pepper the night sky. It had taken part of the dividing wall down with it, exposing the main bedroom in Charlie's house where he could see that flames were already taking hold.

With fear and grief gripping his innards, Charlie dashed forward towards the Heavy Rescue crew and fire brigade crew who were battling to get the blaze under control. As he reached his house, a fireman, face scorched red with the heat and wearing his breathing apparatus, stepped in his path.

'Sorry, chum, it's too dangerous!' he yelled above the noise and extending his arms to bar the way.

'I think my son is still in there!' Charlie shouted as he pushed past him. He kicked the broken front door aside and headed into the house.

The hallway walls were still standing but the fire in the bedroom above had already burnt through the floorboards. The flames were now catching hold on the main beams, bathing the hallway in red light. The kitchen at the back of the house was already ablaze but, thankfully, the stairs seemed to be more or less sound.

Grabbing the upright post at the bottom, and with the heat from above pressing down on his head, Charlie ran up the stairs to the first floor.

The main bedroom door had been burnt away and all the furniture and walls were alight as the night breeze fanned the flames. The air was thick with smoke, stinging his eyes and choking his lungs even though he was breathing through his cotton neckerchief.

Using his jacket to shield his face from the heat, Charlie pressed himself against the undamaged hallway wall and, with burning wallpaper singeing his hair and clothes, he headed for Patrick's bedroom at the end of the hallway.

Charlie tried to open the closed door but something lying behind stopped it after just a few inches. Pressing his face to the wood, Charlie peered through the five-inch gap.

Shining his torch through the black smoke that filled the room, he saw Patrick was lying in his cot clutching his old teddy bear. Unlike the rest of the furniture in the house, which was modern, his son's bed was in fact the old metal-framed cot Charlie himself had slept in a quarter of a century before. Just as well, as a great lump of plaster had fallen from the ceiling and now lay across the top of the cot. Had the bed been made of wood, Patrick would have been crushed beneath the heavy plaster.

Stepping back to gain momentum, Charlie charged at the door with his good shoulder and shoved it open a little further. He managed to squeeze himself through the gap.

Coughing as the acrid smoke filled his lungs, and with his eyes streaming from the same, Charlie crossed the room in two strides, wrenched the plaster aside, and lifted his lifeless son out of the cot. Tucking him beneath his jacket, Charlie hugged the boy to him. He retraced his steps back into the hall.

The bedroom at the top of the stairs was a sheer wall of flames and the fire was now spreading into the hall, curling the rug on the landing black and turning the door frame into a burning arch.

With the beams above his head cracking as they burnt and the smell of his hair singeing as he passed close to the flames that were now lapping the top of the stairs, Charlie ran downstairs and back into the street, hearing a crash as another part of the roof collapsed behind him.

The searchlights were still criss-crossing the sky, highlighting the arrow-shaped formation of enemy bombers droning above them while the ack-ack guns along the Thames tried to shoot them down.

Coughing, Charlie drew in a long breath of the night air then, sitting down on the cobbles, he lifted Patrick out from under his coat.

With blue lips and grey cheeks, his son looked bloodless and was like a rag doll in Charlie's embrace.

Dread gripped him.

Praying like he'd never prayed before, Charlie placed his cheek close to the boy's mouth and held his breath. After what seemed like an eternity, he felt the feathery softness of his son's breath on his skin.

Charlie almost wept with relief.

'Patrick!' he shouted, rubbing his son's chest with the palm of his hand. 'Daddy's here. Wake up, son!'

Patrick gasped and then coughed. His eyelids fluttered for a second and then were still again.

The fireman who'd tried to block his way came over with a blanket.

'We'd better get that little chap to the first-aid station around the corner.'

Cradling Patrick in his arms, Charlie got up from the ground. 'I'm going to take my boy straight to hospital.'

Wrapping the fireman's blanket around Patrick, Charlie held him close and kissed his sooty forehead.

Another bomb landed somewhere nearby. With the ground shaking beneath his feet and the sulphur-laden air burning around him, Charlie set off again at double-quick time, this time for East London's main hospital.

An explosion somewhere close by set the strip lighting above Charlie's head swinging back and forth, making the shadows striping across his son's cot shift sideward.

'Don't worry, son,' whispered Charlie, squeezing his son's tiny hand reassuringly. 'Daddy's here.'

Patrick, who was lying under a blue blanket with a black rubber oxygen mask over his nose and mouth, didn't move.

Tears pinched the corners of Charlie's eyes as he stared through the cot bars at his son's grey and inert face.

Charlie didn't remember much of his dash to the London hospital.

The waiting room was already rammed full with bloodied, blackened casualties when Charlie burst through the half-glazed doors clutching his son. The nurses fetched the medic in charge who immediately ordered oxygen and transferred Patrick to the children's section in the hospital basement.

That's where they were now and had been for the past two hours. Around him, between the lead water pipes, concrete foundation columns and discarded equipment, were about a dozen half-sized beds, each containing a sick child with an anxious parent alongside.

The ground shook again. A couple of children started to whimper as the lights flickered overhead. Reaching across, Charlie smoothed his hand over his son's soft hair and then reached for the small boy's hand again. Other than outside the burning house Patrick hadn't stirred, not even when the nurses stripped him of his smoke-clogged clothes and washed the worst of the soot of his face.

God, if he'd arrived five minutes later…

Cold fear squeezed the breath from Charlie's chest. Without letting go of Patrick's hand, Charlie leant back in the straight-back chair and closed his eyes as he struggled to keep his fears at bay.

There was a light cough.

Charlie looked up to see a fair-haired nurse in a navy uniform and frilly cap standing at the end of Patrick's cot; she had half a dozen manila files clutched to her chest.

Beside her, wearing a three-piece suit, flowery bow tie and a stethoscope around his neck, was a tall chap with a receding hairline and pencil moustache.

'Brogan?' he asked.

Charlie rose to his feet. 'Yes.'

'Dr Ogilvy, consultant paediatrician,' the man replied. 'Dr Kemp from Casualty has asked me to take a look at your little chap.'

'Thank you, Doctor,' said Charlie.

The consultant turned to the nurse. 'How's he now, Sister?'

'He seems to be breathing a little better now he's on oxygen,' she replied.

'Good.' Ogilvy held out his hand and the nurse gave him one of the files she was carrying.

He took it and, removing his spectacles from his inside pocket, perched them on his nose. He scanned down the notes for a moment, then snapped the file shut and handed it back to the waiting nurse.

Taking his Hunter watch out, he flipped open the top and took hold of Patrick's wrist. He studied the dial for a moment, then gently put the child's hand down. Removing his stethoscope from around his neck, he put it on and then slipped the rounded end under the pyjamas the nurse had dressed Patrick in.

He moved it a couple of times, then flipped it back around his neck and pulled out a pencil torch. Raising Patrick's right eyelid, he flickered the dot of light across it a couple of times before doing the same to the left one.

A dour expression settled on the consultant's lean features.

Switching off the torch he returned it to his pocket then looked across at Charlie.

'He turns one on the twentieth of this month, doesn't he?'

'Yes, next Saturday,' Charlie replied over the lump in his throat.

Dr Ogilvy pursed his lips. 'I won't beat about the bush, Mr Brogan, your son is very lucky to be here and not in the morgue,' he said, as Charlie felt sick and faint in quick succession.

'Very lucky indeed,' continued the consultant. 'Thankfully he's breathing by himself, but he has inhaled a considerable amount of toxic smoke and there's no way of knowing at this stage how much lasting damage might have been done to his immature lungs.'

'But he's going to be all right, isn't he, Doctor?' Charlie said, willing the consultant to agree.

'Although people often regard smoke as being like steam with no substance, it can suffocate a person as surely as placing a pillow over their face,' said the doctor. 'Although your son's observations are satisfactory, these are just the most basic of brain functions. Only time will tell if there is any permanent injury.'

A black void opened at Charlie's feet.

'You mean he might have brain damage?' he asked.

'I'm afraid so,' the consultant replied. 'The next few days are crucial. I've placed him on the danger list so you will able to sit with him outside the usual visiting times, but although children's bodies mend quicker than ours, your son will need complete rest if he is to have a hope of recovering.'

Grief crushing his chest, Charlie said, 'Is there anything I can do?'

Compassion flickered across the consultant's face. 'Pray, Mr Brogan, you can pray.' Another bomb shook the ground again, and Dr Ogilvy moved on to his next patient.

Taking Patrick's hand again, Charlie stared blankly through the metal bars of the cot at his son.

He wasn't even one until next week. For pity's sake, he was just a baby.

Tears distorted Charlie's vision.

He tried to pray but couldn't as the feel of Patrick's arms around his neck, the sound of his laughter and the sensation of cradling his son in his arms, flooded through Charlie.

In his mind's eye he saw Patrick reaching for him, Patrick opening his mouth for the spoon Charlie held, Patrick blowing him a kiss goodbye as he went off to the yard. Then the happy images of his son were replaced with the one of Patrick, scared and crying as bombs dropped around him, and then Charlie pictured him lying unconscious in his cot as the house burnt.

Blood pounded through his ears, muffling the sound of the ward around him and his knuckles cracked as he gripped the top of the cot rails.

He tried to clear his mind and pray to the Mother of God but instead of Ave Maria, a roar of fury filled his mind as it fixed on Stella.

A hand rested on his shoulder.

Charlie lifted his head and saw a round-faced nurse in a lilac-striped uniform standing beside him.

'I'm sorry, Mr Brogan,' she said, her voice barely penetrating the howling emotions flying around in his mind. 'The all-clear has sounded so perhaps you should find your wife and tell her about your son.'

Charlie stared blankly at her for a moment, then rose to his feet.

'Thank you, nurse,' he said. 'Perhaps I should.'

Chapter thirty-one

'AH, AH, AH,' shouted Stella, contemplating the lampshade as Master Sergeant Elijah Forrester Lee Moffit pounded away between her legs.

The all-clear had gone off an hour ago, which was a pity as the bombs landing were the only things that had stirred her all evening.

Granted, Donny had arranged for a bottle of champagne to be chilling in Eli's billet but, as she'd walked into the Excelsior Hotel on the overweight sergeant's arm, she'd fancied the fresh-faced American Military Police officer guarding the entrance had given her a pitying look.

She barely understood Eli Moffit's thick Southern accent, but it didn't matter as he hadn't been interested in conversation; his piggy eyes had been glued to her cleavage as he scoffed down his dinner.

Thankfully, the fat master sergeant wasn't interested in bedroom play either, but he had insisted on having the lights on, which meant not only was she forced to watch him strip off his clothes, she'd also had to pretend to be impressed when he did.

Still, this was his third go so, with a bit of luck, after knocking back almost a bottle of whiskey, he'd soon slump into a stupor and she'd be able to slip out before sun-up.

'Oh yes, keep going, keep going, cowboy!' she shouted, feigning breathlessness as he sweated and grunted his way to a climax.

Curling her fingers on his blubbery shoulder she noticed the polish had chipped on one of her fingernails and she was just wondering if she'd have time to have them done before she collected Patrick after lunch tomorrow when the door opened.

She looked over Eli's bobbing rear and fear gripped her.

In the doorway, a wild, frenetic look in his red-rimmed eyes, stood Charlie; holding a rifle.

Their eyes met and Stella's heart jumped into her throat.

Charlie stood motionless for a moment, then raised the gun to his shoulder.

Stella screamed.

The roaring in Charlie's head ran down his right arm to his index finger as it hovered on the trigger.

The rifle he'd taken from the GI at the front door was a M1 Garand semi-automatic which could fire eight rounds in quick succession, which would be more than enough to send his hateful wife to kingdom come, more correctly, to Hell.

The fat man on top of Stella froze mid-thrust and, scrambling for the dishevelled sheet at his feet, yanked it over his lower portion and rolled onto his back.

'What the…?'

Charlie adjusted his hold on the rifle and the American's loose lips clamped shut.

As the smell of stale whiskey and sex filled Charlie's nose, his gaze ran over the open packet of French letters on the bedside table and the used ones on the floor.

Charlie's mouth pulled into an ugly line.

Stella swallowed hard. 'Charlie, I can explain—'

'Do you know where our son is?' he yelled. 'Do you?'

Sweat broke out on the overweight GI's forehead as he shifted away from Stella to the end of the bed.

'Now look, pal,' he said, 'if I'd known she was your old lady I wouldn't have—'

'Fighting for his life in the London hospital, that's where,' Charlie continued, without glancing at the man beside her.

The colour drained from Stella's face. 'What's happened?'

'What do you care?'

'Patrick's my son too,' she replied. 'And I waited as long as I could but when you didn't turn up, I—'

'I was trapped for two hours on the underground, but you couldn't be bothered to wait, could you? Or even take him to my mum in the shelter. No, you just left our son, a defenceless child, alone in the middle of an air raid.'

'How was I to know there was going to be an air raid?' Stella snapped back.

'We're in the middle of a fucking war!' Charlie hollered.

She shot him a resentful look but didn't reply.

'So, while you were shagging money out of this tub of lard,' Charlie indicated the man trying to retain his dignity with just a crumpled sheet, 'Patrick was being suffocated by smoke in his cot as the house burnt down around him.'

'He's all right, isn't he?' she asked. 'I mean, I didn't think—'

'He's still alive, if that's what you mean,' Charlie replied. 'But no thanks to you.'

Hatred and pain started howling in his head again and his finger tightened on the trigger.

Fear flashed across Stella's heavily made-up face.

'You're right, Charlie, I shouldn't have left him,' she whispered, her terrified eyes fixed on his face. 'It was wrong. And I swear I'll never do it again.'

Raising the gun to his shoulder, he pointed it at her. 'No, you won't.'

'Don't do anything stupid, Charlie,' she said, her faltering voice barely permeating the pounding in his mind.

Tucking the butt of the rifle into his shoulder he looked down the barrel at the petrified face of his wife clutching the sheet.

As he studied her, the woman he'd trusted and who had deceived him, pain ripped through him.

He could have borne the humiliation of his wife's profession and unfaithfulness. Even if he was forced to live a lifetime with the crushing pain of losing Francesca, he could have done it, just, but only because he had Patrick. The one good thing in his life was now hovering between life and death. Because of her.

'They'll hang you, Charlie!' she screamed. 'Take Patrick! I don't care. You can have him. I'll even get something signed by a brief, just don't shoot, Charlie. Don't shoot!'

His finger squeezed the trigger but, as it connected to the firing mechanism, the image of Francesca hunkered down beside Patrick materialised in Charlie's mind.

The roaring in his head vanished and he raised the barrel. He emptied all eight of the .30 carbine bullets into the ornate Edwardian cornice ten feet above his wife's head.

The American threw himself onto the floor as Stella let out another piercing scream. Fragments of plaster rained down on the pair of them.

Drained of emotion, Charlie's arms fell to his side and he dropped the empty rifle.

The door burst open as three white-capped USA Military Police rushed in. Two grabbed Charlie and pinned his arms behind him, while the other went to assist his senior officer to his feet.

Grabbing the sheet from the bed, Stella's American friend dragged it around his bloated pink body. Barefoot, he stomped over to Charlie.

They stood there eyeball to eyeball for a moment, then the naked GI punched Charlie in the gut.

Charlie pitched forward, gasping for breath.

'I'll make sure you have the book thrown at you for this, boy,' he drawled, as Charlie studied the man's flat feet and misshapen toes. 'The whole Goddamn book.'

Chapter thirty-two

'DO YOU LIKE it, *mia cara?* asked Leo, as Francesca studied the sparkling diamond and emerald ring on the third finger of her left hand.

Francesca pursed her lips. 'Isn't it a bit…big?'

It was just before ten o'clock on the Saturday morning after her visit to Mattie's and they were in a small jeweller's shop situated in a narrow alley behind Hatton Garden.

'Perhaps madam would like to try the three-stone sapphire one again,' suggested the shop assistant, a long-nosed man who, in black coat and pinstriped trousers, was dressed in the livery of the exclusive shop.

'I'm not sure,' Francesca replied, taking off the ring and placing it back on the soft cloth that had been spread across the glass counter.

'Perhaps you could show my fiancée some different settings,' said Leo.

The shop assistant's narrow nostrils flared slightly as he gave a tight smile. 'Very good, sir.'

'I'm sorry, Leo,' Francesca said, as the assistant glided though the heavy curtain. 'I just can't decide.'

'Don't worry,' he replied, slipping back into their usual Italian. 'If you want to try a thousand rings, I don't mind as long as you're happy with it.'

'Plus, Leo, they are all very expensive,' she added.

He laughed. 'Don't look at the prices, just pick the one you want.'

The shop assistant returned with another tray of rings and placed them on the counter next to the other two.

'Now, my love, what do you think?' asked Leo.

'They are all so beautiful,' Francesca said, as she ran her eyes over the rows of twinkling diamonds and gemstones.

'Perhaps madam would like to try this one,' the assistant said, plucking a three-stone ring from the top. 'It's a grade AA step ruby flanked by two baguette-cut near-flawless diamonds.'

Francesca slipped it on.

'Do you like it?' asked Leo.

'It's beautiful,' she said, studying the ruby with sparkling diamonds nestled on either side.

'What do you think?' asked Leo.

What *did* she think? It was utterly beautiful.

'Try on some others, if you like. I want you to be sure it's the one you want. After all...' Raising her left hand, Leo pressed it to his lips. 'You're going to be wearing it for the rest of your life.'

Francesca stared at the exquisite ring twinkling on the third finger of her left hand for a second, then twisted it off. Her eyes were blurry with panic.

All but throwing it on the plush velvet jeweller's cloth, she fled the shop.

With black spots crowding into the edges of her vision, she staggered into the street. Francesca leant against the shop's brickwork in the shade of the striped awning with her head swirling and her knees about to buckle. Closing her eyes, she drew in a deep lungful of fresh air to steady her pulse.

The shop bell jingled.

Francesca looked up to see a worried-looking Leo hurrying out of the shop.

'I'm so sorry, Leo,' she said, tears gathering in her eyes. 'I just can't—'

'It Charlie Brogan, isn't it?'

Francesca paused, trying to steady her breathing before she nodded. 'I'm sorry.'

Pain twisted Leo's handsome features. 'But why, Francesca?'

'Because it's always been him,' she replied.

'But he's married,' said Leo.

'That doesn't matter,' Francesca looked into his eyes, aware of the pain she must be causing him. 'Because he loves me and that's enough.'

Leo raked his fingers through his hair. 'But I love you, too, Francesca.'

'I know, and I love you, Leo, but not in the same way I love Charlie,' she replied. 'I wish I could, but...'

Leo took her hand. 'Perhaps, if we were married, Francesca, you could grow to love me and, once you have a home of your own and children, you might—'

'I thought so too,' she cut in. 'I really did, but I'm sorry, Leo, I just can't.' With guilt clawing at her, Francesca reclaimed her hand. 'I never intended to play you false or hurt you, but my heart is with Charlie.'

As the thumping of feet overhead threatened to match the thumping in her head, Ida took the cold flannel off her forehead and looked at the ceiling.

'Will you boys go out and play!' she yelled, feeling her ear drums reverberate.

The noise above stopped as two sets of feet thundered down the stairs.

Billy and Michael, dressed in their rough clothes, burst into the lounge and headed for the kitchen.

'Make sure you're back for lunch,' Ida yelled as they sped past the sofa where she was lying. 'And if we're not here, go around to Cathy's and—'

The back door slammed.

Ida sighed. Repositioning her feet on the arm rest, she put the flannel across her forehead and let her head sink back into the chenille cushion.

The baby inside her shifted and a ligament in her left side protested at the movement.

The ten-fifteen morning service started on the wireless. Hoping a little spiritual calm might calm the terrors that had been swirling in her head since she'd found Queenie's note on the table, Ida closed her eyes.

The short service finished, but as Victor Silvester started playing the opening bars of *Music While you Work*'s signature tune, the back door banged again.

'Charlie!' Ida shouted, swinging her legs down and sitting up.

The kitchen door opened, and Queenie walked in looking all of her sixty-four years.

'How's Patrick?' asked Ida.

'Still clinging to life, bless his sweet little heart,' Queenie replied, collapsing into one of the fireside chairs. 'I left my mother's rosary with him, so he has the Virgin herself to protect him.'

'Have you seen Charlie?' asked Ida.

Queenie shook her head. 'But Jerry said he's not listed as a casualty in the town hall, so that's a mercy. He's staying at the hospital for now but I said one of us would be in later to relieve him. Hopefully by then we will have found Charlie.'

'Isn't Stella with Patrick?'

Queenie shook her head. 'I haven't seen hide nor hair of her. I expect she's still sleeping off last night's gin in some gobshite's bed.'

'Even so,' said Ida, her mother's heart feeling for her worthless daughter-in-law despite everything. 'Having a child so close to death would break any mother's heart.'

'Only if she had one,' Queenie replied. 'The Devil take her. But what I'm wild to know is, where has our Charlie gone?'

'I'll tell you where your precious bloody Charlie's gone!'

Ida and Queenie turned to see Stella, dressed in a crumpled cocktail dress, scuffed high heels and laddered stockings, standing in the kitchen door.

'Fucking locked up in West End Central nick, that's where,' she said.

'Charlie's under arrest!' said Ida, her head reeling. 'What for?'

'Attempted murder. Or at least it will be by the time the American Army's brief explains how he tried to kill one of their senior officers when Charlie's in front of the Bow Street magistrate on Monday,' Stella replied, with undisguised relish.

'One of your tricks, was he, this senior officer?' said Queenie.

A flush coloured Stella's powdered cheeks and she was about to say something, but Ida stood up and waddled over to her daughter-in-law.

'I'm sorry, Stella,' she said, placing her hand on her arm, 'but Patrick was caught in a bombing raid last night and is in the London hospital.'

'I know,' Stella replied, as the smell of stale perfume and body odour turned Ida's stomach.

Ida looked puzzled. 'You know?'

'Yes she does, Ida,' said Queenie, getting up and coming to stand beside her. 'Because when Charlie found out she'd left Patrick alone in the house while she went to meet her pimp, he went to find her. She knows about Patrick because Charlie told her.'

Anger shot across Stella's face.

'He tried to kill me!' she yelled. 'Your bloody precious Charlie tried to kill me.'

'Who would blame him?' said Ida, wishing not for the first time her son had never set eyes on the loathsome blonde.

'I wouldn't put money on that if I were you, Ida,' said Stella, adjusting her handbag. 'Well, I just popped by to tell you that your Charlie's looking at a twenty-year stretch at His Majesty's pleasure and, now I have, I'm going to sit at my dear little boy's side and when he wakes up, I'm going to tell him about the nice new house we're going to live in.' Looking at Ida, Stella gave her a syrupy smile. 'A long, long way away.'

Ida clasped her hands over her mouth.

Seeing her bolt had hit the mark, a smug expression spread across Stella's face. She turned to walk to the back door but before she could take a step, Queenie sprang in front of her, blocking her path.

Raising both hands, she pointed a bony index finger and jabbed it in Stella's face.

'May the Devil take you to the grave, Stella Miggles,' she said. 'And…'

'You've cursed me before, you old cow, so don't waste your breath,' said Stella. She went to brush past her, but Queenie stood her ground.

'… and make you a load for four men to carry on their shoulders before the moon is full again.'

Jumping down from the 15 at eleven thirty, just an hour after she'd left a stunned Leo outside the jeweller's shop, Francesca hurried across Commercial Road and entered the top end of Watney Market.

Although the market itself seemed fairly untouched by the pounding the Luftwaffe had given the area the night before, the ARP wardens had set up an information post by the Lord Nelson and there was a queue of people trying to locate loved ones lined up alongside.

Treading carefully over the slithers of glass and splinters of wood from the bombed-out windows, Francesca made her way between the stalls towards the railway arches at the bottom of the bustling street.

With her heart fluttering in anticipation of feeling Charlie's arms around her again, Francesca practically skipped down to Feldman, the stationer's at the corner of Chapman Street.

Hurrying beneath the damp arches, with the pigeons cooing above in the girders, Francesca turned east into Cable Street. There was a thick cloud of smoke hanging over the houses a few streets away but, as she turned into Mafeking Terrace, she was pleased to see that other than a few cracked panes of glass, the Brogans' street had escaped the worst of the Luftwaffe's most recent visit.

Francesca slipped down the side alleyway and the memory of Charlie's loving words and his lips on hers as he held her in this very place flooded back, sending her heart into another little flutter. Reaching the gate, she entered the backyard and then opened the back door.

'Only me,' she called cheerily, as she stepped in.

However, although a wisp of steam showed the kettle was still hot, the cosy hub of the Brogan household was completely deserted.

Baffled as to why at this time of day Queenie wasn't getting ready to dish up the midday meal or why Ida wasn't stirring a cake for Sunday-afternoon tea, Francesca continued through to the parlour.

Jo was lying on the sofa in her ambulance uniform with her feet up and her eyes closed.

As Francesca walked in, Jo opened her eyes and sat up.

She looked baffled. 'I thought you were out choosing rings with Leo.'

'I was, but…' Francesca gave her a nervous smile. 'Is Charlie around?'

Jo stared at her, hollow-eyed for a moment, then burst into tears.

Chapter thirty-three

WITH HIS BACK resting on the whitewashed brickwork behind him, Charlie counted the bricks along the top of the wall opposite him. There were a hundred and three. He already knew that as he'd tallied their number half a dozen times. It was tedious for certain, but it saved him rushing screaming at the cell door.

He had no idea what the time was but a police officer had taken his dinner tray away about half an hour ago so Charlie reckoned it was almost two in the afternoon.

Of course, it was his own stupid fault he was in here, in West End Central police station, and not at Patrick's side, but God… Other than a vague memory of getting the hotel's address from the BonBon club's doorman, everything else about the previous night was a dense grey fog of confusion, that is until the three American Military Police officers burst into the room.

To be honest, he'd gone to the hotel with every intention of killing Stella. However, when the police wrested him from the GI police, and he'd arrived at the police station, he was astonished that he was only being charged with common assault and causing a breach of the peace and not murder. He couldn't remember what had brought him to his senses at the last minute but thank God it had!

Footsteps sounded in the corridor outside, then a key jangled in the cell lock.

It opened and the fair-haired, fresh-faced constable who'd brought Charlie his corned beef hash and spuds earlier walked in, this time carrying an enamel mug.

'I thought you might like a cuppa, chum,' he said, offering it to Charlie.

He took it. 'Thank you, Officer.'

'I put a couple of sugars in it,' the policeman added.

'Just the way I like it,' Charlie replied. 'And thanks for letting my mum and dad in earlier.'

'That's all right,' the constable replied. 'It's the least I could do under the circumstances. How is your little fella?'

'Holding up,' said Charlie.

His parents had arrived half an hour before the midday meal, his mother in tears and his father, as ever, solidly, completely in Charlie's corner. Through them he'd learnt that although Patrick was still unconscious, he had been coughing up tarry-coloured muck, which the nurse had said was a good sign. His son had also had a tube passed down his nose to his stomach so the nurses could give him milk.

'Good,' said the young officer. 'I'm sure he'll pull through.'

Charlie forced a smile.

'The station sergeant would have let you out on police bail,' continued the constable, 'but he's had some bloody Yank general threatening hell and high water—'

'I understand,' said Charlie.

'I tell you straight, none of us in the nick blame you for what you did,' continued the police officer. 'Bloody Yanks. Flashing their money. If it ain't hard enough to keep a lid on the local tarts, we've now got women flooding in from all over the place to turn tricks for doughboys. You know, we had a woman from Scunthorpe picked up last week; tooting a GI's flute in a doorway in broad daylight she was. Scunthorpe! I ask you. Bloody GIs.' He turned and headed towards the door but, before he left, he paused. 'Oh, I almost forgot. You've got another visitor downstairs, a young lady; once I've finished the afternoon checks I'll fetch her up.'

'Thanks, Constable,' said Charlie.

The young officer gave him a sympathetic smile. 'Don't mention it, and the name's Mills.'

His footsteps faded away.

Charlie resumed his seat on the hard wooden bench. Resting back against the wall, he put his feet up.

Wondering which of his sisters was downstairs, Charlie took a mouthful of tea.

He raised his eyes to the top of the wall opposite and was just studying a spider's web in the corner when the cell door lock jangled again.

Putting his mug down, Charlie swung his legs around and stood up.

As the door opened, Charlie forced a cheery smile.

'Hello, sis—'

Charlie's jaw dropped as he started in disbelief.

He could hardly believe his eyes but there she was, dressed in a red flowery frock, green jacket and narrow-brimmed summer hat.

'Francesca!'

Her lovely dark eyes locked with his for a couple of heartbeats then, as the cell door closed behind her, Francesca crossed the space between them.

'Charlie!' she said, throwing her arms around him.

'What are—'

Her lips captured his, stopping his words.

Charlie stood stupefied for a second then, closing his eyes, he parted her lips with his and kissed her back. Her hands moved up his back, hugging him even closer and Charlie's arms tightened around her as her shapely body moulded into the contours of his.

After a breathless, head-spinning moment, Charlie reluctantly tore his lips from hers.

'Francesca?' he said, still not quite believing she was actually in his arms.

'I love you, Charlie,' she said, her eyes confirming her words.

Charlie's gaze ran slowly over her face, taking in every gorgeous detail for a moment then, wrapping her in his embrace again, he pressed his lips onto hers and kissed her deeply.

He didn't know how or why she was here. All he knew was Francesca, the woman he loved, and in whose hands all his happiness, hope and future lay, was in his arms. And she loved him and that was all he needed to know for now.

Waiting until the bus stopped outside the Blind Beggar public house, Francesca stepped down from the running board. Although it was just after five in the afternoon, Waste Street Market was still busy and there were bargains to be had as stallholders offloaded the last of their perishable stock.

Through the window of her father's cafe Francesca could see there were still a handful customers finishing up their late-afternoon cuppa and cake before it closed in half an hour. She also spied her father taking money at the wrought-iron till at one end of the counter.

However, instead of pushing open the front door and going in, Francesca walked past. Turning down the side alley, she headed for the rear of the shop.

Turning the key in the lock, Francesca opened the back door and walked into the square hall at the bottom of the stairs. She removed her jacket and hung it up on the coat rack then, after extracting the pin that secured it to her head, she lifted off her hat. Placing it on the hall table, she looked in the mirror.

Smoothing down her hair, Francesca studied herself for a moment in the reflection, then she ran her finger lightly over her lips, which were still tingling from Charlie's kisses. A shiver of excitement ran through her as the memory of his strong embrace flooded over her.

'Francesca, is that you?' a voice called through the parlour door.

'Yes, Papa,' she replied.

Taking a deep breath to steady her racing heart, she opened the door and walked into the cafe.

Her father had a wide smile on his face. 'Francesca,' he said, tilting his head. 'I thought you'd be back ages ago.'

'Sorry, I was delayed.'

He glanced behind her. 'Where's Leo?'

'Back at the hotel by now, I expect,' she replied.

A puzzled expression replaced his happy one. 'But I thought you were both—'

'I've broken off the engagement.'

His jaw dropped. 'You broke off the engagement?'

'Yes,' she said flatly.

He looked perplexed for a moment, then a sentimental expression crept across his sallow face. 'I suppose you had a lovers' tiff.'

'No, I—'

'It happens,' he continued. 'It's quite natural just before a wedding. It's just nerves. Knowing Leo there'll be a bouquet arriving for you on Monday and it will all be forgotten about in a day or two.'

Francesca squared her shoulders. 'I can't marry Leo, Papa, because I love Charlie Brogan.'

He looked incredulous.

'And he loves me,' she said. 'It would be wrong of me to marry Leo when I don't love him.'

'And when did you decide this?' he asked.

'This morning in the jeweller's shop,' she replied. 'Truthfully, although I tried to tell myself otherwise, deep down I've known all along that I love Charlie too much to marry anyone else.'

'But Leo could give you so much more than Charlie Brogan ever could,' he said. 'For goodness' sake, Francesca, he's a proper aristocrat with money. He's the perfect husband for you.'

'It's for me to say who my perfect husband is, don't you think, ?' Francesca replied, holding her father's furious glare.

'Well, in case you've forgotten, Charlie's already got a wife,' her father continued. 'And what about your job at the BBC? I doubt they'd be too happy employing someone living in sin with a married man.'

A lump formed in Francesca's throat. 'I'll deal with my job when the time comes and Charlie's going to try and get a divorce.'

A furious expression contorted her father's face.

'Divorce!' he shouted. 'How can you shame your family name by even considering marrying a divorced man?'

'I'm not marrying a divorced man,' Francesca replied calmly. 'I'm marrying Charlie.'

'Well, there isn't a Catholic priest in the land who'd perform the ceremony,' he said.

'Then we'll get married in a registry office,' Francesca retorted.

Chewing the inside of his mouth, her father studied her thoughtfully for a moment, the spoke again.

'And what if he can't get a divorce, Francesca, have you thought about that?'

Francesca's heart jumped in her chest, but she held her father's angry gaze. 'Then we'll have to make do without.'

The colour drained from her father's face.

'It's not what either of us wants,' she continued hastily. 'But we want to be husband and wife and if there's no other—'

'You know what people will call you, don't you?' her father bellowed. 'And what if you have children? They'll have to live with the stigma, too.'

'As I said, it's not what either of us want, but—'

'And where is Charlie Brogan? If he's going to shame my daughter before the whole world, surely he should face me like a man instead of leaving you to do his dirty work.'

Francesca's mouth pulled into a firm line. 'Charlie would be here, Papa, but he can't because…'

She told him what had happened the night before.

'I don't know what's going to happen at the magistrates' court on

Monday, but we'll cross that bridge when we come to it,' Francesca concluded. 'And he's to report for duty on Friday so chances are he'll be shipped back to North Africa before the month's out in any case. But when Charlie returns, I'll be setting up home with him. I'm sorry you're disappointed, but I've got to change and then get across to the hospital.'

'But you've only just got in,' he replied.

'I know,' said Francesca. 'I promised Charlie I'd be at Patrick's bedside in case he wakes up. I'm going to take my turn at caring for him. Ida's been there all afternoon so I'm going to relieve her as she's got to get the boys to the shelter. Queenie will take over from me when the blackout starts so I'll be back then.'

Sorrow replaced the anger in her father's eyes and he suddenly looked as if he'd aged a decade.

'All I want is for you to be happy,' he said softly.

Francesca put her arm around her father's sagging shoulders.

'I know, Papa.' Giving him a squeeze, she kissed his forehead. 'And now I have Charlie, I am.'

Chapter thirty-four

CHARLIE STEPPED THROUGH the cell door and followed the police officer down the corridor that was lined with iron doors on either side.

He'd been in the holding cell in Bow Street Magistrates' Court for almost two hours, having arrived in the back of a Black Maria along with a handful of drunks and pickpockets just after ten o'clock.

His travel companions for the mile journey from Savile Row to Covent Garden had all been dealt with and now, finally, it was his turn.

The police officers at West End Central, where he'd been held for the last forty-eight hours, had all been very accommodating and although a police cell must be the most unromantic place on earth, with Francesca in his arms it was something close to Heaven.

She was going to telephone her office to tell them she was going to take a few days off and then come to court, but Charlie had asked her to stay at Patrick's side instead. She was at the hospital now and, hopefully, once the magistrate had dealt with him, he could return to them both. After all, common assault and breach of the peace weren't hanging offences.

With that thought fixed in his head, Charlie set his shoulders straight and marched briskly along the corridor and through the open doorway at the end.

'Good luck, son,' said the court's officer, a sergeant with a grey handlebar moustache, as Charlie emerged into the high-ceilinged courtroom.

He indicated the enclosed area to his right in which sat three American officers.

Each of them was dressed in their formal pink 'n' greens with a collection of bars and stars on their shoulders, their steely eyes focused on him.

Charlie glanced behind him at the public seating area. There were about a dozen people packed into the boxed-off area at the back of the court. Amongst them was his father, who gave him an encouraging thumbs-up.

He stepped into the raised dock and was just about to face the magistrate when the man sitting at the far end of the public gallery caught his eye.

Tucked into the corner behind a couple of women sat a sandy-haired GI with a bull-like physique. Unlike his fellow countrymen sitting on the lawyers' benches, he was an enlisted man and had the three chevrons of a sergeant on his upper arm.

As Charlie's gaze reached him, the sergeant took the cigar from his mouth and blew a stream of thick smoke towards the skylights above.

Charlie didn't know who this cocky doughboy was, but he lay a pound to a penny that he was Stella's fancy man and he knew enough about army life to know that sometimes those in charge didn't have pips in their epaulettes or gold braid on their caps.

A feeling of unease crept up Charlie's spine as he turned his back on the American and faced the magistrate, sitting behind the bench under an arched canopy.

As a youngster Charlie had been, on one or two occasions, brought up before Sir Randolph Ewing, the resident magistrate at Thames Magistrates' Court, for the sort of tomfoolery young men with too much energy were prone to get involved in. Sir Randolph was renowned for being an unsympathetic magistrate and, looking across at the dour-faced man in a horse-hair wig and black gown, Charlie concluded that Sir Malcolm Bevington-Cox was cast in the same mould.

The magistrate studied Charlie for a second, then glanced at the chief clerk who sat at the desk in front of him.

'Mr Salthouse, if you please.'

The clerk, a flat-faced individual with receding hair, stood up and looked at Charlie.

'Bombardier Charles Patrick Brogan,' Mr Salthouse said.

Charlie snapped to attention.

'You are charged with common assault and breach of the peace,' continued the clerk. 'How do you plead?'

'Guilty,' Charlie replied.

'Stand easy, Bombardier,' said Sir Malcolm.

Clasping his hands behind his back, Charlie took a half-step.

The magistrate looked at Sergeant Hanson, Charlie's arresting officer, who was standing beside the witness box.

With his helmet tucked under his arm, the sergeant took the stand. After placing his headgear on the seat behind him, he took the oath.

'In your own time, Officer,' said the magistrate, when he'd handed the Bible back to the clerk.

Sergeant Hanson, a stout officer in his mid-fifties with wiry red hair, took out his pocketbook.

He cleared his throat. 'I was on patrol with PC Jones when, at ten minutes past three in the morning on Saturday 14th, we were called to the Excelsior Hotel in Hay's Mews where gunfire had been heard. We arrived to find the accused being held by three American Military Police officers. On investigation we discovered that Bombardier Brogan was supposed to have collected his son from his wife, Mrs Stella Iris Brogan, from the family home at around six o'clock. However, Bombardier Brogan was delayed on his journey home from his appointment at the Middlesex hospital for several hours because of a power failure on the Central line.'

'Hospital?' asked the magistrate.

'Yes,' the police officer replied. 'He was injured on active duty in North Africa. When Bombardier Brogan didn't turn up at the allotted time, Mrs Brogan, who was due on stage at eight, set off to work at six thirty leaving their one-year-old son in the house alone in his cot.'

'Is Mrs Brogan an actress?' asked the magistrate.

'An exotic dancer,' Sergeant Conroy replied. 'In the BonBon strip club. When Bombardier Brogan finally returned home at ten he found there had been an air raid and his son was trapped in the collapsed house, which was on fire. Having rescued his son, he took him to the London hospital where he is now in a critical condition. After discovering Stella Brogan had gone to the Excelsior Hotel, he followed her and, after a short struggle with Private Abraham, who was guarding the hotel's entrance, Bombardier Brogan took his gun and went into the hotel. There he found his wife in bed with Master Sergeant Elijah Forrester Lee Moffit. Bombardier Brogan let off eight rounds into the ceiling above their head after which he was apprehended by the three GI MP officers.'

'Thank you, Sergeant.' The magistrate turned his attention to Charlie.

'And where else have you served, Bombardier?' the magistrate asked.

Charlie stood to attention again.

'Northern France and Dunkirk,' he said. 'Then on an ack-ack gun in Hackney Marshes during the autumn of 1940 after which I shipped out to Algiers in May last year.'

The magistrate's unyielding gaze softened a little. 'And have you anything to say in your defence?'

'No, sir.'

'Well then—'

'Excuse me, Judge,' said one of the three American officers, leaping to his feet.

Sir Malcolm's bushy eyebrows rose. 'And you are?'

The American officer saluted. 'Captain R. J. Milkwood, of American Army Advocate Corps. And this is my assistant, Lieutenant Warren. And I'd like to submit evidence in this case.'

A pleasant expression lifted the magistrate's long face. 'Would you now?'

'Indeed, I would,' said Captain Milkwood, a lean man of about Charlie's age with a shock of white-blond hair and startling blue eyes. 'I have here –' he held his hand out and his assistant handed him manila file – 'witness statements which I would like to submit to you, Judge, which prove that Bombardier Brogan should be facing a charge of attempted murder and aggravated assault.'

Charlie's blood seemed to turn to ice in his veins.

The magistrate looked astounded. 'Statements from who?'

Milkwood gave a smug smile and raised the file like a lawyer in a B-rated courtroom drama.

'Mrs Brogan,' he boomed, his eyes scanning across the handful of police officers and onto the spectators in the galley, 'who has been so deeply traumatised that she has yet to recover from her brush with death. Master Sergeant Elijah Forrester Lee Moffit, an officer in the United States of America's supply corps with an exemplary service record and Private Abrahams, who had his M1 Gerand rifle ripped from his hands and was beaten to the ground during Brogan's violent rampage through the Excelsior Hotel, have also testified. It is only by the good Lord's grace that those eight bullets missed their target.' His gaze flickered briefly towards the public gallery where the lone GI sat. 'And we further ask that as the Excelsior Hotel is under American control as a secure billet for its service personnel, you hand the bombardier over to a US authority.'

A lump formed in Charlie's throat as images of himself facing a line of American officers in a military court flashed through his mind.

Leaning forward, the magistrate studied the American officer for a moment, then spoke again.

'Might I say something, Captain?'

Milkwood's smug smile spread a little further. 'Please, Judge.'

'This is a British court, not some Hollywood film set,' bellowed Sir Malcolm. 'So who the hell do you think you are, coming in here and throwing your damn weight about?'

The American captain blinked with surprise. 'But I have evidence—'

'Get out!' yelled the magistrate, his jowls quivering with rage as he grasped the bench in front of him. 'Get out before I have you both arrested for contempt of court.'

A flush coloured the fair-haired American captain's cheeks and he glanced nervously towards the GI at the back of the courtroom again.

'Officer!' shouted Sir Malcolm.

The court's resident police officer stepped forward.

Captain Milkwood thrust the file at the man beside him who, after shoving them into a briefcase, stood up.

'I shall be reporting this to Colonel Greywood,' the captain said, pulling down the front of his jacket.

'As will I when I meet Major General Ingram at the club later,' Sir Malcolm replied.

With as much dignity as he could muster after being roundly balled out in front everyone, Captain Milkwood and his lieutenant walked across the courtroom.

'And I'm a magistrate, not a judge, so you address me as "your worship" not "my lord", you pair of goons!' Sir Malcolm hollered as they left the courtroom.

The door slammed shut and the magistrate turned back to Charlie.

'Now we have command of my courtroom again, let's move on,' he said. 'Bombardier Brogan.'

Charlie stood to attention again.

'Having pleaded guilty to common assault and a breach of the peace you're bound over on both counts for a year.'

Relief swept over Charlie.

'Thank you, sir,' said Charlie, sending a small prayer skywards that, unlike the magistrate at the Thames Magistrates' Court, Sir Malcolm had actually listened to the evidence and shown some compassion.

'Also, Salthouse,' continued Sir Malcolm, 'send a note to the superintendent at Arbour Square police station regarding Mrs Brogan. Her conduct towards her son sounds like child endangerment to me.'

'Yes, sir,' the clerk of the court replied, scribbling on his notes.

'And, Brogan!' said the magistrate, as he looked over his spectacles at Charlie. 'I hope your son recovers.'

'Thank you, sir,' he replied.

'Next!'

Charlie turned and, stepping out of the dock, he looked at the sandy-haired GI who was now shoving his way through the crowd towards the exit.

He caught Charlie looking his way and paused.

Charlie held the stocky GI's enraged glare for a moment, then the not-so-cocky-now doughboy left the public gallery.

'So, thanks to Kep, Jemima Puddle-Duck was safe back on the farm,' said Francesca, closing the children's book on her lap.

Patrick, who was lying with his eyes closed and the rubber oxygen mask over the lower half of his face, didn't respond.

She looked at her watch. It was two thirty. Ten minutes later than when she'd looked the last time.

Damping down her anxiety, Francesca reached across and stroked Patrick's springy curls. As she withdrew her hand, Charlie strode past the side-room's window and through the door. He was unshaven and grey with weariness but, when they rested on her, his eyes lit up.

Setting aside the book, she stood up and flew into his arms.

'Charlie, I was beginning to—'

His lips closed over hers as his arms tightened around her.

Francesca gave herself up to the magic of his kiss but, after a couple of heartbeats, broke away.

'What happened at court?'

'I was bound over on both charges,' he replied.

Francesca let out a long breath. 'Thank goodness. When you weren't back by midday, I was worried that something had happened.'

He gave a wry smile. 'There was a hiccup, but I'll tell you about it another time.'

He kissed her on the forehead, then crossed the room to his son. Perching on the edge of the chair she'd just vacated, he reached across and held Patrick's motionless hand.

'How is he?' he asked in a tight voice.

'Better,' Francesca replied. 'The nurse said he still had a good colour despite them reducing the oxygen level and she also said he's more or less stopped coughing up black muck, which means his lungs must be almost clear. And I'm sure his eyelids flickered a little as I read to him.'

'You've been reading to him?' he said softly as he smoothed his son's hair.

'Yes, there was a talk on the wireless about how people who are unconscious can still hear so I thought it might help if I read him Jemima Puddle-Duck,' Francesca replied.

Charlie kissed his son's forehead, then stood up.

Taking Francesca's hand, he drew her to him and enveloped her in his embrace again.

'Do you know how much I love you?' he asked, smiling lovingly down at her.

Francesca smiled back. 'As much as I love you, I expect.'

Kissing her briefly on the lips, he pulled up the other chair in the room and then sat down on the one closest to his son.

Picking up the book from the bedside locker, Francesca sat down next to Charlie and handed it to him.

'Your turn.'

Charlie gave a low laugh then, crossing one long leg sideward over the other, he opened the book.

'What a funny sight…'

Sitting in the chair beside him, Francesca rested her head and closed her eyes to listen to his deep voice telling them about the maternal duck's problems with her eggs.

'When she reached the top of—'

A strangled gasp cut across Charlie's words.

Francesca's eyes flew open to see Patrick awake and choking.

Splaying his large hand across his spluttering son's back, Charlie sat him upright as she screamed 'nurse' and dashed out of the room.

As he held his choking son upright, fear gripped Charlie.

'It's all right, Patrick, Daddy's here,' he said, patting his son's back and feeling utterly useless. 'Daddy's here.'

When the nurse, in a lilac pin-striped uniform, dashed in, with Francesca on her heels, Patrick was red-faced and retching.

'It's the tube,' said the dark-haired nurse calmly.

Grabbing the stainless-steel kidney bowl containing a handful of gauze swabs, she came over.

'It's all right,' she said, smiling at his snotty son. 'We'll soon have that nasty old thing out.'

Holding Patrick firmly, Charlie pressed his lips on the lad's head as the nurse extracted the rubber tube from his nose.

'All done,' she said, dropping it in the kidney bowl.

Charlie went to hug Patrick.

'I'd hold back for a moment, Dad, if I were you,' said the nurse, holding the kidney bowl under the boy's chin.

Patrick shuddered, then vomited into the bowl.

'That's better,' said the nurse, wiping his mouth. 'You can hug him now.' She gave the little boy a soft look. 'I reckon this little lad deserves a bit of hugging after what he's been through.'

'I couldn't agree more,' said Charlie, lifting Patrick out of the cot.

'I'll make him a bit of scrambled egg in the kitchen,' she said, gathering up the soiled equipment. 'Poor baby, he must be starving.'

'I'm sure he is.' Charlie kissed his son's hot, damp cheek. 'Thank you, nurse?'

'Sullivan,' she replied. 'I'll let the doctor know.'

She left.

Holding his son in his arms, Charlie looked across at Francesca, who had fat tears shimmering on her lower lids.

'Thank God,' she said, as one escaped and rolled down her cheek.

He crossed the space between them and, taking her in his free arm, hugged both the woman he loved and his son in one embrace.

'Well, ain't that touching?'

Opening his eyes Charlie saw Stella, dressed up to the nines, standing in the door.

'That's a nice thing to do, ain't it, Charlie?' she continued, her furious eyes fixed on him. 'Canoodle with your bit of fluff in front of your sick kid.'

Keeping his arm around Francesca, Charlie turned to face her.

'Although you haven't said, I'm sure you're pleased to see, Stella, that Patrick is out of danger,' he said.

'Of course I bloody am!' she snapped. A sickly smile spread across her face.

'Hello, baby,' she said, wiggling her painted fingers. 'Mummy's here.'

Patrick stared wide-eyed at her, but didn't respond.

'Of course, he only spent the last three days unconscious in hospital because of you,' he replied. 'I'm surprised you've got the nerve to show your face, Stella, after the little stunt your fancy man tried to pull in the court this morning. Not to mention all that bloody cock and bull you told the Yank solicitor in your witness statement.'

'I don't know what you mean,' she replied, struggling to hold his gaze.

'Don't think I didn't see your GI at the back of public gallery,' he replied. 'I suppose it was him who had those goons pop up to argue with the magistrate.'

Stella's lips twisted into an ugly scarlet line.

'You should have been done for bloody attempted murder,' she snapped.

Francesca gasped, but Charlie gave her a reassuring hug.

'And you *will* be done for child cruelty,' he replied. 'Oh, didn't your doughboy tell you that the magistrate sent a note to Arbour Square's senior officer asking him to investigate you? You'll be the one doing time, not me.'

Alarm flashed across her face for an instant, but a smirk replaced it.

She took a step closer and Patrick's arms tightened around Charlie's neck.

'Even if I was!' she screamed, jabbing her finger in Charlie's face. 'I'd still be your bloody wife so you can forget putting a ring on 'er finger.'

Patrick started howling.

Letting go of Francesca, Charlie rocked his son.

'What the blue blazes is going on?'

Looking over Stella's shoulder, Charlie saw a very tall middle-aged man, in a three-piece suit, a club tie at his throat and a stethoscope draped around his neck, standing in the room with the ward sister hovering behind him.

'I'm sorry,' said Charlie, as the doctor studied him through his horn-rimmed spectacles. 'Things got a little heated.'

'Indeed they did,' the doctor agreed. 'I take it you're the boy's father.'

'I am,' Charlie replied.

'Dr Shepherd.'

He offered his hand and Charlie took it.

The doctor turned to Stella. 'And you are?'

'Patrick's mother,' she snapped, glaring at him.

Dr Shepherd's heavy eyebrows rose, and he looked at Francesca, who was standing beside Charlie. 'I thought—'

'Naw,' Stella interrupted. 'She's just my husband's bit on the side.'

Francesca lowered her eyes as a blush coloured her cheeks.

Charlie gave her a hateful glare, which Stella answered with a sweet smile.

'Well, your domestic arrangements are your own concern,' the medic said, studying them down his sharp nose. 'Mine is the little chap in the bed who, despite having a jolly rough time, seems to have come through none the worse for it.'

'So I can take him home?' asked Charlie, as relief swept over him.

The doctor shook his head and gave him a sober look. 'I'd like to keep him under observation until Friday. Just to be sure.'

Charlie looked bleakly at him. 'But I return to base tomorrow.'

'I'm sorry,' said Dr Shepherd. 'It's just a couple of days and if he's still as right as ninepence by Friday, he can go home. I'm sure you'll understand; I have to put my patient's well-being first.'

Unable to speak, Charlie nodded.

'Well, thank you, Doctor,' said Stella. 'And Friday it is, then.'

Dr Shepherd cast his eyes over the three of them again and then left the room with the ward sister in his wake.

Francesca slipped her arm through Charlie's and gave him a little squeeze.

Stella's smug smile returned.

'What a pity you're not going to be here on Friday, Charlie,' she said brightly. 'But don't worry, I'll fetch him home.' Opening her handbag, she took out her compact and snapped it open. 'Not my old home, of course,' she continued, checking her face in the mirror. 'But somewhere nice and away from all the bombing.' She dabbed her nose with the small powder puff. 'So you can tell your mum she won't have to worry about Patrick any more because I'll be looking after him from now on.' Looking up, she smiled. 'Bye-bye, Patrick,' she said, wiggling her fingers at him again. 'Mummy will see you soon.'

Snapping the case shut, she dropped it back in her handbag and closed it.

'Have a nice trip back to North Africa, Charlie,' she said, then turned and trotted out of the side ward, the click of her heels fading as she walked towards the ward's main door.

Charlie stared bleakly after her for a moment, then looked down at Patrick nestling in his arms. Resting his head lightly on Patrick's, Charlie closed his eyes.

Francesca wrapped her arms around them both. 'We will get Patrick back, Charlie,' she said, pressing her lips to his forehead.

'I know,' he said, praying to God and all his saints above that she was right.

Chapter thirty-five

THE RATTLING OF the old water pipes running up the wall behind Francesca woke her from a light doze. She looked around and found Charlie studying her in the low lighting of the hospital basement.

Dressed in his battle dress he was sitting next to her on an old mattress on the floor with his packed kit bag beside him. He was cradling Patrick in his arms as he had done since Stella marched out the evening before.

'I must have nodded off,' she said, rubbing her eyes to drive the sleep from them.

'I got you a cup of tea when the WVS trolley came by a while back.' Charlie indicated the china mug sitting on the concrete at their feet. But I expect it's cold by now.'

She looked surprised. 'How long have I been asleep?'

'A while.'

Ida had arrived half an hour after Stella left and wept on Charlie's chest for a full minute when she'd found Patrick sitting up in the hospital cot. Jo and Cathy had popped in after that, bringing Patrick a few treats and to say goodbye to their brother. Mattie had arrived shortly after her sisters had left. After hugging her big brother and nephew, Francesca's lifelong friend, who knew how long she'd loved Charlie, clasped her in a warm embrace. Jerimiah, wearing his Fire Auxiliary uniform, had dropped by on his way to work to see his grandson and bid his son farewell. The last Brogan to arrive was Queenie, who'd walked into Patrick's side-room as the day staff were departing at seven. She'd come to spend the night with her great-grandson but after finding Francesca with Charlie at Patrick's bedside, she'd said her goodbyes to her grandson and had left them to be alone.

The warning siren on the hospital's roof had started wailing about half an hour after she'd gone so instead of spending the night in an uncomfortable upright chair at Patrick's bedside they were now in the relative comfort of the hospital's basement, along with dozens of patients and staff.

A bomb crashing to earth shook the ground and set the dangling strip lights above them bouncing.

'Did you manage to get some shut-eye?' she asked.

'I'll sleep later.' He smiled down at her.

'What?' asked Francesca, grabbing her thick plait and pulling it over her shoulder.

'I was just thinking how beautiful you are,' he said softly.

She laughed. 'What, with my hair all messed up and my mascara smudged?'

'Even so,' he replied. 'And…'

'And what?' she asked, as she tucked her hair back into the snood and re-pinned it.

'And I can't wait until I can watch you sleeping beside me every day,' he replied, giving her the look that always set her pulse racing.

'The war won't go on for ever and then…' She looked shyly at him from under her lashes. 'Then we can be together, properly, with Patrick.'

Charlie frowned and opened his mouth to speak.

'And don't ask again if I'm sure,' she continued. 'Because, yes, I am, totally. I love you, Charlie, and if us living in sin is the only way we can be together as husband and wife, then that's the way it has to be. And it's not as if we'll be the only couple in the area living together without marriage lines. I could name half a dozen right off the top of my head.'

In the muted light of the basement's strip lighting his blue-grey eyes darkened, as the ground trembled again.

'Good,' he replied, in a low voice. 'Because I can't imagine a future without you by my side.'

Adjusting his son in his arms, Charlie leant forward and kissed her. Francesca's hand slid up his chest and held the back of his neck as they kissed for a couple of electrifying moments, then he released her.

A grim expression spread across his face. 'It's five o'clock, Francesca.'

'Already?'

Tears pinched the corners of Francesca's eyes, but she blinked them away.

'You'd better get going then,' she replied, forcing a bright smile. 'You don't want to be AWOL on your first day back.'

Closing his eyes, Charlie pressed his lips to his son's forehead, then transferred him into her arms.

Patrick snuffled and pulled a face at being disturbed but then drifted back to sleep as Francesca settled him across her lap. She gave him a peck on the cheek, then tucked the hospital's blue blanket around him.

Charlie ran his fingers across Patrick's unruly curls, his gaze soft as he looked at his sleeping son, then his attention shifted to Francesca.

'If only I had—'

'What's done is done, Charlie,' she cut in. 'And it doesn't matter. All that matters is that you come back to both of us.'

Charlie's gaze locked with hers for a heartbeat then, leaning across, he placed his lips on hers in the tenderest of kisses.

He stood up. He swung his kit bag over his shoulder then, as another explosion set the water pipes behind her rattling again, he turned and walked away.

*

'I'm guessing you like them, huh?' said Donny, as Stella's fingers caressed the three-row string of pearls draped around her neck.

'I do,' she replied, enjoying the warm feeling of them on her skin.

Donny swallowed a large mouthful of his drink. 'Well, they cost a pretty penny, so—'

'And I earned every bloody one of them, didn't I?' Stella replied, giving him a sour look.

Leaning forward, Donny placed his hand on her thigh. 'You sure did, baby. You sure did.'

Too right I did, thought Stella, as the memory of the gun pointed at her chest and the reverberation of the rapid fire over her head flashed back through her mind.

It was nearly midnight on Thursday, just six days since Charlie had burst in on her and Eli Moffit. She and Donny were in some club with dark walls and low lights, just off Wardour Street. It was in the cellar of one of the houses and, like every club in the West End and Soho, it was packed with American servicemen and almost as many doe-eyed young women working hard to spend their money.

As always, she and Donny were in the best seats which, in this case, were in a raised booth at the back of the club. This gave them an unhindered view of the dance floor and the small jazz band who were doing their best to drown out the sound of the bombs crashing to earth close by.

The siren warning had gone off just after they'd left Donny's rooms a couple of hours before and the first wave of enemy bombers had followed soon after.

Stella swallowed a large mouthful of her G & T. Returning her cigarette to her lips, she drew in a lungful of smoke.

'He should have gone down for it,' she snapped, as the image of Charlie holding a rifle flashed through her mind again.

'That's life, I guess,' Donny replied with a shrug.

'Can't you do something about him getting off almost scot-free?'

persisted Stella. 'After all, you're the one who's forever telling me you've got the goods on the top brass.'

He looked puzzled. 'Got the goods?'

'Know their dirty little secrets,' Stella explained.

'I do but if you stir up a hornets' nest you're gonna get stung, babe,' Donny said. 'So perhaps better to let sleeping dogs lie because someone up top starts poking around, they might start looking into how we're mixed up with Eli. They might even start poking around in the PX accounts and checking dockets. And we don't want that, do we? Not when Eli still wants in on our little arrangement with Len, especially now that he's lining up buyers for the lorryload I'm sending his way next week.'

'I suppose,' said Stella moodily.

Reaching across, Donny squeezed her knee.

'Hey, look on the bright side,' he said. 'The money's rolling in and your kid's on the mend, right?'

Stella nodded and drew on her cigarette again.

'Did you see him today?' Donny asked.

'I popped in,' she replied, flicking ash into the ashtray in the middle of the table. 'But I didn't stay long as Charlie's sodding family were there.' A spiteful smile spread across her face. 'Still, they'll be smiling on the other side of their poxy faces when I take Patrick away from them tomorrow.'

The band finished their number and the dancers drifted off the floor. A hefty-looking girl with red hair and red lips wearing a stylised ATS costume and high heels wriggled out from the wings and stood in front of the microphone.

As the musicians behind her played the opening bars of 'Don't Fence Me In', Donny downed another slug of bourbon and then took his cigar case from his inside pocket.

'You're not thinking of bringing him back to the Hibernian, are you?' he asked, flicking a flame from his lighter.

'Don't be daft.' Stella laughed. 'One of the dancers at the club knows some woman over Bermondsey way who looks after kids from time to time. He can go there tomorrow until I sort out getting him evacuated.'

Puffing on his smoke, Donny gave her a measured look. 'Tell me to butt out if you like, babe, but wouldn't it just be easier to let your old man's folks have the kid?'

Stella's flame-red lips pulled into a tight line.

'I suppose it would, but I wouldn't give them the satisfaction. Not after the way his bloody family have treated me over the years.'

The image of Patrick clinging to Ida when Stella tried to take him from her when she arrived at the hospital that afternoon flashed through her.

'No, let them suffer for turning Patrick against me like they have.' Stella gave a mirthless laugh. She flicked the cigarette ash again. 'And, anyway, I'm doing it for Patrick. He'll be better off in the country, ain't that what the ruddy government's always telling us?'

Donny shrugged.

Stella knocked back the last of her drink and placed the glass on the table.

'Do you want another?'

'Not here with all that caterwauling going on,' Stella replied, as the singer hit a duff note. 'Let's go to that one behind Swan & Edgar.'

'You mean The Deuce?' he asked.

'That's it,' Stella replied.

Donny downed the last of his Scotch and threw a brown ten-bob note on the table. 'Well then, baby, let's go.'

They emerged onto Wardour Street, which, despite the air raid warnings, was filled with men and women who, like them, were also out enjoying London's lively nightlife.

The drone of enemy planes overhead stifled the noise in the street. Above them the searchlights criss-crossed the sky. In Green Park the ack-ack guns pumped a shower of shells in an arc across the black sky as the unmistakable thud of bombs dropping reverberated through the ground under Stella's new patent wedges.

Donny turned on his torch and shone it on the ground in front of them. Stella slipped her arm through his and trotted along beside him, pools of light from passers-by also adding a little more illumination to her path. They turned into Brewer Street and, despite the blackout, Stella could see little twinkles of light as the hooded headlights of the buses and service vehicles moved along Regent Street.

She was just wondering if she should get Donny to buy her a bracelet to match her new necklace when an explosion rocked the street. Stella staggered as people around her crashed to the pavement.

She tried to grab Donny but he was no longer beside her. Another blast, that seemed to lift the whole ground, boomed, throwing up a screen of earth from between the pavement slabs.

Stella opened her mouth to scream but, as she did, a flash of light seared her eyes. Blinded, she stood stock-still for a second, then a rush of scorching air lifted her off her feet and tore her breath from her lungs.

There was a moment of unbearable heat and agonising pain then Stella Brogan, née Miggles, ceased to be.

Chapter thirty-six

AS FRANCESCA STEPPED out on to the third floor of Bush House, she yawned.

Hardly surprising really, as she'd hadn't had a wink of sleep all night. She was worrying about Patrick because Stella would be collecting him from hospital today and worrying about Charlie, who could do nothing to stop her. And she was worrying about facing Leo again.

Gripping the handles of her basket firmly, Francesca headed towards Radio Roma's office at the end of the corridor. Then she paused.

Although she wasn't relishing facing Leo, as they worked together she would have to face him at some point so perhaps better to do it sooner rather than later. Clear the air.

She was only glad she'd insisted they keep their courtship secret as it would perhaps save his pride being too dented.

Taking a deep breath, Francesca grasped the handle and, steeling herself, strode in.

'Good morn—'

She stopped dead and her jaw dropped.

Instead of the half a dozen desks in the office being piled high with recording discs and manuscripts, they were bare, with even the pencil trays and blotting paper removed. In addition, the pinboards behind them had been stripped of the notes and schedules, plus the grey filing cabinets had been removed, leaving squares of brighter-coloured Lino where they had stood. The telephones had vanished, too, along with Francesca's typewriter.

Footsteps sounded behind her and Francesca turned as Miss Kirk walked into the office.

'Oh hello, Francesca, how are you?' she said, beaming at her.

'I'm a little tired but well enough?'

'Splendid, splendid,' said her supervisor. 'I'm so glad to hear it but I wasn't expecting you back until Monday. Is everything all right?'

'Yes, thank you,' Francesca replied. 'But I could ask you the same question. What on earth has happened?'

'Oh, you mean the office?' said Miss Kirk.

Francesca nodded.

'I'm afraid the director of the Overseas department has pulled the plug on Radio Roma,' Miss Kirk laughed. 'It's been on the cards for a while but when Signor D'Angelo phoned in on Monday and said he was taking indefinite leave—'

'He's gone?' cut in Francesca.

'Yes,' said Miss Kirk, cheerfully. 'Off into the wild blue yonder, it seems.'

'But he was so committed to making Radio Roma a success,' said Francesca, feeling more than a little responsible for the station's demise.

'Well, obviously for all his fine words Signor D'Angelo couldn't have been that committed, or he wouldn't have just upped and left like that but, after the Old Servants on the fifth floor, got to hear about it that was the last straw as far as they were concerned. The directive came around on Tuesday and the porters came to take the equipment the following day.'

'What about us?'

'We're going to be deployed to other departments,' Miss Kirk replied. 'Mr Whyte has already been sent to Drama and Mr Crozier, who was only on loan anyhow, has returned to Sport at Broadcasting House. I've asked Miss Frobisher, who's in charge of the personnel department, if I can move to News.' She gave Francesca a jolly smile. 'I'm quite looking forward to getting dispatches hot-foot from the front line. Oh, and don't worry,' she continued, seeing Francesca's troubled look, 'I put in a good word for you. Told her you were hard-working and would be an asset in any department.'

'Thank you,' said Francesca. 'Perhaps I should pop along and speak to her now.'

'She's gone to Alexandra Place studios today, so I suggest you see her on Monday and put in your request,' Miss Kirk replied.

'I will,' said Francesca. 'But what shall I do today?'

'Well, there's nothing for you to do,' Miss Kirk replied jollily. 'So I suggest as you've been putting in a lot of extra hours recently, you take the time back and go home.'

'If you're sure,' said Francesca.

'Yes, I am,' her supervisor replied. 'I'm just popping down to the stores so before you do, make sure you've taken anything you want to keep out of your desk drawers as the porters will be coming for them later.'

She picked up the dozen or so files. 'Oh, I almost forgot.' Juggling the files in one hand, Miss Kirk fished around in her jacket pocket. 'This arrived from the post room for you this morning.'

She handed Francesca a cream envelope with a heraldic shield instead of a stamp on the top right-hand corner.

'Thank you,' Francesca said, taking it from her. 'I must say, you seem to be taking this very well.'

'Well, these things happen and I'm sure it will be for the best in the long run,' Miss Kirk replied. 'And I've had a bit of good news too.' Her expression went from happy to blissful. 'I had a phone call last night from Professor Giulio telling me that not only will he be coming back to work soon, but also…' Behind her metal-rimmed spectacles Miss Kirk's pale-grey eyes grew wistful. 'Not wanting to speak out of turn, mind you, but as his insensitive wife has gone to live with her sister in Cheshire, Bruno has invited me over to keep him company tonight and is cooking us both dinner.' She gave a heavy sigh and adjusted the files in her arms. 'Have a nice weekend, Fran, and I'll see you Monday.'

Opening the door, the supervisor left.

Putting her handbag on her now-empty desk, Francesca sat down behind it and turned over the expensive-looking envelope. The flap had a wax seal securing it with the Pontadera family crest pressed into it.

Sliding her finger underneath, Francesca broke it. Then, opening the envelope, she took out the single sheet of paper.

Dear Francesca,

    As always, I hope you are in the finest of health.

    By the time you read this letter I will be many miles away staying with old university friends in Scotland. I may stay with them for some time so it is unlikely our paths will cross again.

    Therefore, I am taking my leave of you the coward's way in a letter. And I am a coward because as much as I desperately want to see you, I dare not. I dare not because I know, my darling, I would just fall on my knees and beg you to reconsider. I know you cannot, and I have accepted that even if my broken heart has yet to reach that state of being.

    You ask me to forgive you but, in truth, there is nothing to forgive as I know to my cost love cannot be denied. Your love is leading you on a narrow, rocky road for a respectable young woman and I hope it won't be too long or too painful a journey.

    I will finish now by assuring you of my best wishes for your future, which I pray will be a long and happy one.

    Your most devoted servant
    Leonardo D'Angelo, Count of Pontadera

As she read Leo's signature, sadness rose up in Francesca.

Folding the letter, she placed it back in the envelope and laid it on her desk before retrieving her fountain pen, pencil case and notebook from her top drawer.

Standing up, she dropped them into her handbag, then hooked it over her shoulder and, picking up Leo's letter, stepped out from behind the desk. She glanced down at the stiff cream envelope for a moment, then tore it into quarters. Dropping it into the half-full wastepaper salvage bin, Francesca shook the pieces to the bottom.

Another time, another place, she and Leo might have had a chance, but he was right. Love cannot be denied. She loved Charlie. That was all and everything.

Walking to the door, Francesca grasped the brass handle, opened it and walked out to face her future with Charlie, the only man she would ever love.

Stacking the last of the washed crockery from the midday meal on the draining board, Queenie picked up the tea towel but, as she reached across to take the first plate, one of her rings slipped off her finger. It spun around a couple of times then landed flat next to one of the upturned mugs.

The thin, nondescript silver band lying on the scrubbed wooden surface had been her mother's wedding ring. Queenie had taken it off her mother's finger and put it on her own as her mother lay in her coffin almost half a century ago and it had sat there ever since.

Queenie stared at it for a moment then looked around.

'Well now, that's a sign from the other side if ever I saw one,' she said, picking the ring up and putting it back on her finger.

Prince Albert, who was perched on the top of the dresser bobbed his head up and down in agreement.

'But the meaning of it and all the other happenings this morning escapes me,' she added, running the tea towel over a plate.

The grey bird trilled his reply.

Queenie put the dry plate on the table and picked up the next one.

'First there was meself being all a-fussy and a-fizzling,' she continued, remembering the floaty feeling surrounding her since she'd opened her eyes that morning. 'And then there were the chickens all skittery around the pen like a group of nuns lost in one of those nuddy camps.' She placed the second dry plate on the first. 'Not to mention the wind blowing a multitude of formless sentiments around me head as I was hanging the washing in the yard.' Running the tea towel around the inside of a pot, Queenie looked up at the forty-watt light bulb hanging from the ceiling. 'If you lot, skittering around up there, could impart your foretellings in a mite less bamboozling way, that would be grand.'

'I suppose you're talking to the spirits again, Ma?' Jerimiah said, as he walked into the kitchen in his dressing gown and boots.

He'd been on duty the night before and had staggered in, sooty and exhausted, as the boys were leaving for school. He had been in bed ever since.

'Well, who else would I be talking to as there's not been another soul in the house these past hours other than yourself snoring your head off upstairs?' she replied.

A gust of something swept across her mind. Queenie put her hand to her forehead.

'Are you all right, Ma?' Jerimiah asked anxiously.

'Of course I'm all right!' she snapped, feeling anything but. 'Now, you're making the place untidy so sit yourself down and I'll make you a cup of tea.'

He gave her a dubious look, then spotted the parrot. 'You'd better not let Ida see him. Not after he shat in her ironing basket last week.'

Queenie waved his words away and re-lit the gas under the kettle. 'Ida's gone around to Mattie's so she won't be back for hours.'

The back door opened and Ida, with her five-month-gone belly, waddled in, pushing Patrick's pushchair in front of her with a dazed-looking Patrick strapped in it.

Seeing her, the little boy waved his hands. However, as Queenie waved back, the miasma of emotions swirled around her head again.

Ida spotted Prince Albert hovering over her best china on top of the dresser.

'What's your parrot doing out of his cage?' she asked, bending over and unhooking her grandson from his harness and setting him on the floor.

'Having a spread of his wings,' Queenie replied. 'But I've a better question for you to answer. How is it you have Charlie's lad with you? I thought his hussy of a mother was fetching him from the hospital.'

'Thankfully, Mattie had given the hospital her number and they phoned just before I arrived to ask when he was being picked up,' Ida replied, setting Patrick on his feet.

'Do you know where Stella's got to?' asked Jerimiah.

'Sprawled under some fecking American and still plastered, I shouldn't wonder,' said Queenie.

'Don't swear in front of Patrick,' said Ida, glancing at her grandson who was bouncing his Auntie Jo's old wooden horse across the Lino.

'He'll hear far worse than that from his mother,' said Jerimiah.

'Well, he won't,' said Queenie, as the swirling sensations started again. 'We promised Charlie we would move heaven and earth to get Patrick back and now we have him, he's staying with us.'

Ida's mouth pulled into a firm line. 'Yes, he is and when Stella does arrive, we'll tell her to sling her hook.' Her attention shifted to her husband. 'Jerry, go and get dressed. If it ends up being a screaming match on the doorstep, I don't want the neighbours seeing you in your dressing gown. You can use the washstand, so take the kettle with you.'

'But—'

'I'll boil another when you get down,' she added.

Jerimiah gave a sigh. Rising to his feet, he trudged back upstairs.

Through the window Queenie heard the back gate open and close.

She and Ida looked at each other for a second, then Ida scooped up Patrick.

Queenie stood shoulder to shoulder with her daughter-in-law and they faced the back door.

The handle turned and the door open.

'Francesca!' said Ida in surprise as she stepped into the kitchen.

'Hello,' replied Francesca, looking a real treat in her flowery summer dress. 'What's Patrick doing here?'

As Queenie's eyes rested on the lovely young woman who had captured her grandson's heart, the storm of emotions that had swirled around her head all morning vanished in an instant.

Queenie smiled. 'Come in, me darling, and we'll tell you over a cuppa.'

'So I dashed straight around to the hospital and picked him up,' said Ida, as Francesca finished her last mouthful of tea. 'And when she does turn up I'm going to tell her to push off cos we're going to look after him properly until Charlie comes back. Isn't that right, Queenie?'

Francesca's attention shifted to Charlie's gran, who was sitting in her usual chair by the hearth.

'That we are,' the old woman replied, a soft, sentimental expression on her face as she looked across.

In fact, Queenie had been gazing at Fran in much the same way since she'd arrived half an hour ago.

'Lovely though it is to see you, Fran,' said Ida, who was sitting opposite her mother-in-law with Patrick on her lap, 'I thought you were at work.'

'I went in this morning but...well, they've been having trouble for weeks with the Italian authorities blocking the broadcasts so the bigwigs on the top floor have pulled the plug on Radio Roma. We're being kept on but, as I can't find out where until Monday, Miss Kirk sent me home,' she said. 'I was going to help Dad with the midday rush but, as I stepped off the bus, I had the strangest notion that I should pop in on you first, Mrs Brogan,' Francesca added.

'Sure you did,' said Queenie, with a knowing, wistful sigh.

Patrick wriggled off his grandmother's ever-shrinking lap and toddled over to Francesca and tried to climb up. Putting down her empty cup, Francesca lifted him up and settled him on her knee, giving him a tender kiss.

Queenie's expression slid from sentimental to downright soppy, a look which was somewhat peculiar on a woman who could turn the handle on a cast-iron mangle as if it were an egg whisk.

The door opened and Jerimiah walked in, buttoning his shirt.

'Your tea's on the mantelshelf, Jerry,' said Ida.

'Ta, luv,' he said. 'Hello, Fran. We weren't expecting to see you today.'

'No, we weren't,' said Queenie. 'But the spirits brought her so 'tis right she should be here just now.'

She winked at Francesca who, for the first time ever, wondered if Ida was right about the old woman's state of mind.

Crossing to the fireplace, Jerimiah picked up his cup and took a slurp.

'I ought to get down the yard,' he said, glancing at the clock.

'Wait awhile,' said Queenie.

'But I've a crateload of—'

'I said, wait a while!' snapped Queenie, glaring at her son.

Ida rolled her eyes and gave her husband a long-suffering look.

There was a knock at the door.

Ida jumped up off the chair. 'It's her!'

'Don't worry, Ida,' Queenie said, a determined expression

tightening her wrinkled face. 'We're more than a match for the likes of her.'

Shuffling forward so her dangling feet could touch the rug, she stood up.

Putting down his tea, Jerimiah went into the hallway to open the front door.

Tucking her arm around Patrick, Francesca rose to her feet. 'Perhaps I should go.'

Queenie winked again. 'You're just grand where you are, me darling.'

The door opened and Francesca's heart thumped uncomfortably in her chest as she braced herself to face Charlie's hostile wife. However, when the parlour door opened again it was a police sergeant with his helmet tucked under his arm, not Stella, who walked into the parlour with Jerimiah behind him.

'Sergeant Bell?' said Ida, looking puzzled as the well-padded officer with deep-set eyes stood in the middle of her rug.

'Afternoon, Mrs Brogan,' he replied, a sober expression on his face. 'Sorry to disturb you, but as Queenie and I are old acquaintances, I thought I'd come and tell you myself.'

'Tell us what?' asked Jerimiah.

'That your daughter-in-law, Stella Brogan, is dead,' Sergeant Bell replied. 'The morgue in Queen's Square sent the names of the casualties from last night's bombing through to the station and she was on the list,' the police officer continued, from what seemed to be a long way away. 'A high-explosive bomb landed just off Regent Street and she was caught in the blast.'

The ground seemed to shift under Francesca's feet. Sitting down, she hugged Patrick and stared at Sergeant Bell.

He cleared his throat. 'I know your family didn't always see eye to eye with her, but—'

'Don't worry, Sergeant, we'll take care of the arrangements,' said Jerimiah.

'Yes, we will,' agreed Ida. 'When all's said and done, she was our Charlie's wife. And thank you for taking the trouble to let us know.'

'Yes, we're obliged to you,' chipped in Queenie, looking positively cheerful.

'Well, I'll bid you good day then,' he said, flipping his police hat back on his greying hair. 'Nice to see you, Queenie.'

He touched the rim of his helmet and Jerimiah led him out. Patrick fiddled with the buttons on Francesca's cardigan.

Jerimiah came back in the room, shrugging his jacket on. 'Well, I suppose I'd better go to Tadman's on the way to the yard.'

'Don't be daft, you great lummox,' said Queenie, slapping her son's arm lightly. 'You're going to drive to the dead house at Queen's Square and get Stella's death certificate.'

'But the funeral directors can do that when they collect the body,' he replied.

'They could,' said Queenie, 'but we need it before that. Now, just go and do as I say.'

Jerimiah rolled his eyes but trudged out, nonetheless, and went to start his lorry.

Queenie watched him for a second, then her coal-black eyes fixed on Francesca.

'Now, my darling girl,' she said, placing her gnarled hand on Francesca's sleeve, 'you go home and get what you need along with your birth certificate and I'll have Patrick packed and ready to go when you get back.'

'Ready to go where, Queenie?' asked Ida.

'Go to Southampton because Charlie doesn't ship out until Sunday.' She squeezed her arm. 'Does he, sweetheart?'

Francesca stared at the old woman for a moment, then she stood up and handed Patrick to his great-grandmother. 'I'll be back in three-quarters of an hour,' she said, snatching up her handbag from the sideboard as she dashed across the room.

'Wait!' called Queenie, as she reached the doorway.

Francesca turned.

Setting Patrick on the floor, the old woman hurried over.

'Take this.' She twisted off a thin silver ring and handed it to her. 'And blessings be upon you, you beautiful, beautiful girl.'

Chapter thirty-seven

SPITTING ON THE toecaps of his newly reissued army boots, Charlie scuffed the bristles of the shoe brush across them briskly.

In the early light coming through the window of the corrugated-iron Nissen hut, he wondered if he was wasting his time polishing his boots to a shine because, although it was the third Saturday in June, the heavens had opened the moment he'd stepped off the troop train two days before and hadn't let up, turning the transit camp into a muddy quagmire.

After a bumpy half-hour ride in the back of a Bedford lorry he and the dozen or so other men returning to active duty had been deposited in C barracks, somewhere on the southside of Southampton Waters, across from the docks.

He'd been allocated to 8 hut, where he was sitting now, getting his kit in order with the rain lashing the window.

There were twenty men billeted in the hut and after parade at six and breakfast two and a half hours ago, most of the occupants were taking advantage of a free morning. Many had gone to the recreation hall for a showing of a Will Hay film but a handful like Charlie, who preferred to use their time more productively, were sitting on the beds around him, while the tinny sound of the rain striking the metal above their heads echoed around the enclosed space.

To be honest, the miserable weather suited his mood perfectly as not only was he being shipped out tomorrow but today was Patrick's first birthday. His only consolation was knowing that his family and Francesca would find where Stella had taken him and move heaven and earth to get him back. And if they couldn't,

Charlie swore that when he returned from the war, even if he had to drag Stella through every court in the land, Patrick would be brought up by him.

Of course, the other thing that kept him from wallowing in depression was Francesca. She loved him and that was the beacon of light which lit his world.

Charlie lightly passed the brush over the toecap again. He put the boot down and was just about to pick up the other one when the door at the far end of the hut opened and one of the second lieutenants from the staff offices walked in, his all-encompassing khaki mackintosh dripping rain onto the bare boards.

'Bombardier Brogan!' he barked, scanning the half a dozen men in the room.

Charlie stood up.

'Major Lawry wants to see you in the CO's office,' he said. 'Quick as you like.'

He left.

Speedily tying on his newly cleaned boots, Charlie stood up.

Grabbing his waxed brown-and-fawn poncho from the peg behind his bed as he passed, Charlie dashed out of the hut after the junior officer.

With the wind throwing rain into his face, Charlie hurried up the gravel path between the rows of semi-circular structures toward the barracks' entrance.

The supplies for the troop's embarkation tomorrow morning were already being loaded into trucks on the other side of the parade ground, so by skirting around the edge of the soggy drill square Charlie arrived at the senior staff's offices.

Opening the door, he walked in.

The WAC bashing away at a typewriter looked up from her work as he walked in.

'Bombardier Brogan,' he said, taking off his soaked outerwear and hooking it over the coat stand. 'Major Lawry sent for me.'

'He's in the Old Man's office,' she said.

Charlie marched along the corridor until he reached the last door on the left with Colonel Banfield's name painted in gold on it. Charlie knocked.

'Come!'

He walked in.

Major Lawry, a stocky chap in his mid-forties, was sitting behind the camp commander's desk. He looked up.

Charlie double-stepped to attention and gave his senior officer a brisk salute.

'Bombardier Brogan, sir, you —'

Charlie's head reeled. He must be hallucinating.

There, sitting on the chair in front of the desk, with Patrick on her knee, was Francesca.

She was wearing the same outfit she'd worn at Jo's wedding but with a light-green plastic raincoat over the top. Patrick was also dressed for the weather in a nylon poncho much like the one Charlie had just hung up outside, except his son's was sky blue instead of desert camouflage.

Francesca's legs were splashed with mud, there were damp tendrils plastered to her forehead and the rain had smudged her mascara but, to Charlie, she'd never looked so beautiful.

'Stand easy,' Lawry said.

Charlie relaxed his stance.

'I'm sorry to drag you in here but I'm afraid there's been a bereavement in your family,' said the major.

'Bereavement,' said Charlie.

Charlie looked at Francesca, panic-stricken, imagining which of his beloved family had been lost to the Luftwaffe.

The major rose from his chair. 'I'll leave Miss Fabrino to fill you in on the details.'

Taking his flat cap from the end of the desk, Charlie's senior officer left the room.

'It's not Gran, is it?' Charlie asked as the door closed behind him. Francesca shook her head.

'Don't say it's Mum or Dad?' Charlie said, taking his son in his arms.

'It's not.' Pulling out a sheet of paper from her pocket she unfolded it and offered it to Charlie.

He took it from her and read what Francesca had given him.

It was a death certificate. Charlie read across the entries, heart thumping painfully in his chest.

He read it again, then looked at Francesca.

'We only found out yesterday morning,' she said. 'Your dad went up to the morgue in Queen's Square to identify her.'

'Ruptured lungs?' said Charlie, as Patrick fiddled with his lapel button.

'She was caught in a bomb blast on Thursday night,' Francesca explained. 'I'm sorry. Even after everything she's done to you and Patrick, I can't help feeling sorry for her dying like that.'

'How did you find out?' he asked.

'Sergeant Bell arrived at your mum's yesterday and…' Francesca told him what had happened the day before. 'So by the time I got back from the cafe, your mum and Queenie had Patrick's things ready. Your dad drove us to Waterloo, and we caught the last train to Southampton last night. I got a room at the Star Hotel in the High Street and then caught a bus to the camp first thing this morning. And your gran also packed these.' She pulled out three folded notes. 'It's your birth certificate, your baptism and communion certificates too. She thought you might…' She gave him an uncertain smile.

Charlie stared at her for a moment then a dazzling bright light burst through him, lifting his soul to Heaven.

'Don't worry, Charlie,' she continued in a hesitant voice. 'I'll understand if it's too soon—'

'No, it's not.' He crossed the space between them and slipped his free arm around her waist. 'Not at all. In fact, the suddenness of Stella's death is exactly why we should snatch every moment of happiness.'

'If you're sure,' she whispered, her lovely brown eyes gazing up at him.

Charlie smiled and pressed his lips on hers in reply.

Francesca's arms wound around his neck and around Patrick who they hugged between them as she returned his kiss.

After a moment, Charlie raised his head. 'I love you.'

'And I love you, Charlie Brogan,' she replied. 'I always have.'

Charlie kissed her again and, as her mouth opened under his, his world fell back into place.

The door opened and Charlie looked around to see Colonel Banfield standing in the doorway.

The transit camp's CO had survived the last war with Germany and had delayed his retirement to help with this one. He looked like a tall Winston Churchill but with a yard-brush moustache.

With his arm still around Francesca, Charlie stood to face his senior commanding officer.

'Sorry, sir,' he said. 'Major Lawry called me into your office.'

'Yes, yes,' the colonel replied, his moustache quivering as he spoke. 'Damn roof's sprung a leak, flooded half the block. I hear you've had a bereavement, Bombardier.'

'Yes, sir,' Charlie replied.

'Well, condolences and all that but there is a war on,' said the colonel.

'So they tell me,' Charlie replied.

Banfield's moustache shifted back and forth again. 'Well, even so. If there's anything we can do, then—'

'Well, actually, sir,' Charlie cut in. 'Can I request a twenty-four-hour pass to get married?'

*

With her head resting in the dip of Charlie's shoulder and her fingers threaded through the hairs on his naked chest, Francesca listened to the steady beating of her husband's heart.

They were lying in a cast-iron bed in a second-floor room in the Star Hotel, which although it now had a massive crater across the road from it, was one of the few buildings in the High Street to have survived the port's Blitz the year before. Raising her hand slightly, Francesca looked at Charlie's great-grandmother's ring on her finger that he'd placed there just a few short hours before.

Having been given an eighteen-hour pass from midday, Charlie had cadged a lift. They'd loaded Patrick's pram, with him in it, into the back of an army supply truck then headed back into Southampton. Although it had been raining solidly for the past three days, as they climbed from the truck onto the quayside, the clouds had parted and the sun had burst through.

They'd had a hasty midday lunch in a cafe a few streets behind the docks, then headed for St Joseph's Catholic church and pitched up on the rectory doorstep as the nearby clock struck one.

The housekeeper had given them a cup of tea while they showed the priest their identity cards and their certificates, after which he'd walked them across the road to the church.

Having secured the church's verger and a passing ARP warden as witnesses, she and Charlie, carrying Patrick in his arms, had walked out of the church door as man and wife at ten minutes past two in the afternoon.

Arm in arm, they'd strolled between the wreckage of the shops and businesses along the High Street. While Patrick had his afternoon snooze, they'd located a telephone box and Charlie had phoned Mattie so she could tell his family their good news, after which Francesca had telephoned her father.

Charlie had spoken to him too and assured him that he loved Francesca and would do everything in his power to make her happy.

When she'd taken the receiver back from Charlie, her father had seemed a great deal happier.

By then, as it was the middle of a very sunny summer afternoon, they'd stopped for an afternoon cuppa at the WVS canteen near the front.

The motherly woman in a forest-green uniform behind the counter heard that not only had they just got married but that it was also Patrick's first birthday, so when their order arrived there was a small blue candle in the middle of one of the rock cakes.

They'd returned to the Star just before five and after producing their crisp new marriage certificate for the receptionist, she'd handed over the room key.

As Charlie dealt with Patrick's soggy nappy, Francesca had freshened up and then changed into the pink and green flowery dress she was wearing the day Patrick took his first steps.

Duly changed and ready for their evening meal she and Charlie, carrying his son in his arms, had headed down to the hotel restaurant. After beef stew, boiled potatoes and carrot followed by a bowl of treacle pudding, Patrick, who had somehow managed to get custard in his hair, had started grizzling.

The waitress had brought them a beaker of warm milk for him while Francesca and Charlie had finished their wedding meal with a cup of tea. Then, just after nine, they had taken a very tired Patrick back to the bedroom.

Positioning two chairs in front of the cot, Charlie had draped the quilt from the bed across them to give them a little privacy. After putting his son to bed, Charlie had left to have a beer at the bar. With Patrick sucking on his thumb behind the improvised curtain, and in the soft glow from the nightlight by the cot, Francesca had got ready for her wedding night. She'd sat in bed fiddling with the lace on her nightie and straightening her hair until Charlie returned twenty minutes later.

She'd expected him to pull a pair of pyjamas out of his kit bag but instead he'd removed his boots, then took her hand and gently pulled her to her feet.

With his eyes locked on hers, he'd torn off his tie and unbuttoned the front of his shirt, pulling it free from his trousers. Taking a step closer, he'd lifted her nightdress over her head and thrown it behind him. Suddenly shy, she'd shaken her unbound hair to cover her a little, but he'd smiled and smoothed it back over her shoulders.

As his gaze ran slowly over her, Francesca had understood for the first time that the tight sensation below her navel that Charlie always triggered was just a pale foretaste of what was to come. So much so that when he'd stepped forward and placed his lips lightly on hers, she'd practically torn the shirt from his back.

That was about an hour ago. Charlie now lay naked beside her with his left arm around her, his eyes closed and the hint of a smile lifting the corners of his lips.

Resisting the urge to stretch up and press her lips on his, Francesca let her gaze run over him, studying every little detail from his broad chest with its covering of dark hair down to his flat stomach, then to the sheet that was draped over his hips and the tops of his thighs.

Her gaze lingered for a few moments, then she stole a glance at Charlie's face.

Satisfied he was snoozing, Francesca caught the sheet between her toes and tugged it towards her. As the cotton fabric glided over Charlie's right hip it escaped her hold so Francesca gripped it again and repeated her action.

The sheet slid off.

Francesca raised her head slightly and studied the portion of Charlie that had been concealed beneath.

Several actions that had never entered her head before dashed in rapid succession through her head and she suddenly felt quite hot.

'Do I meet with your approval, Mrs Brogan?' Charlie said in a low, rumbling tone.

Francesca looked around to find him grinning at her.

Her cheeks flamed as she lowered her eyes.

'Oh, I'm sorry, I—'

Drawing her into his embrace and rolling over her in one swift movement, his mouth closed over her. Francesca put her arms around his neck and gave herself over to the pleasure of it.

After a long moment he lifted his head and smiled down at her.

He repositioned a stray tendril of hair with his index finger. 'I love you.'

She gave him a languid smile. 'I know.'

'And I never want you to be embarrassed to look or touch or do anything with me,' he said softly.

Francesca nodded and gave him a shy smile. 'And...and the same goes for you, if you like.'

That quirky smile of his lifted the corner of Charlie's mouth but, as he lowered his head, Patrick gave a little cry.

Giving her a quick peck on the cheek, Charlie rolled off and got out of bed.

Sitting up, Francesca gathered the sheet over her breast. Resting back against the headboard, and in the muted illumination of the nightlight, she watched Charlie.

He stood by the cot watching the sleeping child for a moment before coming back to the bed, allowing Francesca to appreciate his hard, muscular body from a different perspective.

'Just a bad dream,' he said.

He stood looking down at her for a moment then, grabbing the sheet, pulled it towards him.

Francesca hugged it close, but Charlie smiled and raised an eyebrow, so she relinquished it.

Charlie's gaze ran slowly over her, setting off a sensation she hadn't known until an hour ago.

She waited breathlessly for him to look his fill then, after several heartbeats, he sat back on the bed. Shuffling closer, he placed his hand on her thigh.

'I'm sorry it was a bit swift before,' he said, looking into her eyes.

Francesca was puzzled. 'Was it?'

An enigmatic smile spread across Charlie's face.

Francesca sighed. 'Well, I thought it was perfect.'

He laughed. Hooking his arm around her waist, he drew her under him.

'What are you doing, Charlie?' giggled Francesca.

Charlie gave a smile and passion darkened his eyes.

He placed his hand low on her stomach. 'I'm going to show you, my perfect, perfect wife.'

Stopping behind the crowd of women and children waiting in the early June sunshine at the Southampton dock, Francesca kicked the brake of the pushchair. She unclipped Patrick from his harness and lifted him out.

'Let's go and wave Daddy goodbye,' she said, settling him on her hip.

Her stepson wound his arms around her neck. Holding him close, Francesca squeezed through the melee and found a space at the front. She sat Patrick on the railings just as the first column of soldiers marched along the concrete, their army boots echoing in the space between the troop ship tied up on the quayside and the warehouses behind her.

Women further along the row from Francesca started shouting and waving at the passing troops. As they drew nearer to the crowd of women and children, men broke ranks and rushed to give their sweetheart, wives and children a last hug before marching up the gangplank.

Coiling her arm tightly around the one year old to keep him

from wriggling off his perch, Francesca shaded her eyes with her free hand.

'Where's Daddy, Patrick?' Francesca said, as she peered down the line of khaki.

Patrick turned his head and followed her gaze.

She'd told Charlie she would be wearing her red suit so he could spot them. As the formation of men came towards them, Francesca's eyes searched the ranks.

And then she saw him. Charlie.

Her husband of less than twenty-four hours and the only man she had ever loved.

'There he is, Patrick!' she shouted, pointing to the third block of soldiers. 'There's Daddy. Wave so he can see us.'

'Dada,' said Patrick, shaking his hands and swinging his legs.

Francesca's heart leapt into her throat as she watched Charlie's tall frame draw nearer, then he spotted them.

His eyes locked with Francesca's for a heartbeat, then he stepped out from the line and dashed towards them, the billy can and tin cup lashed to his bulging backpack bouncing as he ran.

He threw his arms around them in an all-encompassing embrace, kissing her and Patrick in quick succession. With tears gathering in her eyes, Francesca hugged him to her as she imprinted the feel of him into her mind to sustain her for God only knew how long.

Closing his eyes, Charlie kissed his son again, then turned to Francesca.

'I will come back,' he said.

'I know,' she replied.

They looked at each other for a long moment then, hugging her tightly, Charlie pressed his mouth on hers in a crushing kiss before releasing them both and running back to his place amongst the marching troops.

Patrick continued to wave but Francesca stared after Charlie, her heart already aching for his return.

As the last few companies of men marched past, women started gathering their children and drifting away.

Giving Patrick a kiss on the cheek, Francesca lifted him off his improvised seat.

'Come on, sweetheart,' she said. 'Let's go and have a nice cup of tea at the station cafe before we catch the train back to Nanny's.'

She went to lower him into his pushchair but, as she did, Patrick put his arms around her neck.

'Mama,' he said, and pressed his small mouth to her cheek.

Epilogue

UNSCREWING THE TOP of his canvas-covered canteen, Charlie gulped down a mouthful of water. It was warm, which was hardly surprising as, despite it being 1 November, it was eighty degrees plus.

It was just after noon and Charlie and his men had spent the first hour of the day making sure their Howitzer was in A1 condition and well stocked with ammunition.

When he'd returned to the Eighth Army just over five months ago, he'd been allocated to six gun in C company. Its seven-man crew were from a Lancashire regiment and had lost their previous bombardier after he strolled off to have a pee and stood on a landmine a few weeks before Charlie arrived. Their acting bombardier, Roy Unworth, a skinny twenty-year-old from Skipton, had taken command and done a pretty good job. Understandably, the crew were a bit wary of having an outsider in charge of them but now, after two days of trading shells with the Germans, it was as if they'd been together since the off.

Having sorted out their gun and topped up the truck with water and petrol, Charlie headed off to the Sunday service conducted by Reverend Robert Fisher, the battalion's padre, in the mess tent. Before Hitler had set his sights on Poland, Reverend Fisher had been a vicar somewhere in Lincolnshire. As the nearest Roman Catholic priest was with the infantry battalion ten miles away, Charlie reckoned God wouldn't hold it against him for attending an Anglican Mass under the circumstances.

While he'd been otherwise engaged, Unsworth and the rest of the crew had set up an improvised shelter over their sandy bivouac, which was where he was sitting now.

They'd dug in opposite the mess tent and now that Father Bob had vacated it, Bombardier Milligan from another Howitzer gun crew was entertaining his fellow squaddies by playing popular tunes on his trumpet.

Although he was tempted to join them, Charlie was instead sitting on his kit bag with his back against the gun's wheel.

His division in the Eighth Army were... Well, truthfully, he didn't know exactly where they were right now. They were surrounded by sand and rocks and the last road sign he'd seen was pointing to El Alamein, some twenty miles north of them.

They had made camp as the sun set two days before and, after almost three weeks of pushing the enemy west, Charlie for one was very grateful. Not only because the mess tent had sprung into action almost as soon as they'd stopped, but also because the battalion postal service had finally caught up with them, bringing with it Francesca's last four letters.

She'd written as regular as clockwork every week, sometimes twice, and her letters were never less than three pages long. He read each one daily, memorised each word until the next one arrived. They were all now locked safely in his tin chest amongst his personal items.

Reading Francesca's neat words, it was as if he were standing there beside her. Through her eyes he watched Patrick as he settled into his new life in her father's cafe and saw how he was quickly becoming the apple of Grandpa Enrico's eye. Through Francesca's letters he heard all his son's new words, saw him enjoying his favourite toys and running everywhere. He was able to celebrate the arrival of every new tooth and he smiled when he heard of the fun Patrick had each day with his Auntie Cathy and Cousin Peter while his mummy was working in the BBC's Schools' Broadcasting department now that Radio Roma had been disbanded.

Reading between the lines he felt Francesca's love for his son as he pictured her singing to Patrick, soothing his hurts, tucking him into bed in the shelter under the cafe and kissing him goodnight, and it warmed his heart.

She kept him up to date with family news too, telling him all about his gran's chickens, his father's business, Mattie's family and Jo and Tommy's new home. She also told him that Michael had been made a class monitor, and how he and Billy were getting on at Parmiter's secondary school, plus that his mother had secured shelter tickets for them all, including Cathy and Peter, in Bethnal Green station so they were convenient for the school. Also how his mother and father were still arguing about names for their new offspring, which was due to arrive any day.

However, as he read this last bit of news a small pang of regret niggled at Charlie. Even though they'd only had one night together as husband and wife, he had hoped that they might have started another little Brogan.

It was stupid, he knew, because couples sometimes waited months, even years, before they heard the patter of tiny feet and now, after almost five months with no word from her in that regard, Charlie had accepted that their much-wanted family might have to wait for the duration.

Charlie turned the page of Francesca's letter and smiled as he read through the last paragraph, where Francesca told him again how much she loved and missed him and how she, like him, was counting the days until they were together again.

As he reached her rounded signature, he pulled out the photograph he kept in his inside pocket.

Francesca had bought two copies of the family photograph taken at Jo and Tommy's wedding and she had carefully cut out the image of him, Francesca and Patrick so it would fit into his pocket. It had arrived in a letter at the beginning of September and he had kept it close to his heart ever since.

Holding it in the palm of his hand, Charlie gazed down at the image for a second or two, then slipped it back where it came from.

Refolding the tissue-thin sheets of paper, he placed them back in the envelope and put it with the others he'd already read. He picked up the last letter.

Taking the knife from his belt, Charlie slipped the tip under the gummed edge and opened the envelope. He saw it contained a picture. It was a studio photo of Francesca standing beside a smiling Patrick who was wearing a sailor suit and sitting on a tall stool.

Charlie set it aside and opened the letter itself.

Dearest Charlie,

I hope you are well and I'm happy to tell you, other than a grumbling back molar making him a bit fractious, Patrick is still full of beans and seems to be growing taller and more like you every day.

I hope you like the photograph of us. I only had it done a week ago and, as you might be able to see, I'm well too, blooming in fact.

Holding his breath, Charlie's gaze shifted down to the next paragraph.

Forgive me for not writing to tell you sooner, my love, but I wanted to be sure. I'm now past four months…

Charlie picked up the photo again. And he saw it. The distinct roundness of Francesca's stomach that clearly showed a growing child. His child. Their child.

Charlie stared at it for a moment then, feeling as if his heart would burst, he threw back his head and laughed.

'Oi, Brogan!'

Charlie looked up and found the bulldog-like Sergeant Turner running towards him.

'Wipe that silly smile off your face and get your bunch of fairies together; we're moving out,' he barked as he jogged past and onto the next Howitzer crew.

'Where?' Charlie asked as he stood up.

'Right through Rommel's line to Tripoli,' Turner shouted over his shoulder. 'Now shift yourself.'

Charlie took a last look at the photo of Francesca and Patrick, then, scooping up her letters, he slipped them and the photo into his shirt pocket.

Ducking his head under the awning, Charlie looked around and spotted Unsworth sitting on an ammunition box in the shade of the medical tent, reading a book.

Curling his right thumb and index finger together, Charlie put them in his mouth and let out a long, two-tone whistle.

Unsworth looked across.

'We're off to give the Germans what for, so gather the men!' Charlie shouted. 'And be quick about it. I've got a family to get home to.'

Acknowledgements

As always, I would like to mention a few books, authors and people, to whom I am particularly indebted.

In order to set my characters' thoughts and worldview authentically in the harsh reality of 1942 I returned to *Wartime Britain 1939-1945* (Gardiner), *The East End at War* (Taylor & Lloyd), *London's East End Survivors* (Bissell), *The Blitz* (Gardiner), *Living Through the Blitz* (Harrison) and *The Blitz* (Madden) to give me a feel for those dark days.

I also reread *Wartime Women: A Mass Observation Anthology* (Sheridan), *Millions Like Us* (Nicholson), *Voices from the Home Front: Personal Experiences of Wartime Britain 1939-1945* (Goodall) and *The Wartime House* (Brown & Harris).

For Francesca's time at the BBC Overseas Department I used *Auntie's War: The BBC During the Second World War* (Stourton) and *Human Voices* (Fitzgerald).

Along with my father's memories of the Eighth Army, to ensure the authenticity of Charlie's experiences as a gunner in North Africa I went to Spike Milligan's entertaining *'Rommel?' 'Gunner Who?'* and *Monty: His Part in My Victory*.

For Donny Muller's background and the impact of the American's arrival in war-torn London I delved into *Overpaid, Oversexed, and over Here* (Gardiner), *A Village in Piccadilly. Reminiscences of Life in*

Shepherd Market (Henrey) and the US War Department's *Instructions for American Forces in Britain 1942*. For Stella's shenanigans at the BonBon club I explore *Remembering Revudeville: A Souvenir of the Windmill Theatre* (Shapiro).

I would also like to thank a few more people. Firstly, my very own Hero-at-Home, Kelvin, for his unwavering support, and my three daughters, Janet, Fiona and Amy, who listen patiently as I explain the endless twists and turns of the plot. I'm grateful to the Facebook group *Stepney and Wapping living in 60s early 70s* and the *Saga Girls Facebook Group* plus Peel Agency and P&O who have given me half a dozen opportunities this past year to write *A Ration Book Wedding* while sailing the seven seas as a enrichment speaker.

Once again, a big thanks goes to my lovely agent Laura Longrigg, for her encouragement, and Louise Davis, whose incisive editorial mind helped me to see the wood for the trees. A big thank-you to the wonderful team at Atlantic Books, Jamie Forrest, Karen Duffy, Patrick Hunter and Sophie Walker for all their support and innovation. Lastly and by no means least my lovely editor Poppy Mostyn-Owen who helped turned my 400+ page manuscript into a beautiful book.

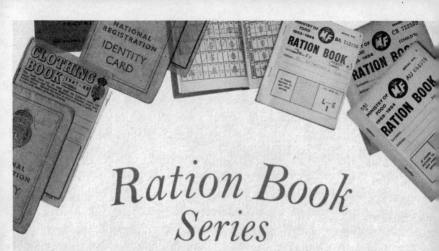

Ration Book Series

FALL IN LOVE WITH THE PAST...

A Ration Book Dream

The Blitz will never destroy their spirit

JEAN FULLERTON

A Ration Book Christmas

Love is never in short supply

JEAN FULLERTON

A Ration Book Childhood

When war is on your doorstep, family is everything

JEAN FULLERTON

A Ration Book Wedding

Can love conquer all?

JEAN FULLERTON